Song
of the
Highlands

Song
of the
Highlands

Sharon Gillenwater

PALISADES
PREMIER

MULTNOMAH BOOKS
SISTERS, OREGON

Also by Sharon Gillenwater
Antiques
Love Song
Love Wanted (A Christmas Joy)
This is a work of fiction. The characters, incidents, and dialogues
are products of the author's imagination and are not to be construed
as real. Any resemblance to actual events or persons, living or dead,
is entirely coincidental.

SONG OF THE HIGHLANDS
published by Palisades
a part of the Questar publishing family
© 1996 by Sharon Gillenwater
International Standard Book Number: 0-88070-946-4
Cover photo by Michael Hudson
Cover designed by Catherine Bergstrom

QUESTAR PUBLISHERS, INC., POST OFFICE BOX 1720, SISTERS, OREGON 97759

LIBRARY OF CONTRESS CATALOGING-IN-PUBLICATION DATA
Gillenwater, Sharon.   Song of the highlands/by Sharon Gillenwater.
p.cm.   ISBN 0-88070-946-4 (alk. paper)   I. Title.   PS3557.I3758S6   1997
813'.54--dc21   96-50930   CIP

97 98 99 00 01 02 03 — 10 9 8 7 6 5 4 3 2 1

In loving memory of Aunt Marie—
No one ever loved like you.

...he hath sent me to bind up the brokenhearted, to proclaim
liberty to the captives, and the opening of the prison to them that are
bound...to give unto them beauty for ashes,
the oil of joy for mourning, the garment of praise for the
spirit of heaviness; that they might be called
trees of righteousness, the planting of the LORD, that
he might be glorified.

ISAIAH 61:1b, 3 (KJV)

1

England, April 1810

A GREEDY EYE NE'ER GOT A GUID PENNY WORTH.

WITH THE OLD SCOTS PROVERB running through his mind, Kiernan Macpherson, the tenth earl of Branderee, slumped in the seat of his rented gig and stared at the sprawling building before him. Part castle, part manor, part who-knew-what, the country house of his new estate had been plucked from an architect's nightmare. His gaze moved slowly over the structure, beginning with a lone, narrow tower, the remnant of a medieval castle. The large elm growing amid the rubble indicated it had been in ruins for centuries.

Attached to one wall of the tower were three stories built at a later date, each level separated from the next by rows of carved stone gargoyles, fruit, and flowers. The artist had been sorely lacking in talent, thus even the flowers appeared grotesque and frightening.

The third wing slanted off to the right at a forty-five degree angle, then jogged again in a slightly different direction, disappearing behind a copse of trees. He could not tell much about the style of this wing from where he sat, only that it was two stories high and made of the same honey-colored Cotswold stone as the rest of the house.

"And Glenbuck put on such a grand regret at losin' the place," he muttered, deploring the day he had set foot in the famous White's Club in London. Its prestige as the oldest and finest gentlemen's club on St. James's Street no longer impressed him. Nor did he care that the names of the richest and most distinguished men of society graced its membership roster. Caught up in his first—and last—high-stakes card game, Kiernan had only been thankful for winning. Now, he suspected he would have fared better by losing.

The hope of a quick sale vanished. He doubted he could give the monstrosity away. Using his fingers, he combed his black hair back from his forehead and sighed in disgust. "The man was just waitin' for a pigeon." He expected better of a fellow Scot. "Half Scot," he amended, remembering that Glenbuck had an English mother. "A deceitful lot, the English."

Kiernan drove through the grass and weeds shrouding the grounds, carefully guiding his horse around the large tree limbs broken in yesterday's storm. He estimated the third wing to be seventy-five to a hundred years old. The roof sagged in one corner, and many of the windows on the second floor were covered with gray, weathered boards. To his surprise, a faint plume of smoke rose from a chimney at the back of the building.

He drew the horse and gig to a halt, surveying the landscape with a frown. The windstorm had uprooted a huge oak and sent it crashing across the yard, smashing shrubs, a dozen rosebushes, and all but one corner of a vegetable garden.

A movement on the other side of the tree caught his eye. Kiernan climbed down from the vehicle and walked through a narrow strip of tall, wet grass, barely noticing the cold drops of water splattering his bare legs between kilt and hose. He worked his way around the tangle of roots and a gaping hole where the tree had once stood, and paused. Across the yard, a slender young woman tugged on a heavy branch, dragging it out of a flower bed. A saw and hatchet lay on the broad tree trunk, and he wondered if she intended to dispose of the behemoth by herself.

The early afternoon sunlight shimmered across gold and copper glints in her red hair. Kiernan waited, silently admiring both her crowning glory and her determination. When she dropped the branch and straightened to catch her breath, he said quietly, "That's a mighty chore for such a wee lass."

Gasping, she whirled toward him. Her mouth fell open as her gaze slowly traveled from the red, green, and blue plaid thrown over his shoulder past the matching kilt and down his legs to the red tartan hose.

Since many Englishmen considered him a barbarian—until they discovered he was a wealthy, titled lord—he half expected her to scream or make a dash for the hatchet. Instead, she smiled, her face lighting with pure joy and a hint of wistfulness.

"I did not think I'd ever again see a man in Highland dress," she said, with the faintest touch of broad Lowland Scots in her lilting voice.

Kiernan walked toward her as she stepped away from the bough. "You're a long way from home." His smile deepened when he noted the sparkle in her lovely gray eyes.

She nodded. "I've been in England since I was thirteen, but time and distance can never take Scotland from the heart."

Though he had left Scotland only a month before, a wave of homesickness washed over him, as keen as any he had known during his many years in one foreign land or another fighting Napoleon. "Truer words were never spoken." He grabbed the heavy branch. "Where do you want this?"

"To the left of the house. Thaddeus will cut it into firewood when he has the time."

As she gathered up an armload of small branches, Kiernan dragged the limb around to the side of the house, enjoying the physical effort it took to move it. *I've been living the pampered life for too many months,* he thought. "Is Thaddeus your husband?"

She laughed and tossed her bundle on top of an already large pile. "No, he cares for the cattle and tends the cider orchard, as well as lending a hand with the things I can't do." Resting hands on hips, she looked back at the tree with a scowl. "Such as remove that monster from my vegetable garden."

Frowning, Kiernan straightened. "You're the housekeeper?" he asked, surprised that the previous owner, the earl of Glenbuck, would spare the money for someone to stay in such a ruin.

A blush tinted her cheeks as she shook her head. In the blink of an eye, despite the simple brown woolen gown with frayed hem and shiny fabric at the elbows, she became every inch a regal lady. "No, ramshackled as it is, Stillwater is my home. Please forgive my manners. I fear I've been tucked away in the country too long. I am Lady Mariah Douglas, Glenbuck's sister."

Kiernan drew a harsh breath. The uneasiness he always experienced in the presence of a lady of the aristocracy swept over him. Towering over her, he suddenly felt cumbersome and unrefined. When he spoke, his tone was more gruff than he intended. "Then we have a problem, my lady. I'm the earl of Branderee—and the new owner of Stillwater."

She stared at him, her face growing pale, her eyes darkening like a storm-tossed sky. "You cannot be," she said, shaking her head. "No one would buy an estate sight unseen."

"I didna buy it. I won it in a game of whist." He opened the leather sporran hanging at his waist and withdrew a folded sheet of paper. "Here is the record of the transaction. You'll find your brother's signature at the bottom."

10

With a trembling hand, she took the paper, unfolded it, and quickly read the official verbiage confirming the change in ownership.

"I...I see," she murmured, handing the deed back to him, her eyes dulled with confusion and worry.

When she shivered, he carefully took hold of her arm. "Let's go inside, out of the chill." She did not protest as he steered her around the corner of the house to the back door and followed her into the kitchen.

"Pryse never could stay away from the gaming tables, even when he didn't have ready cash." Lady Mariah stared at the small blaze in the fireplace. A lightly steaming teakettle hung from an iron hook suspended over the fire. Kneeling beside the hearth, she carefully laid another log on the grate, took a deep breath, and squared her shoulders. "Would you care for a cup of tea, my lord?"

"Aye, thank you." Kiernan glanced around. Near the hearth, two scarred mahogany drawing room chairs with faded blue velvet cushions sat on either side of a small mahogany table. Only a Bible and an oil lamp occupied the dust-free old table. A rickety spinning wheel stood in front of one chair, with a basket of wool and another of yarn sitting alongside it.

An ancient kitchen table and four sturdy chairs filled the center of the room. A workbench and shelves ran along one wall. On the opposite wall, an open door revealed a small, neat bedroom. *Either the lady is eccentric or no' worth a bean,* he thought.

Lady Mariah stood and faced him. "I should have known it would come to this, but I've been here so long..." Her voice trailed off as she turned abruptly and walked over to the workbench. "I apologize for having nothing stronger to offer." She opened a small canister and sighed. "It appears the tea will be rather weak as well."

"It will do." Kiernan moved to where he could see her face and leaned against the wall, crossing his arms. "How long have you lived here?"

"Nine years." She emptied the tea leaves from the canister into a china teapot and carried it to the table, where she filled it with boiling water. Returning the kettle to the fireplace, she hung it on a different hook at the edge of the fire.

He waited for her to explain why she was there, but she didn't. When she set two delicate china cups and saucers on the table, he almost told her to forget the tea. Considering his taut nerves, the cups appeared far too fragile for his big hands. "Glenbuck didna say anything about a sister."

"Of course not. If you had known about me you would not have accepted the property as payment of the wager. In all likelihood, he forgot I was here."

"Why?"

Lady Mariah glanced at him, her expression filled with soul-deep sorrow, and he regretted his bluntness. She pulled out a chair from the table and sat down. Kiernan did likewise, waiting in silence.

She poured the tea, placing the cup and saucer in front of him without meeting his gaze. "I hope you don't mind it plain. I have no sugar or cream."

And no' a penny to your name, Kiernan thought grimly, feeling guilty for drinking the last of the expensive tea. He leaned back against the chair, studying her thoughtfully, wondering what she had done to put herself in such a difficult situation. It didn't take much to ruin a young woman's reputation and bring disgrace to the family name. Some mistakes could not be rectified. Others could—providing family and friends rallied around the unfortunate lass. Obviously, her brother had turned her out instead.

"Tell me about the estate," he said, striving to make his voice light. "Glenbuck's solicitor didna know much about it."

"And I'm sure Pryse's description was exaggerated."

"Highly," agreed Kiernan with a slight smile. "He painted such a glowing picture that I knew it couldna be true. How many tenants are there?"

"None."

His smile faded. "Glenbuck mentioned at least three families."

"Their leases were up months ago, and they moved on. I don't blame them. They had done their best but could not make enough to provide for their families. Two of the cottages were falling down around their heads, and Pryse refused to part with a penny to help them. He wouldn't even hire an estate manager, just sent his man of business out from London when the rents were due or when Thaddeus took some cattle to the market."

Carefully picking up his cup, Kiernan studied her delicate features—high cheekbones, a small, straight nose, heart-shaped face. She appeared as fragile as the cup in his hand, yet she had to possess fortitude to survive in such circumstances on her own.

Her soft voice, filled with concern for the tenants, soothed his uneasiness. She was different from most Society ladies he had met. They seemed only to care about impressing their peers. He expected some of her compassion came from her situation, but not all of it. Kiernan set the cup back on the saucer. They might as well have been drinking plain hot water. "So he drained everything he could from the estate without putting any money into it."

"Practically. There is a small herd of cattle left and five new calves. The cider orchard is productive most years, but the profits go to Thaddeus in lieu of a regular wage." Lady Mariah took another sip and made a face. She set her cup down also, her expression growing thoughtful. "Pryse doesn't give a fig for this place. He won it, just as you did. He is a poor businessman and reckless with his gambling. He can also be quite devious."

"As in foisting this pile of rubble off on me."

"He has tried to sell Stillwater innumerable times, but his asking price has always been far too high. I still have a few friends left among the *ton* who let me know what mischief he is up to if they hear of it. This isn't the first time he has tried to use the estate to pay off a debt."

"But I'm the only dupe to take it." He scowled, picturing her dandy of a brother laughing at him behind his back.

"I doubt you are a dupe, Lord Branderee, but are you new to London?"

"I'm new to all this," he muttered. Kiernan pushed back from the table and paced around the kitchen. "I've spent most of my adult life with the Gordon Highlanders fighting Napoleon. We knew the patent allowed the title to pass through the female line, but there was no reason to ever expect I would inherit it. The last earl, Malcom, was a distant cousin on my mother's side. He had three sons who were followed in the line of descent by another cousin and his son." He stopped by the fireplace, leaned his hand against the mantel, and stared into the fire.

"The earl and his cousin were close friends and avid sailors. Last spring, they took their families on a trip along the north coast. They were caught in a storm off Cape Wrath, and both yachts went down." He closed his eyes, haunted by the images in his mind, faces he knew only from the portraits hanging in the great hall of a castle that would never be a home. "All were lost."

"How tragic!"

"'Tis hard to ken a whole family gone so sudden." He took a deep breath, exhaling slowly.

"Were you close to them?"

"Nae. Supposedly I met Malcom when I was young, but I dinna remember it. If he'd been a piper, bard, or soldier, I might have been more impressed."

14

She tipped her head to one side, studying him. "You wish you were still with the regiment, don't you?"

"Sometimes. I served with them for twelve years. It was a hard life but a less complicated one. Now I have lands to look after, a castle so big I canna find my way from one end to the other, and far too many people depending on me—tenants and servants who deeply resent me."

Kiernan dropped into the chair. "I know I'm an ungrateful lout. I should be thankful for all I've been given." Exasperated, he hit the table with his hand, rattling the teacup and sloshing a few drops of the pale liquid over the side and into the saucer. "And I am, but I'm no fancy gentleman. I dinna know the first thing about running estates or hobnobbing with the aristocracy." He shook his head. "Or games of chance where a man can lose a fortune." Heat rushed to his face at his outburst, and he called himself an idiot. *Now she'll think I'm a clod for sure.*

"Being born into the aristocracy doesn't guarantee success, my lord. Even the most careful can be snared by the dangers in our midst."

He looked up, uncertain whether he should squirm or take comfort from the sympathy he saw in her gaze. He wanted to ask what trap had caught her but decided it would be rude. "My friend warned me about the game. Gabriel said the stakes would be high, but I thought he was joking. I couldna see how anyone would take such risks. It started out reasonable enough, but before I knew it, I had several thousand pounds on the table." He grimaced. "I willna gamble again. Next time it might go the other way."

"Then you are wiser than many in Society. There are a vast number among their ranks who are in debt way over their heads."

He straightened the cup in the saucer, absently pushing his finger against the handle, turning it round and round, until he glanced up and found her watching the movement with a trace of apprehension.

"Are you going to try to sell the estate?" she asked as he rested his hand on the table.

"That was my plan. The solicitor said your neighbor, Sir Edgar Pittman, might be interested in it, but I canna see why he would be."

"The land is valuable and could be made profitable with some judicious improvements. Sir Edgar is very knowledgeable about farming in this area. He has practically worked miracles on his estate. He made Pryse a standing offer years ago, but my brother wanted twice the amount. Sir Edgar's offer is probably low, but what Pryse wanted was far too high. He was not willing to negotiate. Sir Edgar is a fair man. I expect he would be willing to settle on something in between."

"I'll talk to him then. My land in Scotland is enough to worry about."

"Would you care to see some of the other rooms?"

He nodded. "I suppose I should, but I hope the other wing looks nicer on the inside than it does on the outside."

"Unfortunately, it's in terrible condition. I've only dared go in there once. But there aren't any gargoyles," she added with a smile.

"Good. They remind me of the old tales the lads used to tell around the campfire. I dinna believe such things, but still, on a dark, windy night, my imagination might rule over my common sense." Kiernan stood and carefully pulled out her chair as she rose.

She glanced up at him as if surprised by his manners. Delicate pink touched her cheeks as she softly thanked him.

"I'm no' completely uncivilized, ma'am," he said with a half smile. He noted a few tiny lines at the corners of her eyes and wondered if they were caused by laughter, or squinting in the sunlight.

16

The sprinkling of faint freckles across her nose indicated that, unlike many ladies, she ventured outside without a bonnet at times. He liked the idea that she might enjoy the heat of the sun upon her face. Even more, he hoped she had laughter in her life.

"I didn't think you were at all uncivilized, Lord Branderee," she said hastily. Her blush deepened, and she looked down as she stepped away from the table. "It's been a long time since anyone showed me such courtesy. I have few visitors, so I fear my manners have grown rustic."

"Nae, Lady Mariah, you're as fine as any duchess in London."

She shook her head but smiled shyly at him. "You are too kind, sir." The skin around her eyes crinkled as she smiled, minutely deepening the tiny lines.

So you have found many reasons to smile, he thought, wondering why it pleased him so much.

Opening a door, she led him down a long hallway. "I expect that a hundred years ago, this was a beautiful home. The villagers tell me it belonged to a wealthy baron, but when he was honored with an earldom for some valiant deed, he and his family moved to a much larger estate in Kent. Stillwater fell into disuse and changed hands several times until Pryse won it."

She stepped into an empty room where sunshine beamed through numerous tall windows and reflected off the polished hardwood floor. "This is my favorite place in the house."

Kiernan barely spared the room a glance. He was more interested in watching the light cast a warm, golden glow across her skin and set her hair aflame.

"It would make a wonderful sitting room. It's so easy to picture a family here on a summer afternoon, enjoying the sunshine and the view of the flowers through the windows. The father would sit in a big chair over there, reading yesterday's *Morning Post* or *Gazette.* The mother would occupy a smaller chair opposite him, working on her stitchery."

Drawn by her soft voice and the subtle yearning in her expression, Kiernan moved to her side. "And the children?" he murmured. "What are they doing?"

She pointed toward the window. "The young master is sprawled on the floor over there, lining up his soldiers for battle. The little lass is sitting by her father's knee, dangling a string in the air while her frisky kitten tries to catch it."

He was tempted to trace his finger along her cheek to see if her skin felt as soft as it looked, like a rose petal. "And is the babe asleep in the cradle beside her mother?" When she smiled and nodded, his throat tightened. *So much love to give. Why is she here alone?* "A wee bairn with fiery red hair like her mother's?" he asked softly.

She moved her head as if to nod but halted and looked up at him. Agony flashed in her eyes, even as her face turned scarlet. "Please forgive my foolishness," she whispered, turning away.

He caught her arm. "Why are you no' married, milady?"

For an instant, she stood still as a porcelain figurine, and Kiernan caught another glimpse of the pain she could not quite hide.

She composed herself and met his gaze, her countenance devoid of emotion. "I was married, my lord," she said in a controlled, even tone. "Unfortunately, my husband neglected to mention that he already had a wife."

2

MARIAH FELT THE EARL'S FINGERS SLIP from her arm as he stared at her in disbelief. She had grown used to the expressions of shock followed by revulsion when others learned of her past. Lord Branderee, however, did not respond as expected.

His black brows wrinkled in a scowl as he clenched one fist at his side. "Who was the cur?"

She had the oddest impression that he would like to thrash the man who had so maligned her. It should not have been of great consequence, but to one who had been shown far too little kindness in a very long time, his concern was a precious gift.

A lump formed in her throat, and she swallowed hard. Her voice held an unusual huskiness when she spoke. "He said he was the great-nephew of an elderly viscount who lives in Wales. The old man is eccentric but highly respected, so his letter of introduction, though a fake, quickly gained Shelton's entry into Society. When I met Shelton, he had lived in London for over a year, moving in the best circles of the *ton*. He said he had had a bit of success in Jamaica and was ready to find a wife. I doubt anyone suspected otherwise.

"It was my first Season, and Pryse was adamant it would be my only chance on the marriage mart. He wouldn't spend another farthing dressing me up."

"I'd wager he didna part with much in the first place."

"Actually, he spent more than I expected. He was as anxious to be rid of me as I was eager to be free of him." The earl's dark eyes had grown black in his anger. She looked away, no longer able to meet his penetrating gaze. "Shelton captivated me with his attentions. He was very charming, always pleasant, and highly considerate."

"The opposite of your brother."

"Yes, completely." She had been so naive, so desperate for love. But no longer. "Shelton was a consummate actor."

Mariah walked over to the window. As if nature reflected her change of mood, a heavy cloud blocked the sun, turning the landscape wet and dreary. Fear knotted her stomach. *Where will I go? How will I live? Why did I ever think Shelton was sincere?*

"Such foolish dreams," she whispered, not realizing Branderee had followed until he spoke at her side.

"Dreams of sun-filled sitting rooms and bairns playing at your feet?" he asked quietly. "From what I've seen, that isna the way the rich care for their children."

"No, they are usually banished to the upper floor with a nurse or governess, spending only a few minutes a day with their parents, if they see them at all." She glanced at his wavy hair, black and shiny as a raven's wing. He wore it slightly longer than most gentlemen, combed back on the sides and curling softly against the nape of his neck.

"Many parents travel much of the time, as did mine. I hoped that when I married, my family would be close to each other, like the tenant families on our estate in Scotland."

A tiny smile lifted one corner of his mouth. "The whole family living in a one-room hut and probably sharing it with the cows?"

His twinkling eyes, now brown-black in his lighter mood, dispelled some of her tension and gloom. He didn't seem like the kind of man who would simply throw her off the property. She smiled, shrugging slightly. "Well, not quite that close." *Please, Lord, let him be merciful.* They did seem happy and relaxed in their affection toward each other.

"But I digress. Our courtship and engagement were far briefer than most. Shelton and I had known each other only a few weeks when we posted the banns. Pryse was all too happy to give the marriage his blessing as long as I was content with a private and inexpensive ceremony."

"Didna your brother check on the man?"

"I assumed he did. Afterward, he admitted that he had not bothered. I don't think he was being malicious, only lazy. Everyone accepted Shelton for who he said he was. We learned later that Shelton was not kin to the viscount at all but had served as his valet for a time. He forged the letter of introduction, using the viscount's signet ring to make it appear legitimate."

Mariah was surprised by her openness, telling this stranger things she had shared with only a few others long ago, but she couldn't seem to stem the flow of memories or the need to speak of them. Perhaps it was because he seemed genuinely concerned about what had happened to her. Most people only wanted to hear the story because they relished the scandal.

"And your dowry? Was nothing done to protect you?"

"My portion was entirely monetary, and every bit went to my husband on our marriage. Father had not made any kind of separate provision for my welfare. I never thought to question whether or not he had done so. I doubt if it ever occurred to Pryse to arrange something different."

The earl made a disgusted sound deep in his throat and crossed his arms. "So this man pretended to marry you, got his hands on the money, then abandoned you. Probably took all your jewelry, too, if you had any."

"I only had a few pieces besides my wedding ring, and he took those. He was not brave enough to try to slip the ring off my finger. I pawned it to travel back to London."

He slanted her a sharp look. "Where were you?"

"In Brighton. We spent three weeks there on our honeymoon." Those days had been the happiest of her life, filled with laughter, passion, tenderness, and total joy—right up to the morning she awoke to find the bed empty beside her, and a note of farewell on her beloved's pillow.

Reliving those first horrid moments of abandonment, Mariah closed her eyes. Despite the vicar's assurance that God could heal all wounds, she had not found it so. A heart torn asunder could not fully mend; its scars merely served as sentinels, ever-present guardians to protect against further hurt. Jesus had sustained her and given her peace in many things, but not in this. Nothing could erase the pain of Shelton's betrayal and the destruction of her self-assurance. Never again would she believe promises of love and faithfulness. *Never again!*

When she felt the earl's large hands gently clasp her shoulders, she looked up, trying to suppress her misery. She drew a shaky breath. "I beg your pardon, my lord. I am rarely given to such maudlin thoughts or unseemly displays of emotion."

Branderee stared at her for a minute before stepping back. He moved his hand to the belt around his waist, as if reaching for a sword. Frustration flickered across his face, and he muttered something in Gaelic. From his thunderous expression, Mariah decided it was good she did not know the language.

His gaze captured hers. "My dungeon is dank and empty, if ye care to use it. There be room for this thief of hearts and dreams, and for your brother as well."

A fierce Highland warrior stood before her, as solid and strong as

22

Scotland's rugged Grampian Mountains and just as unyielding. She had read and heard of the Highlanders' bravery and victories in battle. Now, she understood why the French often fled when the Scots advanced. How easily she could picture him as a fearless chieftain of old, courageously leading his men into the fray, banishing his foes to the dark depths of the castle dungeon where they would no longer be a threat. *He protects those in his care,* she thought. *Surely he will give me time to find my way in the world.*

"I suspect your wife would object to Pryse's wails of despair over his dirty clothing," she said with a smile. "As for Shelton, he disappeared long ago with his wife and children somewhere in the wilds of America."

"What a pity. I hate to miss the perfect chance to put the dungeon to good use. I understand it has been empty for nigh unto a century." He relaxed his stance, and a tiny smile lit his eyes. "Since I have no wife, Glenbuck could still be my guest. The walls are thick so his complaints would be like the squeak of a mouse, no' even the teeniest irritation. It would serve him right for sending you here to rot."

Mariah laughed. "He did say something about letting me molder away in the country. I'm sure he would be disappointed to learn life has not treated me so badly."

The earl nudged aside the bottom of her skirt with the toe of his shoe, looking pointedly at her boots. Gaping cracks in the brown leather revealed her white cotton stockings and proclaimed her a liar.

Embarrassed, Mariah flicked her skirt back into place. "These are quite adequate for working in the garden. We should continue your tour," she said briskly, moving toward the door. As she stepped into the hallway, she thought she heard him chuckle.

She entered the dining room, walking halfway across it before she looked back to see if he had followed. Her footprints made a clear path in the thick dust that covered the floor, and she almost groaned out loud. Though she only used the kitchen and bedroom, she tried to sweep the rest of the ground floor occasionally. Evidently she had neglected the chore longer than she had realized.

Branderee's expression remained passive, and he said nothing as he scanned the room. He turned abruptly and walked back to the hall.

Mariah caught up with him as he entered the drawing room. Large chunks of plaster littered the floor in a dozen places, surrounded by smaller debris and a fine white powder coating the darker dust. She gasped at the sight. "Oh, my goodness!"

"It probably fell when the tree was uprooted last night."

"The house shook terribly. I spent most of the morning cleaning the kitchen and bedroom, then went outside to work in the fresh air. I have yet to check the rest of the house."

A quick inspection of the other ground-floor rooms in that wing revealed two more with plaster damage. All needed a thorough cleaning. Mariah had never been more conscious of the unkempt floors, smoke-filmed windows, and dusty windowsills. As they moved up the narrow staircase to the next floor, she could see the earl's disgust in his frown and the stiffness of his back. With each step, embarrassment over her poor housekeeping grew more acute.

"I doubled the size of my garden last year so it took much more of my time. But I had more produce to send to the market in Cheltenham. The raspberry vinegar sold especially well. The dried fruit and preserves—twice as much as I'd ever had before—also sold well.

"Mrs. Henderson, one of Sir Edgar's tenants, taught me how to spin. I spent most of this winter trying to improve enough to sell some of my yarn." She knew she was babbling, but his silence and ever-deepening frown made her nervous. "I'm not very good yet, but now she is teaching me to knit. At least I will have a warm shawl for next winter."

Mariah opened the first door they came to, glancing back at him as she walked into the room. "It has been years since I've been up here. I fear it is a terrible—"

Her right foot plunged through the floor and ceiling below as the wood crumbled. Her left leg buckled, slamming her knee against the floor. A loud cracking sound echoed around the room as the wood began to give way. Crying out, she reached frantically for the door, but it was beyond her grasp.

Branderee lunged forward, grabbed her beneath the arms, and lifted her free. Moving backward, he hauled her against his solid frame, holding her firmly with one arm, and stepped into the hall. Leaning against the far wall, he enveloped her in a protective embrace. "Are you hurt?" he asked, breathing rapidly.

"Only bruised, I think." Mariah clung to his hand and rested the back of her head against his shoulder, grateful for his support. She was shaking too much to stand on her own. Her heart pounded so hard she could barely breathe. "I'm too scared to know."

His arms tightened minutely. "I should have warned you the floor might be rotted away." Anger shaded the regret in his voice. "There are dozens of water stains on the ceiling downstairs. The roof has probably leaked for years."

"It has. I just didn't think about it when I opened the door."

"You were too busy worrying that I'd find fault with your housekeeping. I know ye couldna have kept the place clean by yourself, lass," he said quietly.

"Thank you," she whispered, more relieved than she liked to admit. When he rested the side of his jaw against her temple, Mariah welcomed the comfort he offered and drew on his strength.

The earl held her for a few moments, giving her a chance to calm her rattled nerves. Gradually, she began to notice things—the light scent of vanilla and orange flowers in his honey-water cologne, the smoothness of his skin against her temple, the heat of his body warming the chill of her own. To her dismay, she realized it felt nice—very nice, indeed—to have Branderee's powerful yet gentle arms around her. *Oh dear, this will not do!* She lifted her hand from his, and the earl instantly released her.

"You'd better check your leg," he said gruffly, turning his back to her.

She discreetly lifted her skirt. Two puffy red marks near her knee would probably be ugly bruises by nightfall. Several scratches of varying lengths ran along the outside of her calf, but none were deep. Most had barely broken the skin. "No great damage," she said, dropping her skirt back into place. "My poor old boot saved my leg." As he turned around to face her, she soberly met his gaze. "And you saved my life. You have my deepest gratitude, my lord."

He shook his head. "I should no' have put ye in danger in the first place. Stay here while I check the rest of this floor."

He took off at a brisk pace, not giving her an opportunity to object. Throwing open one door after another, the earl peered into each room from the hallway, his scowl increasing as he progressed down the corridor. When he reached the last two rooms, which were directly above the kitchen and her bedroom, she heard him exclaim something in Gaelic, then mutter in the same language all the way back down the hall. He stopped at her side, looking as if he impatiently awaited some action on her part.

"I do not understand Gaelic, my lord. Is something amiss?"

He put his hand against the small of her back and propelled her toward the stairway. "The whole roof above your quarters could come down with the next rain, and another storm is brewing. I canna allow you to remain here, Lady Mariah. You must pack your things immediately."

I liked it better when you called me lass, she thought, and became instantly annoyed at her foolishness. "And where do you suggest I go?" she snapped, wincing as her battered leg protested at their race down the stairs.

Branderee slowed his step and offered her his arm. "Are any of the tenant houses livable?"

"There may be one that does not leak. Thaddeus would have a better idea of their condition than I do."

"I'll find him while you collect your things."

"Is it really necessary, my lord? I will be leaving Stillwater anyway, as soon as I can make arrangements."

"I willna risk you coming to harm," he said sternly. "If there is somewhere else you had rather go, I will see you safely there."

She shook her head. "There is no place else at the moment. I need to send inquiries to friends before I can proceed with a more permanent move."

When they entered the kitchen, Branderee went straight to the back door. "Where do I find Thaddeus?" he asked, opening the door and stepping outside.

"Follow the road past the orchard and turn left. His cottage is not far. He should be there or perhaps in the barnyard." She walked to the doorway and looked up at the cloudy sky. The earl was right. They would have another storm before nightfall. "Ask him to bring over the wagon. I would like to at least take the bed."

"We'll take whatever you need, but make haste."

She smiled wryly. "One advantage to being poor as a churchmouse is that I have little to move. It will not be more than a wagonload."

The wind picked up, and the earl glanced at the leaves rustling in a nearby tree. He looked as if he was about to say something but changed his mind, nodding curtly before striding to his gig.

Mariah stood in the doorway and watched him drive down the road until a sudden chill overtook her. Shutting the door, she sagged against it, rubbing her arms, her mind in a whirl. "Living in the cottage can only be temporary. I must think of somewhere else to go." She closed her eyes, fighting her apprehension. "Father God, give me the faith to trust in you. Please give me the wisdom to know what to do."

She set the teakettle on the edge of the stone hearth to cool and went into her bedroom, quickly stripping the linens from the bed, folding and stacking them into a neat pile.

Opening her trunk, she removed her two best day dresses and laid them on the mattress. Though no longer quite the fashion, they were in excellent condition, as were the shoes she placed beside them. Like the frocks, the shoes had been reserved for the day she was forced to venture out into the world again. At least when she left Stillwater, she could do so with a shred of dignity.

Her gaze drifted to the much-worn pelisse hanging on a peg near the foot of the bed. "So much for my pride," she muttered. "The dresses might pass minor scrutiny, but that coat will shout my penniless state to the world."

Memories assailed her as she withdrew the last item from the trunk, a beautiful evening gown. The creation had been made for her first ball. Oh, how she had feared no one would ask her to dance!

With a rare twinge of gratitude to her brother, she remembered how one of his friends—a noted rake, but the least disreputable of the lot—had come to her aid, claiming two dances early in the evening so she would not be condemned to hiding behind the potted plants. He had also introduced her to other, more respectable

28

members of the *ton,* both male and female, so that her narrow sphere of acquaintances, as well as dance partners, had widened considerably during the evening.

Shelton had not been at the ball, and she supposed that had been one reason she kept this particular gown. "Perhaps I can sell it to some country miss for enough to buy a new coat. Or one that isn't quite so worn."

Laying the gown beside her day dresses, she put the bedding in the bottom of the trunk along with the clean towels from the rickety washstand. She dragged the trunk into the kitchen and carefully tucked her small set of mismatched dishes between the folds of the linens.

Then she added other things that might be broken in the move, including a small silver mechanical bird that sang when wound up. Her father had given it to her when she was a child.

The rest of her clothing came next, with the nicest things placed carefully at the top. By the time Thaddeus arrived with the wagon, she had all her possessions gathered and ready to move.

Thaddeus doffed his hat as he came into the kitchen, his expression pensive. "Is it true, milady? Is that Scotsman the new owner of Stillwater?"

"It's true."

"He says you have to move right away." He looked up at the ceiling, frowning at the fresh circles left by the rain the day before. "Suppose he's right." He picked up a couple of kitchen chairs. "He goin' to sell to Sir Edgar?"

"Probably, although I don't believe he has talked to him yet."

"Where will you go then?"

"I don't know. I've barely begun to think about it." She studied the heavy table, wondering if she and Thaddeus could move it. The burly man would not have a problem, but she wasn't sure she could lift her end. "Is the earl coming back?"

"He said he'd be along soon to help with the furniture." A sudden grin eased the strain on her friend's face. "He's not your typical lord, that one. Not high in the instep at all. Right now, he's sweepin' out the cottage."

"Sweeping out the cottage?" Mariah stared at him.

"Knew what he was doin', too," he said, laughing as he walked out the door.

She picked up a chair and carried it out to the wagon, her thoughts lingering on the earl. The image of the large Scot wielding a broom evoked a bemused smile. He said he was no fancy gentleman, yet surely he must have been part of the gentry with servants to do the menial work. Even as a regimental officer, he likely would have had a personal servant. Branderee was definitely not a typical lord.

The ton will make mincemeat of him.

3

THE FOLLOWING AFTERNOON, Kiernan sat in Sir Edgar Pittman's study, watching the lanky gentleman shift restlessly in a large leather arm chair.

"Then we are agreed?" asked the knight. "The offer is acceptable?"

Kiernan nodded, halfway expecting his host to hop up and dance a jig. He was practically giving the land away, but he did not care as long as he could be free of it.

"Splendid!" Sir Edgar stood and shook Kiernan's hand, pumping his arm up and down. "A splendid deal for both of us, and a good jab at that popinjay, Glenbuck. The land is mine at a jolly good price, and you are making more than you risked."

Laughing, Kiernan eased his hand free. "I had a feeling you knew the terms of the wager."

"To the penny, milord." Sir Edgar grinned. "I've kept my ears on the twitch for years, just waiting for Glenbuck to lose Stillwater. Would you care for a glass of port to celebrate our mutual victory?"

"Just a swallow. There is another matter we must discuss."

"Lady Mariah." Sir Edgar poured half a glass of wine for Kiernan and a full glass for himself. "Unfortunately, it will be impossible for her to remain at the estate," he said, handing the drink to Kiernan with a grimace. "My wife is a very jealous woman. She would make Mariah's life intolerable. Did Mariah mention any employment prospects or have any positions in mind?"

Kiernan frowned, focusing on his host. "She said she needed to write to some friends. I assumed she intended to stay with them."

"Not Mariah. She'd rather starve than take anyone's charity. My sister, Prudie, and I have tried to help her on numerous occasions, but she firmly rebuffed our efforts. I can't blame her. She is an earl's daughter, after all. And from what I hear, her father was quite plump in the pockets. The fortune didn't last long after her brother got his hands on it."

"What kind of work would an earl's daughter do? There canna be many acceptable choices."

Sir Edgar tapped his fingers on the arm of the chair. "No, indeed. She is well educated, so she could be a governess." He curled his lip in distaste. "But that is seldom a pleasant position. Perhaps a house-keeper on some country estate? She's certainly frugal."

"Ever met a housekeeper with a title?" Kiernan stood and walked over to the window, relieved to see sunshine replacing the clouds. Lady Mariah intrigued him and seemed to have taken up permanent residence in his mind. "What about being a companion to an older lady or perhaps a chaperon?"

Sir Edgar joined him at the window. "Either would probably do. She knows how to go about in Society well enough. She must be around seven-and-twenty, old enough to be considered on the shelf. It's well known that she is penniless. With no money and her wastrel brother for a liability, there is little hope of her finding a hus-band on the marriage mart. Even if she wanted one.

"But she still has friends and allies in the *ton*. More than she real-izes. At the time, the scandal was the latest *on dit*, the talk of the town. No doubt she felt completely ostracized, though I know of many who stood up for her. In their minds, she was a victim, not someone to be scorned." He grimaced. "Unfortunately, the ones casting stones cried the loudest."

"They usually do."

"Someone is bound to bring up the past, but it shouldn't cause more than a momentary ripple. The story is too old to be of any consequence. Generally, I believe she would be welcomed back into Society's midst. Some doors will be closed to her, of course, but few people gain access everywhere."

"My mother and sister are in London. I'll ask Lady Mariah to be our guest until she has something worked out."

"That is very generous of you, sir." Sir Edgar frowned. "But I doubt she will do it."

Kiernan set his glass on the desk. "My mother is homesick. She will enjoy sharing stories with a fellow Scot."

He bade Sir Edgar farewell and drove back to Stillwater. Mariah was not at the cottage, so he traveled around the estate until he found Thaddeus in a pasture, checking on the new calves.

"After a long, hard rain, the little ones sometimes get stuck in the mud, but they were smart enough to stay away from the bog today." Thaddeus pulled off his hat and swiped his sleeve across his forehead. "Did you sell the estate, milord?"

"Aye. As soon as the paperwork is drawn up, Sir Edgar will be your new landlord."

"He'll be a good one."

"You willna mind working for him?"

Thaddeus shrugged. "Things will be different, but I won't mind working for him."

Kiernan understood what the other man left unsaid. When they helped Mariah move, Kiernan had swept the cottage and laid a fire in the hearth, deeds much appreciated by the lady. Thaddeus, however, had diligently watched over her. He had been one step ahead of Kiernan most of the time, relieving her of heavy loads when she tried to carry them inside, quietly insisting she rest at the first sign of tiredness, and hauling in water from the well. He had also made certain Kiernan left her cottage before he did.

Kiernan suspected the man harbored a deep affection for Lady Mariah, perhaps even loved her. It was obvious, however, that though the lady considered Thaddeus a good friend, she was unaware of his feelings. Nor did she look upon him in a romantic light. Kiernan was sorry for him but also relieved—a feeling he found unsettling. Still, he could think of no one who would see to her safety more than Thaddeus.

"Ever work with horses?" asked Kiernan.

"I spent a couple of years working for the ostler at the Old Tower Inn. Took care of horses day and night. You need a groom?"

"I do, but I also need a man who could be intimidating as a guard. My mother, sister, and I will be staying in London for a while." *And perhaps Mariah, too.* "I have a coachman to drive them about, but I'd feel better having a guard go along. Can you handle yourself in a fight?"

Thaddeus smiled. "Aye, milord. I've never been to London, but I bashed a few heads at the inn when I had to. And I can look mean if need be." His expression turned serious. "But I can't leave until Lady Mariah does."

"I understand. We can work out the details later if you're interested."

"And after London, sir? Would I still have a job?"

"If you are willing to go to Scotland. I'll be staying in London only through the Season. We will go home by June."

"Always wanted to see Scotland." Thaddeus looked across the pasture as the cattle wandered away. "I've poured enough of my sweat into this plot of ground. I'd rather spend my time with horses than cattle. I'd be pleased to work for you, Lord Branderee."

"Good. I'll talk to Lady Mariah and see what her plans are. Do you know where she is?"

"Saw her walkin' toward the village about twenty minutes ago."

Kiernan nodded, guiding the horse and gig around in a circle, and proceeded back toward the main road at a fast clip. He caught up with Mariah a short distance from the village.

Slowing the horse, he stopped beside her, giving her green muslin dress a quick but thorough glance. He suspected the frock was not quite the current fashion and that the color might have faded slightly, but the graceful lines of the simple empire style flattered her slim figure. Green ribbon trimmed her straw bonnet, ending in a pert bow beneath her chin, complementing her red hair and delicate complexion.

He was glad she was not forced to wear a tattered gown to the village and expose her deplorable situation for all to see. The walk had put a touch of color in her cheeks, and when she smiled up at him, her sparkling eyes shone like silver. She made a very fetching picture.

"Good morning, my lady. May I drive you the rest of the way?"

"That would be most kind, sir."

He kept the horse steady and, leaning toward her, held out his hand in assistance. When she placed her foot on the small step and her hand in his, he tugged gently, pulling her lightly up into the carriage. Noting her sensible kid walking boots, he gave them his silent approval. Though they showed signs of wear, they were in much better condition than the ones she had worn the previous day.

Once she was seated, he whistled lightly to the horse, and they continued toward the village. "After last night's storm, I didna think today would be sunny. It's a nice change."

She lifted her face momentarily toward the sun. "A welcome change. I enjoy the sunshine much better than the rain. Speaking of rain…"

When she looked at him, Kiernan was mildly taken aback by the seriousness of her expression. He smiled wryly. "You noticed the roof as you walked by the manor."

"I noticed the lack of a roof. Lord Branderee, I owe you my most profound apology."

"How so?" The gig hit a pothole, one of many left after the heavy rain, and her shoulder bounced against his upper arm. Though he found their close proximity quite pleasant, he had no intention of jarring the teeth out of her head. He slowed the horse to a walk.

"Yesterday, I questioned the necessity of moving to the cottage. I thought you were overreacting to the situation."

"And overbearing," he said with a grin.

She returned his smile, a twinkle lighting her eyes. "That, too. But I am very glad you did not relent."

"Ah, lass, you've been away from your homeland too long. Have ye forgotten that stubbornness is an honored Scottish trait?"

Her smile wavered and the light faded from her eyes. "My brother seems to have been born with a double measure of that particular characteristic, although he is only half Scots. I learned early on that stubbornness on my part only heaped coals upon my head. Life was more tolerable if I complied with his commands."

Kiernan frowned. "Such as being banished to Stillwater with nary a penny to survive?"

"I came here of my own accord. It was my sanctuary, a quiet balm to my soul. I knew he would not take time away from his pleasures to follow me. I thought he would provide a small income so I might live here quietly and not cause him further discomfort. Unfortunately, that proved to be a very unwise assumption. In my distraught state, I didn't think about the depth of his disdain. When people smirked at my failure, Pryse could only think about how he had been made a laughingstock. He had always considered me an embarrassment anyway—"

"Why?"

"I'm his half sister, you see; the offspring of Father's second marriage. In his opinion, it was bad enough that Father married again at the advanced age of fifty, but to wed someone so far beneath him— the daughter of a mere country squire—and a woman three years younger than my brother, was beyond the pale.

"When I was born, it was too much to bear. He considered Father an old fool and felt he had been made to look the fool, also. Pryse could not tolerate my mother. Because of his harsh criticism of her, the once close relationship between him and our father dwindled away completely."

"He thought she was after the money and title?" asked Kiernan. When she nodded, he added, "That is often the case when a young woman marries a much older man."

"It was true of my mother, and Father knew it. In return, he wanted a beautiful wife, one he could display proudly to the *haut ton*. They got along well despite the differences in their ages.

"After Mother died, I thought perhaps Father and Pryse would mend the rift between them. Unfortunately, they were both too proud. Neither one would make the first move toward reconciliation."

"Glenbuck is a fool." Kiernan thought of his father and deep sadness filled his heart. "We never know how long we'll have our loved ones with us."

"You've lost someone dear?" she asked softly.

"My father died fourteen months ago, right before the regiment came back from Portugal. A fever took him so quickly, Mother didna even have time to send word that he was ill. He wasna an old man. I thought he'd be here after the war was over. I was twenty when I went away. I deeply regret being gone so long."

"But you served your country well, my lord. Without you and the others who have fought so valiantly, Napoleon would have taken England long ago."

"I dinna regret fighting, only that I canna make up the time I lost with my father."

"I think that is part of my brother's problem, too. He truly grieved for Father. In the presence of others, he was cold and remote, but I heard him weeping the night he arrived and again late at night after Father's funeral. He loved him in his own way. Perhaps that is one reason he disliked me so much. I suspect I served as a constant reminder of his mistake."

Kiernan took her hand and turned it over, running his thumb across her callused palm. "He punished you for his sins." Feeling a slight tremor ripple through her, he released her hand and glanced at her face, worried that he had frightened her. He saw confusion and wariness in her eyes but not real fear.

Turning his attention back to the road, he guided the horse around a particularly deep pothole. "What errands have you today, milady? Where shall I take you?"

"To the inn. I have some letters to post."

"You intend to visit friends, then?"

"Not exactly." She sat up straighter. "I'm hoping one of them will know of a suitable position for a lady of refinement." She pursed her lips. "I believe that is the proper term for someone in my situation. I should think I would be acceptable as a companion for an elderly lady who spends most of her time in the country or perhaps someone who wishes to travel to foreign lands."

She withdrew five letters from her reticule. "I've also written to an employment agency which is said to be reputable. Hopefully, I shall be happily working within a few weeks."

"Perhaps much sooner than that." Kiernan drew the horse to a stop in front of the inn and handed the reins to a groom. "Would you take luncheon with me, Lady Mariah? I have a matter I wish to discuss with you before you send off your inquiries."

A tiny frown wrinkled her brow. "I suppose it wouldn't hurt to wait. The mail coach does not come until three. And I admit I'm hungry."

Kiernan grinned. "I'm starved." He climbed out of the gig and went around to assist her. When she stood, he put his hands around her waist and lifted her easily to the ground. "I'll expect you to eat plenty. You're light as a feather."

"Hardly," she said with a laugh. "But I promise to do the meal justice."

"Good." He offered her his arm, smiling when she took it. "The food here is excellent, but it will be even more tasty when eaten in such fair company."

"Oh, well done, milord." She smiled up at him. "You're learning the *ton's* bantering ways already."

He raised an eyebrow and lowered his head a bit nearer to hers. "Know well, Lady Mariah, that I only speak the truth."

She blushed prettily. "Then I thank you for the compliment, sir. But pray tell, what would you have said if I had been a crotchety dowager?"

"In such *exalted* company," he replied promptly.

"Not bad." She grinned. "You might be able to hold your own after all."

The door to the inn opened and two young blades, dressed to the nines, sauntered out. One of the men held the door for them as the other stepped aside. Kiernan missed neither the appraising looks they gave Mariah nor their politely murmured greetings. There was nothing precisely improper in their behavior, but he still had the urge to toss them into the nearest mud puddle.

Since his arrival in the area, Kiernan had taken his meals in the common taproom. Once the locals found out who he was, where he was from, and why he was there, he had not caused much of a stir. Walking in with Lady Mariah on his arm, however, brought an instant lull to the noisy room. Her fingers twitched against his arm, but her calm expression revealed none of her apprehension.

The innkeeper hurried across the room, greeting them with a bow and sincere smile. "Lady Mariah, how nice to see you again."

Mariah quietly acknowledged the proprietor's greeting. A buzz rippled through the room as the neighborhood busybodies assessed the situation and voiced their opinions. Though she kept her attention focused on the innkeeper, she could well imagine the speculative looks they were receiving.

"Do you have a private table?" asked the earl, interrupting the owner's comments on the fine quality of apple cider produced by Stillwater's orchards.

"Yes, my lord. Of course." The man showed them to a smaller room adjoining the taproom. "I'll send the girl right in with your meal." He left, closing the door behind him.

Branderee met Mariah's gaze. "Would you be more comfortable with the door open?"

"For propriety's sake it should be open, but I'm more comfortable without everyone staring at me."

"Perhaps we can have both." He set two of the chairs out of the way and moved the table over against the wall, near the door. He added a chair on either side, indicating that Mariah should take the one in the corner. After she sat down, he opened the door and took his seat. "Better?"

"Yes, thank you." She smiled in approval. "Now, their vivid imaginations can't run quite so amuck, but you are still blocking me from view. I hope you can bear dozens of eyes boring into your back."

"They will tire of it soon enough. If no', they'll go cross-eyed from staring at the plaid."

Mariah laughed and told him about the village and its various shops until the serving girl brought their food. When they were alone again, she met his gaze. "Is Sir Edgar buying Stillwater?"

"Yes. The paperwork has to be drawn up, but that should be taken care of shortly."

"I'm sure you are relieved not to be burdened with a run-down English estate." She cut a bite of roast beef and glanced up to find him watching her with a small frown of concern. "This is excellent," she said with a smile.

He relaxed and they ate in silence for a few minutes. "Did I tell you that my mother and sister are in London?"

"You might have mentioned it. I've been a bit muddled the last twenty-four hours," she said.

He paused, looking up at her. "It seems longer. You've done well for having your life turned upside down."

"I spent much of last night in prayer. Placing myself in God's hands has helped greatly to lift my spirits." She smiled ruefully as she scooped some broccoli up on her fork. "Although I'm afraid I have a tendency to try to peek between his fingers and see if I can't sort things out by myself."

The earl chuckled. "Most of us do the same. Except for my sister Jeanette. I've never seen anyone with as much faith as that lass."

"The Bible says we should have faith like a child."

"She's nineteen and definitely no' a child."

"Then you'll be staying for the Season?"

41

"We hadna planned to, but Jeanette's new friend has filled her head with dreams of parties and handsome admirers." He smiled, obviously fond of his sister. "She is such a levelheaded lass, it never occurred to me that she would be interested in fancy dresses and dancing 'til dawn."

Mariah laughed. "You must not have spent a great deal of time around women. Most young ladies I know would love to go to a ball." She sobered. "As the sister of a wealthy earl, she will be considered quite a catch. Even if she is cow-faced and tongue-tied, there will be fortune hunters of all ages hanging out for her."

"She's neither, but she is green and far too trusting. Jeanette sees only the good in people. If a thief picked her pocket, she'd offer him the change in the other, believing only desperation would have driven him to crime."

"Drill it into her head that she must never go anywhere alone."

"I have."

"And hire a large bodyguard."

"I've done that, too. Thaddeus has agreed to come work for me."

"I didn't think he would leave Stillwater," she said, surprised.

"He willna leave as long as you are there, but he said he is ready for a change. He will probably be going to Scotland with us when we return home."

"Thaddeus is a good man." A wave of sadness washed over her. "He has been a good friend. I shall miss him." She forced a smile. "He will protect Jeanette well. When I first came here, I kept running into scoundrels in the village. There really weren't that many, though it seemed like it. Most were merely annoying, but a few were more persistent. Thaddeus always appeared when I needed him. Only one confrontation came to blows, and he broke the man's nose. Other times, he drove off the rogues with the threat of a thrashing. There are not many men who will stand up to his challenge."

"Yet you were going to the village alone this morning. Have the villains all disappeared?"

"No, but I'm more adept at avoiding them now. If someone seems as if he might cause problems, the shopkeepers are good to either have a helper drive me home or send someone after Thaddeus. I usually wait and ride in with him anyway. I only walked this morning because I would not be buying anything."

Mariah frowned. "A bodyguard won't do Jeanette any good at a ball or other parties. Such a gentle soul could be sorely trounced amid Society. I hope you plan to stay close by her side."

"I do. I think I can handle the men—" He halted when she grinned. "What's so funny, minx?"

"The image of London's finest beaus quaking beneath your glare. You realize you are probably a head taller than most of them, don't you?"

"I noticed. I'm also taller than many of my countrymen. Just made me a bigger target on the battlefield.

"What I dinna know how to handle are the ladies. I'm no' sure I'll be quick enough to fend off the barbs should they decide to throw them. Some of those women have devilish sharp tongues."

"Yes, they do." She looked down at her plate. "They can be unpardonably cruel if they take a mind to."

"Which is why I was hoping you would help us."

"Me?" Frowning, Mariah met his gaze. "How?"

"By being Jeanette's chaperon and acting as companion to my mother."

Mariah shook her head. "No, I cannot. I will not throw myself back into that den of vipers."

He ignored her protest, continuing as if she hadn't even spoken. "Mother came from the gentry, but she fell in love with my father when she was seventeen. He was a forester who worked for my grandfather's friend. My grandparents liked him well enough and thought love more important than status. She married and never went to Edinburgh for a taste of Society parties and such.

"She frets that none of us have town polish, including her. After their marriage, she was perfectly content living in Badenoch and rarely ventured to Edinburgh. Never to London."

He pushed his plate aside and leaned toward her, resting his forearms on the table. "Mother is naturally shy, but since my father's death, she has retreated more and more within herself. I had hoped this trip would put a little spark back into her. She did seem happier and more interested in life, until Jeanette asked about staying for the Season.

"Mother is torn between wanting to race back to Scotland and wanting Jeanie to have this special time. She is in such a quandary that I fear she might become ill. It would help her greatly if she had a trustworthy woman to accompany my sister to the balls and parties—someone to guide her through the maze of functions and the endless rules of comportment. I believe you would guard her feelings and her reputation.

"You could also boost my mother's confidence by accompanying her when she goes out, which at the moment is never. Hopefully, with you to lend her support, that would change. Sir Edgar assured me you can do both."

"Lord Branderee, how can you ask me to chaperon your sister? Guard her reputation? She would be ruined merely by associating with me!" She lowered her voice, though she felt like shouting. "I destroyed my life because I fell for the first man who whispered sweet words and tender promises in my ear. I was stupid and gullible, blind to his deception. You cannot trust your sister's welfare to such a fool." She threw her napkin on the table and glared at him, shaking her head. "I thought you had more intelligence."

"You are no' a fool or stupid, Mariah. And I am no' an idiot. You were young and green when it came to men, with no one to guide you. Yes, you made a grave mistake, but because of it, you will be all the more diligent to keep Jeanette safe."

"I cannot. If I attempted to go about in Society again, it would stir up the scandal anew. I will not go through the vicious gossip and the cuts, and I will not put your sister and mother through it. You do not know how cruel they can be."

"Sir Edgar does no' share your opinion. He says the story is old news, and most people will pay little attention to it. According to him, you have many allies in the *ton*, many who felt you were a victim. He believes that you would be welcomed back into Society by most people."

"He only wishes it were so." *What if he is right?* Mariah knew her friend was an excellent judge of people, and he kept an astute eye on the *ton*. Had her self-imposed exile, her trying existence been unnecessary? A picture of Pryse's livid face flashed across her mind. If she had stayed in London, he would have made her life far more wretched than it had been.

It would be nice to see my friends again. There were a few who had kept in touch through letters, although she had turned down their invitations to visit. At first, pain and shame had kept her isolated. Later, pride kept her hidden away; she could not bear for them to see her poverty.

"I would not want your sister or mother hurt by even one person, and that is bound to happen."

"It will probably happen whether or no' you are with us. Do you trust Sir Edgar's judgment?"

"Yes." She toyed with her knife, moving the handle back and forth on the tablecloth. Pride was still her captor. Two good frocks and one ballgown would never suffice in Town. She would be an embarrassment to Lord Branderee and his family.

He seemed to read her thoughts. "I'd pay you well, enough so that you willna have to scurry to find another position when we go back to Scotland. Perhaps you might accompany us. Mother is lonely even there. She is no more at home in that castle than I am. We would also provide clothing and other necessities for you." When she started to protest, he held up his hand. "It would reflect poorly on Jeanette and Mother if you were no' suitably dressed.

"We have met a few people here in England, but our acquaintances are sorely limited. If you introduced us to others, Jeanie might have a better chance of being invited to a ball and some of the other parties. I'd hate to stay for the Season and have her no' get any invitations. Wouldna you like to see your friends again? Surely, there are some you have missed."

"Yes, there are friends I would like to see again." She was also acquainted with several people—if they would still speak to her— who could open Society's doors to Branderee and his family. And he was right that she would diligently guard his sister from silver-tongued rogues. Troubled, she met his gaze. "I'm afraid," she said quietly.

"It is an honest feeling." He reached across the table and gently covered her hand with his. "I'm afraid, too. Afraid I'll make some blunder or that Jeanette or Mother will be hurt in some way. It would be easier to go back to Scotland, but we are also a part of this world, now. We must learn how to live in it."

"And you think I must, too." She eased her hand from beneath his and began folding her napkin.

"You canna keep hiding."

She placed the napkin on the table and looked at him, asking the question that burned in her heart and mind and frightened her most of all. "Why are you helping me?"

He shrugged. "Because you need me to, and I would be plagued with guilt if I didna. Besides, the arrangement would be beneficial to us both."

He made it sound so simple, as if it were an ordinary thing to go about lifting people from the mire. It could be she was only one of many he had helped. Perhaps she had only imagined the flare of interest—or was it desire?—she had seen in his eyes as he considered her question. "I would like to think about it."

"Do you have any other errands in the village?"

"No."

"Wait here while I fetch my bagpipes. I'll take you back to Stillwater, and you can think while I play." He smiled as he pushed back his chair. "I canna go long without my music. The pipes are a wee bit loud for Londoners, and I'd probably frighten the wits out of the villagers. I hope you and the cows can put up with it."

She returned his smile. "I don't know about the cows, but I'll enjoy it."

"Good." He stood and started to turn away, then looked back at her. "I must return to London within a few days. I'll need your answer soon."

4

ENCHANTED, MARIAH SAT ON A WOODEN BENCH outside the thatched-roof cottage, listening as Branderee played a lively tune on the great Highland bagpipe. When she had been in boarding school in Edinburgh, the teachers had taken her and her classmates to several exhibitions, both that of the great pipe and the smaller Lowland bagpipe, which was blown with bellows. If her memories were correct, the earl's ability was equal to the best of the pipers she had heard.

He was certainly more handsome than any of them. He had discarded the coat and plaid as the day warmed, and his white shirt displayed the powerful muscles in his arms and shoulders. Current English fashion showed the shape of a gentleman's leg in narrow trousers or tight pantaloons, but there was something rather appealing about seeing the actual leg from the top of his knee to his upper calf. She smiled to herself, thinking she might not find a skinny Highlander's legs nearly so attractive.

As the last note floated away on the breeze, the earl began a new song. Slow and beautiful, the haunting melody sent a shiver skittering along her skin and evoked images of the great Scottish mountains she had seen only in paintings. Lord Branderee closed his eyes, and she wondered if he pictured those brooding peaks, or if he yearned for a special Highland lassie.

The raw emotion reflected in his face made her feel as though she intruded in his private world. She averted her gaze, but the music enveloped her, deepening the fragile bond between them, stirring a longing in her heart that had as much to do with the man as with her homeland.

Mariah leaned her head against the side of the cottage and closed her eyes, remembering the green, rolling hills of the Border country, the Scotland she had known and loved. Pryse still owned the family land, but the manor had been left desolate as year after year he plundered the furnishings to pay for his lavish lifestyle.

Her thoughts turned to the Highlands, land of misty mountains, glistening lochs, and heather-covered glens. She pictured Branderee striding toward her through the heather with his self-confident, determined gait, his kilt swinging slightly with each step. With a warm, inviting smile, he held out his hand.

Startled by her vivid imagination, she gasped softly and opened her eyes. Branderee captured her gaze, and heat flooded her face.

The earl took the blowpipe from his mouth and stilled his fingers on the chanter. The music lingered in the air as he walked over to her. "Is something wrong?"

"No, nothing. I was just thinking of Scotland."

Glancing at her flushed cheeks, he arched one eyebrow, questioning her statement in silent eloquence.

"Tell me about Branderee," she said quickly. "Where in the Highlands is it located?"

"It is no', at least no' in what most of us consider the Highlands." Sitting down beside her, he rested the pipes on his thigh. "It is on the northeast coast, near the small town of Cullen, about fourteen miles west of Banff. The castle is built on the edge of a small cliff overlooking the Moray Firth. The area right below us is rocky and a favorite nesting place for seabirds."

"The scenery must be grand."

"It is, but when a gale hits, you'd best be inside. Many was the time last winter when I wished the castle had been built farther inland, rather than perched where it receives the brunt of the storm. Though I admit the storm clouds rolling in from the sea and the waves crashing onto shore are a sight to behold."

"I can only imagine how it would seem. What a majestic reminder of the Creator."

"And humbling. A man quickly develops a healthy respect for all that power."

After a short pause, Branderee continued. "Generally the land is slightly rolling, although there are some hills, and the mountains can be seen off in the distance. The land is fertile. Oats, turnips, and cattle do well there. Some of the tenants are also fishermen, sailing out to the sea to catch herring and other fish."

It struck Mariah that the earl felt no kinship with the land he had inherited. There was no pride of ownership in his voice, no sense of belonging in his words. He could have been reciting from a travelogue.

"The first Lord Branderee built the first tower in 1360. Over the next two hundred and fifty years, additional towers and wings were built."

"How big is it?"

"It has nigh unto fifty rooms. I canna see why anyone would need so much space, even a large family. The three of us rattle around in it like old bones."

Mariah laughed, although it was easy to see the earl did not like his new home. "When you have a house party, you must be glad for the extra space."

He shifted his weight. "We have no' had any house parties.

Mother would take to her bed if I even mentioned it. I thought she might invite some of her friends from Laggan to pay us a visit, but so far she has declined. I suspect she fears they will think she is trying to show off. Gabriel has been with us since we moved to Branderee, and his parents visited for a fortnight. Besides a few cousins, we've had no other guests."

"Are you and Gabriel related?"

"He's a Macpherson, so we probably share some ancient ancestor, but no' one close enough to count. We grew up together, and though his parents have much more money than mine did, they approved of our friendship. They generally moved in higher circles than our family, but his mother and mine are good friends." He frowned. "They think Branderee is grand."

"You do not?"

"It's a fine estate," he said with a shrug.

"But you do not like living there."

"Nae. I had always planned to return to the Highlands, to the mountains around Loch Laggan. They are my home, no' some moldy castle on the coast. I carried the image of the mountains and lochs with me into every battle. I intended to go back and work beside my father, hopefully fill his shoes when he decided to slow down."

He sighed heavily. "I'm no' certain I will ever be content in Branderee. Even with Mother and Jeanie there, it is lonely, empty. For the most part, the servants and tenants dinna trust me. I've left things as they were until I feel confident that any changes I make will be the right ones. There are a few servants I probably should dismiss, but I'm hoping in time their attitudes will change. I do think Mother enjoys the scenery and climate better there than in the Highlands. She grew up on the coast near Aberdeen."

"That explains why your English has a bit of Lowland Scots

mixed in. I had wondered. Most Highlanders I've met speak the language as precisely as the English themselves."

"Since Gaelic is our native tongue, those who speak English usually learn from an English tutor or governess. Sometimes they are even sent away to boarding schools in England."

A smile brightened his expression. "My father spoke little English or Scots. Just enough to communicate his feelings to my mother soon after they met. We learned Gaelic, some Scots, and Mother's version of English from the very beginning.

"Her parents had not strictly adhered to the theory that Scots is a second-class language and that English is the only proper language for the aristocracy, gentry, and educated. She mixed them both together. Now my sister and I do, too. Gabriel's mother also came from the Lowlands with a similar view toward Scots so he tends to do the same. I like to think we are preserving a wee bit of a grand language."

"You are. Unfortunately, my parents and teachers felt that speaking Scots made them sound uneducated. I loved the language and learned what I could from the servants, only to have my knuckles rapped if I slipped around the wrong person. After I came to England, it was purged for good."

"It's a pity."

"Yes, it is. Perhaps I'll go back someday and learn it again." She smiled, relaxing against the side of the cottage. "You play beautifully."

He smiled and gave her a shadow of a bow. "Thank you. I would hope to meet your expectations, since I've spent most of my adult life playing for my supper."

"You were a piper in the regiment?"

He nodded, the warmth of pleasant memories evident in his smile. "When Gabriel decided to purchase a commission, I went along."

"Then you purchased your colors at the same time?"

"Me?" He chuckled softly. "Nae, lass, I didna have the money nor the aristocratic background and gentlemanly qualities to be an officer is His Majesty's army."

"You are as much a gentleman as any man I know," she said indignantly.

"And you are a very gracious lady. Perhaps I'm learning better than I thought. Gabe will be pleased. He has been trying to pound the niceties into my thick skull for years." He began taking the bagpipes apart, placing each piece carefully in the wooden case on the ground beside him.

"Pipers are no' officially part of the military. The officers of the Scottish regiments, usually the captains, hire them to serve with their company." Though he dismantled the instrument with ease, there was respect and care in every movement.

"Then you could have left at any time?" she asked.

"Yes. I didna have to sell a commission like the officers, and unlike the enlisted men, I wasna bound for life. More often than no', those lads didna know what they were getting into. The recruiters plied them with drink, put a coin in their hands, and shipped them south. When they sobered up, they discovered they had signed papers pledging their lives to the army until they died or were too old to fight." Anger glinted in his eyes. "Their only hope was that the war would end, and the regiment would be disbanded. Their lot was often pathetic, with inadequate supplies and no pay for months at a time. Still, none fought with more honor or bravery."

"Was your lot much better?"

"Usually, but no' always. Gabriel took good care of me, but even an officer canna provide food when there is none to be had."

"Yet you stayed for twelve long years."

He looked mildly uncomfortable. "Other men have fought

longer, and far too many have sacrificed much more. We canna let Napoleon take the rest of the world, for he willna leave Britain alone. My duty was to play the men into battle and keep playing as long as I could. It gave them something of home to hold on to, a reminder of why they were fighting—to keep Scotland free." His eyes twinkled. "And England, too."

Mariah smiled. "Yes, please. England, too." The fact that the earl had been a piper instead of an officer did not lower her opinion of him. If anything, he grew in her esteem, though she reminded herself not to exalt him too highly. From what she had seen, most men had feet of clay.

The piper led the company into battle, stirring their hearts as deeply as the ancient war cry, "Scotland Forever!" His music roused the Highlanders to fight, sustained their courage through the fray, and comforted them afterwards. It occurred to her that by carrying the pipes, he could not have held a musket. "How did you protect yourself?"

He grinned as he latched the case. "I danced a jig and dodged the bullets."

"You can't dance and play at the same time." Mariah laughed, enjoying his banter entirely too much. "And I don't think anyone could dodge all the bullets." With a fingertip, she traced a narrow white scar that ran across the back of his hand. "Or other weapons," she said softly.

"I didna come away unscathed, but that scar is from my youth. Gabe and I were racing home, and I slipped off a log that bridged a narrow stream. When I fell, I cut my hand on a sharp rock on the bank." He laughed softly. "I was sure I'd bleed to death, but there was barely a trickle by the time we reached home.

"As for protecting myself in battle, I carried two pistols and a dirk in my belt and another dirk in my hose. Sometimes I took a sword instead of the dirk in my belt." He met her gaze. "And there were times I needed them."

"Were you ever badly hurt?"

"A bayonet wound in the leg was the worst of it. Bad enough, but better than taking a round or being hit with grapeshot or a cannonball. It laid me up for a while."

Mariah sensed he did not want to talk about the fighting or his wounds. "I was told that the duchess of Gordon gave each man a kiss when he joined the Gordon Highlanders." She smiled mischievously. "Is that the real reason you went with them?"

Branderee leaned back against the cottage wall. "She was lovely, and her arguments to fight for our country were most persuasive. Many a man was recruited by her grace's kiss and the gold guinea she placed in his hand. I heard that sometimes she put the coin between her lips, but I canna say if it is true.

"When the regiment was first raised in 1794, she came to our district recruiting with her husband and their son, the marquis of Huntly. He was the Lieutenant Colonel Commandant. I was barely sixteen, and my mother didna want me to go, but oh, I was tempted—by the grand lady's kiss to be sure, but more by the six pipers who accompanied her. I had played the pipes since I was ten and decided then and there to be a company piper if I could find a way. I practiced long and hard. Four years later, Gabriel bought his commission, and off we went to war."

"Where is Gabriel now?"

"In London with my mother and sister. I didna want to leave them alone. He's nursing a nasty cold anyway, but even sick, he will make sure they are safe."

He stood, stretching his arms over his head, then out to the sides. Lowering his hands, he rotated his shoulders. "I think I'll go find Thaddeus and see what work needs to be done." He looked down at her and winked. "A ditch to dig or hay to toss. Maybe a field to plow. Something besides sitting around and being lazy."

Smiling, Mariah shook her head. "My lord, earls do not dig ditches."

He rested his hands on his hips, his expression arrogant. "Earls can do anything they want…almost." A tiny smile hovered about his lips. "Or so I'm told. I would be pleased if you call me Kiernan. I'm weary of my lord this and my lord that. No' even quite used to being called Branderee." He tapped his chest with his fingertips. "In here, I'm still Kiernan Macpherson, common man. No' a nobleman at all."

You have no idea how noble you are. "You are anything but common." She paused, not wanting to let him see how he affected her. "I really shouldn't call you by your Christian name. We haven't known each other long enough."

"What does time have to do with it?"

"It would be highly improper should I go to work for you."

"Are you going to work for me?"

"I haven't decided yet. I was enjoying your music too much to think about the situation."

"Dispense with the formalities, Mariah. They are a false shield, no' needed between friends. I will be your friend, whether or no' you work for me. If it would make you more comfortable, you can milord me all you want when we are around others—except for my family and those close to me. I'll show you equal courtesy."

He picked up the pipes. "May I leave these in your cottage? I would just as soon no' carry them around with me."

"Of course." She stood and led the way inside the small house, pointing to a spot near the door where he could set the case. "I may walk over to Sir Edgar's in a while. If I'm not here when you return, please feel free to come in for them."

"Would you like me to drive you?"

"No, thank you. The walk will do me good and give me more time to sort out my thoughts."

He looked around the cottage, frowning when he saw an empty bucket and two large kettles stacked by the wall on the floor. "Did the roof leak?"

"Only in a couple of places."

"Those are big kettles."

"They were big leaks." She smiled wryly. "If I'd had a barrel handy, I could have collected wash water. Since the roof is thatched, though, I don't believe it will cave in anytime soon."

"Mariah, this is no' good." He looked at her, still frowning. "Even if you decide no' to work for me, please come to London. You can be our guest until you find something else."

"I could not impose on you."

"It wouldna be an imposition. It would be much more bothersome to worry about you drowning in your sleep or the roof falling in."

"I'll think about it."

He nodded, clearly not satisfied with her answer but willing to accept it for now. He left and Mariah closed the door after him, watching through the window as he drove away. She knew she should be more suspicious of his intentions. "Do you truly have a sister and mother waiting in London?" she murmured. "I know nothing about you, except what you've told me." It troubled her that she found it so easy to trust him, but even worse, how much she wanted to.

She plopped a bonnet on her head and automatically tied the ribbon beneath her chin. In all likelihood, Sir Edgar would know whether or not the earl of Branderee spoke the truth.

Mariah did not rush to Sir Edgar's house. She strolled at a comfortable pace and talked to God. "Lord, I know you watch over me.

Since I gave you my life, you've always protected me and provided for my needs. But I know how easy it is for me to make mistakes, to think that what I'm doing is right when it's not. Please give me wisdom, Father. Help me see the situation correctly and make the right decision.

"I cannot stay here, and I don't know where else to go. If you have some other place in mind, please show me quickly. It frightens me to think about going back into Society, but if I could keep his sister from being humiliated—or worse—then shouldn't I do it?"

As she followed the road up a small hill, she spotted Kiernan standing at the edge of the woods with Thaddeus. She paused when Thaddeus handed the Scot an ax. The earl stepped up to a tall tree and began to swing the ax with a proficiency that surprised her, until she remembered that he had said his father was a forester. He worked on one side of the tree, then the other. A short time later, Kiernan stepped back, and the tree teetered for a few seconds, then crashed into the meadow.

When his short, triumphant yell reached her, she laughed and waited to see what he would do next. He talked briefly to Thaddeus and pointed to a large, dead tree. Thaddeus shook his head, but Kiernan walked around the tree, looking up. He stopped and studied the terrain. From her vantage point, Mariah could see there was only a narrow clearing in which the tree could fall. If not cut properly, it might become tangled in the two large trees on either side of the clearing, causing a potentially dangerous situation.

The men talked again, and moments later Thaddeus took a coiled rope from the back of the wagon and climbed the tree. Slightly more than halfway up, he tied one end of the rope around the trunk, throwing the other end free. When he reached the ground and moved out of the way, Kiernan began chopping the tree. He worked for several minutes, then handed the ax to Thaddeus.

Kiernan took the free end of the rope and walked into the clearing until the rope was stretched tight.

Mariah tensed. The rope did not appear long enough for Kiernan to be clear of the tree when it fell. Thaddeus began chopping the tree again, then shouted and jumped out of the way as a loud crack split the air. Mariah held her breath as the tree leaned slowly, drifting too far to the right.

Her gaze flew to Kiernan as he gave a powerful tug on the rope and ran to the left, pulling the tree to the center of the clearing. He dropped the rope and raced toward the meadow. The falling giant picked up speed, its heavy branches sweeping down toward Kiernan. Mariah cried out, certain he would be crushed, but at the last second he dove free of the danger, the leaves at the tip of one thick branch landing a few inches from his feet.

Shaking and her heart pounding, Mariah waited for the earl to get up. He didn't move. She tore down the hillside as Thaddeus ran up to him. By the time she reached them, Thaddeus had helped him to his feet.

Kiernan leaned over, resting his hands on his knees, gulping in air. When he straightened, he slapped Thaddeus on the back. "We did it!"

"You were almost killed! That tree could have broken every bone in your body!" Mariah stormed around in front of him but stopped short at the sight of his broad grin, gleaming white in a black, mud-covered face.

"Lass, I cleared the tree with room to spare."

"It missed you by inches. That was the most foolhardy thing I've ever seen." Her gaze moved over him, and amusement slowly pushed aside her fear and anger. His front was black, literally from head to toe. The pristine white shirt, as well as the bright red, green, and blue kilt, tartan hose, and black shoes were completely covered in mud. So were his arms, hands, and legs.

"The tree was dead. It needed to be taken down, or it might have fallen on someone."

"That's true, but you still took too great a risk."

He swiped his hand across the back of his kilt and wiped his face. "I knew I could outrun it." He grinned again. "But I didna plan on suffocating in the mud."

"What if you had slipped and fallen? Did you think of that?" She wanted to put her arms around him and hold him tight, mud and all.

"I thought of it, but it wasna a great concern. I'm steady on my feet." He wiped his face again and winked at her. "And I'm good at dodging, remember?"

The wink did it. She smiled in spite of her efforts not to. "You had better find a pond and go for a swim."

"What? I thought you'd let me use your hip bath."

She shook her head. "And track mud in my house? I think not."

Kiernan looked at Thaddeus. "No' very hospitable, is she?"

Thaddeus grinned. "Can't say that I blame her, milord. There's a pond near my cottage. You can borrow some clothes if you want. You'll be laughed out of the taproom if you go back to the inn like that."

"True. Very well, I'm off to the pond." He walked toward the gig, chuckling as his feet made squishing noises in his shoes. When his horse craned her neck to give him a second look, Mariah and Thaddeus burst out laughing. Kiernan joined in and was still laughing when he drove away.

"I understand you're going to work for Lord Branderee." Mariah walked with Thaddeus back to where he had dropped the ax in his rush to reach the earl.

"I won't leave until you're settled somewhere, milady. His lord-

60

ship has agreed to it." He picked up the ax and turned back toward the farm wagon.

"Thank you for your thoughtfulness." Mariah walked beside her friend in silence for a few minutes. "He's asked me to go to work for him, too, as his mother's companion and his sister's chaperon."

When Thaddeus met her gaze, she caught a flicker of hope in his eyes.

"It would be nice to still be able to talk to you sometimes, milady."

"Yes, it would. It would also be nice to know I have a friend near should I ever need help. I have not given Branderee an answer. I want to find out what Sir Edgar knows about him first."

"That's wise."

"Thankfully, he's a patient man."

"For now."

"What do you mean?"

Thaddeus laid the ax in the back of the wagon before climbing up on the seat. "He's attracted to you, milady. He seems nice enough, but what if he's the type of lord who expects a little dalliance along with your other duties?"

"Then I shall leave."

"I'd take you wherever you wanted to go."

"Thank you." Mariah reached up and squeezed his hand. "I know I can count on you, Thaddeus. No one ever had a more loyal friend."

He merely nodded and drove off in the direction of his cottage.

Mariah struck out for Sir Edgar's, walking quickly. She did not think Kiernan would ever make such an improper demand, even though it was common enough among the aristocracy.

And if he did?

"I'd turn him down," she said firmly, glancing up as a bird fled at the sound of her voice. The tenderness she had seen in Kiernan's eyes and the memory of his embrace sent warmth rushing through her. Those brief moments in his arms had stirred feelings she had never expected to know again.

You'd refuse him? taunted the small voice in her mind.

Mariah stopped, inhaling deeply. "Yes." She sighed. "But not without some regret."

Sir Edgar's sister, Prudence, offered Mariah a biscuit to go with her tea. Some ten years older than Mariah, Prudence had accepted her life as a spinster. She found fulfillment in overseeing the running of her brother's house, leaving her sister-in-law free to engage in charitable and frivolous pursuits.

"It's unfortunate Eddie isn't here for your visit. He is ecstatic at finally being able to purchase Stillwater. He and Celeste drove off to Gloucester shortly after Lord Branderee's visit this morning. Eddie was anxious to see his solicitor, and as usual, Celeste never misses an opportunity to visit friends. They will not return for several days."

"Did he say what he thought of Branderee?" asked Mariah, relieved that Celeste was not at home. She took a bite of lemon biscuit, absently noting the flaky texture and sweet, yet tart taste.

"Oh, yes. He was very impressed with him, and you know he seldom misjudges a man's character."

Mariah nodded, silently agreeing that Sir Edgar was usually accurate in his assessments. However, even he had been fooled by Shelton.

"Of course, Eddie received a letter yesterday afternoon from one of his London cronies, Melville Hood, telling him all about the Scotsman winning the wager."

"How did he know the earl wanted to sell?"

"Well, he didn't know for certain, but he thought it was a reasonable assumption. Mr. Hood found out what he could about Branderee. He said it was rather difficult because the earl is new in London and doesn't know very many people."

Prudie took a sip of tea and leaned a little closer to Mariah. "Mr. Hood was at White's during the game and said the earl was cool as a cucumber, even though the stakes were high. Your brother actually had to take out his kerchief and mop his dripping brow," she said gleefully. "Branderee didn't even break into a sweat." Prudie grinned mischievously. "Of course, a lady shouldn't say sweat, but the word sounds so much more manly than perspire. Besides, I'm relating the tale as Mr. Hood told it."

Mariah grinned. "It would lose something in the telling if you changed it."

"Precisely. It seems that it took Branderee a few minutes to accept Stillwater as your brother's wager, and Glenbuck became exceedingly nervous."

"Did he say anything else about the earl?"

"Oh, yes. He is fairly new to the title, inherited it sometime last year. His predecessor didn't come to London often so no one knows very much about him, either. I do remember hearing that he and his entire family were killed in a boating accident of some kind. The present earl had been in the military until right before that time, but Mr. Hood did not know what rank."

"He was a piper." Mariah quickly explained his duties and the unique situation of pipers in the service.

"How interesting." Prudie smiled. "And romantic. Lord Branderee must be a very brave man."

"Foolhardy," murmured Mariah, remembering how close he came to being killed by the falling tree.

"Pardon?"

Mariah thought of how he caught her when the floor gave way. He could have stayed out of danger. Instead, he risked his life to save hers. "Yes, he's very brave."

"Why do I have the feeling you've seen this valor firsthand?"

Knowing how Prudie enjoyed an exciting tale, Mariah told her about falling through the ceiling. She judiciously decided not to mention that Kiernan had held her for several minutes. "I'd appreciate it if you would not spread the story around. The fewer people who know my sad state of affairs, the better. And somehow I think it would make the earl uncomfortable."

Sighing, Prudie placed her palm on her chest. "The man will have all the ladies swooning at his feet. A handsome earl, brave, flush in the pocket—do kilts have pockets? And humble as well. All the mamas and their daughters will be vying for his attention. I assume he is staying for the Season. Mr. Hood mentioned that his mother and sister accompanied him to England, and that his sister looked to be of an age to make her come out. He allowed as he'd only seen her once, and that she is quite pretty. Branderee had taken her to the theatre, but their mother wasn't with them. Mr. Hood said he had heard the mother doesn't go out much."

Relieved at this confirmation that Kiernan had been telling the truth, Mariah relaxed. "Lord Branderee's father died a little over a year ago, and it's been very hard on his mother. She's shy to begin with. London and the *ton* are somewhat overwhelming to her." She finished the tea, setting the cup and saucer on the table in front of her. "His lordship has offered me a dual position as his mother's companion and his sister's chaperon."

"Wonderful! You are going to take it, are you not?"

"I haven't made up my mind."

"What is there to decide? You would be perfect, and it's a gift from heaven. You'll move about in Society once again, renewing old friendships and making new ones, which means we can see you when we're in Town.

"You will not have to beg recommendations from anyone, although you know Eddie and I would be honored to vouch for you. Nor will you suffer through who knows how many interviews only to end up as a dauntless but overworked teacher at a boarding school. Or worse, become the much-put-upon companion to an eccentric curmudgeon who'll make your life miserable," said Prudence in a mildly joking manner.

Mariah laughed. "You're being a trifle melodramatic." *But not much.* All too often, young women in similar circumstances lived just as Prudie described.

"Besides," said Prudence with a smug smile, "I think Branderee is quite taken with you."

Mariah tried to ignore the little jump in her heartbeat. "Why do you say that?"

"Eddie said Branderee was worried about your welfare."

"That is just his way. He has already hired Thaddeus to work for him."

Prudie tapped her lips with her index finger, her expression thoughtful. "At first, the earl assumed you would go live with friends, but Eddie set him straight on that misconception. Then, he said he would invite you to be their guest until you found something. How delightful that he asked you to work for him instead."

Mariah tried not to reveal how much his thoughtfulness touched her. She didn't even want to admit it to herself. "He is a considerate man. It was kind of him to think of me."

"I expect kindness had something to do with it," said Prudie with a sly smile.

Mariah shook her head. "Prudie, you're a hopeless romantic. I'll be his employee." *And friend.* She would enjoy becoming better acquainted with the earl of Branderee—and his family, she added hastily.

"Then you are going to work for him?"

Mariah hesitated. Though the prospect evoked fear as well as excitement, it seemed to be her only choice. A sense of peace entwined with her other emotions; an assurance she hoped came from God and not merely from reaching a decision. She took a deep breath and met her friend's bright gaze. "Yes, I am."

5

THE EARL ARRIVED AT HER COTTAGE at the crack of dawn in a private coach, the Branderee crest emblazoned on the door. In a matter of minutes, her trunk and Thaddeus's two smaller bags were loaded, and they set off with Thaddeus riding outside with the coachman.

The trip to London took over ten hours, but Mariah enjoyed it well enough. She could not say she was completely at ease with the earl, even though his friendliness and relaxed attitude should have made her so. Riding alone with him in a closed carriage would be frowned upon, although she thought perhaps it wasn't so much a taboo for someone her age as it was for a younger miss. It was, she reasoned, much more comfortable and safer—in some ways—than making the trip in a rented gig.

They kept the curtains opened wide, but she could still appreciate Society's wariness of such a situation. Sitting across from him in such close proximity for hours provoked too keen an awareness of the man. The resonance of his voice and deep rumble of his laughter. The hard muscles in his leg when a rock or rut jostled her against him. His strength as he caught her when a particularly violent jolt threw her practically onto his lap. The spark in his dark eyes and the moment of hesitation before he settled her safely back onto the seat and released her.

She began to wonder if anything would escape her notice—certainly not his neatly trimmed nails, tanned cheek, and the creases that ran across his forehead when he pondered some point.

As the day warmed, he lowered the windows a few inches. Unlike the other noblemen of her acquaintance, he actually enjoyed the wind ruffling his black hair, which made her smile. She could not remember seeing him wear anything on his head, not even the round, flat woolen bonnet usually donned by the Highlanders.

"Do you ever wear a hat?" she asked.

"Sometimes, if it's cold or raining. When I was with the Gordons, the Scottish bonnet was part of the uniform and had to be worn whether the weather was hot or cold. Now, I wear it only when I want to, which isna very often."

"How refreshing, a gentleman who is not a slave to fashion."

He flicked the edge of his kilt. "If I worried much about being fashionable, I wouldna be wearing this." A tiny frown touched his brow, and he looked away.

Mariah suspected he often received derogatory comments about his choice of apparel, but she had the impression he did not want to discuss whatever troubled him. She would have preferred to keep talking. With the lull in conversation came memories.

Leaving Stillwater was more difficult than she let on. Though the house itself had been little more than a ruin when she occupied it, the grounds, woods, and fields had sustained her, providing food for her soul as well as her body. The estate truly had served as her sanctuary, not merely a refuge from a hateful world, but a garden of renewal for her spirit. She had found God there, in the beauty of his creation and in the teachings of a young country vicar who loved Jesus with all his heart.

She would greatly miss Reverend Jordan Wylde—friend, counselor, and gentle soul. He had been her confidant; she had been his.

Mariah was one of the few people who knew of his secret longing to be a man of business rather than a minister. She also knew his heartache and understood it well.

"What saddens you, lass?"

Mariah met Kiernan's concerned gaze. "I was thinking of Reverend Wylde. Thank you for taking me by to say farewell."

Something flickered across Kiernan's face as he glanced out the window, an expression she could not quite classify. Irritation, perhaps?

"You will miss him."

"Yes, I will. He is a dear friend."

"Only a friend?"

She noted the tension in his jaw that had not been there moments before. "He has also been counselor, teacher, confidant. I was dying. He saved me."

"Dying?" Kiernan's gaze shot to hers.

"Figuratively speaking, although it could easily have been literal without his help. After I learned the truth about Shelton, I was cast into the depths of despair. I didn't think I could sink any lower. Then Pryse turned his back on me. Even though I had been running my brother's household for two years and overseeing the staff, I discovered I did not have the slightest idea of how to function on my own.

"Besides the typical classroom work and an effort to rid me of my deplorable Scottish accent, the focus at Miss Eversham's School for Young Ladies had been on how to behave. I could dance without missing a step, carry on an intelligent conversation, flirt with my fan, and quote the rules governing a young lady's behavior to perfection, but I could not start a fire, boil an egg, or grow a bean."

"And the good reverend taught you all that?"

She laughed. "He showed me how to lay a fire, but he cooked

the eggs far too long. Since he has a housekeeper, Jordan was no more educated in that area than I was. The eggs were inedible, hard and rubbery, so once they cooled, he juggled them. When one fell on the floor, it bounced like a ball, and he chased it across the room."

Suddenly, Mariah's eyes misted. She blinked rapidly. "He acted so silly that I laughed. Until then, I thought I'd never laugh again. That moment of joy gave me hope. I resolved to rise above my desolation.

"He told me I was not alone. Jesus loved me and would always be with me if I would but turn to him. I did not truly comprehend what he meant until much later, but in seeking to understand, I found another reason for living.

"Each day brought new challenges. I learned to cook, do my laundry, and clean house. But not without many mishaps," she said with a wry grin. "I swallowed my pride and asked the tenants to teach me to grow vegetables and put up the produce. Eventually, I became rather self-sufficient and made some good friends at the same time.

"I had attended church services most of my life, but I had seldom paid attention to what was said. I began listening to his sermons, although I must admit, at times it was difficult. He does tend to ramble when he's in the pulpit. In private, Jordan bemoaned his lack of booming voice and great oratory prowess, especially when the squire's snores had drowned out half the sermon. He gave me a Bible, and I read it when I had time. We started meeting a couple of times a week to discuss what I had read."

"Alone?" Kiernan frowned.

She smiled at his disgruntled expression. "He is a man of the cloth, Kiernan."

"Underneath that cloth, he's still a man."

It was a true enough statement. She was not so naive as to believe that ministers did not suffer the same temptations as other men. "He always treated me quite properly."

"He hugged you today," he muttered.

"We were saying good-bye. He is one of my closest friends, and I'll probably never see him again," she said sadly, looking down at her lap, toying with the ribbon on her dress.

"I wish he could find another position, one to which he is better suited. He really isn't meant to be a vicar. He is a godly man and tends his duties diligently, but he only went into the ministry because his mother wanted it so badly. She's gone now, and he has decided it is time he followed his own interests."

"Such as?"

"His talents are handling business affairs and dealing with people. He has been assisting Sir Edgar while his regular secretary is on a trip to America. He says Jordan does excellent work and could go well beyond the duties of a private secretary." She peeped up at him. "Do you have a man of business?"

"I do," he said curtly.

Taken aback by his sharp tone, she tried to imagine how he must feel, suddenly thrust into the role of wealthy, titled lord. No doubt he had been plagued by people wanting to share in his good fortune. Did he think she was trying to take further advantage of his kindness? "If you know someone who needs an assistant, perhaps you could suggest Reverend Wylde? Sir Edgar would vouch for his ability and integrity."

"I'll keep it in mind."

But not for long, if his scowl was any indication. *What made him such a cross-patch? He almost sounds jealous.* The idea was ridiculous, but she decided further explanation might help her friend's cause.

"Jordan needs a new challenge, work he truly enjoys. A few years before I moved to Stillwater, his wife died giving birth to their first child, a stillborn. Jordan loved her deeply and his heart still belongs to her. Her death, and that of the baby, devastated him. I'm not sure he will ever risk loving someone again."

To her amazement, Kiernan's face softened and his stiff shoulders relaxed. "I'm no' sure I could, either, after such a terrible loss," he said somberly. He was quiet for a few minutes, lost in thought. "If I hear of anyone needing a secretary or man of business, I'll suggest him."

"Thank you."

"Every dream deserves a chance." Kiernan met her gaze and held it. He did not speak, but she could read his thoughts as clearly as if he said the words. *Even yours.*

Rattled, Mariah merely nodded and turned toward the window, barely noting the passing scenery. Her dreams had died in the stark reality of a lovely little cottage by the sea, though the need for love remained hidden in her heart. She angrily denied her longing, burying it even deeper beneath the regret and bitterness of a hard lesson well learned.

The earl's description of Portugal was entertaining, but as they arrived in London, her thoughts drifted until his words became merely a pleasant drone. Apprehension crept through her, tightening the muscles in her neck and bringing on a dull headache.

What if she made a cake of herself? Or Kiernan's mother and sister took an instant dislike of her? Even if they accepted her, would she be able to handle the snubs that were certain to come? And most of all, what if she had only imagined God's peace about the situation? Was she making a terrible mistake?

"We rode the most interesting flying horses," said Kiernan.

"Soared from rooftop to rooftop and town to town without so much as a hoof touching the ground."

When his words penetrated the jumble in her mind, she met his amused gaze. "What?"

"It would seem the description of my foreign travels needs more drama."

"I'm sure your description is quite fascinating without the flying horses." She tried to smile. "I apologize for not attending."

"There is no need to be nervous, Mariah."

She took a deep breath, blowing it out with an ungraceful puffing of her cheeks. "You aren't the one who has hidden from the world for nine years. I haven't even been to Cheltenham for fear someone would recognize me."

"I thought you sold your produce there."

"Thaddeus handled it. He also bought most of the things I needed. Prudence, Sir Edgar's sister, purchased the rest."

Mariah shifted restlessly as they reached Mayfair, the fashionable area of London reserved for the aristocratic elite's sojourns in the city. Though the spring social whirl was yet to begin, some members of the *ton* remained in residence much of the year or arrived early for the Season. They passed a townhouse with a string of coaches lined up in front, the elegantly dressed passengers disembarking and strolling up the steps of the lavishly lit mansion.

Wishing she had dimmed the lamps on the inside of the carriage, Mariah drew back from the window and tried to hide from view by turning her head. Her courage all but deserted her. "Kiernan, this was a mistake. People are staring."

Kiernan chuckled softly. "Of course, they're staring. It is an unfamiliar coach, and you are a lovely lass. I doubt they caught a glimpse of you, but if they did, the men are already plotting to meet you, and the women are sizing up the competition."

She practically snorted. "Competition, my slipper." She glanced out the window, her face flaming as two couples craned their necks in an attempt to see inside the coach. "I'm nine years out of fashion." *And riding alone in a closed carriage with a man.* Suddenly she almost laughed out loud. *Who chaperons the chaperon?*

"There isna much difference between your dress and others I've seen around the city."

"There isn't," she admitted. "I just don't like being stared at."

"You had better get used to it. It seems to be what Society does best."

"True." The goal of many of the upper ten thousand was not to enjoy a social function or entertainment but to be seen, which meant that others had to look. "I had forgotten how utterly frivolous this all is."

"Gabe says it's an important way to meet others in my new social class. So far, few have impressed me." He stretched across the coach, dimming first one lamp, then the other.

Relieved to be sheltered in the shadows, she murmured her thanks. "He is right, though it may not seem so now. It is wise to know those who wield power, whether they be prominent landowners, leaders in government, or dictators in the social realm. Will you have a seat in Parliament?"

"No. Though I think it is unfair that all of England's lords can sit in the House of Lords when Scotland is allowed only sixteen seats, I'm thankful I dinna have to face that challenge. I have no desire to be elected as one of Scotland's representatives. I may change my mind someday, but now I would be like a coach without a wheel. Or two."

They passed another house where several guests were arriving. As before, Branderee's carriage did not go by without close inspection. Still leaning back away from the window, Mariah could see out but hoped no one could see her. She noted that the women didn't even glance toward her side of the coach. Their gazes were riveted on the earl as the bright lights shining from the house illuminated his face.

Of course, the women are looking at him. They probably already know how handsome he is. Even if they had not seen him in person, word of a handsome, eligible earl traveled fast. She shook her head, smiling at her foolishness.

"What's so amusing?"

"Here I am worrying about what the women will say about me when they are too captivated by you to even look in my direction."

"Is that a compliment?"

"Of course it is. You're a braw man, Kiernan Macpherson, and you know it."

He smiled, his eyes sparkling. "I know no such thing...but I'm glad you think so."

"How could I not?" she asked, almost managing a nonchalant shrug. When the coach halted in front of a townhouse, a new wave of worry assailed her. "Kiernan, if your mother and sister are not comfortable with our business arrangement or do not like me, I'll leave immediately."

His smile vanished. "Where would you go?"

"I have no idea, but I'll think of something." She frowned and added softly, "I might have to borrow some money. Just enough to get by until I can find another position. I will pay you back every penny."

Kiernan leaned across the narrow space between them and covered her hand with his. "They will like you, Mariah."

She wondered if he was confident of her or of his ability to bend others to his will.

She met his gaze, but the warmth she saw there unnerved her

further. She looked down and eased her hand from beneath his. "I hope you are right."

"I am." He straightened and gave her a cocky grin. "Didna I tell you? I'm always right."

"Humble, too," she said dryly.

"Rarely."

A footman raced down the steps and opened the coach door. "Welcome home, Lord Branderee."

"Thank you, Simms." Kiernan stepped out and turned to help her down.

Mariah placed her hand in his, once again aware of his strength as he bore part of her weight when she stepped to the ground. Calling herself a coward, she let her hand linger in his until he offered her his arm.

Smiling when she tucked her hand around his forearm, he whispered, "Relax."

As they walked up the steps, the stately, silver-haired butler opened the door, greeting them with a somber half-bow. "Good evening, my lord, madam. I hope you had a pleasant trip. The ladies and Mr. Macpherson are in the drawing room," he intoned in a deep, rumbling voice, with the precise diction and projection of a thespian.

"Thank you, Wilton. Please have Lady Mariah's trunk sent up to a guest room."

"As you wish, sir." Wilton nodded, ordering a footman to his side with a flick of his hand. "Shall I have Cook prepare a light supper?"

"Perhaps later."

Kiernan escorted Mariah down the hall. She fought to control a giggle. "I feel as if I should be dressed for the theatre. Wherever did you find him?"

Kiernan grinned. "The staff came with the house when we rented it. He is a wee bit pompous, but I like him."

"A wee bit? I'm glad I'm working for you and not him," she said with a grin.

"He rules us all with an iron hand." Kiernan smiled down at her, his eyes twinkling. "He keeps everything and everyone running on schedule."

He paused just inside the drawing room door, and Mariah took a calming breath, quickly scanning the room. It had been painted pale green to complement the green marble fireplace and white plaster vines in the ornate ceiling. A man and young woman, obviously Kiernan's sister, sat at a small Queen Anne walnut table on the other side of the room engrossed in a game of chess.

Except for a feathery layer of bangs, Jeanette's light brown hair was drawn into a cluster of curls at the back of her head. Her features were softer than Kiernan's, but the resemblance was unmistakable. Her peach muslin dress set off her coloring and gently rounded figure. She was not a ravishing beauty, but even without a wealthy brother, she would have had her share of suitors.

Mariah felt certain her companion was Kiernan's friend, Gabriel. He wore a soft creamy shirt and a kilt of the same red, green, and blue tartan Kiernan favored, but his plaid and jacket had been discarded in the warm room. Broad-shouldered and slim, he looked as if he might be an inch or two taller than Kiernan. He combed his straight auburn hair neatly back from his tanned face, and the brilliant smile he flashed at Jeanette was only slightly dimmed by the pink around his nose. *Even with a cold, the man is a charmer.*

Near them, an older woman dozed, her head lolled against the back of the yellow silk covered armchair, her feet resting on a small matching walnut footstool. An open book lay across her lap. Her dark brown hair, liberally sprinkled with gray, was pulled back into a bun. Dressed in black and small in stature, she seemed too thin for her height. Mariah suspected she had not always been so delicate, to the point of appearing frail. Grief had taken more than the joy from his mother's life.

Mrs. Macpherson's eyelids fluttered, then lifted. Smiling sleepily, she looked straight at Kiernan, her dark brown eyes warming. "I didna hear you come in," she said, straightening and setting the book on the table beside her. Her gaze slid to Mariah, then back to her son. "And I see you've brought a guest. Welcome, miss," she said with a smile.

"Thank you," murmured Mariah, attempting to lift her hand from where it rested on Kiernan's arm.

He pressed her hand firmly against his side and drew her across the room, finally releasing it when they stopped in front of his mother. Dropping a kiss on her wan cheek, he searched her face. "Are you well, Mother? You are no' taking Gabe's cold, are you?"

"I'm fine, dear."

"You're pale."

She waved away his concern. "I'm spending too much time indoors. I'll be fine when I'm back in Scotland's clear air."

Mariah did not believe the excuse. Mrs. Macpherson's skin had almost a grayish cast, and there were dark circles beneath her sad eyes. Mariah wondered if she suffered from more than a broken heart. She sensed Kiernan did not believe her either, but he refrained from questioning her further.

"Now, introduce me to your friend, laddie."

"Yes, ma'am. Mother, may I present Lady Mariah Douglas, the earl of Glenbuck's sister. Lady Mariah, my mother, Ailsa Macpherson."

Surprise crossed Mrs. Macpherson's face, but it vanished in a polite smile. "It is a pleasure to meet you, milady."

"The pleasure is mine, ma'am. Lord Branderee has spoken very fondly of you." Mariah thought she saw suspicion creep into the other woman's eyes, but then wondered if she might have imagined it. "I hope you are enjoying your visit to London."

"The city is interesting, although we have no' been out a great deal since Kiernan left."

"I'm afraid I have been a poor escort," said Gabriel, moving to Mrs. Macpherson's side, resting his hand on her shoulder. Jeanette joined them, smiling at Mariah.

Mrs. Macpherson reached up and patted Gabriel's hand affectionately. "You've been too sick to go out."

"I'm well enough, now. I'll take you for a drive in the park tomorrow." Gabriel smiled at Mariah. "I hope you will join us, milady."

"Not tomorrow," said Kiernan, briefly meeting her gaze. "Lady Mariah will be busy."

6

"LADY MARIAH, MAY I PRESENT my little sister, Jeanette, and my good friend, Gabriel Macpherson."

After the three exchanged greetings, Kiernan asked Mariah to sit on the terra-cotta silk brocade sofa. He sat down beside her, knowing she was nervous, wishing he could ease her fears. He wanted to take her hand in his. Instead, he smiled, momentarily capturing her gaze, silently reassuring her that all would be well.

As Jeanette and Gabriel sat down across from them in matching chairs, his sister sent him a questioning glance.

"Aye, lass, I know you're about to pop with curiosity."

Jeanette laughed, her topaz eyes sparkling. "Forgive me, milady. My brother does no' often bring ladies home with him."

"I take it he has done so on occasion," Mariah said graciously.

Kiernan saw the strain in her smile.

"Yes, on occasion." Jeanette grinned at him. "Last November, a lady's coach broke down not far from the estate. She and her maid spent several days with us until it was repaired. A couple of other times, he rescued some young women from rather unpleasant circumstances. They now work as maids at Branderee Castle."

Kiernan frowned, not sure he liked the light in which his sister cast him. Mariah would think he took in every misbegotten soul he came across, which was not true. Sometimes he felt a need to help, sometimes not.

With Mariah, it was not simply a matter of lending a hand. She would have found some way to go on without his assistance, but at what cost? He felt responsible for her welfare. Because of him, she had been forced to leave Stillwater. Yet he knew he would not have left her behind even if he had not been to blame.

He wanted to be around her, to learn what she liked and disliked, to watch her move and hear her voice. He needed to know she was safe from harm, with a warm bed, good meals, and decent clothes. Anything less would doom him to more sleepless nights filled with worry. Now, she would think she was no different from the others he had brought home.

"Ah, a rescuer of damsels in distress," said Mariah with a smile. "He has done the same for me."

To Kiernan's amazement, she seemed to relax somewhat. *Very well*, he thought, *if it puts her at ease, let her think I go around like some knight on a white charger.*

"When I arrived at Stillwater, I discovered Lady Mariah living there," said Kiernan.

"Did Glenbuck know?" asked Gabriel with a deep frown.

"I believe so." Mariah looked at him, her cheeks turning pink. "My brother and I are not on good terms. We have had no contact in several years."

"Why didna you simply let her stay?" asked his mother.

"It was no' possible."

"Stillwater is in deplorable condition, Mrs. Macpherson. Even if Lord Branderee made vast improvements, it would take years to see any return. I could not have made enough from the land to pay the rent, much less hire someone to work it. His lordship is fortunate that my neighbor, Sir Edgar Pittman, has long wanted to acquire the acreage."

"You sold her home right out from under her?" Jeanette exclaimed, staring at Kiernan in disbelief. His mother looked at him as if he had taken leave of his senses. Even Gabriel glared at him.

Irritated, Kiernan shifted his position, resting his arm along the back of the sofa. He could see no way of explaining the situation without embarrassing Mariah or painting himself as a blackguard.

"Please, do not fault your brother, Miss Macpherson," said Mariah quietly. "If I had stayed at Stillwater, my home would have been a leaky, one-room tenant cottage. The roof on the manor collapsed two days ago." She glanced at Kiernan, her expression filled with gratitude. "If his lordship had not recognized the danger and insisted I move to the cottage, I would have been killed."

Jeanette gasped. "Oh, my goodness! Was anyone hurt?"

"No, I lived alone." When Mariah faltered, Kiernan started to speak, but she quickly shook her head. She took a deep breath, looking directly at his mother. "Years ago, I made a grave mistake and lost my inheritance, causing a scandal. My brother disowned me, and I fled to Stillwater because I knew he hated the place and never went there."

Her gaze shifted to Jeanette. "For the past nine years, I have lived in two rooms of a ramshackled manor house that should have been demolished long ago. I could not afford servants, but by the grace of God and the others who lived on the estate at the time, I learned to manage on my own."

When she glanced at Kiernan, it was all he could do to keep from putting his arm around her. He had wanted to spare her humiliation by explaining her situation as briefly as possible, going into the details only after she had retired to her room. Judging from the others' sympathetic expressions, however, it was best that she tell her own story. *Such a brave lass.*

"The truth is, ma'am, I haven't a feather to fly with. In all likelihood, I could not have held out at Stillwater much longer, perhaps a year at the most."

"You poor lass." Ailsa dabbed her eyes with a lace kerchief. "Thank you for being so forthright with us. You are welcome to stay here as long as you need."

"Thank you, ma'am, but I cannot take advantage of your hospitality." Uncertainty swept over her face, and she hesitated.

Kiernan curled his hand into a fist to keep from touching her. "I think I have a way for Mariah to support herself and to help us in the bargain. I've asked her to be your companion, Mother, as well as Jeanie's chaperon." When his mother's eyes shone with relief, he knew he had made the right decision. "Though she has been away from London for some time, she has friends in the *ton* and knows how to manuever through the maze of Society. She could be a great help to us while we are here." He grinned at Gabriel. "I know you'd be grateful for the rest. You are an old hand at this, but I think we are exhausting you with all our questions and mistakes."

Gabriel rolled his eyes. "I beg you to stay, milady. The blunders these two make are going to put me in my grave."

Jeanette swatted him playfully on the arm. "We have no' been that bad." She sighed and looked at Mariah. "Though I worry that I will do something that is perfectly fine at home but will put me beyond the pale here. I've already discovered I canna even go for a walk in the park by myself without causing an uproar." A quick grin flashed across her face. "I dinna know who was more put out when they learned I'd gone off on my own, Gabe or Wilton."

"Jeanie, I told you that you canna go out without an escort," Kiernan said sternly. "You must take a footman or groom with you."

"I know you said I should, but they were busy, and Gabe was too sick to go. It was such a beautiful morning, the first sunny day we'd had all week." She shrugged, her expression chagrined. "The park is only three blocks away," she said to Mariah. "I didna think it would hurt anything, and it didna except to cause everyone here great consternation. No one accosted me, and I had a very pleasant time with two nannies and their little charges. Such precious bairns. They didna have a footman or groom with them."

"But they had gone together, no' alone." said Gabriel. "I think she learned her lesson. Wilton went after her and brought her home."

Kiernan raised an eyebrow. "Did he ring a peal over your head all the way back?"

"Wilton? Never. No' in public. He very politely informed me my presence was required at home. He escorted me here without another word." Jeanie grimaced. "But when we arrived, he spent a quarter hour explaining in exact detail how my behavior could ruin me before I even made my come out." A blush spread across her face. "Then he spent the next quarter hour explaining what else might have happened—things such as being robbed or kidnapped and held for ransom or sold to a brothel in the East End."

Kiernan tensed, scowling at the door as he wondered if Wilton was anywhere close by. This time the man had gone too far. The butler had no right to speak to Jeanie of such things.

"Dinna yell at him, Kier. He didna go into great detail, but he opened my eyes to the dangers here. He was kind but reminded me that I am far too trusting and green. Speaking in that dramatic way of his, he made a far greater impression on me than either you or Gabe have. I apologize for no' heeding your warnings and doing as you directed."

Jeanette smiled sweetly at Mariah. "So you see, Kiernan is right. I do need a guiding hand. I dinna try to get into mischief, but I seem to land in it anyway."

"You are all very kind." Mariah took a deep breath and squared her shoulders. "But you need to know of my past before you agree to Kiernan's suggestion. You may change your mind."

One glance at her pale face, and Kiernan forgot all about the butler. "Mariah, you've had a long day. Why dinna you retire and let me explain?"

She shook her head and looked at him, her eyes silently asking for his understanding. "I could not rest anyway. You all must understand what you may be up against if I stay." When he nodded, she began her story.

"I had my come out nine years ago. About midway into the Season, I met a very handsome, charming man who swept me off my feet."

As she briefly described her short courtship and marriage, Kiernan listened in silence, watching the others' expressions. Curiosity turned to horror as she related how she awoke to find herself abandoned and the marriage a sham. His mother gasped audibly, and quick tears filled Jeanette's eyes. Gabe scowled, muttering an appropriate description of Shelton in Gaelic.

Mariah closed her eyes and lowered her head, a small tremor shaking her body.

Kiernan slid his arm around her. "Enough, Mariah. Let me tell the rest later."

She raised her head, her expression once again composed. "No, I'll do it."

When he held out his hand, she curled her fingers around it, gripping tightly. Kiernan caught a surprised, speculative look between his mother and sister, but to his relief they said nothing.

"I returned to London, reaching my brother's house in the morning. By nightfall, the scandal was all over town. The next morning, an article appeared in the *Times*. Although I was not mentioned by name, Shelton's name was given as the paper proclaimed to the world that he was a bigamist and a thief, warning other young women to beware so they might protect their innocence and their inheritance. Though written sympathetically toward me, it was horrible to have my shame displayed so publicly."

She paused and Kiernan tightened his arm around her shoulders, willing her to stop.

"My brother was livid at my stupidity. He conveniently forgot that he had given us his blessing. He decided the only way to weather the storm was for me to go to the next social function for which we had an invitation. He said it would show the *ton* that I did not care what they thought, that I could still hold my head high."

"He was right in a way," said Gabriel. "You were the one wronged. You had no reason to be ashamed. Yet, how did he expect you to pretend nothing had happened when you had been hurt so deeply?"

"He wasna thinking of her feelings," said Kiernan angrily. "Only his place in Society."

"Did you go?" asked Jeanette.

"Yes. We attended a ball that very evening. I was so numb I didn't think anything else could hurt me. I was wrong. Some people were sympathetic to my plight and praised my courage. Others refused to speak to me or brushed their skirts aside so they would not be tainted by the touch of my gown. Some turned their backs on me, giving me a direct cut.

"Yet my friends surrounded me with their support. I managed a couple of dances without tripping my partners and thought perhaps I might make it through the evening. Then my next partner slyly offered to comfort me during my distress since his wife was conveniently out of town for a fortnight."

"Such audacity!" exclaimed Jeanette.

"It was only the beginning. I quickly realized several of the men gazed at me in that same demeaning way, and one even went so far as to offer me *carte blanche*, promising to set me up in a nice little house of my own and shower me with jewels.

"When I angrily refused, he declared it was all I should expect. He said it was common knowledge that I had known Shelton had a wife, but that I'd gone through with the illegal marriage anyway in the hope of taking him away from her. We later learned the rumor had begun to circulate shortly after our arrival. In the eyes of many, I was ruined."

Kiernan fought to remain calm in spite of a hot rush of anger. Though she had mentioned the snubs and cuts, she had not told him of the propositions and disgraceful treatment at the hands of *gentlemen*. Now he was certain he did not want to be included in their ranks.

Mariah pulled her hand from his, slowly looking up at him with sad eyes. "Now, you know the whole of it, what I could not bring myself to tell you before. It may have blown over as Sir Edgar says, but it is also possible that my presence will stir things up once again." She looked first at his mother, then Jeanette. "If I stay here, you may find yourselves outcasts or, at the very least, the subject of gossip.

"Now, if you would be so kind as to have someone show me to my room, you can discuss this situation freely." She stood, turning toward Gabriel. "Mr. Macpherson, you are familiar with Society's whims and ways, I trust you to give your friends good advice."

Kiernan rose from the sofa, intent on escorting her upstairs.

"Nine years is a long time, Lady Mariah," said Gabriel quietly as he stood also. "I dinna think there will be much of a stir."

"And if there is, we will ignore it," said Jeanette, jumping up and linking her arm through Mariah's. "Come, Mariah, I'll show you to your room. I know you must be exhausted. When you are rested, we will go shopping. We shall have great fun spending my brother's money on clothes for the Season."

Mariah halted, her gaze going to his mother. "Mrs. Macpherson?"

"Of course, you should stay, dear. You canna know how it eases my mind to have you here to watch over Jeanie. I suspect no one else would be more careful of her reputation than you. What's past is past. We will no' worry overmuch about it."

"I dinna believe in coincidence, Mariah," said Jeanette gently. "God brought you to us. He allowed Kiernan to be in that card game with your brother, knowing he would be the one to win Stillwater. He knew we needed you as badly as you needed us."

"I want to believe that," said Mariah with a faint smile. "I try to trust God, but sometimes I worry that I may not see the way."

"We all have our moments of doubt." Jeanette started walking, pulling Mariah along with her. "But I'm certain you are supposed to be here."

So am I, thought Kiernan. He had hoped that when his mother and sister heard her story, they would welcome her, but seeing it accomplished was a great relief. He could not bear the thought of her going anywhere else.

"How do you know?" asked Mariah.

Jeanette grinned at Kiernan. "Because I've seen the way my brother looks at you."

Clearly startled, Mariah glanced at him over her shoulder. He said nothing but winked and flashed her a joyful smile.

The wooing begins.

7

A CARRIAGE RATTLING ALONG the cobblestone street in front of the townhouse awakened Mariah the next morning. After Jeanette's teasing comment and Kiernan's roguish wink, she had expected to toss and turn. Sheer exhaustion, aided by a warm bath, had overcome her turbulent emotions, however, and she had slept soundly all night.

She stretched lazily beneath the covers in the four-poster bed, staring at the yellow and white brocade canopy above her. Though the fire burned low in the fireplace, the room remained comfortable. There had been no need during the night to draw the matching curtains around the bed. Sliding her hand from beneath the feather quilt, she touched the tip of her warm nose with her finger and grinned. *Much better than a cold, dripping castle or leaky cottage*, she thought happily.

"And no holes or mends in the sheets," she said softly, running her foot across the width of the bed. Scooting up, Mariah plumped the pillows against the mahogany headboard and leaned against them, letting her gaze roam around the cheerful room.

A wardrobe occupied one corner, and next to it stood a mahogany chest of drawers. A satinwood dressing table and matching washstand with a blue printed basin stood along the opposite wall. The two outside drawers pulled out and pivoted, revealing an adjustable mirror in each one so she could see the back of her head as well as the front. A rectangular cheval mirror stood in the corner for a last-minute head-to-toe inspection before leaving the room.

Near the window a cheerful pink, chintz-covered armchair had been positioned to catch the morning sun. Beeswax candles secured in porcelain holders on a table by the chair provided light for reading on cloudy days or in the evenings.

"Beeswax candles, a washstand that doesn't wobble, thick carpet on the floor...Heavenly Father, I could grow used to this. It's the nicest room I've ever had."

Her thoughts drifted back to the nursery at Glenbuck Castle with its simple furnishings—a small bed for her and another for Nanny; two chairs and a table where she ate, played, and learned to read; a wardrobe; a dresser; and shelves for books and some old toys. It had been an austere room, brightened only by the wildflowers she and Nanny gathered. Adequate for a girl, her father had said.

Her gaze fell on a vase filled to overflowing with tulips on a table in the small sitting area of the room. The flowers had been waiting the night before, a welcoming gift by the thoughtful housekeeper.

Her rooms at Miss Eversham's School had been somewhat better than the one at Glenbuck. Pink rose wallpaper had adorned the walls, and the furniture, though heavy and ornate, had been polished until it glistened. She had shared a room with another girl most of the time, but at the start of her last year, she was given a room of her own, as befitted an earl's sister, Miss Eversham had said.

Then she had moved to Pryse's London home. He liked expensive, beautiful things, but usually only those rooms guests might see were decorated elegantly. Her room had been comfortable but certainly not as pleasant as this one.

Mariah sighed, remembering the twinkle in Kiernan's eyes as he winked at her the night before. "If I had any sense, I'd go to the employment agency straightaway." But she knew she wouldn't.

Gratitude and a sense of responsibility kept her with the Macphersons. It would be impossible to find another position with the same financial benefits. Nor, she suspected, would she ever find another family who welcomed her so warmly.

"Because they think Kiernan is interested in me." A little shiver ran down her spine, part trepidation and part anticipation. Mariah would never give her heart to another man, nor would she marry. She had lived alone and by her wits too long to bow to the complete control granted a husband by English law. But could she not enjoy his friendship and a light flirtation? *Pleasant but dangerous.* "But not likely to go too far with his mother and sister in the house."

It would not be easy for Kiernan to find Jeanette a chaperon who would not try to stifle the girl's independent, joyful spirit. Mariah understood the freedom inherent in growing up in the country and knew well the perils awaiting the innocent amid the *ton.* "I think this is where you want me, Lord, but not completely for the same reasons Jeanette thinks."

A soft knock on the door broke through her reverie. "Come in."

The door opened and a young maid carrying a small tray stepped into the room and bobbed a quick curtsy. "Good mornin', milady. I'm Elise. I've been assigned to be your abigail."

Mariah started to protest until she saw the girl's sparkling eyes. "I take it that this is a move up."

"Oh, yes, milady." Elise shut the door and hurried across the room, setting the tray on the bedside table. "I've been the upstairs maid for the past year, but Miss Jeanette's abigail, Sukey, took a likin' to me, she did, and she's been teachin' me. When his lordship asked Wilton to find a lady's maid for you, he recommended me. I was ever so grateful."

She spread a linen cloth across Mariah's lap. "I didn't know whether you would want tea or chocolate so I brought both."

"Tea, please, with a spoonful of sugar and a touch of cream." A perfect pink rose in a crystal bud vase sat beside a plate of toast on the tray. "The flower is lovely, Elise, and I appreciate your kind thought, but there is no need to pretty up my tea tray."

The maid handed her the translucent china cup. "Oh, the rose wasn't my idea, milady." Elise grinned, her eyes sparkling. "Wilton said his lordship ordered it from the florist first thing this morning. Lord Branderee put it on the tray himself, he did. He said he noticed all your rosebushes at Stillwater and thought you might enjoy it."

"How kind of him," murmured Mariah. *And how romantic.* Suddenly, a light flirtation seemed more disquieting than appealing.

"He left a note, too." Elise handed her the folded piece of ivory stationery edged with gold and discreetly moved over to open the drapes.

Her pulse quickening, Mariah set the cup on the tray and unfolded the paper. *To celebrate your new beginning. Welcome to our home. Kiernan.* Sweet, but not as romantic as she had feared—or had she been hoping? She didn't want to delve too deeply into that question, nor make too much of an act of thoughtfulness.

Elise's giggle drew her attention. The maid stood in front of the wardrobe, holding a petticoat and shift in her hand. Taking a sachet from amid the small stack of Mariah's underpinnings, she lifted it to her nose and sniffed. She tucked the small bag back into place and grinned at Mariah. "Now, I think I know why his lordship said he had recently developed a great fondness for roses."

"Oh, dear." Mariah threw back the covers and hopped out of bed. "This will never do. I must speak to him."

"You can't, ma'am. He's gone off on business and won't be back until this afternoon. But Mrs. Macpherson and Miss Jeanette will be goin' down to breakfast soon. They said for you to come down whenever you wanted. You'll let me style your hair, won't you, Lady Mariah? I'm very good at it."

Mariah sighed, torn between enjoying Kiernan's interest and knowing it was foolish to allow it to continue. "I'm sure you are, Elise. Of course, you may do my hair. It appears there is no need to rush."

Half an hour later, Mariah walked downstairs to the breakfast room, wearing one of her two best day dresses. The short-sleeved calico frock in bright turquoise always lifted her spirits. Jeanette and Mrs. Macpherson had just taken their places at the table. They greeted her warmly.

"Did you sleep well, Mariah?" asked Mrs. Macpherson. "I wondered if the noise would wake you too early. I have no' yet grown accustomed to the heavy wagons lumbering past just after dawn. As you can see, we are still keeping country hours somewhat."

"That will change when the balls and parties begin. Going to bed at two or three in the morning quickly changes one's sleeping habits." Mariah picked up a plate and stared at the variety of breakfast dishes displayed on the sideboard. There were sausages, bacon, poached eggs, boiled eggs, grapes, toast, muffins, butter, marmalade, and several kinds of preserves. There were pots of coffee, tea, and chocolate on the table.

Jeanette asked quietly, "Is something wrong?"

"I had forgotten how many choices there are. I've grown used to simpler fare—a bowl of gruel or an egg and piece of bread." She shook her head in bewilderment. "I fear stepping back into the aristocracy is going to be more difficult than I realized."

Jeanette smiled. "I expect you will fall into step quickly enough. We always had a variety and plenty to eat before Kiernan became wealthy, but I confess it has no' taken me long to delight in some of the things money can buy. Such as the confections from Gunter's. The first time I tasted their strawberry ices, I thought I'd gone to some magical land. Now, eat up. We have a busy morning ahead of us."

The food looked so good, Mariah was hard pressed not to take some of everything. With the silent reminder that she could eat something different on the morrow, she took sausages, a poached egg, a muffin, and some grapes. "What are we doing today?"

"First off, we have an appointment with Mrs. Haveland, the dressmaker, so you can be measured and pick out the material for some new dresses and a pelisse. Kiernan insisted we see to it right away. He said after being in the country so long, your wardrobe is bound to need updating." Jeanette glanced at Mariah's dress. "Although maybe he is wrong. You look lovely this morning."

"Thank you." Mariah smiled ruefully. "And I'll look fine tomorrow after Elise washes and presses the dress I wore on the trip." She sat down and poured a cup of tea, adding sugar and cream. "But the next day, I'll be back to this one. Kiernan is right. I only have two nice day dresses, ones I've kept tucked away. I have a couple of others that are presentable enough to wear here in the house as long as we don't have company and no one looks too closely." She took a bite of sausage, barely restraining a sigh of contentment.

"After the dressmaker's, we may visit a few other shops. We will definitely stop off at the milliners." Jeanette grinned. "Everyone has to have a new bonnet when they first come to Town."

Mariah laughed. "My best bonnet is still pretty but sadly out of fashion."

"Save it for Scotland. No one will know the difference there. If you go back with us," Jeanette added quickly.

"Kiernan mentioned the possibility, but I don't think we should plan on it." Mariah smiled at the young woman. "I've only been here one night, and much can change in a few months."

"Do you have friends in London, Lady Mariah?" asked Kiernan's mother.

"I'm not certain they are here yet, although I have friends who usually come for the Season." Mariah wrinkled her brow in a slight frown. "I should have calling cards made up."

"I believe Kiernan is seeing to that today," said Mrs. Macpherson. "He said he would be going close by the printers."

"He seems to have thought of everything," said Mariah, flattered but still unnerved by such attention.

"Gabe mentioned the cards. He keeps us up to the mark on that kind of thing. Kiernan told Jeanette to purchase anything you needed." Mrs. Macpherson placed her fork on the edge of the plate. "And to spare no expense."

Heat rushed to Mariah's face under the older woman's concerned gaze.

Jeanette smiled mischievously. "I've also been instructed to buy twice what you ask for since my brother thinks you'll try to make do with the barest of necessities."

"I only need enough so as not to embarrass myself or your family." Mariah put down her fork and carefully folded her napkin, suddenly no longer hungry. "I'm uncomfortable with him purchasing anything for me. If you will keep a thorough accounting, I'll repay him out of my wages."

"He willna take your money, nor would I want him to." Mrs. Macpherson rested her hand on the table. "He has much; you have little. It is right that we share God's blessings.

"Being in charge comes naturally to my son. He sees a need and tries to help, discovers a wrong and seeks to right it." A tiny smile touched her lips. "He was that way even as a wee laddie and landed himself in many a scrape."

Her smile faded, and her expression became troubled. "The power and wealth that came with his title have unsettled him. He moves in a new world, one with different values than what his father and I taught him. My prayer is that he will find his bearings in remembered words of Scripture and no' be led too far astray.

"Be careful, Lady Mariah, for he is greatly attracted to you. A year ago, I would have had no doubt that his intentions were honorable, but I canna be sure any longer. Here, men can do as they choose so long as they have money and are discreet." She shook her head sadly. "I dinna quite know what to expect from him anymore. I never thought he would come home drunk or spend all night in a card game risking thousands of pounds, but he has done both."

Mariah pondered Mrs. Macpherson's words, knowing they reflected some of her own worries. "I thank you for your concern, ma'am. Before I agreed to come to work for you, I carefully considered and prayed about the possibilities of the situation. I have not been acquainted with your son for long, but my instincts—honed through bitter experience—tell me he is an honorable man. As for gambling, he told me that he has no intention of ever being in a high-stakes card game again."

She pictured him making that declaration and smiled. "Of course, that was moments after he first saw the manor at Stillwater. Winning it would make all but the most avid gamester question his folly."

Mrs. Macpherson smiled. "It does seem he was being taught a lesson. Let's hope he heeds it."

"He will, Mam." Jeanette patted her hand. "You worry too much. Kiernan isna going to become a reprobate," she said gently. "He may wander a bit, but his heart is good, and God will watch over him."

"You're right, Jeanie." Mrs. Macpherson's eyes held deep sorrow as she looked at Mariah. "Without my husband to reassure me, I do worry too much. I didna realize how much I depended upon him until he was gone." She took a deep breath and forced a small smile. "Go get your bonnets on or you'll be late. Mrs. Haveland willna like to be kept waiting."

Mariah smiled. "Now we know who truly rules Society."

Mariah soon learned that Jeanette had not been exaggerating when she said she enjoyed spending her brother's money, especially when it came to making purchases for her "dear friend." Nothing was said to indicate that Mariah was a paid chaperon or companion.

When she quietly protested the cost of a particular piece of silk Mrs. Haveland suggested for a ball gown, Jeanette merely grinned.

"Stubble it, Mariah. You'll sparkle like a jewel in bishop's blue."

Bemused and silently thrilled at the prospect of wearing something so beautiful, Mariah decided to keep quiet. They picked out material and patterns for four day dresses, two more evening gowns, a pelisse, and a mantle, which was similar to a cloak and made of a large rectangular piece of fabric gathered at the neck with no sleeves. Mrs. Haveland then led her to the back room where detailed measurements were taken.

As Mariah stood in her shift, short stays, and petticoat in front of a mirror, the dressmaker draped the various pieces of material around her to make certain she was satisfied with the fabric. Mariah gasped softly when she pinned the bishop's blue silk, a purplish-blue shade, in place. "Oh, my, this is lovely."

"Milady, we could not have picked a finer color for you," said Mrs. Haveland. "You will turn heads in this gown." She drew the fabric lower, exposing a generous amount of cleavage.

"I'd rather not make their heads spin right off their shoulders," said Mariah dryly. "A more modest cut, if you please."

"But Lady Mariah, this is quite acceptable for a lady not fresh from the schoolroom. You are not limited to the sedate fashions of your first Season."

Mariah glanced at her sharply. So far as she knew, there had been no mention that this was only the second time she had taken part in the Season. "I prefer a sedate neckline, Mrs. Haveland."

"Of course, milady." The dressmaker raised the cloth until just a hint of bosom was revealed and studied Mariah's reflection. "Yes, this is best. You will look regal and serene." She met Mariah's gaze in the mirror and smiled kindly. "The dress will help you feel the same. You are right to come back, Lady Mariah, and hold your head high."

"You remember?" Mariah's heart sank. If Mrs. Haveland remembered the scandal so well, she had no hope that Society would forget.

Mrs. Haveland nodded as she removed the silk. "Mainly because it was the first year I had my own shop. The events of that Season seem to have been stamped in my memory much more clearly than most in the years since. I'm often amazed at how some ladies will chatter when they come for a fitting." She carefully folded the material. "As I recall, many felt you had been grievously wronged, both by the man you thought you married and your brother. I certainly did. Still do." She glanced at the silk and smiled. "If I have anything to do with it, you shall return in triumph."

"I'd rather hide in the shadows," said Mariah, her words muffled as she slipped her dress over her head.

"Well, since that is not possible, only a grand entrance will do." Mrs. Haveland smiled and fastened the tiny buttons that ran down the back of the dress to just past the high waist. "I will have an assistant deliver the mantle in the morning. It will take almost no time at all to stitch up, and at least one of the day dresses should be ready late tomorrow afternoon."

"So soon? Surely you have other orders ahead of mine."

"Two of the patterns are quite simple, and his lordship said he would pay extra for due haste. So due haste it is. I'll hire another seamstress or two. Besides, unlike most clients, he pays upon delivery of the goods, so I am more than happy to provide special service." Her eyes twinkled. "I expected a man would look silly in a kilt, but Lord Branderee changed my mind. A fine figure of a man, even in a skirt."

Mariah stared at her. "He came here?"

"Oh, yes. The first time his mother and sister visited the shop, he came along to set up an account. He also stopped by early this morning to advise that you would be taking Miss Macpherson's appointment and to assure me that he approved the purchases. I appreciate his consideration. I've run into problems a few times when an impulsive young lady thought to help a friend, only to discover that her papa would not foot the bill."

She picked up the folded silk and opened the dressing room door. "I look forward to serving you again, milady." Mrs. Haveland bustled from the room.

Mariah sat down and slipped on her shoes as Jeanette stepped into the room, leaning against the doorjamb. "Did you know your brother came by to see Mrs. Haveland this morning?"

"No." Jeanette smiled. "But it sounds like something he would do. He likes to make sure everything is nice and tidy."

"We need to train your brother." Mariah smiled at the impossibility. "He should send his secretary on this type of errand."

"He didna bring him. Fiske was beside himself at the thought of coming to London. He is more of a house steward than a secretary, though he is excellent at correspondence. He keeps the household records in minute detail, but he is older and set in his ways. He is uncomfortable around new people or in new situations.

"Kiernan drives him to distraction, and I believe it terrified him to think of trying to deal with my brother and the city at the same time. He is slow and methodical. Kiernan likes to do things quickly. Unfortunately, if you try to hurry Fiske along, he falls completely into a dither."

"But Kiernan puts up with it." Mariah picked up her reticule, and they left the shop.

Thaddeus and the coachman, Angus, were waiting at the curb with the Branderee carriage. Thaddeus opened the door and helped them inside. "Where to, Miss Jeanette?"

"I think first to the linen-drapers. Angus knows which one."

"As you wish, miss." Thaddeus bowed and shut the door. The carriage dipped slightly as he climbed into place, then it began to move.

"Kiernan tolerates Fiske simply because he canna bring himself to dismiss anyone. I did point out on the way here that Fiske is old enough to pension off. Personally, I think he would do well to let both him and Macnair go."

"Who is Macnair?"

"The factor. I dinna know what it is about him that makes me ill at ease. He is always polite and respectful and seems to run the estate efficiently, but something isna quite right. I've talked to Kiernan about it, and he has the same feeling, but he canna find anything amiss. Keeping accounts isna Kiernan's strong suit, and he is still learning about the estate."

"Could Fiske help?"

"Kiernan had him go over the ledgers, but Fiske said he didna know enough about farming to determine if the figures are accurate." She shook her head. "Just going over the estate records caused him great distress. He said it was because it made him think about the late earl. The housekeeper told me he had worked for the earl for ten years. She said they were very close."

"That could explain why it has been so hard for him to become accustomed to working for Kiernan."

Jeanette nodded. "I expect so. Here is our next stop."

They spent half an hour at the linen-drapers, buying stockings, petticoats, shifts, nightgowns, and dressing gowns, not only for Mariah but for Jeanette and Mrs. Macpherson as well. Mariah was pleased with the quality of her purchases but relieved when Jeanette did not insist on buying only the most costly. Having Kiernan pay for her underclothes embarrassed her.

They paused briefly to glance over the selection of dress fabrics, then strolled down the street to the milliners with Thaddeus accompanying them to the door. Angus drove the coach to the establishment and parked in front. They purchased Mariah a new straw bonnet trimmed in yellow ribbon and a cluster of tiny daisies at the front of the crown. After ordering her two more hats for day and three for evening wear, they departed the shopping district before it became a man's domain in the early afternoon.

By the time they arrived at the townhouse, Mariah had developed a nagging headache. She longed for a bite to eat, a quiet room, and a long nap but felt obligated to join Jeanette in telling Mrs. Macpherson about their shopping expedition. Hope of escaping to her room vanished when Wilton announced the arrival of Miss Clarissa St. John.

As her mother instructed the butler to show the young lady in, Jeanette leaned over and said quietly, "Viscount and Lady St. John's only daughter. She is one of the few women near my age I've had an opportunity to meet."

Mariah tensed. Years earlier, when news of Shelton's deception had reached the *ton*, Lady St. John had been one of Mariah's most outspoken critics. She had no reason to hope the woman's feelings had mellowed over time.

Clarissa would all too likely tell her mother that Mariah was now situated in the earl of Branderee's household. Before midnight, most of Society would learn she was back in Town.

I wonder how the viscountess will embellish the tale this time.

8

THIN AS A WILLOW, CLARISSA MOVED with grace and confidence. Her short-sleeved, soft pink muslin gown brought gentle color to her fair complexion. A bright pink ribbon and bow adorned her short, blond curls. Though her hair was several shades lighter than her mother's, the girl favored the viscountess considerably and was even more of a beauty.

"Lady Mariah, may I present Miss Clarissa St. John. Clarissa, I would like you to meet Lady Mariah Douglas. She is joining us for the Season."

"How nice. It is a pleasure to meet you, milady."

Mariah murmured a polite greeting as Clarissa sank into a perfect curtsy before sitting gracefully in the yellow silk armchair. She wondered if the girl had chosen that particular chair because the terra-cotta ones would clash with her dress. Clarissa inspected her from head to toe, a slight smirk lifting the corner of her lip as she noted her outmoded shoes. Mariah suspected the chit knew her gown was as old as the shoes, even if it did not look it.

Her headache intensified underneath the girl's barely concealed disdain. An angry elf pounded out his frustrations against her poor brain, keeping rhythm with the staccato beat of her heart. She longed for the peaceful, drippy cottage at Stillwater, or any quiet place where she did not have to deal with women such as Clarissa and her mother.

"I do not believe I've heard Mama mention you, ma'am," said Clarissa.

That was a relief, although Mariah knew it was only a slight reprieve. "I prefer living in the country. I have not been to London in several years."

"I see," said Clarissa, glancing once again at Mariah's shoes. "And what brings you here now?" she asked in a sugary voice.

Mariah hesitated. She supposed her position of employment would become common knowledge, but she did not particularly feel like sharing the news at the moment.

"Business," said Kiernan smoothly, strolling into the room with Gabe.

Mariah's heart sank. What business could someone like her have, other than earning a living?

"Oh?" Clarissa smiled at Kiernan as he sat down in a chair across from her. "Mama says ladies should not trouble themselves with business matters." She fluttered her lashes at Kiernan before demurely lowering her gaze. "She is right, of course. Such things should be left up to men. They are so much more capable than we are." She glanced up, first at Gabriel, then Kiernan. "Do you not agree, Lord Branderee?"

"In some instances," he said dryly, his gaze flickering to Mariah.

The twinkle in his eyes drew her smile.

"A woman should be aware of business matters which might affect her," said Jeanette. "Though I trust my brother to see after my best interests, I want a say in whatever involves me."

Clarissa laughed delicately. "My dear Jeanette, don't let any of your suitors hear you say such a thing. You will frighten them off."

"If they are frightened away by intelligence and common sense, then I'm better off without them."

Clarissa shook her head, sending Gabriel a flirty look. "Such outspoken behavior won't do. Mr. Macpherson needs to give you further instruction on how the game is played. You'll never find a husband."

Gabriel smiled lazily at Clarissa. "I dinna think she is looking for a husband."

Jeanette laughed as Clarissa feigned surprise. "And you know it. I only want a taste of Society and a bit of fun. When I'm ready for a husband, I'll look for a good, solid Scotsman."

Clarissa's half smile hinted at womanly wisdom beyond her years as she met Kiernan's gaze. "Well, there is certainly something to be said for Scotsmen."

He chuckled. "I thought your interest lay Gabriel's way."

Gabriel pulled a long, sad face. "You wound me deeply, Miss St. John." Then he grinned, his olive green eyes dancing impishly.

"The Season is yet to officially begin," said Clarissa, directing her comment to both men with a honeyed smile. "I'll bide my time. I, too, would like a bit of fun before the business of attracting a husband grows serious."

"Fickle woman." Kiernan winked at Jeanette and gave Clarissa a make-'em-go-weak-in-the-knees smile.

A distinct twinge of jealousy pricked Mariah. With difficulty, she schooled her expression to what she hoped would convey mild amusement.

"La, sir," breathed Clarissa, laying a hand lightly on her chest.

Mariah wondered how many times the girl had practiced that graceful little mannerism in front of the mirror.

"You'll have the ladies swooning left and right," said the young blond with a beguiling smile. "Do have a care, Lord Branderee. A fit of heart palpitations in women of a certain age—" her gaze darted to Mariah "—might prove too much for them." She looked back at

Kiernan, her expression wide-eyed and innocent.

Kiernan tilted his head slightly in what Mariah decided was an attempt to keep a straight face. The vicious little elf using her head as an anvil worked himself into a frenzy, wielding two hammers at once.

Don't you dare laugh, Branderee, or I'll throttle you both. A deed bound to earn her the boot out the front door. At that moment, she didn't care. It probably would be best all the way around.

The well-timed entry of Clarissa's maid politely reminding her mistress that she was expected at home saved the earl from making a comment. The instant Clarissa left the room, accompanied by Jeanette to see her out, Mariah sprang to her feet.

Pleading the headache, she excused herself and dashed up the stairs. The exertion heightened the pain in her head, and she stopped in the second-floor hallway and leaned against the wall. Closing her eyes, she rubbed her forehead. "Stupid, stupid, stupid!"

"You, me, or Clarissa?" asked Kiernan softly from beside her.

His warm breath whispered across her temple, and the faint fragrance of orange blossoms and vanilla teased her. For an instant, she wanted him even closer and craved the shelter of his embrace. It struck fear in her heart.

"You," she snapped, "for coming up with this harebrained scheme." Weary, she let her shoulders droop. "And me, to consider even for a minute that your idea had merit."

"It does." Kiernan wanted to promise to make her world a safe, wonderful place, but he doubted his ability to slay all her dragons. He would protect her as best he could and try to ease her burdens. "Dinna let Clarissa trouble you. The girl is young and has much to learn."

"Don't fool yourself. She knew exactly what she was about." Mariah rubbed her neck with one hand. "And well she should with her mother as the teacher."

Kiernan looked down at her and frowned, noting the dark circles beneath her eyes. With all that had transpired in the past few days, no wonder she had missed sleep. The changes he had forced upon her surely had caused much tossing and turning. He couldn't help wishing some of her restlessness had been due to the attraction between them. She certainly had lingered in his thoughts, both waking and sleeping.

"You know her mother?" he asked, nudging her hand aside so he could rub her neck. He smiled as her head lolled against his chest, and she sighed softly. He slid his other hand around to the small of her back, holding her in place.

"We've met, although I can't say we are well acquainted. I spoke to her a few times years ago, always brief but pleasant exchanges. That did not stop her from greatly maligning my reputation when the scandal reached her ears. With Shelton out of the country, I was the only one left to attack. Evidently, she did not consider bigamy and betrayal sufficient fodder for the gossip mill, so she added spice to the tale."

His rage rose swiftly at the hurt and bitterness in her voice. "Such as?"

"She was the one who started the rumor that I had known Shelton was married but went through the false wedding anyway."

"So you could steal him from his wife."

She nodded. "She said I had developed such an attachment for him that I was willing to risk everything for a moment of passion, hoping to lure him away from her."

"That's ridiculous!"

"I agree. Unfortunately, her ladyship can be very persuasive." She looked up, laying her hand upon his chest. "What is important now is that Jeanette and Clarissa are friends. My presence may well jeopardize their relationship."

"Dinna worry too much about that. The lassies are no' all that close." He grinned. "Clarissa and her parents are more interested in Gabriel's money—or my title and money—than they are in whether or no' we have a hoyden in our midst. It seems the viscount invested heavily in an American plantation thriving more with mosquitos and water snakes than crops. He, too, was taken in by a swindler, so Lady St. John has no room to talk."

He lowered his hand. "Does your neck feel better?"

"Yes, but my head feels beastly."

"A good nap will set you to rights. A woman of a certain age needs plenty of rest." He smiled into her eyes.

She glared back. "I am not in my dotage yet, even if Clarissa thinks so."

"I've no complaint with your age, Mariah." Kiernan smiled at her in much the same way he had smiled at Clarissa, only this time sincere admiration warmed his eyes. He was rewarded by a small gasp. His gaze fell on her soft, slightly parted lips, and he felt a compelling need to taste her sweetness. He lowered his head.

"Kiernan," she whispered, her voice frantic.

He halted the movement of his head, then straightened, gazing into her wide eyes. Had she wanted him to kiss her? He decided she had. Was she afraid? Without a doubt.

"This is madness."

He shook his head. "To deny that I'm attracted to you would be madness."

She closed her eyes, as if it was the only way she could break away from his searching gaze. "Lord Branderee—"

"Shhh, Mariah." He touched her lips with his fingertip, and her eyelids flew open. "True, this isna the time nor the place."

She turned her head, moving away from his touch. "There will never be a time—"

"Yes, there will be." He cradled her face in his hand. "Dinna be afraid of me, lass. I will never bring you shame."

"Your mother is afraid you might. And so am I," she added in a rush.

Frowning, he dropped his hands and took a step back. He could understand her fear, but not his mother's. "What has my mother said?"

"She warned me to be careful. She worries that your newly attained power and wealth are corrupting you."

"I'm no' corrupt." True, he had done things he was not proud of. Gambled a few times, but no longer. Drank too much on occasion, which he did not plan to do again, unless a certain redheaded lass drove him to it out of sheer frustration. That answer would not satisfy his mother; probably not Mariah either. *And certainly not the Father,* prodded his conscience. It had been talking to him a lot lately, but he did not want to think about it now.

He turned on the charm. "Well, maybe I've strayed from the path a little—at least the one my mother wants me on—but I'm no' a wicked man."

"With a smile like that?" She crossed her arms, frowning. "Not likely."

His confidence slipped a notch. "What's wrong with my smile?"

"It's enticing, honey-sweet, shamefully persuasive, and altogether too confident. You're too sure of yourself, Kiernan Macpherson. You think all you have to do is snap your fingers, and every woman within sight will come running to do your bidding."

"They usually do," he teased, hoping to make her smile.

"La, sir, you'll have them swooning left and right," she said with a sigh, laying a hand on her chest in an imitation of Clarissa's theatrics. "Be careful not to step on a duchess or trip over this Season's simpering misses," she added sarcastically.

Bemused, Kiernan studied her irritated expression. *The lass is jealous!* He didn't even try to hide his grin.

She practically growled. "Add smug to the list."

"What list? Oh, aye, the description of my smile. Let's see, there was enticing." He leaned a little closer. "Honey-sweet." A little more. "Shamefully persuasive." Closer still.

"And altogether too confident," she murmured, her gaze lingering on his mouth.

"No' now," he whispered, settling his hands at her waist. "You have no' swooned yet."

"I can't. You're holding me up," she said softly.

"Do ye want me to let go?" He lowered his head slowly.

"No." So much emotion in that tiny, whispered word—yearning and regret, trust and fear, hope and hopelessness.

Tenderness filled his heart, a feeling so powerful his chest ached. He kissed her gently, telling her in the only way he knew how that she touched his soul. His lips lingered, but she did not seem to mind. When he finally raised his head, he saw that she had curled her fingers against his chest, gripping his jacket in one hand and the plaid in the other.

He looked at her face—the dewy lips, softly flushed cheeks, hint of a smile—and knew both pride and humility. Pride because his touch had brought radiance to her countenance. Humility because she had allowed his kiss, even welcomed it.

Mariah frowned and opened her eyes. Why had she ever thought she could indulge in a light flirtation with this man? How could one kiss stir so many longings and revive so many dreams? "I don't think we should have done that."

"Mariah, I give you my word I willna dishonor you."

"I know you won't." She brushed her fingertips along his jaw. "You're too good a man to intentionally bring me shame."

"But?"

She laid her hand on his chest. "I don't know if I can be the woman you need."

"And I may no' be the man you need, but I would like to find out. There is something between us, Mariah. I felt it that first morning when I held you. I tried to blame it on the danger and fear for your safety, but I couldna get you out of my mind. You filled my thoughts, my senses, then and now.

"I lay awake last night thinking about what Jeanette said, about how God brought you to us. It seems strange that he would use a card game to lead me to you, but I guess he can use any situation at all for his purpose.

"I was about to join another game when I happened to glance across the room. Two gentlemen were leaving your brother's table. Glenbuck looked at me and nodded in greeting. I thought perhaps I'd met him at some time and couldna place him, so Gabe and I went over. He introduced himself and invited us to join him, bein' fellow Scots and all."

He took her hand, then turned and slowly walked with her down the hall. "We played several games with reasonable wagers. I won a time or two and so did your brother." He smiled. "We even let Gabe win once. We talked about Scotland, and I actually enjoyed Glenbuck's company. He had seen me with Jeanette at the theatre and asked if we would be staying for the Season."

"Do you think he might be interested in her?" Mariah thought her brother was in for a set down if he was. Jeanette was far too levelheaded to be the least bit attracted to someone as shallow as Pryse.

"No, I didna have that impression. He seemed merely to be making conversation. When I mentioned that Mother was skittish about going to social functions, he suggested finding someone to act as chaperon."

"He gave you the idea?" Mariah stared at him in disbelief. She suddenly wondered if Pryse had suggested her for the position. Surely Kiernan would not have feigned his surprise at finding her at Stillwater. "Is that why you asked me to work for you?"

"Yes, although I didna think of it until after I arrived at Stillwater and learned of your situation. He hadna mentioned you. I believe it was a casual observation on your brother's part, which Gabe agreed to, by the way. I forgot all about it because, soon after, the wagers greatly increased and the game became intense. Half an hour later, I was the new owner of an unwanted English estate."

He smiled down at her and lightly squeezed her hand. "I was pleasantly surprised to see you that morning. Did you know the gold and copper in your hair glisten in the sunlight?"

"No, I didn't." She returned his smile as they reached the door to her bedroom. "I do not usually spend much time studying my hair in the sunlight."

"You should. It is beautiful."

She laughed. "Why, thank you, kind sir. I'll have to leave it down sometime and wander out in the garden to see for myself."

He glanced at the cluster of curls pinned at the back of her head. "I meant to tell you, I like that style."

Mariah smiled in appreciation. "I'll tell Elise. She will be pleased."

"Do you like her? Is she suitable? Wilton and Sukey thought she would be."

"Yes, I like her, and I think she will do nicely. It will take me a while to grow accustomed to having help again. I'm used to doing for myself."

"So am I. I still have no' hired a valet, though Wilton keeps the footman, Simms, within calling distance if he thinks I might need him. He takes care of my clothes and draws my bath, but I'll be hanged if I'm goin' to let him shave me."

Mariah slid her hand down the sleeve of his coat. "You have more common sense than most gentlemen, my lord. You don't wear your jacket so tight that you need help getting in and out of it."

"I like to be comfortable. Gabe says I need a valet, but I've seen the way his man fusses over him. I'd throttle him after ten minutes or send him into a fit of apoplexy if I threw a shirt on the floor. Though I suppose I should hire someone. Sukey pressed my clothes on the trip, and it isna right to put the extra work on her, even if she says she does no' mind."

Mariah eased her hand from his. "You would have to find the right man, one who is not so worried about fashion that he will try to change you."

"Should I change my manner of dress for London?" A frown creased his forehead. "Would you be embarrassed to attend a ball with me if I wore the kilt?"

"Of course not. I wish more Scots wore the philabeg. It speaks of pride of country and heritage. It seems such a part of you, but you would look dashing in pantaloons or trousers, too."

He made a face. "I have never worn breeches. I went from infant clothes to the philabeg, though it wasna made legal again until I was six. My father wore the plaid and kilt a good ten years before Parliament said he could. Most Englishmen's agitation over it had long passed by then. They should no' have had the power to outlaw it in the first place."

"I heartily agree." She was glad at least some of the wrongs inflicted on the Scots after the Jacobite Rebellion had finally been rectified. For thirty-six years following the Disarming Act of 1746, they lived with the threat of being transported for wearing their traditional clothing, playing the pipes, or carrying a weapon of any kind. The act had been childish retaliation by the English government and had hurt all Scotsmen, including those Highlanders loyal to the Crown.

"Do you feel conspicuous in your kilt?"

He nodded. "It attracts attention. It never bothered me until we went to the theatre. All the women gawked."

She laughed softly. "Of course, they did. Both you and Gabriel are handsome men."

A slight blush highlighted his cheeks as he frowned unhappily. "But they paid more attention to me."

"They would have even if you weren't wearing the plaid and kilt. You have a title. I'd wager that within minutes of your arrival at the theatre, or more likely even before you left the house, every woman there knew you were an earl, rich, and unmarried. Very impressive attributes to those looking for a husband whether for themselves or their daughters."

"I'm no' shopping for a wife."

"You can subtly let that be known by making certain you favor no particular young lady with your attentions. Never dance twice with the same one—"

"That will be easy. I dinna know how to do anythin' but the Scottish reel, and I'd no' be willing to do even that at a fancy party."

"I could teach you some of the other dances. Is the country dance all Jeanette knows?"

"No. I hired a dáncing teacher for her. She does well." A twinkle lit his eyes. "I might let you teach me a few dances, as long as you dinna expect me to do them in public."

She shook her head. "That will never do, my lord. In time, you will probably have house parties, and you will be expected to dance."

"Nae, lass. I'll be playing the pipes."

"They are not suitable for everything. Some dances need a fiddle."

"True. I'll worry about it then. For now, I'll stay away from the dance floor. The only woman I'm interested in holding in my arms is you, and no doubt that would cause a stir."

"It would indeed." *Especially in me.* "You will also need to sit with a different lady at supper each time."

"Must I escort a lady to supper?"

"No, I suppose not. Usually partners for the supper dance eat together."

"And what of the ladies who dinna have a partner? Would it be appropriate for me to escort one of them?"

How like him to think of the wallflowers. "It would be appropriate," she said quietly. He had just knocked another chink in the armor protecting her heart.

Kiernan retired to his room early that evening. Mariah had not joined them for dinner, eating instead in her room. According to Elise, she had gone to bed shortly thereafter.

He, too, was weary, but sleep eluded him. Blowing out the candles, he sat alone in the dimly lit room, staring at the dancing flames in the fireplace. He had spoken to his mother privately that afternoon, reassuring her that he was not falling into ill repute.

She accepted his words as sincere but reminded him that good intentions did not always lead to success. "You need to walk with God, Kiernan. Even then it is hard enough no' to be trapped by temptation. No one can do everything right, but if you put your trust and faith in Jesus and the Father, you will make fewer mistakes."

He knew from experience she was right. For months, the Holy Spirit had been directing him back toward Jesus and the Father, but Kiernan had stubbornly resisted. The last time he had spoken to God was the day he had received word his father had died. Overcome with grief, he had cried out against the Lord in anger and bitterness.

The pain lingered, but he regretted his harsh words. Without being conscious of it, he had gradually accepted his father's death. In his heart, he knew God was sovereign and did all things in his time and for his purpose.

Kiernan slid from the chair to his knees, bowing his head in humility and remorse. "Lord God, please forgive me for being so angry at you and for yellin' at you the way I did. I dinna know why you took Father from us, but I know you must have had a good reason.

"I just wish I hadna stayed away from Scotland so long. When I think of the time I could have spent with him…" A lump clogged his throat and his heart ached. A tear slid down his cheek. He wiped it away as he cleared his throat. Wrestling with his pain, it was a minute or two before he could go on. "Forgive me for turning from you, for trying to shut you out of my life."

A Scripture from Psalm 51 came to mind, one he had learned at his father's knee. His father had often spoken the verses as a prayer in the evening. Kiernan's whispered words were a sincere plea from the depths of his being.

"Lord, hide thy face from my sins and blot out all mine iniquities. Create in me a clean heart, O God, and renew a right spirit within me. Cast me not away from thy presence and take not thy holy spirit from me." He breathed deeply, a shudder rocking him. "Restore unto me the joy of thy salvation and uphold me with thy free spirit."

He kneeled quietly for several minutes, comforted as the peace of God settled over him. He could almost feel an arm around his shoulders, almost hear the words spoken to his heart. *Welcome home, Son. I knew you were never far away.*

"I feel like I've been alone in a desolate land, Lord. So many times I've needed your counsel. So many times I've failed or done wrong. Lord God, I'm worried about Mother. Please restore her health and her joy. Your word says, 'A merry heart doeth good like a medicine, but a broken spirit drieth the bones.' Her spirit is broken and her body is fading away. Ease her pain and give her a merry heart, dear Lord. Help me not to cause her more grief."

When his knees complained loudly about the hard floor, he ended the prayer and pushed himself up into the chair. Kiernan stared at the fire, the leaping flames reminding him of Mariah's hair. He chuckled when he thought of Clarissa's visit. If the girl had caught Mariah's glare—before she hid her feelings behind a polite veneer of civility—she might think twice before making such a comment again.

Clarissa would never be half the woman Mariah was. He wished he had thought to tell Mariah that when they talked in the hall. Talking was not all they had done, he remembered with a smile. Kiernan had never experienced a kiss such as the one they shared. "You gave me a glimpse o' heaven, lass, and I willna turn away."

9

MARIAH AWOKE LATE THE NEXT MORNING feeling completely rested. Fatigue had once again allowed escape from her warring emotions under the guise of sleep. With the new day, however, came the battle.

"I never should have allowed him to kiss me," she grumbled, tugging a brush through a contrary tangle in her long hair. "Even if it was the most beautiful kiss I've ever had." She paused, remembering the sweetness of his touch. Seeing the reflection of her dreamy smile in the mirror triggered a frown. "*Because* it was the nicest kiss I've ever had. I was a fool to kiss him and a bigger one to enjoy it so much."

She wagged the brush at her image in the mirror. "You learned your lesson once. Don't be stupid again." Kiernan was a charmer, just like Shelton. He turned her insides to mush, even more than Shelton had.

"He could never steal my money," she muttered, setting the brush on the dressing table. "But he could steal my heart." Her gaze rested on the little silver bird her father had given her so long ago. "And break it. He could never truly love me, not the way I need him to." *No one ever has*, she thought sadly, again wondering why. Was it a major character flaw she could not see? Or a dozen little things blending together to turn others away?

She had friends such as Thaddeus, Jordan, Prudence, and Sir Edgar, but she had never known the deep bond of love others experienced, not with her family and certainly not with Shelton.

She could probably count on her fingers and toes the number of times she had spent more than five minutes with her parents. Her mother had deemed her a tiresome bother. Her father had never openly called her plain and worthless, but he had suggested as much by basically ignoring her. Her dowry, paltry considering the sums at his disposal when established, and the lack of provision for her welfare in the marriage settlement indicated the level of his regard.

Pryse detested her. As far as she knew, he had never seen her until after their father's death. Her brother had been loath to be saddled with her guardianship. Even when she lived in his house after finishing Miss Eversham's boarding school, he barely tolerated her presence. He treated her politely in the presence of others only because it would have damaged his place in Society to do otherwise.

As for Shelton, she would never understand how he could use someone so cruelly. To think one was loved and then learn it had been a sham brought far greater pain than growing up without affection.

"I will not let myself care too much for him." Tugging on the bell pull to ring for Elise, she silently admitted that might be impossible.

Spring showers kept them indoors that afternoon and thwarted Gabe's plan to take them for a drive in the park. Mariah was grateful for the reprieve in making her first public appearance. They spent their time in the drawing room with Mrs. Macpherson knitting contentedly as the other four engaged in a lively card game. Mariah noticed that Kiernan's mother seemed more relaxed and often laughed at their antics.

119

During the afternoon, footmen dropped off the calling cards of three of Mariah's past acquaintances who were already in Town. Two of them also sent along notes expressing their great pleasure to hear she was in London and begging her to call on them at her earliest convenience. The warmth of their good wishes brought encouragement, not only to Mariah, but to the others as well.

"See, Mariah, you've been wasting away in the country for naught," Jeanette chided gently. "Your friends can hardly wait to see you."

"I must admit I am relieved. I thought they would, but there was always a niggling doubt. I am so glad Delia—the marchioness of Stanwell—is in Town. We formed a close friendship at Miss Eversham's. Delia came out a year before I did but spent as much time visiting the galleries and museums with me as she did attending dinners and balls.

"Neither of us had high expectations. She had a suitable dowry, but does not hide her keen intelligence or education as some expect women to do. Many men considered her quite the bluestocking and went to comical extremes to avoid talking to her."

Mariah slapped an ace of diamonds down on the table, besting Kiernan's king, and laughed when he pretended to snarl at her. "And well they should have as she was far more knowledgeable in connecting history to the current affairs of government than most of them. Fortunately, shortly before summer she met the marquis, who found her intriguing."

"I prefer the company of an intelligent woman," said Gabriel, dealing another hand. "One who can talk about something besides fashion and amusements. Simpering young misses—if they are pretty enough—are diverting for an evening or two. Anything longer is a dreadful bore."

"And here I thought you were encouraging Clarissa," said

120

Jeanette with a twinkle in her eye.

"Merely flirting, lass." Gabriel frowned slightly. "She is a lovely creature with a bit of wit, but I detect a mercenary heart and a wandering eye."

"I suppose she has to marry for money, given her father's poor investments."

"She is his last hope, but after paying her father's debts, the chit will likely beggar her husband."

"And lead him a merry chase," added Kiernan.

"I'm glad I dinna have to worry about saving my family from financial ruin." Jeanette smiled at Kiernan. Her affection and respect for her brother were obvious. "Even if I never marry, I know you'll take care of me."

"That I will, Posy, but I expect you'll have more suitors than you want within a few weeks' time."

Jeanette laughed. "Such confidence. Suitors are one thing. A husband is another." Her expression sobered. "I will only marry a man I love, and the one I know God has chosen for me."

"You are very wise, Jeanette," said Mariah, smiling at her.

"I am blessed because I can make that choice. If I were in Clarissa's shoes, it might be much harder to stand firm in both my resolve and my convictions. It saddens me to think that there are many young women like her who must choose their mates no' on feelings of the heart but by wealth or title."

"Sometimes they find both love and the necessary financial security," said Gabriel. "Now you, little lass, with your money, beauty, charm, and high connections, should be able to snare a duke if you want one."

"No dukes." Kiernan looked appalled. For a moment, Mariah thought he was teasing. When he scowled at Jeanette, she realized he was serious. "I willna have some popinjay orderin' me about."

"Dear brother, I would never fall head over heels for a popinjay, whether he was a duke or no'," said Jeanette with a laugh.

"No dukes." Kiernan crossed his arms. "No one with a higher rank than mine."

"I promise, no dukes." Jeanette rose and walked around the table, hugging her brother's shoulder. "But if a marquis sweeps me off my feet, I might accept. I wouldna let him order you about." She ruffled her brother's hair and dashed for the door. "But I might," she called merrily over her shoulder as she raced up the stairs.

"You wouldna dare!" roared Kiernan, jumping to his feet with a grin and running after her.

He had reached the landing on the staircase when Wilton stepped into the room, cast a glance at Lord Branderee, then announced in a booming voice, "The earl of Glenbuck wishes to speak with you, Lady Mariah."

Mariah gasped and stared at Kiernan, not knowing what to do. He froze in midstep, his gaze locking with hers. In the blink of an eye, he thundered back down the staircase. "Lady Mariah is no' home to visitors," he said curtly to the butler.

Why now, after all these years? thought Mariah. Feeling stupid, she realized she should have expected him to call. She was in his domain now, and a threat to his rather precarious standing in Society. *He will send me away. But where?* Remembering that her brother's guardianship had dissolved when she was five-and-twenty, she reminded herself that he no longer held legal or financial power over her.

Socially, he could try to ostracize her, but in doing so, he might also destroy himself. Seeing the concern in Kiernan's eyes, she felt almost giddy with relief. Pryse might threaten, but he could no longer intimidate her. He might wound her with his words and hatred, but thanks to Kiernan and his family, she was financially

122

independent, at least for the time being.

Wilton looked at her for confirmation. "I will see my brother, Wilton. Please show him into the library."

Kiernan came to her side. "Mariah, let me send him away. Better yet, let me throw him out into the gutter where he belongs."

"Nae, my Highland warrior," she said softly, lightly touching his arm. "This battle I must fight alone."

He grazed her cheek with his knuckle. "I'll be in the hall if you need me."

"Thank you."

Mariah walked into the library with her head held high, silently thanking Elise for cleaning and pressing her travel gown so she had something decent to wear. Pryse stood by the fireplace, staring at the flames. She was struck by his appearance. Though he was immaculately dressed, the years of dissipation had taken their toll.

He looked up when she entered the room. To her surprise, her brother's expression was one more of discomfort than rage. She barely heard Wilton quietly close the door as Pryse straightened, his gaze racing over her from head to toe.

He cleared his throat. "You look well, Mariah."

"I am." *No thanks to you.*

"I'm glad."

"Oh? Why does that surprise me?" The pain and hardships of the past nine years rushed to the surface, exploding in anger and bitterness. "Did you expect me to be withered and worn? My face brown and lined, my back bent from the long, tortuous hours of working in the garden, trying to earn enough to survive?"

He flinched, but she stepped closer, extending her trembling hands so he could see the short nails and red, roughened skin before she turned her palms upward, exposing the hard calluses. "As you can see, I did not come away completely unscathed. I suppose my skin will grow soft again with diligent application of creams and ointments, but in the meantime I can be thankful ladies wear gloves in public."

He looked away without speaking. Mariah stared at the dull flush spreading over his face. At first, she thought it surely must be the heat or a reflection from the flames, but when he turned away, she realized her brother was ashamed. Dumbfounded, she let the tirade die on her lips.

"I heard at the club last night that you were a guest of Branderee and his family."

"That is incorrect. He hired me as chaperon for his sister and companion to his mother."

He turned back toward her, clearly surprised. "You are working for them?"

"Ludicrous, isn't it? The earl of Glenbuck's daughter working. At least this position pays something." Mariah felt a stab of guilt. She sounded like a fishwife. Not at all like the Christian she claimed to be. Sighing heavily, she sat down on a straight-back chair. "Your pardon, Pryse. I shouldn't rail at you."

"Why not?" He too sank into the nearest chair. "You have every right to rail at me, or even have Branderee throw me out." A hint of a smile touched his troubled face. "That's what he wanted to do, wasn't it? Toss me into the street? He seems like a man of action."

Mariah did not know what to think. This was a side of her half brother she had never seen before. "Pryse, why are you here?"

"To confirm that you were in Town." He shrugged. "After half a lifetime of purposefully quelling it, I've discovered of late that I still have a conscience. I wanted to see how you were."

"Better than I have been in several years."

He nodded and averted his gaze. Neither of them spoke for a few moments. "From what I hear, Branderee is a decent man," he said finally. "The night we played cards, he struck me as the type who would rise to a challenge, a man of high ideals. In a way, he reminded me of myself when I was younger."

Mariah coughed, choking on a cynical retort.

"You don't believe me. I can't blame you. You never met the man I once was, the man our father raised me to be. I was very young when I lost my sense of honor, when my dreams and ideals were shattered."

Mariah found it extremely difficult to imagine Pryse having a shred of honor, yet his quietly intense response, so unlike his usual cutting manner, told her he was speaking the truth. "What changed you?"

He grimaced. "It's not a pleasant story, Mariah, but it's one I think you should know. Perhaps it will better help you understand my despicable treatment of you. You are aware that I was three years older than your mother?"

"Yes." Unsure of what she was about to hear, her imagination running rampant, Mariah's heart started pounding.

"I met her a few months before Father did, when I went to inspect some horses her brother had for sale. She was exquisite, and I was smitten from the first moment I saw her. I spent a week as a guest of the family, and by the time I left, I had fallen deeply in love with her. I visited several times and asked Father to invite her and her family for a fortnight at Glenbuck Castle. We invited several other friends to make it a house party.

"He knew I was in love and that I planned to propose while they were there." Sorrow drifted across his face. "Father and I had always been close. I felt I could tell him almost anything. I'd prattled on endlessly about her.

"Within a few days after their arrival at the castle, I could see she was weaving her spell over him. At first, I thought I was being silly and afflicted with petty jealousy. I said nothing, not wanting to offend Father or Veronica. By the end of the week, it was obvious to all that her attentions were directed Father's way instead of mine, with her parents' open approval.

"And why not? She would have waited years for me to come into my inheritance. By marrying Father, she could make the title and wealth hers at once. In fairness to Veronica, I believe her affections were engaged as well. Father was a handsome man, much more knowledgeable in the ways of the world and women than I was. With her he came alive—charming, witty, gentle. He seemed ten years younger."

"I didn't know he had any of those traits. Whenever I saw him, he was either cold or angry," said Mariah, wishing he had been different.

"I'm partly to blame. I confronted him, and we had a terrible argument. He was convinced that my feelings were merely an infatuation, that I was too young to know true love. He would have her for his wife, and nothing I could say or do would stop him. He proposed the same day, and of course, she accepted. He announced their betrothal while we were waiting to go in to dinner."

Mariah was appalled, and for the first time in her life felt sympathy for her brother. "He had not told you beforehand?"

"No, although I knew it the minute they walked into the room. I started to leave, got as far as the door, when he called my name. Like a fool, I hesitated, and in that moment he asked me to wish him happy. Veronica had consented to become his wife."

"Oh, Pryse, how awful!"

His face had grown pale with the telling of the story. "Yes, it was. I hated them both." He met her gaze, his expression one of profound sadness. "Hate is a terrible thing, Mariah. It consumes you, destroys you. Destroys others. I came to London and went on a year-long binge. I had a sizable inheritance from Mother so I did not need any money from Father. Which was just as well because he wouldn't have sent me any.

"Within the year, Veronica was breeding, and mutual friends told me Father had begun to realize I might not soon forgive him and come around to his way of thinking. He intended to shower his love and attention on his new son, making him the delight of his winter years."

"Only I was not a son."

"No, but I assumed it would not matter. There were hints to the contrary from those same friends, but I ignored them at the time. I saw him and Veronica in London over the years at one function or another, but I never spoke to them. He was older, more sedate, but from a distance seemed much as he always had—good company, as the hostesses like to put it."

"And you believed Father and I shared the same close relationship you had when you were growing up."

Pryse nodded. "I was jealous, terribly so. I reasoned that, even if I forgave him and tried to regain the close bond we once knew, it would never happen because he had you. He no longer needed me."

Shaken by how the selfish acts of one or two could affect so many, Mariah drew a quivering breath. "Not long before he died, I slipped into his room when he was gone on a trip. He kept your portrait in his room. One of the maids said he had hung it there about a month after you left. A candle burned in the window by the front door every night in case you came home."

Pryse made a strangled sound and quickly rose to stand by the fireplace, turning his back to her. He rested his hand on the mantel and leaned his forehead against his arm.

Mariah hesitated, unsure whether he would want her comfort, still expecting him to strike out at her any minute. *He's reaching out to you. You should do the same for him.* She stood and walked quietly to his side, laying her hand on his arm.

"I didn't know," he said hoarsely. He cleared his throat and blinked several times. "He never wrote or sent word of any kind. If he had only apologized, or even said he understood how I felt, I might have tried to make peace with him."

"He was a proud man."

"So am I. I don't know if I would have gone back, even if he had apologized. The wounds were so deep, and the hatred so strong." He straightened and she dropped her hand to her side.

"I went back to Glenbuck last month for the first time since his death. I talked to the housekeeper and the caretaker, some of the others who have been there for years. They told me how life was for you there. It all added up. The things my friends said when you were young, the letter I received from Miss Eversham when you arrived at school listing the numerous items you needed, and your small inheritance with its inadequate provisions. I deeply regret the pain we all caused you, Mariah. When you came here after boarding school, I treated you abominably."

"You had been hurt. You were jealous."

"That is no excuse," he said angrily. "You didn't deserve it. You do not resemble your mother greatly, but just knowing you were her daughter reminded me of her. I believed I was over Veronica, but I could not look at you without remembering what I'd felt for her, what she had done, and all I had lost."

He gripped her arm, looking her directly in the eye. "Please forgive me for the way I've treated you. You have every right to hate me, but I hope you can find it in your heart to forgive—not just me, but them as well."

It was all too much to take in at once. The strength went out of her legs, and Mariah groped for the chair he had vacated.

Pryse quickly took her arm, helping support her until she sat down. He watched her carefully. "Are you going to faint? Can I get you something to drink?"

"No, I'll manage." She smiled weakly. "It's just that this meeting is so different from what I thought it would be."

"I dare say." He smiled ruefully. "It is not going exactly as I had planned. I hadn't intended to tell you about loving your mother. I had only meant to beg your forgiveness for my harsh treatment and make one other confession before you got wind of it from someone else. I haven't even gotten to it yet."

"There's more?" When he nodded, she thought she might indeed faint. She looked around the scantily furnished room. "Perhaps you'd better ask Wilton for a glass of sherry."

"Of course." Pryse hurried to the door. When he pulled it open, he found Kiernan glaring at him from across the narrow hall. "Uh, Mariah is feeling a trifle faint. She'd like a glass of sherry."

Kiernan nodded to Wilton, who hovered nearby, then pushed Pryse out of the way as he advanced purposefully into the room. "What have you done to her?"

Pryse followed, surprising Mariah again because he did not take offense at Kiernan's harsh tone. "Asked her forgiveness," he said quietly.

Kiernan halted, his expression thunderstruck. His gaze sought Mariah's.

She nodded and attempted a smile. "It was rather unexpected."

Kiernan continued, studied her face a moment, then stepped behind her and put his arm around her, resting his hand on her shoulder. Pryse clearly noted his message of protection and possession. Kiernan pinned him with his gaze. "Why?"

"Because I have greatly wronged her."

Wilton walked in, stepping around Pryse with unspoken censure. He held the tray containing the glass of sherry out to Mariah.

"Will there be anything else, milady?"

"No, thank you, Wilton." Mariah took the drink, sipping carefully. A sip or two more, and she set the glass on the table beside the chair as the butler left the room and closed the door.

"The word going round is that you are penniless," said Kiernan. When Mariah gasped softly, he slightly tightened his grip on her shoulder.

Pryse looked at Mariah with a self-effacing half smile. "That was the other confession."

"Did you expect to gain my favor—and money—by apologizing to Mariah?" asked Kiernan, his voice hard as steel. "Think again."

"I know it is difficult to believe, Branderee, but my reason for coming here is honorable. I would not ask for your money. I do not want it." Pryse curled his fingers over the back of the chair across from them. Only the whiteness of his knuckles gave any indication of his tension. "I truly wish I could right the wrongs done to you, Mariah, but I cannot. I'm stone broke. I've lost everything, including the London townhouse and Glenbuck estate. I'll be leaving Britain within the week."

"Fleeing your creditors?" asked Mariah. If so, those who held his accounts would camp out on Branderee's steps in hopes of squeezing the money from her. They eventually would learn she had nothing, but in the meantime, the tailor, greengrocer, coal vendor, and no telling who else would constantly be pounding on the door. She doubted anyone would trouble her over gambling debts; a gentleman always paid those, even if the people who fed and clothed him went without.

Pryse shook his head. "No, making a fresh start. I have paid every last one of them, Mariah. If any creditors come hounding you, they are playing you false."

Mariah's thoughts and emotions were a jumble. The whole scene was like a crazy dream, the opposite of anything she had ever expected from her half brother. *Lord, please help me think straight.* "Where are you going?"

"Boston. I visited there last year and struck up an acquaintance with a lady bookseller." He smiled at Mariah, and his grip on the chair relaxed. "I do love books, you know. Always have. She's a widow by the name of Caroline Chambers. Scottish descent, second-generation American. Her grandparents were transported after the Forty-five.

"She's very unpretentious. Wasn't the least bit impressed because I'm an earl. I discovered I was not all that impressed by it, either," he said with a grin. His smile slowly faded. "I'm different there, especially with her. We've been corresponding since I returned to England. Honest, open letters. I've found myself again, or at least the man I'd like to be. She knows I have little more than passage for me and my library—couldn't part with m'books—but she wants me anyway. We're going to be married."

"I wish you happy." The polite response came automatically, although even as she said the words, Mariah realized she meant it. She reached up and briefly touched Kiernan's hand before standing. "I truly do."

"Thank you." For a moment, Pryse appeared immensely relieved. Then he frowned. "I should have done something for you. I meant to. I kept Stillwater because I knew the minute I sold it you would be completely without a home. I've met Sir Edgar's wife and knew she would not allow you to stay. That woman would be jealous if a fishwife gave him a good price on mackerel. I had to sell off the other properties to clear my debts anyway.

"At one point, I even decided I would give Stillwater to you. I talked to my solicitor about a few options, how to protect the estate for you or sell it and set the money up in a trust for you. But before I actually did anything about it, I made one last visit to White's and lost it."

"I will manage, thanks to Lord Branderee and his family."

"I'll send you some money whenever I can."

"Thank you." *I won't plan on it.*

Pryse shrugged lightly. "Here is Caroline's address." He handed her one of his calling cards with the American address written on the back. "I'd like to hear from you, to know how you are faring and how I can get in touch with you." He hesitated, clearing his throat. "Well, I'll be off. No need to see me out." He turned and walked toward the door.

"Pryse, wait." Mariah moved toward him, and he turned around to face her. "I never gave you an answer. Thank you for explaining things to me. It helps to understand better you and my parents. I do forgive you." She clasped his hand in both of hers. "I must also ask your forgiveness for all the times I have wished you'd be picked up by a press gang or run over by a haywagon."

Pryse laughed and patted her hand awkwardly. Quick tears filled Mariah's eyes, but she held the rest at bay. When he pulled his hand from hers, she saw his eyes were moist, too. "May God protect you on your journey and bless your marriage."

"Thank you," he said, his voice thick. Turning, he walked quickly from the room.

Kiernan stepped up behind her and gently turned her around. "How are you, lass?"

"A mess."

He wrapped his arms around her, and Mariah rested her cheek against his chest.

"I tried to eavesdrop but could only understand a word here and there," he said.

She'd expected as much and smiled at his honesty.

"Since you were no' yellin', I didna know what to think. I was about to barge in when he opened the door."

Always dashing to the rescue. She slid her arms around his waist and closed her eyes, giving in to the need simply to be held by him. "He told me what really caused the rift between him and Father." A tear slid down her cheek. Then another. "It's a long story," she murmured, her voice breaking.

"Tell me later."

He tightened his arms minutely, and sadness filled her soul. Mariah thought of her family and wept for love lost, love never born, and wounds too deep for forgiveness.

Kiernan feathered a kiss on her forehead and whispered softly in Gaelic, gentle, loving words her mind could not translate but her heart understood. In spite of her sorrow and pain, she cherished his touch, his tenderness.

As far back as she could remember, no one had ever held her when she cried.

10

THE NEXT DAY, MARIAH AND JEANETTE paid a call on Mariah's friend, Delia, now Lady Stanwell. Wearing her new bonnet and the first of Mrs. Haveland's creations, made of a dark rust calico, Mariah felt quite up to the mark. When the footman showed them into the drawing room and announced their arrival, Delia jumped to her feet and ran to embrace Mariah exuberantly.

"Oh, my dear friend, how good it is to see you." Delia clasped her hand and searched her face. "Are things well with you?" When Mariah nodded, she smiled, her eyes lighting up in delight. "I see a few new freckles. For shame, you've been out in the garden without your hat again."

Mariah laughed. "It's a good thing Miss Eversham is not around."

Delia grinned and hooked her arm through Mariah's, leading her and Jeanette to a blue velvet sofa. "At school, Mariah was forever going outside minus her bonnet, much to the dismay of our head-mistress. I doubt a week went by without a lecture on the disastrous consequences of a freckle."

Mariah introduced her to Jeanette, and they exchanged pleas-antries.

"Tell me, Miss Macpherson, how ever did you persuade Mariah to return to London? I had all but given up hope of seeing her again.

I'd decided she had turned into a country hermit."

"My mother isna up to the rigors of the Season, so we asked Mariah to come stay with us and act as my chaperon," said Jeanette with a smile. "Just having her with us has done wonders for Mother. The two of them can talk for hours about Scotland. My father died a little over a year ago, and it has been very difficult for Mother. They were very close, and his loss has affected her health. Kiernan undertook this trip hoping the change of scenery would lift her spirits and renew her strength."

"And did it? You talk as if she misses Scotland."

"She does. Though she tires easily, I think she enjoyed the visit. Until I started pestering Kiernan about staying for the Season, that is."

"This whole affair can be tiresome, tedious, and terrorizing if one does not enjoy such things." Delia grinned. "I was almost sent home my first year. I kept running off with Mariah so I would not have to go on endless, boring afternoon calls with my mother. I was the proverbial wallflower at the balls until I met Stanwell. We knew right off that we would suit."

"Marriage agrees with you," said Mariah. Her friend did, indeed, seem happy. Since they had corresponded regularly over the years, she knew the only great disappointment in Delia's life was her inability to have children.

"It does, though this time of year Godfrey spends more time at Parliament than I like. It is important for him to be there, so I try not to fuss overmuch. I've become an agreeable hostess, as long as I do not attempt anything too clever—mainly dinners and an occasional literary or historical discussion.

"In fact, we are having a dinner Wednesday evening. I'd be delighted if you both would come." She smiled impishly at Jeanette. "And bring your mother, the earl, and your friend Mr. Macpherson,

135

too, of course. There are several eligible gentlemen attending who would be overjoyed to make your acquaintance, Miss Macpherson. The ladies would forever be in my debt for the opportunity to meet those two handsome Scots. I never heard so many heavy sighs as when Lord Branderee and Mr. Macpherson took you to the theatre. I thought all the lamps would be blown out."

"They are quite the pair," said Mariah, briefly meeting her friend's all-too-discerning gaze with what she hoped was a normal smile. "You have adapted well to your new role. As I recall, you swore you would never become involved in entertaining, and here you are gloating about introducing two notable gentlemen to your friends."

Delia shrugged nonchalantly. "It did not take long to recognize that the social realm is important to Godfrey's standing in the House of Lords. I do believe as many, if not more, political compromises are reached over the dinner table or afterward when the men are left to their cigars and port than they are in government buildings.

"And contrary to my first impression of the women of the *ton*, I have discovered many who are not concerned only with fripperies, but are involved in charitable works. Some are set on improving their minds, but they generally keep it to themselves, especially around the men." She rolled her eyes. "I never have understood why men believe women are inferior creatures."

"It makes them feel superior," said Jeanette. "Fortunately, I received the same schooling as my brother, so I have never been made to feel inadequate. He is much wiser in the ways of the world, for which I'm grateful and respect his wisdom. However, I'm afraid Gabriel despairs that we willna see summer without making some kind of *faux pas*."

"A dinner would be good for your first real foray into the circus...I mean, social whirl," said Mariah.

"I think so, too." Jeanette's expression was sedate. "I willna have to worry about trouncing some poor gentleman's toes. Mother has drilled us relentlessly on which fork to use, and she's reminded Kiernan often enough, I dinna think he will wipe his mouth on his sleeve. At least I hope no'."

Mariah tried to keep a straight face, but when she met Delia's cautious but questioning gaze, she burst into laughter. Delia joined in as Jeanette grinned. "Dear girl, you shall be a hit, though undoubtedly known as an original."

"I would hope everyone is an original."

"Unfortunately, no. You will soon discover that many of our young English ladies have been stamped from the same mold. They are so flighty and senseless, I sometimes think they share the same brain. You, Miss Macpherson, will be a breath of fresh air breezing through the stuffy halls of the marriage mart."

"Then I willna worry. Fresh air is good for people."

"Indeed it is." Delia turned her attention to Mariah. "Will you be shopping, too?"

Mariah understood from the glimmer in her eyes that she meant shopping for a husband. "Only for dresses. Jeanette and I have made a good start. Lord Branderee is very generous with my clothing allowance and my wages. I'm sure you have guessed he is my employer." She glanced at Jeanette. "Delia knows my circumstances have been strained, and that I could not begin to purchase a suitable wardrobe on my own."

"I suspect I only know the half of what you've been through. I will say nothing of your present situation, except to Godfrey, of course. The only secrets between us are state ones, and sometimes he even shares those if he thinks I might have some insight into a problem." Delia frowned. "I am still put out with you for not coming to us. You would have been welcome here for as long as you wanted to stay."

"I know, and I'm most grateful for your offer and your concern. However, you would not have wanted me hanging around forever, and I needed the solitude of the country. It is good to have you here, now, to help us dip our toes into the social waters. I'm nervous, not about Kiernan and Jeanette, but about how my presence will affect them."

"There will be talk, of course. Some people will gossip about their own mother to gain attention. There have been enough scandals through the years to keep yours from being noteworthy, and each new spring brings others." Delia paused, listening to muffled voices in the hall as another visitor arrived. "Drat! I had hoped no one else would call.

"I would love to have a quiet coze with you, Mariah, so we can chatter all afternoon. I'm usually not home to visitors on Mondays. Have to keep some time to myself or lose my sanity. Could you come then?"

"Yes, it would be a treat." Mariah turned to Jeanette. "If you don't mind?"

"Of course, it's fine. If I canna persuade Kiernan to take me out, I'll enjoy spending the day at home." Jeanette's eyes twinkled merrily. "I dinna think you have to chaperon me with Mam."

Mariah laughed. Seconds later, she was hard put to retain her smile when Lady St. John and Clarissa glided into the room.

Spying Mariah, the viscountess halted abruptly, her mouth hanging open in shock. Clarissa smacked into her, almost tripping them both and drawing a glare from her mother.

Mariah suddenly realized that by being afraid of Lady St. John and what she might do, she had given the woman power over her. *I'm not a green girl to be wounded by every whisper and frown. Nor am I the one who invented and spread lies to destroy another's reputation.* She knew God would want her to treat the woman graciously and with kindness, but the best she could do was nod coolly.

Delia's reception was not much warmer. "Good afternoon, Lady St. John, Miss St. John. Do sit down. I believe you know Lady Mariah. May I present Miss Jeanette Macpherson? The earl of Branderee is her brother."

Clarissa sent her mother a nervous glance. The viscountess kept staring at Mariah, her lips pinched in disapproval. "Miss Macpherson and I have met. In fact we're friends," said Clarissa, looking hopefully at Jeanette, as if she were no longer certain that was true.

"We are." Jeanette smiled kindly. "She has introduced me to all the best shops and several of London's more interesting sights."

Lady St. John shifted her gaze to Delia, mustering something of a smile. "We dropped by simply to say hello. Renewing acquaintances that we seldom see is one of the pleasures of the Season, is it not?"

"It can be," Delia said benignly.

The viscountess fidgeted. "How nice that you are also acquainted with Miss Macpherson and his lordship. Have you known each other long?"

"Actually, we just met, thanks to Lady Mariah. She is originally from Scotland, you see, so it is only logical that they should know each other."

What gammon, thought Mariah. To her amazement, Lady St. John nodded as if it made perfect sense.

"Mariah and I are old friends from our school days," added Delia.

Lady St. John paled slightly as she absorbed that tidbit and quickly scanned Mariah's expensive clothes. "Clarissa said they had a guest from the country, but the pea-goose could not remember the name." She finally met Mariah's gaze, hesitating briefly. "I'm surprised you dared come back," she said petulantly.

Clarissa gasped.

"I'm surprised you are still here and not in America, living on your plantation," said Mariah, managing to keep her demeanor cool despite a surge of anger. "Oh, yes, now I remember, Lord Branderee said something about it thriving more with mosquitos and water snakes than crops. Such a pity to be taken in by a swindler."

Clarissa groaned softly and closed her eyes while her mother sputtered.

"You're one to talk," blurted Lady St. John.

"I am glad you realize I was duped," said Mariah. "Unfortunately, now you must have some idea of how devastating it is to trust someone with your hopes and dreams, only to discover you have been deceived."

"Mama, if Branderee knows, then everyone does!"

"Be quiet, Clarissa." Lady St. John lifted her chin arrogantly. "It is only a minor setback. Nothing to be overly concerned about."

"Well, I'm glad to hear it," said Delia. "Stanwell was saying a few days ago that he understood your husband was nearly bankrupt."

"There is absolutely no truth to the rumor."

"I do hope you are able to set the record straight, Lady St. John," said Mariah. "Sadly, such gossip can be terribly destructive to a reputation."

Lady St. John's face turned bright red, and Mariah felt a flash of triumph—until she looked at Clarissa. The poor girl appeared thoroughly confused and on the verge of tears.

"You are a lovely young woman, Miss St. John. In spite of such talk about your father's financial difficulties, or even in light of actual problems, you should find a suitor of substantial means who is more than willing to overlook them. Now, if you will excuse us, Delia, we really must be going."

"It was a pleasure meeting you, Miss Macpherson. I shall look

140

forward to seeing you and your family on Wednesday."

They left without another word, although Mariah saw Jeanette send Clarissa a look filled with compassion. She did not enjoy putting Lady St. John in her place as much as she thought she would, though some vengeful satisfaction lingered.

Neither of them spoke after they left the townhouse, but Mariah's conscience had a great deal to say. After silently arguing with herself most of the way home, she looked at Jeanette and sighed. "That was poorly done of me. I apologize for ending our afternoon on a vindictive note."

"Reminding her of the destructive power of gossip probably wasna such a bad idea. Perhaps it will make her think twice next time before passing on a tale, and especially before adding to it."

"Perhaps. I suspect Clarissa does not have a clue what she may be up against. I'm ashamed that I was not thinking about those things when I brought up their financial difficulties. I only wanted to throw their problems—and the hurtful gossip—in Lady St. John's face."

"Considering what she did to you, it is understandable."

"But not right."

"No, it isna," said Jeanette quietly. "We dinna always do everything right. When we fail, we can only try to do better the next time."

Forgive me, Lord. "I should have forgiven her long ago." Mariah sighed as the carriage pulled up in front of the townhouse. "I thought I had. Seeing her again made me so angry I wanted to pull her hair out."

Jeanette smiled wryly. "That would have been a wee bit much."

On Wednesday evening, Kiernan stopped by the small sitting room on the second floor to speak to his mother. The room served as her retreat when she felt the need for quiet. She had declined the invitation to accompany them to Lord and Lady Stanwell's dinner party. He had expected as much. Even when his father was alive, facing a whole room full of new people had been an ordeal.

He found her on the red velvet chaise lounge, her eyes closed. "Are you asleep?" he whispered.

"No. Merely resting." She opened her eyes and smiled in approval. "Now, dinna you look fine. Come here so I can see your new coat."

Kiernan obliged, pulling a chair over next to the chaise. "Gabe insisted black superfine with a velvet collar was the thing. He suggested the white waistcoat, too. I think he wanted the brighter colors for himself. He's wearing dark green with a blue waistcoat that matches the tartan." He smiled as he sat down. "I think I like the black. It makes me feel quite grand."

"You look quite grand. The coat and waistcoat both go well with the tartan and your hair. You're such a braw lad. Any mother would be proud."

"I'm nervous."

"There's no need to be. You're like your father, Kiernan, good with people. You have a way about you that sets them at ease."

"Only if I remember to speak slowly. If I talk normal, the English have a hard time understanding me."

Ailsa grinned. "Think what they'd do if ye spoke true Scots. They'd staun there and gype at ye and no' ken whit ye were aboot."

"It's tempting. If I made it impossible, no one would expect an answer on things I know nothing about."

Ailsa patted his hand. "You'll do just fine, laddie. God will be with you. So will Gabe and Mariah. I pray that all will go well for both of you. She's a good lass, son. She'll make a good wife."

"Am I so obvious, Mam?"

"To me. I know you care for her. I see it in every glance."

"I do. I'm no' sure yet if it is love or if it will last a lifetime. That's what I want. The kind of love you and father shared."

"And I pray you find it. We had a good life, your father and I. Even when we quarreled, we knew we'd eventually talk it out and settle our differences enough to go on. He was a good man, and so are you."

"I want to be. It comes a little easier now that I'm trying to let the Father guide me." Kiernan took her hand in his. "Mother, your hand is like ice. Are you feeling ill?"

"No, dear. My hands are often cold these days. It's probably because I dinna ever do any work. I dinna move enough to keep the blood flowing. Now, go on or you'll keep the others waiting."

"Can I fetch you a blanket?"

"There is a light one in the chair there. Toss it over me, and I'll be fine. You might tell Simms to come add a bit more coal to the fire."

"I'll do it."

"You will no'. I willna have you getting dirty when you're all dressed for a party. Now, off with you. Have a good time."

"Yes, ma'am." Kiernan covered her with the blanket, searching her face for any sign of discomfort. Her color was not good, but it had not been for months. "Mother, I'd like you to see a physician. I'm worried about you."

"I dinna need a physician. Half the time they canna tell you what is wrong, much less do anything about it. I just need some rest and some fresh air. Tomorrow, I'll let you take me to the park. Wilton says it should be a nice day now that the rain has stopped."

"He should know." Kiernan grinned and leaned down to kiss her cheek. "I think the man knows everything, and some of it before it happens."

Ailsa chuckled. "Never heard of an Englishman with the sight. Do ye ken if he has any Highland blood in him?"

"I doubt it. I suspect a wealth of experience lies behind his knowledge. Promise to send for me if you feel unwell."

"I promise, but I willna have a problem. I'll ask Wilton to read to me. It's as good as going to the theatre but without the crowd."

Kiernan raised an eyebrow. "You've done this before?"

"Dinna go gettin' uppity. He read to me a few afternoons while you were gone. Gabe was sick in bed and Jeanie was off with Clarissa. I was lonely. He noticed and offered to read to me while I knitted." She straightened the coverlet, avoiding his gaze. "He did some acting as a young man and has a flare for drama. I enjoyed it."

Kiernan detected the tiniest bit of defiance in her tone and a slight coloring of her cheeks. As she straightened the blanket for the second time—still not looking up at him—he didn't know whether to be worried or happy. He decided to be glad she had found something to enjoy, but he also intended to learn more about his butler at the first opportunity. "Shall I send him in?"

"Yes, please."

"Is there a particular book or story you wish to hear?"

She considered the question briefly. "No. I'm sure anything he wants to read would be entertaining."

"Very well. I'll see you in the morning."

On his way down the hall, Kiernan met Sukey, his mother's maid. He told her of his mother's request and said he would ask Wilton to come up. "Sukey, I have a favor to ask."

"Yes, milord?"

"Would you check on Mother often this evening? Perhaps just peep in if Wilton is there. I dinna want to disturb her entertainment, but her color does no' seem quite right." Though he preferred her light blush to the paleness of late, that bit of pink could spell trouble. "If anything seems amiss, send for me right away."

"That I will, sir."

11

"YOU'RE TENSE," MURMURED KIERNAN as they waited for the footman to announce their arrival at the marquis of Stanwell's party.

"So are you." Mariah wiggled her gloved fingers where they rested formally on his forearm. The muscles beneath her hand were flexed far more than normal. "You should be escorting your sister."

"And let you walk in with Gabe? Nae, lass. He may be my closest friend, but I willna give him that privilege."

She tried to quell her pleasure at his words.

"Besides, if Jeanie and I tried to do this on our own, we'd make a muddle of it. The blind leading the blind. This way you can guide me, and Gabe can guide her. Seems wise to me."

"It does make sense, but people will jump to conclusions."

"They will think you are beautiful, and I want you by my side. They might even suspect that I find you enchanting." He leaned a little closer, speaking softly as they moved forward one place in line. "You know I do, and I've decided it would be a good idea if the *ton* realized it, too."

"What?" Her voice squeaked before she quickly lowered it to a whisper. "Kiernan, I work for you."

"They dinna know that. Even if they do, it is of no significance. In rank, you are my equal, and you are staying with my family. No'

145

with me, with my family. If the women think I'm interested in you…" He captured her gaze. "…which I am, then they willna be so forward in trying to engage my attentions. It should also help keep the men from making advances toward you, whether proper or improper, and me from breaking too many noses."

She searched his eyes. He was serious, even about breaking noses. She was touched. And more nervous than ever. "How do you intend to, uh, reveal this information?"

They moved to the second place in line. "I thought I might sweep you into my arms and kiss you passionately a few minutes after we are announced."

"You wouldn't." Surely he wouldn't. She looked up at the imps in his eyes. "Kiernan, I'll never speak to you again if you do."

He sighed. "I thought you'd say that. Very well, lass, I'll be more subtle. But it would have been fun. Liven up the party."

Mariah glanced past the couple in front of them. Probably a third of the people in the room were his mother's age or older. "The doctors would adore you. Besides, it will probably be lively enough."

Kiernan followed her gaze and laughed, which drew the interest of several people nearby. His smile faded as the other guests gave them the once-over and conversation instantly picked up. "If anyone cracks a joke about my *skirt,* I'm liable to plant him a facer."

She pressed her fingertips against his arm and smiled. "If they do, it is only because they are jealous. You are by far the most handsome, most manly gentleman in the room."

"Mariah, you can only see about ten people."

"That doesn't matter. I know how you look, how you are."

He smiled tenderly, glancing at her peach satin gown with a cream-colored silk tunic worn open over it. His mother had loaned her a pearl necklace and earrings. Her hair was caught up in a cluster of curls on top of her head with peach satin ribbon artfully woven through them. "Did I tell you how lovely you look tonight?"

"Yes. Three times, and each one of them is appreciated." She took a deep breath, hoping to calm her nerves. "Our turn. Delia is on the right in the dark green dress with the gold turban. Godfrey is by the fireplace talking to the military man with all the medals. Smile, dear man; we're on display."

Kiernan obeyed. Her softly uttered endearment made it easy to be pleasant in spite of his jitters. *Let them be kind to her, Lord, and please dinna let me embarrass her.*

The butler cleared his throat discreetly before loudly proclaiming, "The earl of Branderee and Lady Mariah Douglas. Mr. Gabriel Macpherson and Miss Jeanette Macpherson."

The room fell silent. All heads turned in their direction. Shock registered on several faces as they stared at Mariah. Kiernan felt her fingers tremble. "Steady," he whispered, scanning the room with a stony gaze, settling on one obviously leering man. The man glanced at Kiernan and gulped.

Both Delia and Godfrey moved in their direction. Mariah focused on Delia, letting all the other faces blur as she tightened her fingers on Kiernan's arm. She was thankful he had insisted on being the one to escort her. Gabriel was her stalwart ally, but his presence would not have given her as much courage.

"Mariah, you look delightful," said Delia, reaching them first. She hugged Mariah, murmuring,. "And he's so handsome, I'm all agog." She stepped back as her husband joined them.

Mariah smiled and made the introductions. Though she spoke softly, her voice sounded loud in the quiet room.

"Good to meet you," said Godfrey, holding out his hand to Kiernan. He shook hands with him and Gabriel as they exchanged greetings. He nodded to Jeanette, glancing at her primrose yellow silk dress with approval. "Miss Macpherson, Delia told me you were pretty, but I see that was an understatement. You are lovely, my dear. We are honored to have you." He lifted her gloved hand and, bending down, kissed it lightly.

When he looked at Mariah, his eyes glowed with warmth and understanding. Godfrey took her hand and clasped it in both of his. "You are more beautiful than ever. Welcome, dear friend."

In her heart, Mariah blessed him. "Thank you, my lord. It is good to see you again."

Silently, Kiernan thanked the marquis and pledged him his friendship for life.

"Been too long, my dear," said Lord Stanwell briskly. "Much too long."

Conversations began again, and Kiernan glanced around the room. There were only a few expressions of open disapproval, one from a prune-faced old biddy and another from a woman Mariah's age whose tongue was probably as sharp as her beak. Some eyed them speculatively, and several smiled in welcome.

Lady Stanwell tugged on Mariah's arm. "You have some old friends I am certain cannot wait to talk to you." She smiled sweetly at her husband. "You introduce the gentlemen around while I steal Mariah and Miss Macpherson away."

"Yes, love." Stanwell smiled affectionately at his wife. He turned to Kiernan and Gabriel. "Well, gentlemen, we have been outmaneuvered. I hear you both were with the Gordon Highlanders. Fine fighting men. Were you in the Peninsula?"

Gabriel answered the marquis's question, engaging him in conversation while Kiernan observed Mariah and how she was received. For the most part, the reaction was favorable. A few of the women whispered to each other behind their fans as Delia led her and Jeanette from one small cluster of people to another. Most greeted them both with smiles. Particularly the men.

He decided the majority of men had assumed exactly what he wanted them to regarding Mariah. A few were a little more obtuse, or perhaps they flirted with every pretty lady who came along. Either way, he felt like marching across the floor, grabbing them by their lapels, and pointing out that she belonged to him.

Kiernan suspected most of them believed she had little or no money. If they were not privy to that bit of knowledge, they likely would be before the night was out. In many men's eyes, she was a penniless old maid, or on the shelf as it was often termed. That suited him fine, even though his conscience reminded him he shouldn't allow her to be perceived in such a derogatory way.

She was certainly old enough to be considered beyond the prime marriageable age, but she was no longer penniless. A message rapidly sent to Sir Edgar the night of Pryse's visit had called off the sale of Stillwater. A meeting with Pryse the following morning, and another with him and Sir Edgar three days later, changed the whole transaction.

Kiernan had traded the land back to Pryse for his library, which he promptly returned to him. Pryse sold Stillwater to Sir Edgar. A small portion of the proceeds went to Pryse, and the rest, twenty-one thousand pounds, was in a bank account for Mariah. Kiernan was acting as trustee until Mariah requested a change in writing. *I should tell her.* He knew it was wrong to make her think she had to depend on him, but if she knew about her money, she might walk out of his life. It was a risk he could not take.

He smiled as two more young men drifted over to speak to his sister. That made four around her, all vying for her attention. There would be no living with the girl.

"Your sister is a hit." Stanwell smiled as if he were her proud papa, though he was much the same age as Kiernan. "I assure you that all the eligible gentlemen here tonight, both old and young, are of excellent character and come from the best families.

"When Delia and I first married, she swore she would never put up with the dibble-dabble of playing hostess to more than a handful of close friends. In time she changed her mind, and now is considered a hostess of some importance. She enjoys besting the competition by introducing new faces to Society." He chuckled. "Both ladies and gentlemen."

Across the room, Mariah laughed, automatically drawing Kiernan's gaze. As if sensing his attention, she glanced at him and smiled. Relief and happiness dwelt in that smile—*It's not nearly as bad as I thought it would be*—so did understanding and affection. Not love, but an ever-deepening friendship, a good start.

"Mariah is in excellent hands," said Stanwell quietly. "No one would dare give her the direct cut or say anything rude in Delia's presence." He looked at Kiernan. "I'm glad she has you to watch over her, Branderee. I have the feeling you would be a formidable opponent."

"I can be if there is need."

"Good. Now, I should introduce you around. Later, you can tell me about Scotland and your countrymen's current sentiments toward the war."

Over the next hour, Kiernan met almost everyone in the room, all forty of them. He could not begin to remember all their names, but figured they could sort everyone out at home. He tried to speak slowly and usually succeeded. By doing so, he seldom had to repeat anything. The men were cordial and accepted his comments with interest. He discovered that he received as much respect for having fought in the war as he did for inheriting the title.

The women made a fuss over both him and Gabriel. The handful of single misses cast blushing glances their way and occasionally ventured a question or comment. The married women were more open in their flirting and wore gowns cut so low that they almost made him blush. He was proud of Mariah and Jeanette for dressing more modestly.

The married women, both young and old, were also bolder with their questions. "My lord," cooed an abundantly endowed blonde, "does it not feel strange to wear a kilt?" It was the third time during the evening he had been asked the same basic question. Only once had it come from a man, a red-cheeked youngster fresh from Oxford. The lad was so green he practically had grass growing out of his shoe, so Kiernan had not taken offense.

"No, I've worn the philabeg all my life."

"But..." She fluttered her lashes and her fan. "Stopping just above the knee as it does, is it not drafty?"

A young woman nearby tittered. Another smiled and shook her head.

"It is made of many yards of cloth, so 'tis quite warm. A breeze isna too noticeable. When it is, it only makes us heartier, able to handle the cold better than most."

"I'd wager you could handle anything better than most," replied the blonde with a sultry smile.

"I doubt that, ma'am. If you will excuse me, ladies, I need to speak with my sister." Kiernan nodded to the ladies and made his escape, walking across the room to where Jeanette held court.

She smiled at him as he joined the circle. "Fleeing, brother?"

"Aye." He grinned. "If I'd known a kilt garnered a man this much attention, I would have come to England long ago."

The other men chuckled. "If it's so interesting to the ladies, perhaps we should all take up wearing it," said one.

"Only if ye have Scottish blood in your veins," growled Kiernan. He smiled when the young man's eyes widened in fright. "I'm only teasin', lad. A hundred years ago, the Lowland Scots wouldna have been caught dead in a tartan. Only the barbaric Highlanders wore the plaid. Now, it is gaining popularity all over Scotland and becoming something of a national symbol instead of only a Highland one. It wouldna surprise me if some of the English took up the fashion, too."

Jeanie took a moment to introduce him to the five or six gentlemen around her, a few of whom he had already met. They ranged in age from around twenty to sixty.

"Miss Macpherson was telling us that you play the bagpipes, Lord Branderee. Is it a difficult instrument to learn?"

"It isna easy to master, and it takes a lot of air."

"Then you should do fine, Tony," teased one of the gentlemen. "You're full of hot air."

The young man laughed good-naturedly. "At times, but not when I say how much we appreciate you bringing your sister to London, sir." Tony Drake glanced at Jeanette with admiration. "She is delightful. With your permission, I'd like to ask her to go for a drive in the park tomorrow."

The other admirers groaned, and someone complained about Tony being too quick off the mark. Kiernan merely smiled and studied his sister's expression. He vaguely remembered Stanwell saying Drake was the son of Viscount Somebody. He liked the lad's personality and sense of humor. He also liked his initiative. Judging from Jeanette's smile, she favored him. "You have my permission to ask. It is up to Jeanette whether she goes or no'."

Tony gave Jeanette a brilliant smile. "Miss Macpherson, would you do me the honor of joining me for a drive in the park tomorrow?"

"I would be most happy to go with you, Mr. Drake."

"You are no' driving a high-perch phaeton, are you? I dinna want my sister's neck broken."

152

"Nor would I want to break it. Or my own for that matter. I have a curricle. Nice and safe."

"Good. Dinna be surprised if we are close behind you. Mother has promised to go for a drive tomorrow."

"Then we shall enjoy chatting back and forth," said Tony with an easy smile.

Kiernan made his way to Mariah just as dinner was announced. He offered her his arm, and they fell in line behind others of higher rank to proceed into the dining room. "You look happy."

"I am. There have been a few subtly rude comments, but nothing too vicious. Everyone else has been kind and avoided mentioning the past."

"Then your mind is at ease."

"Not entirely. This is a small gathering. Godfrey and Delia made it clear that I am their friend, and I doubt anyone here would openly do anything to earn their censure. Delia has become a very important political hostess."

"From what I hear, Stanwell is a powerful man in the House of Lords," said Kiernan.

"He is. Seeking what is best for the country has been his passion since he came into the title at one-and-twenty. Delia says he is a brilliant negotiator. She expects he will be deeply involved in the peace conference whenever we conquer Napoleon."

"You have no' been plagued with any unwanted attention, have you? I've tried to keep you in sight, but it is difficult to keep an eye on you and Jeanette, too, while listening to the conversation around me."

"No one has been bothersome. I found some wanted attention sorely lacking," she said softly, looking up at him. "I missed having you beside me."

"I missed being there." They moved along the table looking for their names on the placecards.

She laughed quietly. "You were too occupied to notice."

"Nae, lass. When you are no' near, there is an emptiness that none other can fill."

"You do say the sweetest things."

"I never say anything I dinna mean."

"I hope so." She looked up at him, sadness lurking in her eyes.

"Dinna think of him, Mariah," he said softly. "Dinna let your memories spoil your evening." Under the pretense of checking a placecard, he leaned toward her and whispered in her ear. "Dinna let them spoil what is between us." He read the card and straightened in disappointment. "Here is your place. It appears I am sitting somewhere else."

"That is the custom. If we all sat next to those we came with, we would never meet anyone new."

"I've already met more people than I can possibly remember."

"This way, you'll get to know a few of them better, and those you will remember. I suspect Delia did not put you too far away. Check the other side of the table."

Kiernan did as she suggested and found his seat directly across from her. He was relieved when two older, well-married ladies sat on either side of him. Two kindly-faced, gray-haired gentlemen were seated next to Mariah.

Jeanette was four chairs down. The blushing lad just out of Oxford was on one side and Anthony Drake on the other. Kiernan smiled to himself, wondering if the seating had been planned that way, or if Tony had switched the cards. Gabriel was placed across from Jeanette and between two young ladies, both making their come outs. Though one was much fairer than the other, Gabe took care to balance his conversation equally between the two.

On the way home, they all decided it had been a successful evening. "Now, we should have plenty of invitations from which to

154

choose," said Gabriel, tweaking a curl above Jeanette's ear. "And our fair lassie's callers will fill the drawing room. Be prepared to be smothered with flowers tomorrow. I expect you'll receive some token from every eligible man there."

Jeanette giggled. "I hope not all of them. A few had silver hair and paunches."

"Those you can politely dissuade," said Mariah with a smile.

Arriving at the townhouse, they were surprised to find Ailsa still awake and playing cards in the drawing room with Wilton.

Though she appeared tired, her eyes sparkled when she saw them. "You're all in such high spirits, it must have gone well. I couldna bring myself to go upstairs until you returned, so I pressed Wilton into keeping me company."

"It was my pleasure, ma'am." The butler bowed politely to Ailsa. Turning to Kiernan, he asked, "Would you care for anything, milord?"

Answers to a few questions. "No, thank you. We've been wined and dined enough for one evening. Feel free to retire."

"Yes, milord." As Wilton turned, he glanced at Kiernan's mother.

Kiernan noted that she also stole a quick glance at the butler, but he could not read the look that passed between them. There was no smile, no hint of impropriety; yet something was afoot.

"Jeanie, come sit beside me and tell me all about it," said Ailsa. "Were you swarmed by admiring young men?"

"Yes!" all four answered in unison.

As Jeanie laughed and began to tell her mother about the evening, Kiernan quietly followed the butler from the room. "May I have a word with you, Wilton?"

Wilton stiffened for a second before nodding. "Yes, milord."

"Let's go in the library." Kiernan led the way and sat down in his favorite chair. He pointed at another across from him. "Close the door and have a seat. This may take a few minutes." Wilton complied with his request, his tension obvious.

"Tell me about yourself."

"About me, sir?" For the first time, the unflappable Wilton seemed at a loss.

"Yes. About your family. Where you grew up. What professions you've had. That kind of thing."

Wilton cleared his throat, and though Kiernan didn't think it possible, he sat up even straighter. "My father owned some two thousand acres in York. No title, just land."

Which makes you part of the gentry, thought Kiernan.

"My eldest brother inherited the land. I was the fourth son, and as such, had little expectations of inheritance, which proved to be true. I stayed at Oxford for two years, worked a year as a clerk in a solicitor's office, then ran away to the theatre. I spent ten years on the stage until I realized I would never become a much-sought-after or highly paid performer. Too, I was tired of the life."

His hesitation was so slight, one could almost blame it on drawing a deep breath to continue or to gather his thoughts, but Kiernan suspected he was deciding just how much to tell him.

"Being without occupation or prospects, I created references stating I had served as a butler for two deceased friends of my father. I had stayed with each of them for a fortnight before joining the theatre, studying the work and ways of various servants so I could accurately portray the roles."

Kiernan smiled. "Especially the butler."

Wilton nodded. "There is usually a play around somewhere with such a character. Since leaving the theatre, I have worked in the position of butler for three employers over the past sixteen years. The longest time was spent in service to Lord Merryweather, maintaining this house. When he died some eighteen months ago, his nephew, Lord Briscoll, inherited. Lord Briscoll has a more elegant townhouse of his own, complete with staff, so he decided to rent this one out. Generally, it has been a pleasant situation, although an occasional tenant has proved unsatisfactory."

"But you find my mother quite the opposite," said Kiernan softly.

"She is a gracious lady. May I speak freely, milord?"

"Please do."

"Your mother is the most gentle soul I have ever known. And perhaps the most hurting. Though I try to be mindful of the differences in our positions, I am drawn to her. I feel compelled to do everything within my power to ease her suffering. I am concerned about her health and her emotional state. She grieves too deeply and too long."

"I agree. I am also worried. She and Father were very close, but I thought she would be better by now."

"I think she is at a loss for what to do with her time. She said she tended to much of the work in her own home."

"She did. She had help, of course, but only a housekeeper. No' a whole house full of servants to take care of every little thing. I know she is bored, but she lacks strength these days. She grows weary at the slightest exertion. Although she surprised me tonight. I hadna expected her to wait up."

"I tried to persuade her to retire, but she wanted to hear how Miss Jeanette's first formal party went. I worried that she might over-tax herself, but she enjoyed our games of cribbage. She said she was glad I did not toady up to her and let her win every time. When we switched to Beggar My Neighbor, she trounced me. Took delight in doing so, too," he said with a smile.

"She is very lonely, Lord Branderee. That is why I first suggested reading to her. I stopped by the sitting room to see if she needed anything, and she asked me several questions about London. When

I started to go back downstairs, sadness and loneliness enveloped her like a cloud. I could not walk out of the room and leave her in the dismals. Thus we shared a pleasant afternoon of Shakespeare."

"There have been other times besides tonight?"

"A few. It cheers her so. I cannot see the harm in it."

"Can ye no'? She is very vulnerable, especially to kindness and attention from a gentleman. I see the potential for great harm from such a friendship."

"I would never hurt her, milord. If I can make her smile or bring her pleasure, then surely that cannot be the wrong thing for her now."

"It depends on what kind of pleasure you have in mind."

"Certainly nothing indecent, sir!" Wilton fairly huffed in outrage. "She is a fine Christian woman and far above my station. I would never presume to take such liberties."

"See that you dinna." Kiernan stood, signaling the servant that their exchange was over. Scowling, Wilton stood and bowed curtly. When he reached the door, Kiernan called his name. The butler turned, looking at him with barely controlled anger.

"Wilton, up until ten months ago, my family was much the same as yours. Mother was remotely related to the earl of Branderee, but her line of the family is part of the gentry. Father was a forester and stepped into the gentry class when he married and acquired land of his own.

"If what you have told me is true, there is little difference between us by birth. An unexpected act of Providence, however, has placed me in a position of wealth and power. If necessary, I can destroy you. I dinna take the responsibility lightly, but I will do what I must to protect my mother. I intend to make inquiries about your family and your past. Is there anything you wish to clarify?"

"No, my lord."

"With that understood, if your friendship can brighten my mother's life, then I encourage it. I trust you will be mindful of appearances as well as her delicate physical and emotional health. If you hurt her in any way, I willna be kind."

Wilton relaxed minutely, his expression serious but no longer angry. "I understand."

"Good." Kiernan nodded, and the butler left the room.

Kiernan watched the older man walk quickly down the hall. "If you can take the sadness from her eyes and put the roses back in her cheeks, I will bless you," he whispered. "I will even welcome you to the family, if it will make her happy."

Mariah came down the hall, stopping at the open door. "I wondered where you had disappeared to. Why are you in here talking to yourself?"

He walked over to meet her, directing her to a small blue brocade settee in a shadowed corner. When they sat down, he put his arm around her and clasped her hand in his. He felt like cheering when she did not protest.

"Why were you alone?"

"Until about a minute ago, I was having an intense discussion with Wilton about him and Mother."

"Wilton and your mother? But he goes out of his way to be kind to her."

"Precisely. They are developing quite a friendship." He caressed her hand and absently noted that the calluses on her palm were growing softer.

"Are you worried it might lead to something more?"

"Yes, although if he makes her happy, then I would no' object."

"You wouldn't care if your mother married a butler?" She looked up, studying him dubiously.

He shook his head. "No' if she loved him. He is from the gentry, same as her. The fourth son of a country landowner. He has had to make his way in the world as best he can."

"You are certain of that?"

"No. It's what he told me, but he knows I will check his story."

"Kiernan, she could be hurt."

"If she is, he will pay dearly, and he knows it. I must keep in mind, however, that in affairs of the heart, there is always the chance of being hurt."

"Has anyone ever hurt you?"

"Yes."

"Tell me about her." She ran her finger along the back of his hand.

"Her name was Marjorie Macpherson. Like Gabe, no' kin, or at least no' close enough to claim. Her family lived in the next glen. She had teasing brown eyes and tawny hair. Loved to sing. She wasna very good, but she enjoyed it anyway. I liked it because she made up silly verses to make me laugh. She loved to race across the heath. Most of the time I won, but sometimes she'd trip me so she could win. She knew the woods as well as I did, and we spent hours there. I thought she was the prettiest lass in all of Scotland, and I dreamed of marryin' her."

"What happened?"

"She quit likin' bugs."

"What?"

"And started worryin' about getting dirty. Started noticing other lads, too."

She grinned, her eyes sparkling when she looked up at him. "Older lads?"

"Aye. They noticed her back. It didna help that she shot up overnight. One week we were the same height. The next she was three inches taller than me."

Mariah laughed and laid her head back against his arm. "Kiernan, she couldn't have grown three inches in a week."

"Seemed like it."

"How old were you?"

"Thirteen. She even let Aulay Mackenzie kiss her down by the stream."

She giggled. "Shameless hussy."

"Oh, that's no' the worst of it. He bragged about it, and I called him a liar."

"You fought."

"Aye, gave him a bloody nose, too. Unfortunately by accident. Gabe said I caught him with my elbow when he punched me in the jaw and I spun around. I didna remember because it knocked me out cold. Gabe said he bled everywhere."

She reached across him and poked his bicep through his velvet jacket. "He must have been a lot bigger than you."

"He was, and older, too. Sixteen. That's why Marjorie was so angry when I came to."

"Well, she should have been. It wasn't right for a boy so much older to fight you."

"She wasna angry at him but at me. Told me I was silly. She didna care if he bragged. She said he was a good kisser, and it made the other girls envy her. Afterwards, I wondered who she was comparin' him to, but I didna think of it at the time," he said with a smile.

"Well, she was the silly one. She didn't know what she was missing."

"Oh?"

"You're a very good kisser."

He chuckled. "I wouldna have been when I was thirteen."

"Maybe not, but you are now," she said softly.

"It depends on who I'm kissing." He cupped her chin, tipping her face upward. "Do you think of me?"

"Yes. Too often."

He smiled. "There's no such thing." He ran his fingers down the side of her neck, resting his hand on her shoulder. "You come to mind at the oddest moments. When I smell a rose, or hear a bird sing. When the rain taps against the windowpane, or the moonlight dances across the floor. In a crowd or alone, you're never far from my thoughts."

"I'm a fool to listen to such honeyed words," she whispered, her eyes filled with longing. "And a bigger fool to want to believe them."

"Believe them, sweetheart. They are true." He brushed a kiss across her lips, then another. When she made a tiny sound of pleasure, he deepened the kiss, wrapping his arms around her. She touched his face, then slid her hand around his neck. He let her sense the passion he held in check, the desire he had known for no other. After a few minutes, he slowly eased back, ending as he began, brushing his lips lightly across hers.

She took a shuddering breath and rested her forehead against his jaw. "Marjorie Macpherson had windmills in her head."

Kiernan laughed softly. "I'm glad she did. Otherwise, I might no' have met you."

Someone coughed lightly outside the partially closed door. She tried to pull away, but Kiernan tightened his hold.

"Kiernan, are you in there?" called Gabe softly.

"I'm here."

"We are all going up to bed. You mother thought you would want to know. Mariah, too," he added with humor in his voice.

Kiernan grinned when Mariah rolled her eyes. "Thanks, Gabe. Tell Mam we'll be right up."

"That I will."

Shaking her head, Mariah moved slowly away from him. "You have a very strange household, Lord Branderee. If anyone else knew what went on here, they might send us all to Bedlam."

He stood and pulled her up beside him. "What's so strange about my household? I see nothing unusual, only an earl who is little more than a commoner—"

"Hardly."

Her comment pleased him immensely. "Who would rather be traipsing around the Scottish mountains playing a bagpipe than cavorting—"

"Cavorting?" She raised a delicate brow as a faint smile hovered about her mouth.

He nodded as they started toward the door. "Through elegant London dinner parties with scantily clad ladies who speak in innuendos and say one thing with their lips but another with their eyes."

She halted abruptly. "Who said what?"

"I canna remember her name, and what she said isna important." He put his arm around her, urging her along toward the door. "Now, where was I? Oh, yes, and an earl who canna make sense out of a ledger if he stares at it for hours."

"You need a good man-of-business." She grinned up at him.

"Perhaps. We have an earl's sister who, though she has reached the ripe age of nineteen, does no' give a fig about finding a rich, important husband. We have the earl's best friend who wishes he'd never brought them to London."

"The only sane one in the bunch."

"And the earl's mother who is falling for the butler," he said in a whisper.

"Don't forget the chaperon who has done very little chaperoning, has been showered with gifts by her employer—"

"By her friends. Jeanie and Mother are involved, too."

"A chaperon who sneaks around dimly lit corridors and libraries kissing that same employer."

"Admirer." His amusement faded at the thread of uncertainty in her voice. "Who demands no favors in return for anything given you. I dinna expect a kiss every time you order a new frock or buy a new bonnet. If I did, I'd order ten for you every day. If you were working in this same capacity for someone else, wouldna they provide your clothes or sufficient funds to purchase them yourself?"

"Likely. But they would not be so generous."

"I'm generous because I can be. Mariah, I could buy you ten times what you'll wear in a Season and barely notice the money spent."

Her eyes widened. A few seconds later, she frowned. "Are you certain? You said you do not understand your ledgers."

He laughed softly. "I dinna understand them, but rest assured my bankers know to the penny how much I can spend. I'm no' about to be in dun territory anytime soon. No' even if I picked up the diamond necklace I saw today and fastened it around your lovely throat."

"Kiernan, you mustn't!"

"I know, but I was tempted." He kissed the tip of her nose. "Now, run along upstairs. I need to make certain Wilton locked up. No one is going to send us to Bedlam."

"They may run us out of the country," she muttered as she started up the stairs.

"Then we'll go to Scotland." He grinned when she frowned down at him. "And I can play my pipes whenever I have the whim."

Kiernan turned away, heading for the front door, imagining the diamond necklace nestled against her skin. *Someday, lass, I'll buy you all the trinkets I want to.*

12

As EXPECTED, THE FLORAL OFFERINGS for Jeanette began arriving mid-morning. Every young man who had attended the Stanwells' dinner sent her a bouquet, as did more than a few of the older single men. The tokens of their esteem came in all shapes and sizes, from a basket of pansies sent by an older gentleman to a large vase filled with two dozen red and white roses from the blushing young man fresh from Oxford.

Jeanie was too excited to sit still. She went from one bouquet to the next, admiring them, sniffing their fragrance, and telling Mariah and her mother everything she could remember about the gentlemen who sent them. She studied the basket of pansies with a frown.

"What is wrong?" asked Ailsa.

"I canna place Mr. Bellson."

Mariah remembered him from her first days in London. "David Bellson. I think he is near fifty. Short, wiry, and quiet. He was around when I made my come out. A baron's son. He is a nice man, except he never says anything." She smiled, enjoying Jeanie's happiness. Not every young woman had so many admirers. "He has lost some hair since I met him."

"I recall him now. He told me good evening and stood nearby while everyone else talked. I dinna think he said another word."

"Unless he has changed a great deal, he seldom does."

Simms entered the drawing room with another floral arrangement. It was the most unique, a cut glass vase containing three pale yellow orchids, almost a perfect match to Jeanie's gown of the night before.

"Who sent those?" Mariah smiled as Jeanie looked up after reading the card, pure pleasure written on her face.

"Tony Drake."

"A very astute young man."

Jeanette grinned impishly. "He certainly didna let opportunity pass him by last night. Within a minute after Kiernan began talking to us, Tony asked his permission to take me for a drive. Then he nonchalantly switched the cards at the dinner table so he could sit by me."

"Courageous." Mariah smiled at her young friend. Despite Jeanette's declaration that she was not looking for a husband, her expression became dreamy as she touched a petal. "Handsome, too."

"Yes, he is. It will be so nice to go to the park with him so we can talk without constant interruption."

"There will be more interruptions than you might think. A good many of the *beau monde* should be in Town by now, so the park will be busy. Remember to speak to everyone you know, otherwise they will think you have insulted them, and everyone else will believe so, too."

"What if I canna remember their names?"

"You don't have to greet them by name, and conversation can be mundane. Talk about the weather or how lovely the flowers are. Mr. Drake will probably know almost everyone. If you see someone you recognize but don't remember their names, solicit his help. It will make him feel terribly important."

Jeanette giggled. "Sometimes it does no' take much to make a man feel important."

"I think we have just been insulted," said Gabriel, sauntering into the room. He looked at all the flowers and grinned at Jeanette. "Did we go into the florist business?"

Kiernan wandered in behind him, sifting through a stack of invitations. He looked up, surveyed all the bouquets, and smiled at his sister. "It's a good thing flowers dinna make you sneeze." He walked over and kissed her on the cheek. "I knew you'd be a hit." He thrust the cards and notes into Gabe's hand. "I think everyone at the dinner last night is having a party."

"And then some. No' all of these are from people who were at the Stanwells'." Gabe skimmed one of the invitations. He looked up at Mariah and smiled. "Word has definitely gotten round that you're here with us. This is from the marquis of Altbury, and you are included."

"What kind of party is it?" asked Jeanette, casting one last look at the orchids before turning to Gabriel.

"You have been invited to your first ball, lass."

Jeanette let out a squeal and clapped her hands. "When?"

"Tuesday week. Why the frown, Jeanie?"

"Clarissa said something about having to obtain vouchers from Almacks and go there before we were invited to any balls. Or was it before we went to a ball? I canna remember. She said it was terribly important to receive the approval of the patroness."

"Only if you want to move within the most elite part of the fashionable world," said Gabriel. "There are many peers of the realm and ladies, too, who for one reason or another never gain admittance to Almacks. Knowing you are no' particularly concerned with making a match, I dinna think it is all that important. Besides, Kiernan and I would have to wear knee breeches if we went. No exceptions to the rule."

"I willna worry about it then. I dinna care if the parties we are invited to are the most fashionable. I only want to meet interesting people and enjoy myself."

Gabriel let the invitations slide from his fingers onto the game table. "I do believe, my dear, the door to the magical land has been opened." He smiled at Mariah. "Thanks in no small part to your connections."

They all sat down around the table, going over invitations to dinner parties, musical evenings, balls, salons, and soirees, which was a fancy name for an evening party. Some of the events were on the same dates, but since they knew few of the people well, the decision regarding which one to attend usually came down to a preference for the type of function involved.

"This one has an Italian soprano as the entertainment, and this one is a salon for the purpose of discussing Greek literature." Kiernan grimaced. "I canna stand opera, and I know nothing about Greek anything."

"Then it would be a good night to stay home. We are under no obligation to go out every evening," said Mariah.

The others concurred, saying they would be ready for a rest by then. Although Ailsa was included in every invitation, she asked to be excused from each one.

"Mam, please go to something. You should no' sit home alone all the time." Jeanette hugged her mother. "You need to go out more."

"No' to parties. You know they scare me to death. Though I would like to go calling with you a bit next week." Ailsa smiled at Mariah. "I think I'd like to meet your friend, Lady Stanwell. She sounds very nice."

"She is. I'm sure she would be happy to introduce you to some other ladies whose company you would enjoy. Delia is very good at matching people according to their interests."

"I would also like to go shopping on Monday. I have decided it is time to wear something besides black." Her eyes brimmed with quick tears, but she wiped them away quickly. "My heart will always grieve for your father, but maybe if I wore something a wee bit more cheerful, it would raise my spirits. I'm tired of being blue-deviled."

Kiernan grinned as Jeanie danced around the table. "That, dearest Mother, is the best news I've heard in months." He leaned over and kissed Ailsa on the cheek. "Buy anything that suits your fancy. Maybe bright pink to put a little color in your cheeks."

"I dinna know if I will go that far. I was thinking more on the lines of silver or gray."

"Suit yourself, as long as it cheers you." Kiernan stood, grabbed Mariah's hand, and tugged her out of the chair, putting a little color in *her* cheeks. "Come with me, lass. I need help answering these. You can tell me the polite way of saying we are no' coming because your entertainment would make my head ache."

Mariah glanced at Ailsa, relieved to see she was smiling indulgently. Evidently, his mother no longer feared his intentions were anything but honorable. "Yes, my lord." Still blushing, she smiled at Ailsa as he pulled her toward the doorway. "We will tell them you do not enjoy caterwauling."

"Aptly put. The only female opera singer I ever heard sounded like some poor cat with its tail caught in the door."

"Be kind, children," called Ailsa with a laugh.

"Your mother seems in a good mood today," said Mariah as they walked down the hall, still hand in hand.

"Yes, she does. It would appear spending the evening in Wilton's company was good for her."

"Did you find out anything more about him?"

"No. I went to my solicitor's office this morning and asked him to look into it. He thought the name seemed familiar. Said an acquaintance of his from York is in town on business, and he would see if he knew anything about the family."

Kiernan wrote out the replies as Mariah dictated, often stopping to discuss who had sent them. She knew something about almost all of their hosts and hostesses. "Remember, I may be outdated on some of this information. Delia wrote often, keeping me up on most of the news, but I'm sure she did not pass on everything. It becomes easier to keep up with who belongs to whom and who owns what once you are better acquainted."

"I like a man for what he is, no' how much wealth he has."

"Which is admirable and fine for giving your friendship. However, when it comes to a potential husband for Jeanie—or a potential wife for you—you must be careful of those who are more interested in monetary gain than their intended's happiness." Mariah tried to ignore the hurt that came with the thought of his finding a wife.

Kiernan nodded. "I know I must be ever on my guard for Jeanie's sake, but keep reminding me. Right now, I do well to put a face with a name. These two I canna place at all."

She leaned closer, studying the card. "I don't recognize the name either. Maybe they are the young couple Delia said married last fall. She's tiny, with blond hair—what you could see of it under her hat."

"The one with all the pink feathers?"

"Yes, that's the one. I think her husband sat a few seats down from Gabriel. I can't remember much about him, rather nondescript."

Kiernan nodded. "Average height, average build, brown hair, pleasant enough but quiet."

"Yes, I'm sure we are right. Mr. and Mrs. Norton. What are they having?" She checked the invitation. "A breakfast."

"At three in the afternoon," Kiernan said with a grin. "Where I come from that is no' called a breakfast."

"In the country, you don't stay up most of the night. After a few nights of coming home around three or four, you will be more than happy to have breakfast in the middle of the afternoon."

They finished the replies and walked back toward the stairway, intending to go upstairs and change for the afternoon drive in the park. As they neared the drawing room, they heard Ailsa and Wilton talking. Kiernan drew Mariah to a halt a few feet from the doorway and lifted his finger to his lips.

"I have decided to do as you suggested last night, Wilton. I'm going to put aside wearing black."

"I am glad to hear it, madam. The change will do you good," he said politely.

"Kiernan says I should buy something in bright pink." Ailsa sounded amused.

"Pink would be very becoming." Wilton's voice mellowed. "You would look quite lovely in deep rose."

"You think so? I dinna believe I've ever tried it. I usually wear gray and blue, occasionally green. I do have one purple frock at home." She paused. "I dinna think I could go from black to something very bright. It would be too much of a shock."

"Perhaps something in light gray, with a touch of color in the trim or bonnet."

"I express a wish for salmon, and it appears on my table in the evening. I need knitting needles of a certain size, and you find them for me. Now, you give me sound advice on fashion. Is there nothing you canna do?"

"There is little I will not try, but alas, I am not always successful. Sometimes I fail miserably. Having lived in London almost thirty years, I have learned where to acquire almost anything. As to fashion, I'm not up on the latest trends, but I do know how to combine colors. It is something I picked up in the theatre." His voice

171

dropped and took on a mildly teasing quality. "But be mindful, Mrs. Macpherson, do not go by my suggestions alone. You might find yourself wearing a gown more suitable to the Elizabethan age than our modern times."

"And saying thee and thou and forsooth?"

Kiernan winked at Mariah, his eyes sparkling. Though she was uncomfortable eavesdropping, she also enjoyed hearing Ailsa's merry answer. She began to edge away, pulling on his sleeve. He resisted before taking a step in her direction. He stopped when the butler started speaking again.

"Aye, and the next time you are irritated at someone, you could call them a mewling, motley-minded moldwarp," said Wilton, drawing out the last four words in a rumbling, scathing voice.

At his mother's peal of laughter, Mariah and Kiernan scurried back to the library. The instant he shut the door, they looked at each other and burst out laughing.

"How in the world did he say that without getting it all tangled up?" asked Mariah when she could catch her breath.

"It's in the delivery." Grinning, Kiernan shook his head. "He must have been quite the actor."

"Heavy on the melodrama."

They shared another laugh. Composing themselves, they walked back down the hall, chattering loudly. When they arrived at the drawing room, it was empty.

"Uh-oh. Do you think they heard us?" asked Kiernan with a worried frown, turning toward the staircase.

"How could they help it? Those big feet of yours must have made noise on the tile." Though Mariah shared his embarrassment at being caught eavesdropping, she placed the blame on him.

"My feet are no' that big."

"Bigger than mine." She held out a foot for his inspection.

172

"I would hope so. You're quieter because your shoes are made of cloth. It's the leather shoes that made the noise, no' my feet."

A giggle drew their gazes upward. Ailsa leaned over the staircase banister near the second floor, smiling at them. "Kiernan, you bootless, beetle-headed bugbear, go get the carriage so we can go for our drive."

Kiernan stared as his mother disappeared up the staircase. When Mariah giggled, he frowned at her, which only made her laugh harder. He planted his hands on his hips. "What is so funny?"

"You should have throttled that thundering thespian."

He growled and lunged for her as she scampered up the stairs. Missing, he called out, "Maybe I should lock up a laughing lass." He groaned. "Now, they have me doing it."

Mariah stopped at the first landing and looked back. She had not felt so lighthearted in years, and she silently thanked him for it. He was still frowning. When their gazes met, she winked.

A smile slowly spread across his face. "Saucy woman."

Mariah didn't think he minded at all.

13

"IT'S SUCH A LOVELY DAY FOR A DRIVE." Jeanette smiled at Tony Drake as he guided the carriage into Hyde Park, thinking he looked even more handsome than he had the night before. His closely cropped, rich brown hair fell across his forehead in a casual, windblown fashion, and his bright blue coat and white waistcoat made his eyes sparkle like sapphires.

"Even if the skies were gray, it would be a lovely day in your company," he said with a smile. He glanced at her pink calico frock trimmed in sea green and matching bonnet. "You are far prettier than any flower in the park."

Jeanette laughed. "What gammon, Mr. Drake."

"I admit it is a line oft used, Miss Macpherson, but in your case it is true. Your cheerful disposition would brighten the gloomiest day."

She smiled gently at his obvious sincerity. "Thank you, kind sir, but I take no credit for it. I am cheerful because God has given me a joyful heart."

A tiny frown creased his forehead. "Does God make your heart joyful even in times of trouble? You have never known sadness or pain?"

"I have been blessed with a loving family and a life mostly free of troubles, but no one can escape sadness or pain. When Kiernan left to fight Napoleon, I was sad and lonely for months on end. I missed him terribly even though our ages differ by several years."

She took a deep breath, letting her gaze move lazily across the crowded park. "When my father died a little over a year ago, I thought I would never smile again. I adored him, and to have him taken so suddenly was beyond my understanding. Grief and misery suffocated me. I cried out to God, and he heard me. In time, I could accept his comfort. I found his peace in the countryside, in the Scriptures, in the love of my family and friends.

"The Bible says he gives us beauty for ashes, the oil of joy for mourning, and the garment of praise for the spirit of heaviness. I spent long hours walking the glens and hills, gazing at his creation, seeing the beauty change with each new day. I began to praise him for the things I could—a bird's song, the opening of a flower, a sunset—and gradually my heaviness lifted. Many months after my father's death, I realized God had slowly replaced my pain with joy.

"I still miss my father, of course, and feel pain whenever I think of him. I'm no' sure something like that ever goes away. But overall, I'm happy, so I see no reason no' to be cheerful."

They stopped for a moment as the carriage in front of them halted while the occupants exchanged greetings with two gentlemen on horseback coming from the other direction. Tony shifted so he could look at her more fully. "You are a very interesting woman, Miss Macpherson. I do not believe I have ever met anyone so open about their faith. Are all Scots so religious?"

She laughed softly. "Some are, but no' all. Many grow up attending church regularly and receiving Christian teaching in the home, just as many Englishmen do."

He turned back to the task of navigating through the crowded lane. "The Scriptures were seldom read in our home, although my family attended church regularly. I think my parents viewed it mostly as a social obligation. We never discussed it, so I do not know for certain. After I went off to school, I dropped into church fairly often and found some of the sermons rather enlightening. I occasionally go to St. Paul's on Sunday morning." He grinned. "But I have trouble staying awake."

"That can be a problem. No' all sermons are particularly interesting, especially if you were up late the night before."

He feigned shock. "My dear, all English gentlemen stay up late every night. We would be considered wrong in the upper story if we did not spend half the night at some kind of amusement."

"Do you no' become bored with it all?"

He was quiet for a moment. "Yes, I suppose I do. Especially by the end of the Season when there has been a party of some kind almost every night."

"Just thinking about it makes me tired," said Jeanette with a smile. "We have purposely kept Saturday evenings free, as well as an occasional night in the middle of the week. I should think everyone would become addled if they went out every night."

Tony laughed and shook his head. "Miss Macpherson, I do believe you are the most outspoken young woman I have had the pleasure of meeting."

"I'm glad you still consider it a pleasure, Mr. Drake. Clarissa says I am far too outspoken, that I will never find a husband on the marriage mart."

"There are some men who would be taken aback by your forthright manner, but I enjoy it."

"Then they are no loss to me. I wouldna want a husband who couldna accept me as I am. Besides, I am here only to enjoy the Season, no' search for a mate."

This time his shock appeared real. "You don't wish to marry?"

"Of course I do, but I am no' desperate. I am only nineteen."

"Practically on the shelf," he said with a teasing smile.

"No' even close. I can afford to wait for love."

"You will marry for love only?"

"Yes."

He met her gaze, his expression tender. "Then I shall court you with due haste, for I am already quite smitten."

"We have only just met, Mr. Drake. We barely know each other," she said with a gentle smile.

"A condition I hope to rectify quickly, Miss Macpherson."

They were hailed by some of his acquaintances from another carriage, and Jeanette was not given the opportunity to tell him that she had other requirements for a husband besides mutual love. She had always planned to marry a Scot, but somehow, at the moment, that particular desire did not seem quite so important.

In one essential way, however, he was not suitable for a husband. She had promised both her father and God that she would not marry an unbeliever. Though Tony attended church occasionally, she doubted he knew Jesus in a personal way. She understood how important it was for a husband and wife to share the same understanding and faith. She would not bind herself to a man who did not know the wonder of God's grace and the joy of salvation through Jesus.

They moved on, approaching another curricle. Jeanette recognized the couple from the Stanwell dinner but could not remember their names. "I hope you know them because I canna remember who they are."

"Lord and Lady Mrrmrrph," he said, garbling the last name.

"Tony!" she whispered.

He grinned in triumph. "Now that you've called me by my first name, I'll hear no more Mr. Drake from those sweet lips."

"You willna think they are so sweet when I give you a piece of my mind." She eyed the approaching couple with a nervous smile.

"So there is a bit of spice mixed in with that honeyed disposition of yours. I like that," he murmured. "Good afternoon, Lady Maplethorp, Lord Maplethorp. I trust you remember Miss Macpherson from last evening."

"We do indeed. How nice to see you again."

They chatted briefly about the previous night's dinner before moving on. A similar scene was repeated over and over as they progressed around the park. Soon Tony had charmed himself back into her good graces.

Jeanette glanced back to see if Kiernan and Mariah were still two carriages behind them, where they could chaperon without being too obvious. He had taken their mother for a drive earlier. Her pleasure came from the quiet beauty of the park, not from being seen and meeting untold numbers of people. A drive such as this would have been torture for her.

From Mariah's stoic expression, she was not enjoying it all that much, either. The four people in the landau going past them were pointedly ignoring her and Kiernan, giving them the ultimate insult. They had not stopped to speak to Jeanette and Tony either, since they were not acquainted. They had, however, smiled politely as they passed by.

As they turned a corner, Tony looked back and frowned. "Do my eyes deceive me, or did those people just give your brother and Lady Mariah the direct cut?"

"It would seem so." She glanced back again, breathing a sigh of relief when the next couple stopped beside Kiernan's curricle and engaged them in a pleasant exchange.

"I heard some talk last night that she had been involved in a scandal years ago. Married a man who was already wed."

Jeanette nodded. "She didna know he had a wife when she married him."

"That's the way I heard it, too. Can't see how anyone could blame her, but knowing the hateful nature of some, there are bound to be people who do."

"Generally, she has been warmly received, but it must still be painful to be the object of disdain, even from a few."

Tony took another peek behind them. "She appears better now that Mr. and Mrs. Norton stopped to chat. Your brother, too. He is very protective of her." He smiled at Jeanette. "You should have seen the quelling look he sent around the room when you arrived last night. Only a cabbage-head would have dared look at her with anything but the highest regard. He won my respect, and that of many others, then and there. I envy him. With or without the title, your brother stands out from other men."

Jeanette laughed. "Wearing a kilt might have something to do with it."

Tony laughed with her. "Well, it does draw one's attention." His expression sobered. "I do not think your brother is a man to cross."

"He isna ruthless, but he is fiercely protective of his family, those in his care, and those who canna care for themselves. There are several men living on the estate that he brought home at one time or another. Men who were crippled in the war. They all contribute to the care of the land and castle in some way, but they likely wouldna be able to support themselves anywhere else."

"Men from his regiment?"

"From the Gordons and others. Brave Highlanders who found themselves with nothing when they came home, their families displaced or tilling lands that couldna support another hungry stomach. Those small plots have been home to countless generations, families and clans bound together by blood, tradition, and loyalty."

"And that is changing?"

"Yes, and I expect we will see far greater changes in the future.

All of the chiefains involved in the Jacobite Rebellion of '45 either fled the country or were executed, and their lands forfeited to the government. Nearly forty years later, the government allowed the families to redeem their estates. Most regained their lands, although I understand a few have no'. Some of the returning families didna feel the same kinship with their clan as before. How could they after being gone so long? They set about improving the estates, which sometimes meant displacing a portion of the crofters.

"For that same time period, the Highlanders were no' allowed to carry weapons, wear the tartan and kilt, or play the pipes, unless they were part of a regiment in service to the king. Much of what held the clans together, especially the threat of feuds and war with their neighbors, was abolished."

"Well, that part of it sounds good," said Tony.

"It has helped to unify the Highlands and the country, but it is a harshness almost beyond bearing to take a warrior's weapons from him. Most of the Highlanders were born fighters. It seems to be in the blood."

"As proven by the fine records of the Scottish regiments."

"Yes." Jeanette was silent for a minute, wondering if she was boring her companion. As she looked around at the elegantly dressed men and women congregated in the park, homesickness assailed her. She longed for the mountains, the castle of Branderee, and the rugged cliff on which it stood. Even the sandy dunes along the coast west of Kiernan's estate called to her.

Most of all, she longed for the Scottish people, the common folk she had known all her life. The men who had gone with the Highland regiments, partly because they were allowed to wear the garb of their ancestors, and the women who sent them off with tears, love, and prayers.

"They fight no' only for the freedom of Scotland and all of Great

Britain, but to restore the age-old traditions that decades of repression couldna destroy."

"Which is why your brother became a piper, and why both he and Mr. Macpherson wear the tartan and kilt with such a noble pride." Tony covered her hand with his. "A pride in country and heritage no greater than your own."

Jeanette blushed. "Forgive me for the lecture."

"My dear girl, you cannot imagine how refreshing it is to have a conversation with a female who is not afraid to show her intelligence. Most English ladies are loyal to our country, but many could not begin to tell me why, except that it is expected of them."

"Maybe they think it too heavy a conversation for such a frivolous setting."

He smiled. "Perhaps. I shall take your cue and change the subject. I thought your mother would be joining our frivolity today."

"Kiernan brought her to the park earlier so she could enjoy the quiet and beauty of the flowers and trees without all the crowd. I'm glad to see her go out of the house. She has stayed inside far too much since we came to London. Other than doing some shopping, she has ventured out very little."

"Has she been unwell?"

"A bit. Mostly, she is very uncomfortable around new people, especially large crowds. She has had too many changes the last year or so, with my father dying, and Kiernan unexpectedly coming into the title. We moved from the Highlands to his estate on the northeast coast, which was a tremendous change for all of us. One week we were living in a modest Highland home; the next we moved into a fifty-room castle."

"That must have been a shock."

"It was. We are still no' accustomed to the whole situation."

"I heard the previous earl was a distant cousin."

Jeanette nodded, explaining how Kiernan came to inherit. Having gone the full circuit of the park, they departed to go back to the townhouse. On the way, she told him something of the life they had lived before. "So you see, Mr. Drake—" She grinned when he glared at her. "We are simple Highland folk, no' at all reared to be a part of such esteemed company."

Tony drew the curricle to a halt in front of the townhouse. "My dear Miss Macpherson, if all Highlanders are as wonderful as you, I would happily forsake London for Scotland." He handed the reins to Simms and climbed down, walking around to help her from the carriage. He lifted her from the seat and gently lowered her to the ground. "And I assure you, I hold no one in higher esteem than you."

She started to make a lighthearted quip about how he had flattery down to an art, but when she looked up at him, the thought evaporated. Either he was a great actor or his words were uttered with heartfelt sincerity. "You flatter me, sir."

"I only speak what I feel. I hope that we might go again soon, but if this were the only time I have with you, I would consider it one of the most special afternoons of my life."

"It is special to me, too," she said as they walked up the steps to the townhouse. "You are the first gentleman to take me for a drive in London."

"But not the first to take you for a drive."

"There were several young men at home who came to call, before we moved to Branderee, that is. Going for an afternoon drive was the main form of entertainment. We had occasional dances and parties, but nothing like here."

"There is no one of particular interest, I hope?"

"No."

"Good. I will be out of town for several days. My father has summoned me home for a visit. But I will be back in time for the

Altburys' ball. I trust you will save me two dances?"

"Of course," she said as Wilton opened the door, and they stepped inside the entryway.

"One of them the supper dance?"

"That would be nice. Thank you for a lovely afternoon."

"Thank you for going with me. Now, if you will excuse me, I must be off to Kent." He bowed and kissed her hand before walking jauntily down the steps, stopping for a few minutes to speak to Kiernan and Mariah as they arrived.

"Did you enjoy your afternoon in the park, Miss Jeanette?" asked Wilton as she handed him her hat and gloves.

"It was very interesting. Seeing all the ladies and gents in their colorful finery, with all their preening and chatter, I was reminded of a flock of birds."

The butler smiled. "An appropriate description. And the young man? Was he a suitable companion?"

"Yes, he was very pleasant."

"Your mother is in the drawing room, anxiously waiting to hear all about it."

"Thank you, Wilton." Jeanette went on into the drawing room with Kiernan and Mariah joining her a few minutes later.

They recounted the afternoon's events for Ailsa. Though she did not wish to be involved in person, she enjoyed hearing about the different people they met.

"You missed the most exciting part, Jeanie," said Kiernan. "Just as you and Mr. Drake left the park, a lady flirting with a gentleman on horseback opened her yellow, tasseled parasol and twirled it. It startled the gent's poor horse and the animal bolted in sheer terror, dashing right between two curricles and through a crowd of pedestrians. People ran left and right to get out of the way. It's a miracle no one was injured.

"The horses pulling one of the curricles took off through the grass and flower beds, giving their master and his fair companion a very bumpy ride before another horseman galloped to the rescue and halted the team."

"Drat! That would have been a sight to see. Tony will be disappointed to hear he missed it."

"Tony?" asked her mother, arching a brow.

"Mr. Drake. I'm sticking to the formalities when I talk to him." *Except for the one slip.*

"You've told me about everyone else at the park, but little about Mr. Drake. Dinna you like him, lass?"

"I like him very much. He is intelligent, kind, and amusing. He didna seem the least bit put off by my outspokenness. In fact, he said he enjoyed it. We talked about Scotland, touching on a bit of history and current conditions. We also talked about church and my faith."

"He is a believer, then?" asked Ailsa, her expression hopeful.

"I dinna think so, Mam. His family attended church, but he thought it was only because they saw it as a social obligation. He said he found some of the sermons enlightening, but I dinna think he understands what it is all about. He attends rarely now." Jeanette smoothed a pleat in her dress. "He seems very interested in courting me with due haste. He said as much."

"But you have reservations," said Kiernan. "They probably come from God, Posy."

"Yes, and from myself as well. Though I like him, he is only the first man who has come to call. It seems foolish to encourage him too much at this time, and it is wrong to encourage him when I have pledged to marry only a Christian. Yet I truly enjoy his company and would like to become better acquainted. He seems to understand that my faith is very much a part of me. I hope there might be an opportunity to tell him more about Jesus."

"Mariah, any words of wisdom for my little sister?" asked Kiernan with a tender smile.

"Do you think he will call again right away?"

"No, he was leaving for Kent to spend time with his father. He said he would be back in time for the Altburys' ball."

"Even though he is very interested in you, I doubt he expects you to single him out right now." She glanced around the room at the numerous floral bouquets. "Give yourself time to become acquainted with several gentlemen, including Tony, but try not to show particular favor to any of them for a while. The Season has barely begun, and there are many others you have not met. There is no need to rush."

"Thank goodness." Jeanette smiled at Mariah. "Still, it's all a wee bit overwhelming."

"But in a nice way."

Jeanette laughed. "Yes, a very nice way."

That night, after she had changed for bed, Jeanette threw on her dressing gown and walked across the hall to Mariah's room. "Might we talk for a minute?" she asked when Mariah answered her knock.

"Of course." Mariah waited for her to enter, then shut the door. She sat down on the bed, leaning against a corner post. Jeanie took the opposite corner, facing her. "What troubles you?"

"Tony is too charming."

"And you are enthralled."

Jeanie nodded. "I've never met anyone who was quite so adept at making outrageous compliments sound so sincere."

"Perhaps they are."

"His expression made me think so. But when I think back over what he said, I wonder. Do all English gentlemen use flowery words of praise?"

"Not all, but some are very proficient. I've often wondered if they teach a class at university on how to flatter a lady."

"They must. It seemed as if the men last night were trying to outdo each other with their compliments." Jeanie laughed and shifted her position. "There, it was easy to count it all as banter, but alone with Tony, it was difficult no' to let it go to my head."

"Or to your heart," said Mariah with a sympathetic smile.

"Back in Scotland, several men came to call, most before father died and Kiernan inherited the title. After we moved to Branderee and I was out of mourning, a few Scots of higher rank showed an express interest. Each of those men paid me compliments and flirted; it's all part of the game." She frowned and plucked at a broken thread on the coverlet. "But none of them affected me the way Tony does. Mariah, sometimes when he looks at me, I go weak in the knees."

Mariah leaned over and squeezed Jeanette's hand. "That is attraction, not necessarily love. It is natural to feel it. Thank goodness, not every man affects us in such a way."

"What a quandary we'd be in if they did." She met Mariah's gaze. "Is it the grand passion they talk about in novels?"

"Sometimes. I think more often it isn't so grand, it just seems so at the time because of the intensity of feeling. I used to get all fluttery every time a certain friend of my brother's smiled at me. He was a notorious rake, completely unsuitable for marriage. He was not interested in me in the least and never did more than smile and utter a greeting, but he had such a way about him that I reacted to his charm just the same."

"Do you think Tony is a rake?"

"I expect he has had a romantic interlude or two. In our Society,

186

most men his age have. He is far too charming and handsome not to, but Delia assured me that every unmarried man present last night was considered suitable by even the highest sticklers. I think we could classify him as a charmer, much like Kiernan or Gabriel."

"So you think my brother is a charmer, hmmm?" Jeanette laughed as Mariah blushed. "Can he make you go weak in the knees with just a look?"

Mariah hesitated before grinning and leaning closer. "Don't you dare tell him, but that man turns me to mush."

14

ON SUNDAY, THEY ATTENDED SERVICES at St. Paul's Cathedral. Mariah was greatly blessed by worshiping in the magnificent building. She had attended there occasionally when she lived in London before, but it took on a whole new meaning now that she had a close relationship with Jesus.

As she sat in the pew and listened to the organ and the choir, she marveled at the beauty of the music going up to the heavens. *A heavenly choir will be even more lovely,* she thought reverently, then wondered how it could be.

After the service ended, she led the others up to the Whispering Gallery high above the main floor and immediately below the twenty-four windows of the dome. "While this is the best place to view the frescoes, the acoustics here are also famous. If you whisper against the wall, you can be heard on the opposite side of the Gallery, which is one hundred and seven feet away."

Jeanette tugged on Gabriel's sleeve. "Come on, let's test it." Laughing, they walked around toward the other side.

Wilton appeared at the top of the stairs and wandered into the Gallery as if he were merely sightseeing, too, stopping when he reached Kiernan, Mariah, and Ailsa. "Good day, ladies, milord." He looked up at the frescoes depicting stories from the life of St. Paul which adorned the inside of the dome. "Exquisite, aren't they?"

"I've never seen anything like them," said Ailsa.

"Shall we enjoy them together, Mrs. Macpherson?" he asked quietly.

Ailsa never looked away from his gentle gaze. "Yes."

It seemed to be the most ordinary thing in the world when Wilton held out his arm and Ailsa slipped her hand around it. They strolled off, discussing the Bible story shown in the next painting.

"I think you had better hire him away from Lord Briscoll and give him a more lofty title than butler," whispered Mariah, being careful to face away from the wall.

"I think you're right. Is house steward more lofty?"

"A little. We may have to invent something." Mariah looked up at the frescoes. Ten years ago, they had only been pretty paintings. Now, she understood their significance, and they moved her deeply. "What do you think of St. Paul's?"

Kiernan glanced around the cathedral. "It's a wee bit more grandiose than what I'm used to, but beautiful just the same."

"Just a wee bit?" asked Mariah with a laugh.

"Our chapel at the castle is somewhat smaller and no' quite as ornate." His eyes twinkled. "But neither it nor this can compare to where I often worshiped in the Highlands. There, I praised God in a chapel of his own creation, a windswept moor with the snowcapped mountains as the altar."

"You miss your mountains, don't you?"

He nodded, his expression sad. "The coast is lovely, and it is God's creation, too, but it isna the same."

"You should move back to the Highlands."

Surprise flashed across his face. "And leave Branderee?"

"Find yourself a home suitable for an earl and live in the Highlands part of the year. Move to the coast in the winter, since I expect the weather is not as harsh there. Surely, with all the improvements going on, you can find someone who would like to sell some land and maybe a manor. Your factor could see to Branderee while you are gone, just as he does now."

"I'll think about it." He turned toward her and leaned a little closer. "I'd like to show you the Highlands, sweet lass."

"I'd like to see them." *And have you as my guide.*

"I want to show you the moon glistening on the water of Moray Firth," he said softly, "as we sit in the dunes near Branderee and listen to the waves lapping on the shore. It's beautiful, peaceful, and made for romance."

She dared not look up at him for fear he would see the longing in her eyes.

"Kiernan, turn away from the wall." Gabe's whispered words seemed to come from out of nowhere.

Startled, Kiernan stepped back and looked across the Gallery. Grinning broadly, Jeanie and Gabriel waved at them. Gabe turned to the wall, and they heard him whisper, "Do your sweet talking somewhere else."

Kiernan and Mariah both groaned but relaxed when they saw there was no one else in the Gallery except his mother and Wilton. The butler stood slightly behind her, her head almost touching his shoulder as he pointed to something in the picture. "I could have shouted, and they wouldna have heard me," Kiernan said with an indulgent smile.

Mariah smiled at the older couple. "They look happy."

"Yes, they do." Kiernan watched them for a few seconds, a hint of sadness in his expression. "Father would have wanted her to love again. He always said she wasna one to be alone."

Mariah slipped her arm around his, hugging it to her side. "I wish I could have met your father. He sounds like a wonderful man."

He looked down at her, his eyes misty. "He was. He would have liked you."

Hoping to avoid the melancholy she sensed coming over him, she shifted the subject. "For all your fussing about Branderee, I think you miss it, too."

"I do," he mused. "It's growing on me. The visit to England has been interesting, but I'd go home tomorrow if Jeanie wanted to." He glanced up at the domed ceiling. "I'm glad we came, though." He looked down at her tenderly. "There are treasures here I wouldna have found otherwise."

I'm going to melt into a puddle right at his feet. Not wanting him to see how much he affected her, she sought a way to steer the conversation in another direction. A historical tidbit about the cathedral came to mind.

"Sir James Thornhill painted the frescoes. The story goes that, while working on them, he stepped back to study the effect. He was so close to the edge of the platform that his assistant was afraid to shout a warning. So, with great presence of mind, the man started to smear the painting, which caused Thornhill to angrily spring forward. It probably saved him from falling to his death."

Kiernan met her gaze with one of amusement. "Is there some hidden meaning to that story, applicable to us?"

Mariah laughed and hugged his arm to her side again. "Not that I can think of at the moment."

They spent almost two hours more at the cathedral, taking in the view of London from the Stone Gallery and an even more extensive view of the city from the Outer Golden Gallery. When they overheard Wilton telling Ailsa a detailed history of the building, the two younger couples joined them. Wilton good-naturedly continued, providing a running commentary on everything from the basic structure to the statues, lantern, clocks, and library.

Finally hunger overcame their interest in architecture, and they exited the building. Since the landau was made to carry only four passengers, Kiernan had driven Mariah to church in the curricle. They did not know how Wilton had reached the cathedral, but when it came time to leave, Kiernan suggested that he ride in the landau with the others.

"Are you certain, sir?" asked the butler as Gabriel assisted Jeanette and Ailsa into the carriage. "We might be seen. I would not want to cause talk."

"Surely, a man can give his employee a ride home from church without causing a scandal."

Wilton smiled. "I would hope so, Lord Branderee. My feet thank you." He glanced at Ailsa. "As does the rest of me. I also thank you for this afternoon. Your mother has expressed a wish to go walking in the park tomorrow morning. With your permission, I would consider it an honor to accompany her."

"Please do. The fresh air will be good for her." Kiernan turned toward the curricle but looked back at Wilton with a smile. "Almost as much good as your company."

With a benign smile and a sparkle in his eye, the older gentleman bowed slightly before climbing in beside Gabriel in the landau.

Mariah and the Macpherson ladies paid a visit to Mrs. Haveland on Monday. At Jeanette's insistence, Mariah ordered several more dresses, both for day and for various evening events. She still was not comfortable spending Kiernan's money, but given the number of invitations pouring into the townhouse, the new gowns would be needed.

Ailsa ordered two frocks in light gray, one trimmed in blue, the other in deep rose. Mariah and Mrs. Haveland persuaded her to have a dinner dress made up in mulberry silk and another in bottle green. While she and Mariah looked over ribbons and laces, Jeanette ordered several more day dresses and dinner gowns for her mother, though Ailsa thought her daughter was ordering them for herself.

Mariah knew differently but kept silent. They had received an invitation just that morning to spend a fortnight with the Nortons and some thirty other guests at their estate in Warwickshire. Kiernan and Jeanette had accepted immediately and were determined to take their mother, certain she would enjoy the countryside and the relaxed social atmosphere provided by the visit. The Stanwells, Sir Edgar, and his wife and sister were also invited to the house party. Mariah looked forward to seeing Prudence and Sir Edgar and prayed his wife would not take issue with her being there.

On Tuesday, they remained at home and received guests. Several young men from the Stanwells' party and a few Jeanette had met on her drive with Tony came to call. All the gentlemen stayed the maximum polite length allowed, twenty minutes, but there were never fewer than three at a time, all vying for Jeanette's attention. It made for a lively afternoon.

Delia dropped by, bringing Mrs. Norton and another friend, Lady Templeton, with her. Lady Templeton was only a few years younger than Ailsa and had been born in Edinburgh. Her family had moved to Aberdeenshire a short time after Ailsa married. They were delighted to discover they knew many of the same people, though Ailsa had not seen most of them in years. Lady Templeton and her husband, an English baron, still owned the family estate in the area.

Delia promptly invited Mariah, Ailsa, and Jeanette over on Thursday for an uninterrupted afternoon visit. Lady Templeton promised to bring her daughter, Olivia, who was also making her come out. To Mariah's joy, Ailsa quickly accepted the invitation.

Her happiness turned to worry a few minutes later when Mrs. Norton mentioned how glad she was that they all would be joining them for the house party. Kiernan's mother paled visibly, her frightened, accusing gaze rendering Mariah momentarily speechless.

Lady Templeton came to the rescue with a smoothness that made Mariah suspect Delia had briefed her regarding Mrs. Macpherson's lack of confidence in her new situation. "We are anticipating it with relish. You have such a lovely, comfortable home, Mrs. Norton."

She turned to Ailsa with a smile. "This young couple threw a house party last year only six months after their wedding. We had such a delightful time. They were very relaxed about the whole thing. Though they provided amusements for those who wanted them, the rest were free to do as they wished, whether it was walking through the gardens and woods or simply dozing beneath a shade tree. The only time we were all together was in the evening. I trust you will be doing things much the same this year?" she asked.

"Yes, it worked so well last time, we see no reason to change. I hope you will encourage Lord Branderee to bring his bagpipes and play for us, Mrs. Macpherson. I've never had the opportunity to hear them, and I understand he is a grand piper."

"I expect he would be more than happy to play for you," said Ailsa, her voice bearing more than a trace of pride in her son. "He canna play here without disturbing the neighbors too much." Though still pale, Ailsa managed a faint smile. "No' everyone enjoys the pipes."

"Well, I for one can hardly wait. I wish we were going tomorrow," said Lady Templeton. "You are coming, are you no', Mrs. Macpherson? We can sneak away by ourselves and share tales of our youth," she added with a conspiratorial wink. "Do you remember

Malcom Keith and Catherine Forbes?"

"Yes. Didna they marry?"

"Yes, but no' until after they tried to elope." Lady Templeton laughed. "Talk about a botched endeavor. It will take me a good hour to tell you the whole of it. Then there's the time John Burnett put a cow in the parish school and left it overnight."

"I heard about that," said Ailsa with a smile. "My mother said they couldna have school for almost a week. The teacher made John come in and scrub the floor every day until it didna smell like a cattle pen." She glanced at Mariah, who nodded in encouragement. "I'd be honored to visit you, Mrs. Norton."

Mariah wanted to hug her, but she smiled instead, saving her hug until all the guests had departed.

Later, she and Ailsa relaxed in the upstairs sitting room. "You knew about my children's conspiracy?"

"Yes, ma'am. We all thought you would enjoy getting out of the city." Mariah smiled ruefully. "Kiernan was determined you should go, even if he had to carry you kicking and screaming out to the carriage."

"He wouldna dare."

"Probably not, but he has been coming up with all sorts of plans, testing the ideas out on us." Mariah slanted her a glance. "He even considered asking Wilton to go along as his valet."

"And did he?"

"As far as I know, he is still thinking about it."

"Tell him to quit thinking and ask the man." Ailsa leaned her head back against the settee, gazing up at the ceiling. "On second thought, tell him no' to. It would kick up a dust if we even walked through the garden together."

"I expect so, but I'm learning we often place too much importance in what others think or say about us."

"I have no' asked because I didna want to distress you. How has it been for you?"

"There are a few who pretend I'm nothing but thin air, and a few others who think I contaminate any room they occupy, but generally people have been kind, and many have been friendly. I do not think it would have gone so well if I had tried to reenter Society on my own, or even with my brother's assistance. By having me in your home and taking me about as if I were your guest instead of a paid employee, you have garnered me a place."

"We have done no more for you than you have done for us. Because of you, we are making new friends." Ailsa looked away. "You are helping my son and daughter become situated in this new world." She looked back at Mariah with a sad smile. "And me as well, in spite of my resistance."

"It is not a world any of you need dwell in for long," said Mariah. "Nor is it where I wish to stay, but it helps to see that the wrongs of the past have been left behind. Some of my demons are being overcome as well." *But not all.* She was not certain she could ever conquer her fear of being deceived or abandoned. "Now, if you will excuse me, I think I'll take a short rest before dinner. Tonight is likely to be tiring."

"I canna remember where you are off to this time."

"The Nightingales' rout. Delia says it should be called a nightmare rout. For some hostesses, like Lady Nightingale, it has become fashionable to invite at least twice as many people as a house will hold. They think they are a failure unless it is deemed a mad crush."

"Crush, as in canna move?"

"Precisely. If I had known, I would have told Kiernan to decline the invitation, but it is too late now. If we don't go, it will be considered an insult."

The rout proved to be as big a crush as Mariah feared. They waited in line in the carriage for an hour before they could disembark. Then another hour before they could get in the door and greet their host and hostess. They worked their way a short distance into the crowd—with Kiernan and Gabriel complaining under their breath because they were constantly being stuck with the pins that helped hold the ladies' gowns together—then gave up in disgust and struggled back toward the entry.

After waiting in the hallway and on the steps for another hour until their carriage reached the curb in front of the house, they departed. Kiernan grumbled crossly, both in English and Gaelic, all the way home. Jeanette declared it was the most ridiculous idea of a party she had ever heard of, with which they all agreed.

During the following days the activities, social and otherwise, increased rapidly.

Wilton regularly escorted Ailsa to the park for a morning walk and to feed the birds. With each passing day, her color and energy improved. Kiernan had driven through the park the first morning to make certain his mother had not become too tired to walk home. He found them strolling along at a leisurely pace, laughing and talking, although Wilton carefully maintained the proper attitude between servant and employer.

Kiernan knew Wilton relaxed those proprieties sometimes at the townhouse, for he often heard him tease or even flirt with her. Kiernan did not mind as long as the older man treated her with the utmost respect, which he did.

Kiernan's solicitor completed the investigation of the butler, reporting that Wilton had told the truth about his family and his life. He stated the butler had lived frugally the past ten years, investing in government securities known as Consols, or consolidated annuities.

They could not be redeemed for their face value, but they earned three percent interest per year, and the annuity was paid regularly. They could also be sold. It was a wise investment, providing income when he decided to quit working.

Kiernan decided that buying an annuity for Fiske, his house steward and secretary, might be the best way of dismissing the man from service. He did not know how receptive Fiske would be to the idea, so he decided to write him about it before making the actual purchase.

Jeanette went driving in the park on Wednesday afternoon with young Mr. Giddings. Mariah and Kiernan went for a drive, too, following at a discreet distance. Though it was considered proper for a young lady to drive alone with a gentleman in the park, Kiernan was not yet ready to let his sister out of his sight in the company of a man he barely knew.

On Thursday, she accompanied her mother and Mariah to Lady Stanwell's for the afternoon. Jeanette and Lady Templeton's daughter, Olivia, struck up an immediate friendship.

They attended a dinner party on Thursday night and a musical evening on Friday. Olivia introduced Jeanette to several other young ladies their age, and her circle of friends widened considerably.

The afternoons were filled with making calls or receiving them, driving in the park, or going to a museum or art gallery. In the evenings, there were dinners, soirees, and musical recitals of varying levels of accomplishment. The social whirl had begun in earnest, with one day spinning into the next.

15

KIERNAN ABSENTLY LISTENED TO an elderly lord drone on about the benefits of putting lime on his fields and idly wondered what good it would do to scatter juice all over the ground. His thoughts and heart were across the Altbury ballroom with Mariah as she stepped onto the dance floor for the tenth time during the evening.

Mariah had never looked more beautiful to him. Her gown was a purplish-blue silk—bishop's blue, Jeanie had called it. The color turned her eyes silver, or was it happiness that put the bright sparkle there? Happiness to which he contributed little or nothing.

The wide, square neckline, trimmed in matching ribbon, was attractive yet modest. The ribbon adorned the edge of the short sleeves and the high empire waistline, showing her slim figure to perfection. She had worn his mother's pearls again, and though they looked nice with the gown, he wished more than ever that he could give her the diamond necklace.

He did not know the names of all her partners, but he would recognize any of them even if he met them in a dark alley. She had already danced with one man twice, a golden-haired rogue with silver wings at his temples and the face of a perfectly sculpted Greek statue. They chatted like old friends every time the dance brought them together. Kiernan had been sorely tempted to trip him when he pranced by.

Her partner for this dance was a tall, skinny fellow with a nervous Adam's apple. The man's gaze was focused not on her pleasant smile but on the small amount of bosom exposed by her gown. Kiernan wanted to put his hands around the man's throat, catch that blasted Adam's apple at midswallow, and squeeze until the reprobate's eyes bulged. "That would teach him where to look," he muttered.

"I say, what was that, Branderee? Didn't quite catch it," said the elderly gentleman, holding his hand cupped behind one ear. "A trifle hard of hearing, you know."

Kiernan dragged his gaze away from Mariah. "You should write a book."

The old man's face lit up. "I should. By Jove, that's just what I'll do."

As the man started prosing about the necessity of good fertilizer, Kiernan excused himself. He made his way to the refreshment table, scanning the crowd to check on Jeanette. She was in a dance set with several of her friends, carrying on a running conversation as the steps moved her from one gentleman to the next and with a turn or promenade took her back to her original partner.

Picking up two cups of punch, Kiernan crossed to where Mariah had occasionally been sitting. He was waiting when the lecher escorted her to the chair.

Sir Bobble-throat asked if he could fetch her something to drink.

"She already has something." Kiernan handed her a cup of punch and glared at the man. "When you dance with a lady, look at her face, no' the top of her gown," he said in a low, menacing voice. "Dinna even think of askin' this one again."

The man gulped and spun on his heels, almost knocking another man over in his haste to flee.

Mariah giggled. "I expect every woman he has danced with tonight would like to thank you." She took a sip of punch. "You can

200

quit scowling. He's probably halfway to his hotel by now."

"Who was the rake?"

"Which one?" Mariah laughed softly, linking her arm through his, subtly urging him toward the open French doors. They stopped near them, taking advantage of a mild breeze.

"The one you danced with twice."

"You're counting?"

"Yes, I'm counting," he snapped. "Who is he?"

"Dominic Thorne, a friend of my brother's."

"He looks much younger than your brother."

"Pryse looks older than his fifty years. If I remember correctly, Mr. Thorne would be around nine-and-thirty. He used to visit Pryse often when I was living at his townhouse." She fanned her face with a blue satin and ivory lace fan. "I would practically swoon if he smiled at me."

"And now?" he asked gruffly.

"Not even a flutter."

"No?" He looked down at her in disbelief. The rogue was the type to make any woman's heart race.

"I'm older and very much wiser. He is older and more cynical. Still, it was nice to talk with him for a few minutes. He was very kind when I went to my first ball. I did not know many people at the time and only a few gentlemen, all my brother's friends. Mr. Thorne was the most respectable of the lot.

"Our hostess was slow in bringing eligible gentlemen over for an introduction, making me the proverbial wallflower. When Dominic saw what was happening, he asked me to dance. He made me terribly nervous, but I was ever so grateful to be out of that chair. Afterward, he introduced me to several people, and one highly respected elderly matron in particular, who saw to it that I no longer lacked in partners."

"What does he think of Pryse moving to Boston?"

"He misses him and thinks him a fool for getting leg-shackled."

"I take it Thorne is a gambler and wastrel like your brother was."

"A gambler, yes, but not a wastrel. He rarely loses. Sir Edgar says it's because he never drinks when he gambles. Everyone else gets foxed while he stays sober and takes note of which cards have been played. He is extremely rich, having inherited two profitable estates from a doting bachelor uncle before he was five-and-twenty, and regularly adding to his bank account from his winnings at White's."

"He has never married?"

"No. With his wealth, he was considered a prime catch, a situation bound to raise questions about the sincerity of any young woman's interest. He has no title to be concerned with, so providing an heir or carrying on the family name is not of great importance to him."

"And he soon discovered a surprising number of bored wives more than willing to indulge in a dalliance," said Kiernan, thinking of the subtle and not so subtle offers directed his way since the Stanwells' dinner party.

"Yes, as you no doubt have also discovered."

"You know I willna have anything to do with them." He searched her face, willing her to understand no other woman could tempt him.

"I know. You are too honorable to indulge in illicit affairs."

He drew her out onto the wide garden steps where they could speak more privately but still remain respectably in view. "I have no' always lived as I should, Mariah. There have been women in my life, no' many, but a few, in relationships that didna honor God. I have asked his forgiveness for those sins and given him my promise never to commit them again. I give you that same promise, sweet lass."

She blinked rapidly, and when she raised her gaze to his, tears sparkled like stars on her lashes. "Thank you. Coming from you, I can believe it."

"Shelton said much the same?"

"He was much more flowery, spouting bad poetry he thought was grand because he had written it." She smiled wryly. "I agreed with him at the time."

"The clarity of hindsight." He smiled and nodded toward the doorway. "We'd best go back inside. I like to know how Jeanie fares."

They strolled inside, arm in arm, and spotted Jeanette a short distance away, curtsying to Tony Drake's bow as the dance ended. "I'd say she is having a wonderful time," said Mariah.

"Now, what gives you that idea? Her glowing face or big smile?" Kiernan caught his sister's eye and winked. She grinned and nudged Tony in their direction as they left the dance floor.

"Well, lass, I think we'd best go home. You look miserable."

Jeanie plucked Kiernan's cup from his hand, drained the remaining punch, and handed it back to him. "I canna ever remember having so much fun. Thank you, dearest brother, for staying in London."

"I thank you, too, sir. Miss Macpherson is a joy." Tony smiled at Jeanette. "I only regret that she is a joy to so many. I go away for a week, dreaming of her night and day, only to find she has been so busy she has forgotten all about me."

"Mr. Drake, you know that isna true. I thought about you when I promised dances for tonight," Jeanette said with a teasing smile. "I remembered to save your two, which is admirable, since I had begun to think you wouldna return to London in time to enjoy them."

"Dear one, the plague could not have kept me from you this night." Tony's forehead creased in a mild frown. "Well, maybe the plague, since I would not wish to make you ill."

Jeanette laughed. "Thank you, sir, for your thoughtfulness. We shall see more of each other at the Norton house party."

"How nice that you are invited, too, Mr. Drake," said Mariah. "Will there be quite a few young people attending?"

"I believe about half the party, including you, Lady Mariah," Tony said with an easy smile.

"Such gallantry."

Kiernan caught a knowing glance between Mariah and his sister. He suspected Mariah had told Jeanie to be wary of Mr. Drake's charming manner. At least he hoped so. He liked the man, but he did not want his sister swayed unduly by pretty words and confident smiles. Glancing over her shoulder, Kiernan saw another young man bearing down on them. "I believe your next partner has searched you out."

Jeanie looked over her shoulder. The big man plowed awkwardly through the crowd with dogged determination. "Yes, I'm promised to Mr. Card for this one."

"Watch your toes," warned Tony.

She glanced at the gentleman's feet as he approached and shrugged minutely. "We Scots are stoic," she murmured, turning to greet Mr. Card with a warm smile.

"Another besotted fool," muttered Tony.

Jeanie ignored him. Her toes would probably not survive without a bruise, but she did not greatly regret accepting Mr. Card's stammering request to dance. She suspected it had taken quite a while for him to work up the courage to ask since she had not noticed him dancing with anyone else. She would never embarrass him by refusing.

"I...I believe this is my dance, Miss Macpherson."

"It is, Mr. Card." Jeanie slipped her arm around his, noting the solid muscle beneath her hand as they moved to take their place in line. Another line formed opposite them. "You said you were from Devonshire, did you no'?"

"Yes, ma'am. Family has a nice estate. Raise cattle. Excellent cattle."

"I've never been to Devonshire. Is it pretty?"

He nodded enthusiastically. "Mountains. Hills. Green vales. Bristol channel on the north. English channel on the south. Lots of grass and rivers."

The orchestra struck a chord and began the tune. Her partner took a deep breath and gave her a shy smile as he reached for her hand. Jeanette smiled back and joined hands with the man on the other side of her, too. The line moved a few steps forward, and they bowed to the people across from them. Releasing hands, they moved backward a few steps.

The next part of the dance consisted of sideways hops, similar to sedately skipping to one side and then back again, while partners held hands. She turned and held out both hands to Mr. Card. He grabbed them with a wide smile, galloping to their left with great exuberance. He switched directions with such force that Jeanie felt her neck crack.

She began to worry.

They dropped hands, weaving in and out the line and back again. She clasped hands with Mr. Card in a crosswise pattern at shoulder level, and they turned in a circle. The dancers around them moved with measured grace. Mr. Card's pace resembled a spinning top. The toes of Jeanie's left foot touched the floor once; the right one not at all. They stopped with a jerk, flinging her leg out to the side. She kicked the thigh of the gentleman next to her. Mr. Card whirled around in the other direction, lifting her completely off the floor.

She began to pray.

With the next rapid change in direction, they were doomed. Halfway around in their mad twirl, Mr. Card's long legs became tangled with another gentleman's. Trying to catch himself, he released Jeanie's hands. She flew headfirst toward a blurred wall of dark coats, white starched cravats, and shocked faces.

Her feet landed on the floor, and she stumbled across the slick, polished hardwood. Unable to regain her balance, she braced for a painful crash to the floor.

It never came.

Two strong hands gripped her shoulders. The top of her head smacked into solid but yielding muscle as the man moved backward a few steps to lessen the impact. When they stopped, Jeanie straightened, and he gently put his arms around her. She buried her face in his coat as a tremor swept through her.

"Are you injured?" he asked softly in a deep, rich voice.

She shook her head, turning her face to one side to breathe, not daring to open her eyes and see everyone in the now silent room staring at her.

"Can you stand?"

Jeanie took a deep breath and nodded.

He held her for a heartbeat, maybe two. Slowly, as if with regret, he eased his hold, settling his hands on her upper arms to steady her, and backed a step away.

She raised her head, keeping her gaze focused on him, noting the dark corbeau green jacket beneath her palms, the rumpled snowy white silk cravat, the tiny cleft in his chin.

He was older, perhaps twice her age, but handsome, probably devastatingly so when he smiled. Jeanie glanced up at his golden hair, highlighted by silver wings at his temples, and met his concerned gaze.

"You're certain you are unhurt?"

"I'm fine," she whispered. He had the most incredible emerald-green eyes. She couldn't look away.

Neither did he.

Jeanie felt as if he were looking into the depths of her being, searching her soul. Suddenly, with a knowledge that could only come from God, she sensed his hidden despair, his utter, shattering loneliness. Her heart went out to him, and with it, the love of Jesus.

Surprise flashed through his eyes before they clouded with confusion. He released her with a troubled frown.

Kiernan and Mariah pushed their way through the crowd to her side. Tony was a few steps behind them. "Jeanie, lass, are you hurt?"

"No' at all." She smiled at her brother and looked back at the stranger. "Thanks to this gentleman. He caught me before I sprawled in an ungraceful heap on the floor." She noted they were several feet in front of the rest of the men who had been watching from the sidelines. She had not collided with him by chance. "Thank you for making the effort, sir."

"You are most welcome, miss," he said with a smile before glancing at Mariah.

"Jeanette, may I introduce Dominic Thorne," said Mariah. "Mr. Thorne, this is Miss Jeanette Macpherson, Lord Branderee's sister."

As he bowed and Jeanie dropped into a shallow curtsy, angry mumbling came from behind her. She glanced back to see Mr. Card sitting on the floor, his face beet red, his head hanging down. Another gentleman stood over him, scolding him in a harsh undertone. Her poor partner looked as if he might burst into tears.

"Please excuse me. I think I'd better go pick up Mr. Card."

Amusement touched Mr. Thorne's eyes, and they shared a smile. It did indeed make him startlingly handsome, but it was not a rakish smile used to charm women, though undoubtedly he did. This expression was more basic and open, giving her a glimpse of the real

Dominic Thorne, the one she suspected he hid from everyone. The one she wanted to know.

Scowling, Kiernan glared at the man on the floor. Jeanie laid a hand on his arm. "No, Kier, let him be. There is no harm done, except to him."

With a quick glance at Mr. Thorne, she turned and walked back to her unfortunate partner, forcing her thoughts away from those intense green eyes. It occurred to her that she had hardly looked in Tony's direction, though now she realized he had been infuriated.

She silenced the grumbling man's tirade with a gentle touch on his arm. He looked at her, muttered something about keeping clods in the country, and stomped off. Jeanie leaned down, closing her hand over Mr. Card's. "Come, sir, let us go in search of the refreshment table," she said quietly.

He looked up, his expression wretched. "Miss Macpherson, I am so ashamed. Never had dancing lessons."

"Then I shall give you some."

He stared at her in amazement and pushed himself to his feet. "Truly?"

"Truly. But no' here," she said with a smile, looping her arm around his. "Come by the house tomorrow afternoon, and we will see what can be arranged. I hope you like bagpipe music. It is the only instrument we have, but my brother plays excellently."

She grinned at Kiernan as they walked by. "I'm sure he would be happy to play for us."

Kiernan nodded, silently thanking God for his kind, gentle sister. Everyone else had gone back to their dancing and chatter, now with someone new to talk about. Mr. Card no longer looked like he wanted to crawl into a hole and rake the dirt down over himself. Jeanie seemed no worse for wear, though he expected she would be sore come morning. It could have been far worse.

He turned to Mariah, finding her anxiously watching Dominic Thorne. The man followed Jeanette with his gaze, his expression thoughtful. His eyes held more than a hint of yearning.

"Stay away from her," Kiernan warned softly. There was no response. Thorne was so lost in thought, Kiernan did not think he heard him.

"She openeth her mouth with wisdom; and in her tongue is the law of kindness," Thorne murmured.

Mariah glanced at Kiernan in surprise. He, too, had not expected such a man to quote part of a biblical proverb. "She has a kind heart."

Thorne met Kiernan's gaze. "That and more. She is goodness itself, gentleness and honor. Truly, her price is far above rubies." Regret darkened his expression, and wistfulness filled his eyes. "Guard her well, Branderee." He glanced at Tony and frowned. "Give her only to a man who will cherish her above all else." He walked away quickly, speaking to no one as he left the ball.

16

THE NORTONS' HOUSE PARTY was a wonderful respite from the hustle and bustle of London. The house itself had come as something of a shock since Lady Templeton had described it as a warm, comfortable home.

Spying the vast east wing as they drove up the long, tree-lined drive, Jeanette counted forty-two windows in the front of the three-storied building. They soon learned that wing had been built early in the eighteenth century. It was connected by a long gallery to the original wing built during the fourteenth century, which was of an equal size.

The restoration of the Elizabethan portion of the house had been begun by Mr. Norton's grandfather and completed by his father. Between the two wings there were more than enough comfortable bedchambers to accommodate each guest separately, as well as quarters for their valets and abigails.

Mariah's maid, Elise, said it was quite the most majestic house she had ever seen, and Mariah agreed. Each room was exquisitely decorated. The furnishings in one room might be the heavy style of earlier centuries, while the one next to it might be resplendent in the latest Regency mode.

During the day, the guests had a variety of amusements from

which to choose. They might read in the great library, join others for a chat in several cozy sitting rooms, or take excursions to nearby scenic or historical sights. They could sit or walk in the brilliantly flowered gardens, stroll through the serene woods, or gallop across the green meadows and hills.

The younger members of the party played battledore and shuttle-cock, lawn tennis, and challenged each other to archery contests. In the warmth of the afternoon, couples might be found relaxing beneath the shade of a tree, the gentleman reading from a book of sonnets to his lady.

Mariah particularly enjoyed her chats with Prudence. She had missed her friend and was happy to hear how things progressed at Stillwater. It was good, too, to catch up on the news of the neighbors and various friends.

In turn, Prudence wanted to hear all about what had been happening in London, in the Branderee household, and specifically about the earl himself. Mariah knew she could trust Prudie to keep a confidence, but she still refrained from telling her everything about her relationship with Kiernan. Some things were too private, too precious to share with anyone.

The gentlemen had a rowing race across the small lake, with the ladies cheering their champions on. Kiernan and Tony formed one team, and much to the delight of Mariah and Jeanette, won the first race. They lost on the trip back across the lake, succumbing to the expertise of Gabriel and Fletcher Card.

After his disastrous evening at the Altbury ball, Mr. Card had taken Jeanette up on her offer to teach him to dance. Since the dances required more than two people, she had recruited Olivia, Tony, Mariah, Gabriel, Wilton, and her mother to fill out the set while Kiernan played the pipes. The lessons took an hour or two during four afternoons. By the end of the second session, it was obvious to all that Olivia and Fletcher were developing an interest in each other. A little bird had whispered the fact into Mrs. Norton's ear, and he had been included in the house party.

After the sumptuous dinners at the Norton mansion, they sometimes danced, with Mr. Card participating enthusiastically but gracefully. Other evenings they enjoyed cards and charades, or listened as one of the young ladies sang, played the pianoforte, or both.

Olivia was a talented singer, with a strong, clear voice. Mariah especially enjoyed her Scottish ballads. She expected the young woman could have screeched in Chinese and still earned Mr. Card's approval.

One afternoon, the servants erected two huge open-air tents on the lawn. At six o'clock, everyone, including the tenants and servants, congregated under one tent to hear Kiernan perform on the bagpipes. He played two slow, haunting laments, before beginning a reel.

The servants and tenants hurried over to the second tent to dance, while the Nortons and their guests formed a set beneath the first one. He played one lively tune after another. Finally, he turned the music over to one of the footmen and his fiddle.

Smiling, Mariah handed Kiernan a large glass of punch. He took a long drink before asking her to hold it while he put away the bagpipes. At last he closed the case and sprawled in a chair, watching the dancers with a smile as she handed the glass back to him. Twilight began to fall, and two servants walked around the perimeter of the tent, lighting tall torches firmly set in the grass.

"Tired?" She sat down beside him.

"A little. I'll catch my second wind in a minute." He smiled lazily and looked over at one of the flower gardens where servants were lighting lanterns hung in the trees. "Then I might steal you away for a stroll in the garden."

212

"I'd like that." They had not been alone since their arrival. Mariah looked back at the dancers, watching as Tony drew Ailsa out of her chair and into the large circle. "You mother told me last night she is very glad she came."

"She said the same thing to me this morning, though she admitted missing Wilton."

An older gentleman smiled at Ailsa as he became her momentary partner. He began a conversation as they clasped hands, moving through the steps together. "Lord Idington is interested in her."

"He is the only man her age here who isna married."

"Yes, but I would be surprised if he doesn't call on her when we go back to London. There is a certain glimmer in his eye."

"I dinna think it will do him any good." Kiernan took another drink of punch. "Although I may be wrong. Receiving the attention of another gentleman for a few weeks may show her that she seeks companionship but no' necessarily Wilton's."

They studied the couple for a few minutes. Ailsa's expression was pleasant, but it did not light up as it did whenever Wilton was near. Mariah looked at Kiernan with a grin.

He grinned back. "No' going to happen, is it?"

"Not with this gentleman, at least."

He stood, placed his empty glass on a tray as a servant walked by, and held out his hand to Mariah. "It must run in the family."

"What?" She let him pull her up.

"I'll tell you later. Too noisy here." He offered her his arm, and they walked slowly toward the garden. Several other couples were taking a break from the dancing and doing the same. Jeanette and Tony, along with Fletcher and Olivia, were among them.

He looked up, sighing in contentment as waves of deep rose pink and purple washed across the sky. He pressed her arm a little tighter against his side. "Some of the most beautiful sunsets I've ever seen were on the battlefield, but only if the fighting had ended hours before. Otherwise, there was still too much smoke hanging in the air to see the sky.

"It seemed so odd to behold such beauty above and such carnage below, as if God wanted to remind us who he is. In spite of all our quarrels, large and small, the world belongs to him. Men wage war in selfishness and hatred, destroying ourselves, all that we have made, and much that God has made. We claim victories and count the spoils, but in truth, we have won nothing. We call ourselves kings and lords, but he is still Lord of all."

"Did you ever doubt him? Ever feel completely alone?" Without thinking, Mariah leaned her head against his shoulder as they walked slowly down a secluded path.

"Never when I was with the army. Even after I'd done things I should no' have, I knew he forgave me when I turned away from those sins. I dinna think I ever went into battle, even unexpected skirmishes, that I didna know for certain that he loved me and would see me through.

"But when my father died, I doubted God. I could no' understand why he would take him. I was so angry, I turned my back on the Lord. I'd never felt completely alone before, but I did then."

"You've made your peace with him."

"Yes, no' long after I met you. He had been workin' on me for some time, and I fought him every step of the way. It wasna until Mother was afraid I would try to force myself on you, or coerce you into becoming my mistress, that I saw how low I was sinking."

"You would not have done either of those things."

"I would never have ravished you, but I wanted very much to seduce you." He drew her deep into the shadows of a wide, weeping willow. The draping branches surrounded them like a lacy tent. He put his arms around her. "I still do."

"Sometimes I wish you would," she whispered honestly. She sighed and rested her cheek against his chest, as he ran his hand slowly up and down her back. "But we cannot."

"No' until it is ordained by God." He kissed her forehead.

Mariah's heart began to pound.

"Earlier when I said it must run in the family, I was talking abou falling in love quickly," he said softly, brushing a kiss at her temple.

"Do you believe your mother truly loves Wilton?" she hedged.

"I think so. She will always love my father, but I believe there is room in her heart for another love. She needs a man to share her life."

"Not all women do." She told herself to pull away, but when his lips touched her cheek, she tilted her face upward so he could do it again.

"And no' every man needs a wife." He cupped her chin, easing her face upward until she met his gaze in the faint torchlight. "I do. I love you, Mariah. I think I started falling in love the day I met you."

"Kiernan, don't," she whispered, trying to edge away.

"Even then, I wanted to protect you, shelter you, fight your foes."

"You feel that way about everybody who needs help."

"I admit 'tis my nature to protect others, but never more so than with you. You are the one I want by my side, to share my joys and my sorrows, to hold me in the night and have my children. I love you, sweetheart. I want you to be my wife."

She pulled away, turning her back to him. "No."

He muttered under his breath and released a heavy sigh. "I knew I should no' rush you."

"Rushing me has nothing to do with it." She drew a ragged breath. "Or maybe it does; I don't know."

The sound of quiet voices reached their sheltered hideaway as another couple came down the path. Kiernan grabbed her hand and pushed aside some branches on the opposite side of the tree, opening a way for them to another walkway. He tucked her hand around his arm, and they resumed their stroll.

"I thought you cared for me," he said quietly.

"I do, deeply." *I love you with all my heart.* She could not tell him how she truly felt, or let him know how desperately she longed for his love. Still, she owed him an explanation, one that came at a great price. No one but God knew her secret sorrow and her deepest fear.

They came to a stone bench built for two. The torches were far enough away to give them privacy, but close enough so they could see each other clearly. She glanced around, and seeing no one else, sat down. He sat down beside her.

"I am afraid to love you, Kiernan."

"After the way Shelton treated you, I can understand why. But I'm no' like him, sweetheart."

"I know you aren't. But it wasn't just him." She looked off across the beautiful, manicured grounds, now only shadows in the darkness. "The gardens at Glenbuck once looked like these. My parents were very particular about the estate. They were not home a great deal, but when they were, much of their time went into overseeing its upkeep or improvement. I seldom saw Mother or Father. When Pryse came to see me last time, he explained some things that helped me understand why."

"It had to do with the break between him and your father?"

She nodded. "Pryse met my mother first and was in love with her. He planned to ask her to marry him while she and her family were visiting at Glenbuck."

"Your father stole her away from him?" Kiernan frowned in disgust.

"Right from under his nose, but not without being enticed. As Pryse said, by marrying Father, she did not have to wait years for

216

the title and wealth. He admitted it was not merely a marriage of convenience. They were very fond of each other.

"Unfortunately, Pryse loved her deeply, something Father did not realize until much later. He thought it was merely an infatuation. My brother never forgave either of them."

"So your father gained a beautiful young bride but lost his son. I suppose he was hoping you would be another boy?"

"Yes. Mutual friends told Pryse that he intended to shower his love and attention on his new son. He expected the boy to be the delight of his winter years. Needless to say, I was a tremendous disappointment to him, and I'm sure to Mother too. I was an inconsequential female, someone to feed, clothe, and educate enough to marry off."

"So they ignored you."

"Mainly. Once, Father gave me a beautiful silver mechanical bird. I was overwhelmed and walked on air for days, winding the key over and over to hear the bird sing. I kept it with me every second and played it so much my poor governess thought they'd send her to Bedlam. But I didn't care if I drove her batty. My father had brought me a gift. He had given it to me with his very own hands. It was proof that he cared for me.

"A week later, I overheard my governess and Mother's maid talking. The musical bird had never been intended for me. He had bought it for Mother, but the tune annoyed her so she gave it back to him."

"And he gave it to you."

"Only because his valet suggested it."

"He could have done something else with it. You meant something to him, Mariah."

She shook her head. "I doubt it. A year or so later, he decided to pay a visit to my little domain to quiz me and see how my education progressed. I think I surprised him. I could read and spell quite well, my sums were adequate, and my stitchery was neat.

"Then he spied the silver bird. He did not remember giving it to me and assumed I had pilfered it from somewhere in the house— someplace I had no right to be. When he started to take it, I protested, reminding him that he had given it to me. He called me a liar and a thief. When he started to scold Miss Aimes about letting me run wild, she refreshed his memory, even to the point of mentioning that his valet had suggested he give the trinket to me. Her detailed explanation brought the incident to mind, and he let me keep it."

"You still have it. I've seen it on your dresser."

"I should have gotten rid of it long ago, but it's one of the few things I have left from my time in Scotland." She paused, picking up the ribbon that hung from her empire waist, twisting it around her finger. "Even though I know it held no significance to him, it is the only thing either of them ever personally gave to me."

"The only thing? They never brought you a present from their journeys?"

"Never. My governess had an allowance for my clothing, so I was always dressed adequately. I once asked for a doll like the minister's daughter had, but she said it was too frivolous an expense. I was not lacking in toys or books, but they had all been Pryse's when he was a child. They were of the finest quality, so some things had remained in very good condition. I did have one doll, which had been a present to Pryse from an eccentric great-aunt. I named her Melissa." She smiled at him, smoothing away his frown with her fingertips. "Her gown was a little faded from age, but she was a great companion on a rainy day. We had wonderful chats."

"Did you ever play with other children?"

"On sunny days my governess would sometimes take me into the village or to a crofter's hut so I could spent time with the children. Mother frowned upon it, but Miss Aimes convinced her that I would grow up a complete social outcast if I did not.

"Occasionally, Mother would invite me to her sitting room. It was a lovely room, filled with paintings and sculpture, and all sorts of mementos from their travels. I could have studied the paintings for hours, dreaming of being in an English garden or walking through a Highland glen. I longed to have just one of those beautiful scenes to hang on the bare, white walls of the nursery.

"My visits to her domain were short because I always managed to disappoint her in some way. I'd either wrinkle her gown or drop crumbs on the floor or not be able to talk to her as well as she wanted. Though I tried very hard to think of something clever to say, it never came out right.

"The last time she requested my presence, she took me into the music room and asked me to play her a tune on the pianoforte. Miss Aimes had told her I could play rather well for my age, and I could—with only my governess to listen." Remembering her humiliation, Mariah paused, wondering why, after so many years, the experience was still so painful. "I knew Mother loved music, and I wanted desperately to play well for her. If I could please her in this one thing, maybe she would want to see me more often."

"It didna go well?"

"I made a complete botch of it. Miss Aimes encouraged me to start with something simple because she could see how nervous I was. I made it through the first piece without any mistakes, but Mother was not impressed. She said a six-year-old could play a tune such as that. So I tried something more difficult, a piece I had played to perfection only an hour earlier. I hit one wrong note after another. When I left out a whole phrase, Mother threw up her hands and shouted for me to stop.

"Father heard her and came to see what was wrong. She told him what had happened and went through a litany of the many ways I had disappointed her over the years. She said I was worthless and couldn't learn, and she wanted nothing more to do with me."

"What a hateful thing to say." Kiernan slid his arm around her. "What did your father do?"

"He agreed with her." She had spent a lifetime trying to forget that moment, but the hatred on her father's face was seared in her memory. Mariah took a deep breath, her shaking voice little more than a whisper. "He said he would no longer tolerate the presence of such an ugly, unlovable child. I was shipped off to boarding school in Edinburgh that afternoon. I never saw either of them again."

"Mercy o' heaven, Mariah." He wrapped his arms around her. "How old were you?"

"Ten."

"His own wickedness stared him in the face when he looked at you."

"I know, but he hated me, too, Kiernan. He despised everything about me. So did Mother and Pryse. All for reasons that had nothing to do with me as a person, yet it had a profound effect on me.

"In many ways, being sent away was the best thing that could have happened. It was not an excellent boarding school, not like the one Miss Eversham had, but the headmistress and teachers were kind and fair. I suspect they were told I was a problem child, but I was so terrified of where I might be sent next that I obeyed them instantly."

"How you must have hurt." He tightened his hold.

Mariah's throat stung with the need to cry, but she choked back her tears. Mindful of how suddenly they could be found in a compromising position, Mariah eased from his embrace. "Over the following months, I made a few friends. The teachers were always taking us to see some event in the city, so life was not boring. I saw my first play and heard the bagpipes for the first time." She smiled at him. "And loved them.

"After my parents died, and Pryse brought me to the boarding school here, life was even better. Miss Eversham and her teachers had a way of instilling confidence in even the most self-conscious, timid girl—"

"You."

She nodded. "At first I was afraid of my own shadow, but she wouldn't put up with such missish behavior. Delia helped, too. She never has been afraid to go against convention. By the time I left school, I had gained a small measure of self-confidence. Running Pryse's household gave me more."

"And Shelton increased it still more."

"For a while. Then he destroyed all the feelings of value I had gained over the years." Spying a small group some distance down the path, she stood. "Let's walk." Kiernan quickly fell into step beside her.

"I have not told you all this to be morose, but so that you would understand why I cannot marry you, Kiernan. I'm am deeply touched and honored that you think you want me to be your wife."

"I don't think it, Mariah. I *know* it. Everything you've said makes me want it even more."

"Please understand how difficult it is for me. I want to trust you, to believe that you will always care for me and want me with you, but the lessons of my life have taught me a much different, harsher reality. I do not think I could survive being left or sent away again."

"Deception." His brow wrinkled in a frown. "I think I do understand better, now. I didna know how hard your life had been." He smiled at her. "To see you now, one wouldna think you had suffered so much."

"God has been gracious to me and helped me find value in

myself through him. Unfortunately, our experiences do much to mold us and cannot be easily forgotten."

"Mariah, I give you my promise to always love you and always want you by my side. I understand that you need time to see I am a man of my word, longer than the few weeks we've known each other. I will try no' to pressure you." He smiled wryly. "But you must understand I am no' a very patient man."

"I would never have guessed," she said with a teasing smile. She felt better having him know about her past and her fears. She wanted, needed, only honesty between them.

His smile was fleeting, as a troubled expression settled over his face. "I need to tell you—" A sharp trill of laughter interrupted him. He glanced back and scowled as several other guests overtook them. "Later."

17

THE NEXT DAY, THE WHOLE HOUSE PARTY left early on an excursion to Warwick Castle, the finest remaining medieval fortress in England. While they waited for the carriages to be brought around, Mr. Norton told them something of the history of the magnificent castle.

"When it was first built by William the Conqueror in 1068, it was simply a large mound of earth with timber buildings and a wooden palisade or stockade around the top and base. These structures were replaced with stone ones in the twelfth century. Various additions and refurbishments have been made over the centuries, some by earls of Warwick and some by kings or queens, depending on who owned it at that moment."

"Gone back and forth, eh? A history filled with intrigue," said Lord Idington.

"Indeed, milord. The title and the castle have gone through several families in its seven hundred-plus years. Most of the earls of Warwick were very powerful men, but occasionally they found themselves on the wrong side in the upheavals of kings and queens. When the Greville family acquired the grant for Warwick Castle in 1604, it had been empty for fourteen years and was in a ruinous condition. Why, parts of it were being used as the county gaol."

"Which is difficult to imagine given its wonderful condition today," added Lord Stanwell.

"Upon receiving the grant, Sir Fulke Greville spent the next ten years and upwards of twenty thousand pounds in restoration and in converting it into his county seat."

"My word, in those days twenty thousand pounds was an enormous sum, a veritable fortune," exclaimed Lord Idington.

"It's still a fortune to some people," muttered Tony, as he stood beside Jeanette.

She slipped her arm from around his as a groom brought his curricle forward, stopping it in front of them. "I think so, too."

Tony helped her into the carriage, then walked briskly to the other side to join her.

"Do you know anything about Warwick Castle?" she asked as he settled in comfortably close beside her.

"I studied up a bit before we came, expecting we'd make an outing of it. What do you want to know?"

"I believe someone said the current owner is the second earl of Warwick, but Mr. Norton indicated there had been many of them. Also, why was Sir Fulke Greville just a knight, and no' an earl?"

"The history of the castle and of the title is quite convoluted. There were twenty-one earls of Warwick up until 1590. The line died out and the castle passed into Queen Elizabeth's hands. After James I became king, Sir Fulke applied for the grant to the castle and received it, but not the title. Doubt if he even tried for it. Several years later, he was raised to the peerage as Baron Brooke of Beauchamp Court. In the meantime, King James I had bestowed the title of earl of Warwick on Robert, Lord Rich."

"So he became earl without the castle or lands?"

"Yes. I believe the book said eight members of the Rich family held the title until the mid-1700s."

"I thought titles and lands always went together," said Jeanette.

"Usually they do, but I suppose when dealing with ones that go back hundreds of years, anything can happen. There were several generations of Grevilles who bore the title of Lord Brooke and owned the castle. The current earl's father was very wealthy and had good connections, so when the Rich line died out, he petitioned the crown for the earl of Warwick title and received it. I'm unclear as to why they started counting all over again, but he was considered the first one.

"He had married into the Hamiltons, a powerful political family, which helped him obtain the earldom. His wife's brother was Sir William Hamilton, the British minister to the Court of Naples. Sir William's second wife, Emma, became Admiral Nelson's mistress."

Jeanette laughed, shaking her head. "How do you keep up with all this?"

He grinned. "Pays to know who is sleeping with whom."

Heat rushed to her cheeks. Such things were commonplace among the *beau monde,* but she could not accept them so casually.

Tony was instantly contrite. "Forgive me, my dear, I did not mean to embarrass you. Sometimes, I fear I am much too jaded for your tender sensibilities."

"I know such things happen, but I canna approve of them. God says a husband and wife should be faithful to each other, and I believe it. Even if God hadna commanded it, I would be crushed if my husband had a mistress."

"A man would be an utter fool to have a light skirt if he had you for a wife." His eyes glowed with admiration.

"Tony, may I ask you something very personal?" Jeanette looked down at her lap, rearranging her skirt. She had to know if he had a paramour nestled away in a nice little house in London as many gentlemen supposedly did.

Men like Dominic Thorne. Since they met, she had prayed for him every day, just as she did for Tony. It seemed natural, since she often felt moved to pray for others. But sometimes Dominic lingered in her thoughts in fanciful, romantic ways, which troubled her. He was nearly twice her age and far too worldly. She had met other men of the same type and had never given them a second glance, yet she was drawn to him.

They had attended some of the same parties since the ball, but he had not spoken to her. Several times, she had sensed someone watching her, and when she looked around, her gaze met his. Usually, Dominic merely smiled politely and dipped his head in a slight bow. Twice, his eyes burned with such intensity, she felt his longing and loneliness clear across the room.

According to the gossip, he was very wealthy. He'd had numerous lovers over the years—wives, widows, and courtesans. It was rumored he sometimes even entertained his fancy-pieces at his vast estate north of Worcester or at a smaller one in Sussex.

Dominic had never been known to lead an innocent young woman down the road to ruin, but Mariah and Lady Templeton warned her to stay clear of him. Merely associating with him would cause speculation, possibly even damage her reputation. Consequently, she had never given him any encouragement other than a smile. It did not keep her from wanting to know him better.

Tony leaned closer, bringing her thoughts back to him. "My sweet Jeanette, you have finally called me by my Christian name; ask me anything," he murmured.

A shiver raced down her spine as his warm breath tickled her ear. "Do you have a mistress?" she asked softly.

"I did for a little while, but no longer." He looked at her somberly. "I wish I could be romantic and say I ended it when I met you, but the truth is, I had lost her to someone else a few weeks earlier. I could not afford to keep her in the style she wanted."

"If you had the money, would you still be with her?" When he flinched, Jeanette was instantly ashamed. "Forgive me, Tony, I should no' ask such a thing."

"Do you think so little of me?"

She laid her hand on his arm, pressing lightly. "I didna think you would, but I understand so little of the ways of the *beau monde*." She moved her hand back to her lap. "I have been told almost all the men, young and old, have affairs."

"While it is tolerated, even very common, it is not as acceptable as you have been led to believe. It would be very bad form for me to have a ladybird while I am courting you. It would be disrespectful and a potential embarrassment to you. Any honorable gentleman would strive to avoid both."

An odd expression passed over his face, a combination of sadness, resignation, and anger. It was gone so quickly, Jeanette thought she might have imagined it.

Without looking at her, he lifted her hand to his lips and kissed her wrist just above her glove. "I will do everything in my power to avoid hurting you." Releasing her hand, he met her gaze. Sadness hovered in his eyes. "I truly care for you. I hope you know that."

"I do. Tony, what is wrong?" She unconsciously leaned toward him until her arm touched his.

He turned back to the road. "Do you care for me, dearest Jeanette?"

"You know I do."

"Enough to be my bride?"

Jeanette blinked. It was not quite how she had imagined him proposing. She had considered the possibility several times and had agonized over how to answer him. "You mean very much to me, but I dinna know if I love you."

"Do you think you could grow to love me?"

"Perhaps, but love isna the only need in marriage." She felt him tense.

"I am not a wealthy man, Jeanette. Not now, at least. I stand to inherit a nice little estate in Norfolk from my great-aunt, but she's a spry old bird and, thankfully, will probably be with us for some time. I could promise you comfort, for I currently have a modest income left to me by my grandfather, but I could not come close to giving you the luxuries your brother can."

"Money isna of great concern. Kiernan would provide an exceedingly generous dowry."

He instantly relaxed. "Then what troubles you, my darling?"

"We dinna share the same beliefs in Jesus, Tony. I promised my father on his deathbed that I wouldna marry a man who was no' a Christian."

He glanced at her with a puzzled frown. "But I am a Christian. I always went to church when I was young and go occasionally now."

"Going to church isna the same as being a Christian, Tony. A true Christian is someone who believes that Jesus is God's only Son, that he came to earth as a man and died for our sins. I know in my mind and in my heart that Jesus gave himself as a sacrifice for my sins. By rising from the grave, he defeated death. Because I believe this, I know I'll go to heaven."

"How can you be so sure it's true?" he asked, his frown deepening.

"By faith and by what I feel in my heart and soul. I've always known Jesus loved me. My parents told me every day of his love, and I believed them. I suppose my simple acceptance seems foolish to some, but God has always been there to help me, even when I couldna find him through the fog of my hurt. I see the truth of his existence in the Bible and borne out in everyday life."

She laid her head against his shoulder and hugged his arm. "It isna something that can be explained or understood in a minute or two." They hit a rough spot in the road, and she straightened quickly to keep from bouncing against his shoulder.

"I suppose not, but you can teach me, can't you? You can help me believe?"

"I can tell you what I know, and you can read the Scriptures. If you ask God to reveal his truth to you, he will. You have to seek him honestly, no' just because you want to marry me."

Tony smiled, falling into his easy charm. "It seems like a good reason to start." He shifted the conversation back to Warwick Castle. "Mr. Norton was saying last night that the current earl ran into some financial difficulties in trying to improve the castle. He accomplished a great many things, but was an indifferent businessman. Six years ago, his creditors obtained a judgment order against him, and the bailiffs took possession of the castle.

"He sold off some of the outlying estates and practiced the strictest economy in all areas. However, it appeared he would be forced to sell some of the valuable paintings to keep out of dun territory, until his housekeeper stepped in."

"How could she help?"

"At the time, the good lady had worked there for forty years and had shown many visitors around the castle. They all paid her something for her trouble, and she had frugally saved much of it. She paid his creditors upwards of thirty thousand pounds of her own money to save the paintings."

"My goodness! Did she have anything left for retirement?"

"She hasn't retired," he said, his eyes twinkling. "I understand she will be our guide today."

∽∘∾

The visit to the castle was everything Mr. Norton had said it would be and more. The elderly housekeeper, as promised, supplied fascinating bits of history, and they viewed priceless paintings and tapestries in rooms with elaborate ceilings and finely carved fireplaces.

Countless swords, other weapons, and numerous suits of armor, including one for a horse, decorated the great hall. Exquisite furniture from medieval times up to the most recent Regency styles filled the rooms.

When the housekeeper led them down to the dungeon, Jeanette peeked inside, caught a glimpse of cobwebs, and scurried back up the stairs, saying she wasn't interested in seeing such a ghastly place. Tony followed, laughing because something had finally frightened his intrepid companion. When he realized how badly she hated spiders, he apologized for teasing her.

The highlight of the visit for Jeanette had nothing to do with the castle. After they toured the buildings, they were free to walk about the extensive grounds. She and Tony strolled across the large lawn, laughing as several peacocks strutted in front of them, their beautiful tails spread open like fans. They wandered along the River Avon for a short while, then back up to the shade trees bordering the lawn.

Finding they were alone, Tony grabbed her hand and ran into the middle of a copse of trees. She leaned against a sturdy tree trunk to catch her breath, laughing at his mischievous grin. "I wonder how many knights and their fair ladies have hidden here like this."

He glanced around and smiled. "A perfect place for a secret rendezvous." He rested one hand beside her on the tree and caressed her cheek with the other.

Jeanette's heartbeat doubled in expectation. She had been kissed twice in her nineteen years. The first one had been a quick peck that left her wondering if the lad had even touched her. The other had been a disgusting, sloppy half-miss. Tony had not taken the liberty before, but she knew he would now. She ran her fingertips along his jaw, her breath catching as he closed his eyes and turned to press his lips against the inside of her wrist.

He met her gaze. "My lady fair," he whispered.

She slid her hand around his neck, letting her eyelids drift closed as she tilted her face upward. He cupped the back of her head, his fingers grazing lightly across the nape of her neck. His kiss was gentle and sure, warm and lingering.

He smiled, slowly moving his hand to his side. "I think we shall suit."

She looked up at him and sighed softly. "That was nice."

"Just nice?"

"Very," she said as she started walking away. She smiled back. "The best kiss I've ever had."

He fell in step beside her along the wooded path. "And have you been kissed many times, minx?"

She pretended to deliberate. "I dinna suppose three times would be considered many."

"Two more than I like."

She laughed. "Believe me, you dinna have to worry about the competition."

He grabbed her around the waist with one arm, swinging her in front of him as he pulled her into a tight embrace. "I don't want any competition." He captured her lips with far greater intensity and urgency than before.

Apprehension shot through her. As if sensing it, he eased his hold minutely and softened the kiss, calming her fear and stirring feelings she had barely imagined. Her legs grew weak, and she clung to him for support.

231

He finally raised his head. "No one else, dearest," he whispered, dropping a light kiss on her forehead. "We'd better go before Branderee comes in search of us." His gaze dropped to her lips, his smile self-satisfied. "I do believe we shall take the long way around to the carriages."

"Why?"

"Because, my Scottish beauty, you look like you've been thoroughly kissed." He held out his arm. When she slipped her hand around it, he covered her fingers with his own. "And while I find your flushed cheeks and rosy lips delightful, I'm afraid your brother would not."

When they returned to the Norton estate late in the afternoon, a letter from his father awaited Tony. He went immediately upstairs to his room to read it in private. Half an hour later, Jeanette received a note from him, delivered to her room by a footman. She broke the small wax seal on the folded paper and walked to the window. Holding it to the light, she read:

"My dearest, I must forsake your delightful company this evening. My father bids me go to Warwick on a business matter, which may require an overnight stay. I shall count the hours until I see you on the morrow. I plan to return in time for our excursion. Until then, dream of me, as I most assuredly shall dream of you. Your devoted servant, Tony."

Jeanette lowered the note and gazed thoughtfully out the window. The wind had picked up since their return, and thick, gray clouds threatened rain. She had spent countless hours with Tony during their stay in the country, seeing far more of him than would have been possible in the city.

She had enjoyed hearing about his youth and his time at university and was touched by his deep love for his family. He particularly adored his mother and spoke highly of her intelligence and thoughtful ways. His devotion to her reminded Jeanie of how Kiernan treated their mother.

During their time at the Nortons', she had not once wished he would leave her alone. "Maybe it is good for him to be gone this evening. It will give me time to think. Father, I dinna know what to do about Tony. I know I should no' marry him if he does no' know you, but my feelings for him keep growing stronger. After today, I dinna know if I can keep from falling in love with him. Is he the one you have chosen for me? Help me to know your will and to show him your way."

A movement below drew her attention. Tony hurried along on the path in the direction of the stables, his forehead creased in a troubled frown. He looked up toward her window, and seeing her there, stopped and waved, a smile brightening his face. She opened the window. "Thank you for the note," she called.

"I should be back in time to go to Stratford-upon-Avon." He glanced around and, seeing no one nearby, wove his way through the shrubbery. When he was directly beneath her window, he blew her a kiss.

Laughing, Jeanette leaned over the windowsill and pretended to catch it. "I shall save it for later when I'm lonely."

His smiled at her antics. "Will you truly miss me?"

"Yes, but I think I can bear it for an evening, though it will be difficult. Do wait out the storm in Warwick, even if you finish your business early. May God protect you and bless your endeavor."

His smile vanished, and he stared at the ground for a minute. When he looked back up at her, his expression reflected abject misery. He turned abruptly, plowing through the shrubs.

"Tony, wait!"

Reaching the path, he quickened his pace and never looked back.

18

AT MOST HOUSE PARTIES, there always seemed to be one fly in the broth, and the Nortons' party was no exception. The culprit in this instance turned out to be Sir Edgar's wife, Celeste. To those who barely knew her, she seemed to possess a sweet disposition. Over time, her acquaintances learned it was merely a sugarcoating hiding a vinegar nature.

Mariah had done her best to stay away from the jealous, vindictive woman. Unless she was with Kiernan, she avoided Sir Edgar, too, though he was her friend. He understood, for he knew all too well how his wife felt about Mariah.

Going down to breakfast the morning following the trip to Warwick Castle, Mariah optimistically thought she might make it through the visit without bearing the brunt of Celeste's malice.

She was more concerned about Kiernan. He had been quietly attentive the day before but often seemed distracted. Since this change of mood came after she told him she was afraid to love him and would not marry him, she worried that she had hurt him more deeply than he had let on. She hoped and prayed he would not give up on her. They had not been alone since that night, so she had been unable to ask him what was wrong.

Approaching the breakfast room door, Mariah slowed when she

heard Celeste speaking to the others at the table. *Botheration! Wouldn't you know the one morning I sleep late, she wakes up before noon.* Mariah stopped before she reached the doorway, deliberating whether to skip breakfast or hide in a nearby antechamber until the others left.

"Personally, I think the way she throws herself at Lord Branderee is disgraceful," said Celeste. "She hangs onto the poor man everywhere he goes."

Mariah's face flamed.

"Though I must admit, he is handsome for a Scot, in a rugged, uncivilized way," Celeste added.

"I believe you have it wrong, my lady," said Lord Idington. "It seems to me that Branderee is the one who seeks her out, not the other way around."

"Well, I suppose he does want his money's worth," said Celeste.

"Celeste, be quiet. You don't know what you're talking about," snapped Sir Edgar.

"I know precisely what I'm talking about," his wife said petulantly. "Everyone knows she lost her inheritance to that bigamist, and her brother cut her off without a penny."

Sir Edgar tried to interrupt, but when Celeste was the center of attention, nothing short of a gag could stop her.

"She stayed in that horrible rundown house at Stillwater for years, living hand to mouth and dressing in rags, worse than a beggar on the street. Now, she wears the finest dresses and gowns. You have only to look at her clothes to know the man is spending a fortune on her. Far more than anyone would spend on a mere chaperon. Or is she his mother's companion? Oh, that's right, she is supposed to be both." Celeste laughed. "As far as I can see, she does little of either. It isn't difficult to guess how she really earns all those fancy things. She certainly tried often enough to entice my husband when she lived next to us."

Her tirade was met with stunned silence.

Mariah turned to run, but Kiernan blocked her way. Judging from his clenched jaw and the anger flashing in his eyes, he had heard the whole thing. He pulled her into his embrace, holding her close. "Forgive me, my love," he said roughly. "Forgive my selfishness."

Something hit the table, rattling the dishes. "Be still, wife!" Sir Edgar's voice shook with wrath. "Unlike you, Lady Mariah is a fine and decent woman. She never once tried to entice me. She is a good and true friend, something you would know nothing about."

Mariah buried her face against Kiernan's chest. She knew how much her friend would regret his public outburst, yet she loved him for defending her.

"She is not penniless," Sir Edgar continued. "When her brother sold Stillwater to me, the money was put in the bank for her. She has more than enough funds to buy her own wardrobe, which I am certain she has done."

Shock and disbelief swept through Mariah, chilling her to the marrow, numbing her mind, freezing her heart. She tried to pull back and look at Kiernan's face, but he tightened his hold.

"Dinna hate me, Mariah," he whispered. "Please dinna hate me."

"You said Branderee won the estate and sold it to you," cried Celeste. "And one of the servants said she told Prudence she was going to work for him."

"That was the original plan, but Branderee sold the estate back to Glenbuck." Sir Edgar was calmer, but Mariah had never heard such a hard edge to his voice. "In turn, Glenbuck sold it to me and arranged to have the money given to Mariah. He was moving to America right away and wanted to provide for her in some way."

"And high time he did," declared Lord Stanwell.

Mariah pushed against Kiernan's chest, and he slowly released her. His guilt-ridden face confirmed everything Sir Edgar said.

"How could you?" she asked in a choked whisper.

His dark eyes grew black with despair. He stepped around her and walked into the breakfast room, stopping just inside the doorway. "Though Lady Mariah is a woman of independent means, I did ask her to act as my sister's chaperon and Mother's companion. She is a guest in our home at their request.

"As Lord Idington said, I seek her out, no' the other way around, but no' for the purposes you so crudely imagine, Lady Pittman. It is my fervent hope that one day Lady Mariah will become my wife." He paused. "As for you, madam, you would be wise to mind your tongue before this uncivilized Scot cuts it out."

Celeste shrieked. "Edgar, do something!"

"I intend to. Something I should have done years ago. Pack your things, Celeste," said Sir Edgar quietly. "The coach will depart in one hour to take you to Lancashire for an extended visit with your family."

"Edgar!"

"I will hear no protest, madam," he said sternly.

"How long must I stay?" asked Celeste in a small, shaken voice.

"Until I am convinced you have mended your ways. If you cannot change, there you will remain. My apologies to all of you, especially you, Branderee and Lady Mariah."

Stifling a sob, Mariah fled to her room, rushing past Gabriel on the way.

Kiernan was just far enough behind her to have the door slammed in his face. "Mariah, open the door."

"Never!"

"Please, sweetheart, open the door."

"Go away!"

"No' until I talk to you."

Something hit the door with a loud thud. Since nothing shattered, he decided it must have been one of her walking boots. "Mariah…"

"Go jump off your cliff, Kiernan Macpherson!"

His mother and Jeanette had rooms on either side of Mariah's. They both opened their doors at the same time and peeked out. "Kiernan, what has happened?" asked Ailsa.

"I'll explain later, Mother. Let me be. I have to talk to Mariah."

"I dinna think she wants to talk to you." She winced as Mariah's other boot hit the door. "I didna think the lass had a temper," she said with a tiny smile. "Do you want me to see what I can do?"

"No." He turned the handle on the door, surprised but thankful that in her haste to throw something, she had forgotten to lock it. She probably did not believe he had the audacity to enter her bedroom. He looked at Gabriel, who was leaning against the wall next to Jeanette's door. "See that we are no' disturbed."

Gabe nodded. Jeanette stared at him wide-eyed.

"Kiernan, you canna go in her bedroom!" exclaimed his mother.

"Watch me," he growled, opening the door and jumping inside, slamming it shut behind him.

"Get out!" Mariah wiped her cheeks with her hand, but fresh tears replaced the ones she brushed away.

"No." He felt behind him for the key and turned it in the lock. Pulling it from the keyhole, he slipped it inside the pocket of his jacket as he moved toward her. "I have to try to explain."

"What is there to explain? You lied to me. You deliberately deceived me by not telling me I had money of my own. You wanted me to think I had to depend on you to survive. Did you enjoy seeing me grovel? Did it make you feel important? Did it make you feel like a powerful, benevolent lord?"

Kiernan flinched and turned his head, unable to look at the hurt shimmering in her eyes. His reason for keeping the money a secret was not what she imagined, but he had never been so ashamed.

"Do you know what it's like to have nothing, Kiernan?" she asked softly. "Even when you were fighting Napoleon and went without rations, you knew you could walk away anytime. You had a home, a family, a livelihood waiting for you." She sniffed and grabbed a delicate linen handkerchief from the dressing table, blowing her nose.

Sobbing, she turned her back on him. He tentatively put his hand on her shoulder, but she angrily shrugged it off and wiped her eyes with the scrap of linen. Spinning around, she waved the handkerchief in front of him.

"Until you paid me last week, I couldn't even buy this on my own. Do you know what it's like not to have enough money to buy a kerchief? Or how it humiliated me to have you pay for my underclothes? In spite of my embarrassment, I almost felt obligated to show you what you had purchased. Do you have any idea how guilty I felt every time I ordered an expensive new dress? I told myself it was necessary, that I needed to look nice to go with Jeanette, when in truth something far cheaper would have served just as well for someone in my position.

"Guilt and pride waged a daily battle. I enjoy wearing beautiful clothes and receiving compliments. I loved seeing your eyes light up in admiration, but every time I put on a new frock I was torn by guilt over the cost. I worried that you wouldn't like it, and that I had wasted your money. Remember the stomachache I had a few weeks ago? It wasn't something I ate. I was sick because you didn't like my dress."

"I've never said I didna like your dress. I like them all." Except for the red thing with the high lace collar that completely hid her

240

neck. It made her look like her head was attached to a fluffy, lace flower.

"You didn't have to say anything. I could tell."

"Which one?" He was determined to be honest with her no matter what.

"That lovely scarlet frock with the lace ruff." She lifted her chin and glared at him.

Uh-oh. He wasn't quite sure how the conversation had shifted to dresses, but he had the feeling the way he answered was very important. Honesty tempered with prudence might be wise. "The one with the high lace collar?"

"I knew you didn't like it!" Fresh tears welled up in her eyes.

He slipped his arms around her, thanking the Lord when she did not pull away. "It's a pretty dress, sweetheart, but it hides your lovely neck."

"It's supposed to. It's a ruff, like Queen Elizabeth wore."

"She probably had sagging skin. Your neck, on the other hand, is smooth and slim and graceful." He gathered her close. "I'm very fond of it."

She rested her cheek and hands against his chest. "Why didn't you tell me?" she asked sorrowfully.

It did not take a wizard to realize she was no longer talking about the dress. "I was afraid you would leave, and I'd never see you again. I knew I was wrong no' to tell you about the money. I fought my own constant battle, no' between guilt and pride, but between guilt and need. I needed to be near you, to try to win your love."

"By deceiving me?" She pulled away, scalding him with a glance.

Sick with remorse, he hung his head. When he looked up and saw the contempt in her eyes, he hated himself. "I'm no' trying to excuse what I did, Mariah. It was wrong. I knew it was wrong at the time, but I couldna stand the thought of seeing you walk out the door and never return. I couldna risk losing you."

"I would have stayed. I had made a commitment to Jeanette and your mother. But I would have paid my own way."

"The matter was settled four days after Pryse visited you," said Kiernan. Her shock and silent accusation twisted the knife in his heart. "It took longer for the transaction to be completed and the money deposited, but if you had known it was coming, would you have stayed? Or would you have found a nice home near the Stanwells' country estate or maybe gone back to Scotland? Which would have won, Mariah—your commitment to someone you had just met or your dread of Society's scorn?"

When she hesitated, he knew the answer. "I feared you would seek a haven somewhere away from London, sweetheart, because in the same circumstances, it is what I would have done."

"Yet by not telling me, you forced me to stay." She sat down on a gold silk settee in the corner, her expression one of hurt and confusion.

"I admit my reasons were mostly selfish, but no' entirely. Sir Edgar and your brother were convinced that you would have little problem taking your rightful place in Society. They both felt strongly that it was something you should do, to give you peace of mind and ease the hurts of the past."

"They advised you to keep the money a secret?"

"No, but Sir Edgar was the one to bring up the possibility that you might hide away and no' confront your demons. I hadna thought of it, but I probably would have."

"So you made the decision for me."

"Yes, I suppose I did." He sat down beside her. "I dinna think I realized until later that I hadna given you a choice. I was too busy falling in love to think reasonably. I wanted to be with you, to see you smile and hear you laugh, to steal a kiss at every opportunity. I wanted to shower you with gifts, anything that caught your eye or mine. If I'd had any idea how it hurt you to have me buy your clothes, I never would have done it."

"Was it your idea to give me the money?"

"I had considered it from the beginning, but it wouldna have looked right for me to deposit a large amount in an account for you. I discovered when I first came to London that it isna too difficult to learn the particulars of someone else's finances. When Pryse came to see you, he mentioned that he had considered giving Stillwater to you, but he lost it instead. That set me to thinking.

"He seemed to truly regret no' being able to help you. After he left, I came up with the idea of selling Stillwater back to him, on the condition that he immediately sell it to Sir Edgar and give you the money. Both he and Sir Edgar agreed."

"How could he buy it when he did not have any money?"

"I traded the estate for his library." When she gasped, he smiled and patted her hand. "Since I have many of the same books at Branderee, I gave it back to him as a wedding present. Pryse renegotiated the sale of the estate with Sir Edgar."

"You mean he upped the price?"

"Yes, but I had sold it for a fraction of its value just to be free of it. Sir Edgar was happy to pay more, knowing you would receive most of the money, and he still got a bargain. With some minor improvements, he can sell it for much more if he wants to. We agreed that Pryse could have a thousand pounds. Help him start off better in his marriage.

"Because the transactions would take more time than Pryse had, it was arranged for the money to go directly into an account in your name. He set things up so that you may handle the account yourself or have it administered by trustees. That way, the trustees can take care of it if you marry and want to keep the money out of your husband's hands.

"I was temporarily made a trustee to see that all proceeded as it should. As of last week, everything was completed. You are now the only one with access to your account."

"You wound up with nothing."

"I dinna lose the seven thousand pounds I wagered in the first place, and I'm no' stuck with an English estate. I also have the satisfaction of knowing provision has been made for you, though it is meager consolation."

"Consolation?"

"For losing you. Can you forgive me, Mariah? Or have I completely destroyed my chances of winning your love?"

She was silent so long, he thought all was lost.

"You deceived me." There was no longer anger in her expression, only sadness and disillusionment.

"Mariah, I wish I always made the right choices and never made mistakes. I'm stubborn and selfish and sometimes a daftie, but no other man could ever love you the way I do."

She sighed heavily. "I wish you wouldn't say that."

"Why?" He frowned and cupped her face, carefully tilting it so he could see her eyes.

"Because it makes it hard to stay angry."

"And the hurt?" He grazed her cheek with his thumb and lowered his hand.

"It's still there." She looked down at her lap. "But I'm not going to cling to it. I can't honestly say I forgive you right now, but I know in time I will. Probably not all that long a time, either."

He put his arm around her, and she snuggled up against him. "Have I fallen far in your eyes, lass?" he asked softly.

"A notch or two. But I suppose pedestals are precarious anyway."

"And lonely. I'd much rather be here with you."

"But you shouldn't be. I'm surprised your mother didn't come in

244

and drag you out by your ear."

"She couldna." He fished the key out of his pocket. "I locked the door."

Her eyes grew wide. "Kiernan, you're going to compromise me!"

He grinned and tucked the key back in his pocket. "Now, there's a thought."

"Get out of my room, you fiend." Her murmured words lacked the force to send him running to the door.

"Soon, but no' just yet. I'm still apologizing." He kissed her tenderly.

Afterward, she looked up at him thoughtfully. "You started to tell me about the money the other night, didn't you? Right before the Templetons and Biscoms caught up with us."

He nodded. "You had bared your soul to me, been totally honest, and I felt like a reprobate."

"How much?"

"Like the very worst."

She ran her finger up his neck and down his jaw, tickling his chin.

Kiernan thought about tossing the key out the window.

"I mean, how much money do I have?"

"Twenty-one thousand pounds."

Her mouth fell open, and she stared at him. Her lips mimicked his words but no sound came out. When he nodded, she gave a little squeak and buried her face against his neck. Seconds later, he felt a tear trickle down his collar. "Sweetheart, dinna cry. I'm sorry."

She muttered something about dungeons and the rack, then kissed his neck. And his chin. And finally his mouth, whispering, "Thank you." He thought she added, "my love," as her lips touched his. Or was it only the yearning of his heart?

Her hands slid around his waist, and he lost himself in her kiss.

Too soon, she eased away. "You'd better go."

He sighed. "I'd better."

She stood and pulled him to his feet. Walking backwards, she led him toward the door. "As soon as we go back to London, I'll repay you for my clothes and wages." When he started to protest, she shook her head. "Kiernan, I don't need to work for you."

His heart dropped to his knees. "Then you're going to leave after all?"

"No, I want to be with Jeanie through the Season and to see what happens between Ailsa and Wilton. I would like to stay as your guest, not as your employee."

"And see what happens between us?" He stopped and tugged her to him.

"Only if you behave." Smiling, she twisted away and held up the key. He laughed as she unlocked the door. When she opened it, his mother stood in the hallway, arms crossed, tapping her foot. Gabriel and Jeanette were standing guard near the stairs.

"It's about time. I'd decided if anyone else came upstairs, you were on your own." Ailsa looked at Mariah. "I see you must have accepted his apology." She glared at Kiernan. "For whatever he did. The way you two were yellin', I'm no' sure he deserved to be forgiven."

Kiernan looked at Mariah. "Am I forgiven?"

"Not quite." She glanced at the others. "Do they know?"

"Gabe does."

"Then you'd better explain it to your mother and Jeanette."

"They'll rail at me, too."

"Good," she said with a smile.

That smile was worth a scold from his mother. He suddenly remembered why he had gone looking for Mariah in the first place. "Uh, sweetheart, I have a surprise for you."

"Another one?" she said dryly.

He grinned sheepishly. "Jordan Wylde is waiting to see you in Mr. Norton's study."

"He's here?" A bright smile lit up her face. She turned toward the stairs, but Ailsa caught hold of her arm as she rushed by.

"You need to tidy up, lass. You look like you've been pulling your hair out." Laughter sparkled in her eyes. "Or maybe my son has been pulling the hairpins out."

Blushing, Mariah returned to her room. As Kiernan started to close the door, she stopped and looked back at him. "Did he just drop by for a visit?"

"No, I asked him to come since this is closer to the vicarage than London. I thought you would enjoy seeing him."

"I will. It was sweet of you."

"Thanks." He pulled the door closed and, with a worried frown, walked slowly toward his mother's room. He had expected Mariah to be happy to see Jordan, but she was more excited about the visit than he liked. *I wish I hadna asked him to be my secretary.*

Even more, he wished Wylde had not accepted the position.

19

Jordan greeted Mariah with a grin and a big hug. "What's this? I think you've put on a few pounds," he teased.

"I'm not eating my own cooking." She laughed and leaned back to smile up at him. "It's so good to see you. I've missed you."

"I gathered that from your letters. I've missed you, too. Now, turn around and let me look at you." She stepped back and spun around, ending in a curtsy. "You look lovely, except that you've been crying. What's amiss, my friend?" he asked gently.

"Kiernan and I just had a row."

"That is why it took you so long to come down?" When she nodded, he motioned toward a couple of leather armchairs by the window. "Do you want to talk about it?" he asked as they sat down.

"Later. Right now, I want to hear how you are."

"Doing well for having just spent fifteen minutes trying to console Lady Pittman. She is convinced Sir Edgar will never let her return. I fear she may be right. This has been coming for a very long time, since about a month after their marriage, in fact."

"Perhaps being away from him will help her realize how wrong she has been about him. Poor man, at one time or another I think she believed every woman in the district was trying to snare him," said Mariah, wishing he had married someone with a nicer disposition.

"I feel sorry for him, but I pity her, too. It is her own lack of self-assurance that makes her fear losing him. I've told him as much. I've also told her that she will indeed lose him if she does not change." He sighed. "They have been in my prayers for a very long time. Now, we must lift them up even more than ever."

"I, too, have prayed for them, but it will be difficult to speak kindly of her to the Lord after what she said about me this morning."

Surprise and concern brought a frown to his face. "You heard?"

"I was standing in the hallway. Were you in the breakfast room?"

"No, but Sir Edgar told me word for word what she said, and more or less what he said. Of course, her version was somewhat different." He pursed his lips. "I tend to believe Sir Edgar."

"I do hope they can work things out, but I also never want to see the woman again." Mariah made a face. "Not very Christlike, am I?"

"Forgiveness seldom comes instantly."

"As I well know."

"Lord Branderee confirmed that your entry back into Society has not been too difficult."

"A few sneers and cuts, but not too many. Lady St. John has been terrible. Her daughter and Jeanie were friends until I arrived. Now, she won't let Clarissa associate with her. Jeanie has other friends and tells me not to fret about it, but I know it troubles both of them. And it makes me feel awful. At some recent parties, Clarissa has at least spoken to her, though I don't think she dares sit down for a long chat.

"Delia and Godfrey have taken us under their wings and seen to our success. Jeanette is a prize, and I dearly love Ailsa, Kiernan's mother. She was shy with me at first, but now we sit down almost daily and have wonderful talks. She loves the Lord and is a wise woman."

"You said the same thing about Jeanette in one of your letters," said Jordan. "It is rare for one so young to have such a close walk with the Savior."

"She told me once that he is her best friend. I think God reveals things about people to her that the rest of us miss. They react to her gentle heart, too." She smiled fondly at Jordon. "In both ways, she reminds me of you."

Mariah told him about the Altbury ball and how Fletcher sent Jeanie flying and Dominic caught her. "Dominic was entranced as he watched her walk away. I thought for a minute Kiernan might plant him a facer. He ordered him to stay away from her, but I'm certain Dominic didn't even hear him. He turned to Kiernan and quoted a few verses from Proverbs thirty-one, of all things."

"Her price is far above rubies," said Jordan with a thoughtful nod.

"Yes, and the verse about speaking with wisdom and kindness. He said she was goodness, gentleness, and honor. I've known him a long time, Jordan. He is probably twice her age and the veriest rake, perpetually hovering on the edge of acceptability. I have never seen him when he wasn't charming and in complete control, except for those few moments with Jeanette."

"He sounds like a man seeking God, only he doesn't know it. I expect he sensed the love of Jesus reaching out to him through her. Did you ask her what transpired between them before you reached them?"

"Yes, we talked about it the next day. She said they barely spoke. He asked if she was hurt; she told him she wasn't, that type of thing. But they were certainly looking at each other as if no one else was in the room.

"When I warned her to stay away from him because of his reputation, she said she would, though she admitted she wished she could get to know him. I pressed my point—I am supposed to be a chaperon, you know," she said with a smile. "Jeanie promised she'd do as I asked, but as she was leaving my room, she made the strangest comment. She looked at me with infinite sadness and asked me to pray for him. She said despair and loneliness are destroying him."

Jordan whistled softly. "I look forward to meeting this young lady."

"I think she is still here. She and Tony, as well as several others, are going to visit Shakespeare's home and other sites in Stratford-upon-Avon. Anthony Drake has become a most ardent suitor. I think she cares a great deal for him, though she said when she came to London she was not looking for a husband." .

"Such intentions have a way of changing if the heart becomes involved. I won't trouble her today. I'll have plenty of time to become acquainted."

"You're staying a few days?"

"Only the night. I'll meet her next week when I go to London." When she frowned, he looked puzzled. "Lord Branderee didn't tell you?"

"Tell me what?"

"He has hired me as his secretary. I assume my new duties when you go back to Town. I will be moving to Scotland with them at the end of the Season."

Mariah's frown deepened. "More secrets."

"He said earlier he had not told you because he wanted to discuss the position with me first. It does give me more confidence that he hired me because he thinks I can do the job, not because you persuaded him to do it. However, I assumed he told you when he went looking for you."

"He didn't mention it. Of course, we were discussing something else right then. When we left Stillwater, I told him you wanted to change professions, but he already had a secretary."

"He said they did not work well together. The man is getting on in years and nervous. His lordship says Fiske makes him want to yell and pound the desk after five minutes." Jordan absently tapped the arm of his chair with his finger. "Does he do that sort of thing often?"

She thought of the day she met Kiernan and how he had pounded on the table in frustration over trying to be an earl. "Not often. Did he finally fire Fiske?"

"Pensioned him off. He said the old man seemed delighted when he wrote to him and suggested setting up an annuity. Fiske wrote back and told him to send the money to Edinburgh. Said he was leaving Branderee the next morning."

"My goodness, he was happy to escape."

Jordan laughed. "Mariah, you're making me worry about the wisdom of taking the position."

"Don't mind me. I'm just miffed because he didn't tell me."

"I think he wanted to surprise you. He thought it would make you happy."

"It does. I've missed you dreadfully. Though you won't be a vicar anymore, will you still give me your wise counsel?"

"Such as it is. Want me to start now?"

She nodded and gave him an abbreviated version of the quarrel with Kiernan. She had written him earlier about Pryse's visit, so he was familiar with her brother's transformation.

When she finished, Jordan was beaming. "So he loves you. I had thought as much, given the things you mentioned in your letters about how he treated you. I wondered even the day you left Stillwater. There was something fiercely protective in the way he looked at you." He laughed. "If you could have seen his face when you hugged me good-bye. I thanked the Lord at the time that he didn't have a sword. He looked like he wanted to run me through."

"I should have known you'd take up for him, now that you work for him."

"Mariah, pouting doesn't become you," he chided gently. "Yes, he was wrong not to tell you about the money, but let it go. Build your relationship on the good things between you. Don't tear it apart because he did something stupid. Ephesians says not to let the sun go down on your wrath so you won't give the devil a place. If you harbor this anger and hurt in your heart, it will breed bitterness and distrust."

"Trust comes easier to some than others."

"I know." He was quiet for a moment. "What would hurt you more than anything else? Even more than being deceived?"

She squirmed, adjusting her position in the chair. He knew what it was; they had discussed it several times. Why did he want her to say it again?

"Isn't it being forsaken? Cast aside? Having your love rejected?" he asked softly.

"Yes." Those three phrases summed up her life—until Kiernan came into it.

"In spite of being taught to keep a stiff upper lip and all that rot, men are not immune to the pain of rejection. Some, those with deep and passionate emotions, feel things more strongly than other men. They disdain tradition, welcoming love where they find it. They are the ones who see a need and try to help. They protect and defend, fighting to the death if necessary. They defy the rules to seek justice and honor."

From the distance came the beautiful, lonely melody of a bagpipe. Jordan turned his head toward the window, listening intently, his expression contemplative, wistful.

"They defy the rules to seek justice and honor," repeated Mariah softly.

"And play tunes that make even an Englishman weep."

"It is the song of the Highlands, the cry of his soul, the call of a race and way of life that have been all but lost. It is why he wears the kilt and plaid with so much pride and honor."

"He loves you, Mariah. I think it is safe to assume that when Lord Branderee made those monetary arrangements for you, he was in love with you, or at least falling in love. Perhaps he has not been hurt as you were in the past, but still, don't you suppose his fear of losing you—being forsaken, cast aside, having his love rejected—might be as great as your own?"

His words hit her full force. "I find it hard to imagine him being afraid of anything."

"Love makes even the bravest man weak."

"That's a terrible thought." She scowled at him.

"I'll amend it," he said with a smile. "It makes him vulnerable, though when necessary, even braver."

"I don't like to think of Kiernan as being vulnerable."

"You need to. Even the strongest man can be hurt when he cares for someone. Feeling defenseless breeds desperation."

"That I know all too well." She studied him affectionately. "How did you become so wise?"

Deep sadness washed across his face. "I've loved and lost."

"Jordan, forgive me. I didn't mean to be glib."

"You weren't. Tell me, is Branderee a believer?"

"Yes. He is close to the Lord now, though he struggled for a long time after his father died. Suddenly inheriting the title shortly afterward did not help."

"It must have been difficult. I'm relieved he is a Christian. It will make the transition to my new career easier. Now, will you please go find him and put him in a good mood? If he doesn't play something lively soon, we'll all have a fit of the dismals."

Mariah laughed and jumped up, hurrying to the door. "We'll be back before long."

"Don't rush. I think I'll go introduce myself to his mother. If she is busy, I'll wander around the gardens."

On the way out, Mariah stopped to talk with Jeanette and Tony for a minute before they left on the outing. Lord and Lady Templeton and Fletcher and Olivia had already left for Stratford-upon-Avon.

"I'm shirking my duties," said Mariah. "Kiernan and I should be going along."

Jeanette laughed and squeezed Tony's arm. "I'm in good hands. Tony is a very careful driver, and the Templetons will watch over us, so you need no' worry. Kiernan told me what happened, and why you were so upset." She rolled her eyes. "Sometimes he's such a dunderhead. Do you feel better now?"

Mariah nodded. "Though I think I should go find him and cheer him up."

Tony grinned. "Amen. I saw him heading toward the lake. We'd best be off. I don't want to be too far behind, just enough to stay out of Fletcher's dust. We're already late."

"You should no' have insisted I go back for my parasol," said Jeanie.

"You'll need it if it warms up."

"Enjoy yourselves," said Mariah.

"We will." Tony clicked his tongue and flicked the reins lightly. As the horses sprang forward, Jeanette waved happily.

Mariah watched them drive down the lane, thinking what a nice-looking couple they made. She felt another twinge of concern because she and Kiernan were not going along. "It's not as if they will be by themselves." She started walking toward the lake, unable to shake the nagging uneasiness. "Please watch over her, Lord. Keep her safe. Please keep all of them safe."

Following the sound of the pipes, she found Kiernan in the woods near the lake. He abruptly stopped playing when he saw her. "Did you and Wylde have a good visit?"

"We did. I'm very pleased that you asked him to work for you."

"Sir Edgar recommended him highly." He watched her carefully.

She smiled and stepped closer. "Relax, dear man, I'm not going to start screaming or burst into tears again."

"That's good to hear." He shifted the pipes to one arm. "So you caught up on all the news?"

"If you're asking did I tell him about our argument, the answer is yes."

Kiernan frowned. "I'm no' so sure hiring him was a good idea. I dinna want him to know everything that goes on between us. He will be my secretary, not the local reverend."

"He is still my friend and confidant, Kiernan. Nothing can change that. He is a very wise man, and I trust his counsel."

His frown deepened. "So what pearls of wisdom did he spout?"

She laughed softly and slipped one arm around his waist. The pipes were in the way of the other arm. "He told me not to let the sun go down on my anger."

Kiernan relaxed slightly. "Good advice."

"And he helped me see that even you might have legitimate fears."

"A few. Did he tell you to forgive me?"

"He did. Quite forcefully, in fact." She brushed a kiss across his chin.

"Does that mean you have?"

"Yes." She stretched up and nibbled on his lower lip. "He also told me to put you in a good mood so you would play something lively. You're making everyone melancholy."

He laughed, putting his arm around her. "He is a wise man. I must be bright for hiring him."

"Brilliant." She moved her arms up around his neck. "Will this put you in a good mood?"

"That's nice, but another kiss or two would do better." He leaned down and kissed her deeply.

Squerrrck! A loud note exploded from the bagpipe as Kiernan accidentally squeezed it.

Mariah jumped back, laughing.

"I think the pipes are jealous," he said with a grin as he carefully laid them on the ground.

When he straightened, Mariah stepped into the circle of his arms. "They'd better get used to sharing you."

20

"ARE YOU SURE YOU DINNA MIND TRAVELING AGAIN, Tony? You've barely been off the road an hour."

"I enjoy driving." He glanced up at the clearing sky. "I'm glad last night's showers did not stay around. I cannot think of anyplace I'd rather be than right here with you." He grinned mischievously. "Unless it's in that grove just behind us receiving my welcome kiss. You did miss me, didn't you?"

"You know I did." Jeanette scooted closer, until their shoulders and legs touched. Leaning toward him, she kissed him on the cheek. "Welcome back."

He took a deep breath. "Now I know I should have stopped back there." He looked down at her. "So, did you dream of me?"

"A little." Jeanette couldn't stop her quick blush. It seemed she had spent the whole night thinking and dreaming about him. She had expected to miss him but had been unprepared for the depth of her loneliness. If one night away from him made her so unhappy, what would she do when she went back to Scotland?

Tony grinned. "Just a little? Tell me the truth, darling."

"More than a little, but they were no' all wonderful. In one, we were playing a game of lawn tennis, and you kept hitting the ball too hard for me to return. When I complained, you just laughed. I

258

thought you were mean and selfish and told you so."

He frowned, sending her an uneasy glance. "I may be selfish on occasion, but I'm not mean."

"Of course you are no'," she said in surprise. "It was only a silly dream, even if I did wake up feeling quite put out with you," she added with a grin. "I think I was irritated because you have won every game of lawn tennis we've played, although you have been a gentleman about it."

"Have to keep the game genteel for the ladies," he said, relaxing. "And don't forget, you always win at chess."

She laughed. "With Gabriel around, I have plenty of practice. When I went back to sleep, I dreamed of you again. That one was very nice."

"Oh?" he asked with a roguish smile.

Her cheeks grew hot. "I think we'd better talk about something else."

"Coward," he teased.

"Prudent. How was your trip? Did your business go well?"

"It did. It turned out not to be as tedious as I thought it would be."

"I'm glad. You seemed so upset when you left. I worried about you."

He gazed at her tenderly. "I think I like that. It means you care."

"Tony, you know I do." She looked down, toying with the strings to her reticule. "My affection for you increases every day."

He drew the curricle to a halt. "What are you saying?"

She looked up at him, meeting his gaze and taking a deep breath. "I'm no' sure. I missed you dreadfully and fretted so about you." She glanced away from his burning gaze.

"You looked so wretched when you left, I imagined all kinds of terrible problems and dangerous situations." She laughed softly. "Branderee has a huge library, and I read too many novels over the winter." She looked up at him again. "I couldna bear it if anything bad happened to you, Tony."

"Jeanette, my darling." He embraced her, his kiss triumphant and barely restrained. When he finally released her, he smiled joyfully. "I would turn right around and go back, but I don't want to cause Lord and Lady Templeton undue worry. I'll speak with your brother tonight and ask his permission to marry you."

Jeanette hesitated, her thoughts clouded by his touch. *Do I love him? Do I want to be his wife?* "Not yet. I dinna want to rush into marriage, Tony. We must take time to be certain it is right."

He flicked the reins, smiling broadly as the team started up again. "I know it is right, but I will try to be patient. You will have to meet my parents. They'll adore you. How about next week? Could we visit them next week?"

His excitement was contagious, and Jeanette laughed. "I expect we can."

As they drove along the gently winding, scenic road, he talked about his family and their estate. His father loved the country and hated the city, so his parents seldom went to London. He told how his older brother had built another house on the estate and lived there with his family so they could all be close. He shared a tale of some mischief his nephews had recently gotten into, laughing because he and his brother had done the same thing at their age.

As they approached a crossroads, Tony slowed to let a coach and four horsemen pass. Instead of going on through, the driver halted the older black carriage right in the middle of the intersection in front of them.

Tony quickly stopped the team. The four outriders immediately circled them, pistols drawn.

"What is the meaning of this?" cried Tony. "Let us pass."

"You and the lady are comin' with us, Guv."

Jeanette silently prayed with all her might. *Father, help us!*

The coach door swung open, and a fifth man jumped out. Lowering the steps, he grinned lecherously at Jeanette and bowed with a sweeping wave of his arm toward the carriage. "Your cage awaits, little Scottish birdie," he said with a sneer.

"I'm no' goin' anywhere with you," she said defiantly. Her fingers shook as she slipped them inside her reticule. She eased her small silver bottle of perfume from the handbag, curling her hand around it.

"Cheeky wench, ain't she? You're both comin' with us, and we don't want no argument. Shut your yap, missy, or your brother will be gettin' damaged goods when he pays the ransom."

Tony put his arm around her. "Let her go. I'll give you whatever you are asking."

The man by the coach laughed nastily. "That's noble of you, Mr. Drake, but we know you ain't got the ready. We figure you're worth plenty to your papa, but by the time he forks over the coin for you, he won't have the blunt for the lady, too. She's a walkin' fortune.

"Now, climb down before one of the lads gets nervous and accidentally pulls the trigger. And leave that parasol in the curricle. I don't want you trying to hit me with it." The man glared at Jeanette. "If you want to keep your sweetheart in one piece, cooperate."

When one of the men waved a pistol toward Tony, Jeanie nodded quickly and dropped the parasol on the floorboard. Tony jumped down and helped her out of the curricle, keeping his arm protectively around her. As they walked toward the coach, she hid her hand in the folds of her skirt and dropped the silver bottle in the grass beside the road.

One of the riders dismounted and tied his horse to the back of Tony's vehicle. He climbed into the curricle and, guiding the horse past the coach, sped down the road in the direction from which the kidnappers had come.

"When your brother looks for you, he will find the curricle and our ransom note," said the leader as Tony helped Jeanette into the coach. The man laughed and climbed into the coach after Tony.

"Where are you taking us?" asked Tony, holding her close.

"Where we can keep you well hidden. It's a long trip so you may as well relax. No need to hang onto her. If she bounces over this way, I'll catch 'er."

Tony moved his arm from around her shoulders but kept a tight grip on her hand.

Jeanette held onto his arm with her other hand, more tightly when the coachman cracked the whip and the carriage lurched into motion. Within minutes they were traveling at full speed, around ten miles per hour. They would need to change horses every hour or so if they kept that pace. She worked on a way to elude the kidnappers if they stopped at a posting inn, but she suspected they would not change teams in so public a place.

Father, protect us. Don't let these men hurt us. Please help the Templetons quickly realize something is wrong, and help Kiernan find us. Show us how to get away.

Trying to recognize the scenery, she kept praying as the miles rolled by. Nothing looked familiar. They moved in a general northwest direction, often at less than full speed along the twisting and turning back roads. The turnpikes would have allowed more speed, but they also had many tollgates with pike men who would remember a black coach with three outriders.

Occasionally, Tony would ask how she was, and she would tell him she was fine. They both knew she wasn't; she was frightened half to death. He was calm but also clearly frightened. He offered comfort often with a gentle word or touch.

Father, I know you will protect us. Give me the faith not to be afraid. Help me to keep my wits. Oh, God, please don't let anything happen to

Tony. Don't let him be hurt or die. You've promised not to give us more than we can bear, and that would be beyond endurance.

They changed horses twice, turning off the main road to meet a man and four fresh horses sheltered in the woods. Each time, the gang leader ordered them to stay inside the coach while he got out and talked to the others.

As they pulled back onto the main road the second time, Jeanie hung onto the edge of the window, letting her handkerchief slip from her fingers. When the guards following them did not stop to retrieve it, she breathed a sigh of relief. It might have been trampled into the dust beneath the horses' hooves, but if it was found, Kiernan and her mother would recognize the tiny purple Scottish thistle and her initial embroidered in the corner.

For the third stop, they traveled slightly farther from the road and into an abandoned barn. The leader told Jeanette and Tony to get out and stretch their legs. She left her bonnet and reticule on the seat and moved stiffly down the steps.

"What time is it?" she asked Tony as they walked around inside the building under the close eye of their kidnappers.

He tugged on the gold chain fob, pulled his watch from the small pocket in his waistband, and flicked open the cover. "Half past four." They had left the Norton estate at one o'clock.

"Kiernan will have people out looking for us. The Templetons would have gone back when we didna catch up to them."

He frowned. "We must have traveled at least thirty miles. I'm certain they are searching, but do not raise your hopes too much, darling."

"They will find us, Tony. God will guide them." She started to tell him about the perfume bottle and handkerchief but stopped as the gang leader walked toward them.

"Planning your escape?"

Tony put his arms around her, glancing at the armed men who stood guard at each end of the barn. "We aren't that foolish. I don't suppose you brought anything to eat? Miss Macpherson must be famished by now."

"I didn't, but you did. My man noticed your picnic basket and put it in the boot." The kidnapper looked at Jeanette. "Come, my pretty, show me what rich people eat."

She hesitated, uncomfortable with the way he had stared at her for much of the trip. She had no interest in food, but common sense told her to eat. Reluctantly, she stepped away from Tony and followed the man to the picnic basket which had been set out on a bundle of hay.

The leader opened the basket and looked back at Tony. "You, too, Drake. Such extravagance. You brought enough for all of us." He turned back to Jeanette, his gaze moving over her slowly. "Can't see a pretty thing like you eatin' half of this."

The cook had sent along sliced roast beef, buttered bread, cheese, figs, four strawberry tarts, and the customary bottle of wine. Jeanie put some meat and a slice of cheese between two pieces of bread and took a bite. In spite of receiving a drink of water each time they stopped, her mouth was so dry she could hardly swallow.

Tony made himself a similar sandwich and took a few figs. The leader rummaged through the basket and handed Jeanette a white linen napkin and a strawberry tart.

"Sweets for the sweet," he said with a grin.

"I couldna eat it." She handed it back to him. "Give it to one of your men."

He shrugged, setting it aside. Removing food for himself, the wine, and the two crystal goblets, he tossed the basket to one of his henchmen. He poured two glasses of wine, handing one to Jeanette. "Share with him."

She drank some of the wine, thankful to ease her parched throat, and handed the glass to Tony. He took a long drink, handing the rest back to her.

The kidnapper had already finished his wine and poured himself another glass. He held the bottle toward Jeanette, and she let him refill theirs. Since they commonly drank wine with most meals, she knew she would not become drunk. When the man tipped his glass up, downing the liquid in one long drink, she grew more uneasy.

"Hey, Gray, share that with us," said one of the other kidnappers in a raspy voice. "We've been ridin' in your dust the whole way."

The leader grinned and handed him the bottle. "This will take care of it. Goes down like honey."

Thank you, Lord. Though one man might become drunk on what was left in the bottle, with the four of them sharing it, no one would.

Gray settled comfortably on the hay and watched Jeanette as she ate. "Such polite manners. I didn't think Scots had manners."

"Mind your tongue," snapped Tony, earning a glare from the man. At his sharp tone, one of the other men swung around, pointing his pistol at Tony.

"You mind your tone, Drake." The kidnapper unfolded his lanky frame and walked over to stand in front of them. "Or you'll wish you had."

Jeanette's heart pounded. He looked as if he wanted to bash in Tony's face. "Tell me, sir, why do you have such a low opinion of Scots?" she asked softly, drawing his attention. "Do you know any?"

Gray looked down at her. "Maybe a half dozen. Thieves and cut-throats, all."

"That would explain their lack of manners."

He grinned. "Aye, it would. I suppose a lady like you, raised in a big, fine house with fancy meals, would know how to be polite, whether she was Scottish or English."

Jeanette shrugged. "We were no' raised in a big, fine house or on a grand estate. My father was a forester, but Mother still taught us how to behave."

The kidnapper's eyebrows rose in surprise. "You don't live in a big house?"

"We do now. A drafty old castle. My brother didna inherit the title until recently. Before that he was with the Gordon Highlanders fighting Napoleon for many years. He can easily forget how to be polite," she added quietly. "I dinna envy you when he catches you. He willna be forgiving."

"He ain't gonna catch us." He put his hands on his hips and smiled confidently.

"Oh, but he will. He is relentless and a born warrior, as is his friend Gabriel who is with us. They were raised in the Highlands with my father as their teacher. They can read the land as if it were a travel guide. They will find you, and your payment willna be in money." She caught a glimmer of fear in the man's eyes. "We have a dungeon in our castle, and Kiernan knows many ways to torture a man." Not that he was proficient at them. He had once read a book about some of the gruesome things they found rusting in the dungeon.

"He won't find you until we want him to and where we want him to." He stepped toward her. "We've rested long enough. There's a necessary out back." Gray took hold of her arm, propelling her out the barn toward a wooden privy almost hidden in the weeds. "Use it or suffer. I ain't stopping again."

Jeanette lifted her chin and walked toward the building, hoping she appeared calmer than she felt. She dreaded the filth, the smell...the cobwebs and spiders. *Dinna think about them. You canna fall apart now.* Opening the door, she gasped softly. There wasn't a cobweb or spider to be found. The inside had been thoroughly scrubbed.

When she returned to the barn, she stopped by the wide door where Gray waited. "Thank you for cleaning it."

"Well, now, ain't you easy to please," he murmured, taking a step toward her. She edged toward the opening, but he blocked her way, sliding his hand around her waist, pulling her toward him.

She put her hands against his chest and shoved, but to no avail. "Let me pass."

"Not just yet." Gray held her firmly against him with one hand, touching the soft curls along the back of her neck with the other. He trailed his fingers down her throat, pausing over her thudding pulse. Moving his fingers lower, he brushed them back and forth across her collarbone.

Please, God…

"I ain't never tasted a real lady," he said softly. "I'd wager you're sweeter than other women."

She shook her head. "Let me go," she whispered even as his arm tightened around her.

"Take your filthy hands off her!" Tony grabbed the man's arm, jerking him away from her. She stumbled, falling to the ground as Gray spun toward Tony, swinging at him. Tony ducked and put up his fists, jabbing Gray in the jaw before two of the guards captured him from behind. They pinned his arms, restraining him as he tried to pull free. "Leave her alone!"

"You ain't in any position to give orders," said Gray with a sneer. He punched him in the stomach, and Tony bent forward with a groan. The men kept holding him as their leader drew back to hit him again.

Jeanette scrambled to her feet, flying at Gray, pummeling his face and arm with her fists.

Swearing, he stepped back, dodging her blows. He caught her hands and swept them around behind her, pinning them against the small of her back as he shoved her against the side of the building. "You little wildcat! Be still!"

He gripped her wrists with one hand, pressing her hard against the building. "I'm gonna enjoy tamin' you," he snarled, grasping a handful of hair, rendering her immobile and bringing tears to her eyes.

"No!" cried Tony, struggling furiously to break free.

Gray looked at him, his smile cold and calculating. He turned back to Jeanette, a frightening promise in his eyes. "Oh, yes."

He brought his mouth down hard on hers—bruising, demanding, taking until she whimpered in pain and fear. When he stopped abruptly, she thought she saw a hint of regret in his expression. He massaged her head with his fingertips, then moved his fingers from her hair and wiped a tear from her cheek. "Don't make me angry," he warned in a whisper. "I don't want to hurt you, but I will if you push me too far. Understand?"

Terrified, she nodded.

Still struggling against his captors, Tony swore at him.

Gray tensed, his eyes narrowing in anger.

"Don't hurt him," she pleaded softly. "Please."

He stared at her for a second and nodded curtly. He glanced at Tony and shook his head. "I've never met a bigger fool," he muttered.

"Get in the coach." He released her, stepping back just far enough for her to brush by him. "Put him up top," he ordered. When Jeanette stumbled, he gently grabbed her arm to steady her.

Going pale, Tony looked from her to Gray, his expression filled with fear. For the first time, she questioned whether Kiernan could find them before something horrible happened. She climbed into the carriage unaided, curling up into a ball in the corner of the seat. "Father, I'm so afraid," she whispered.

Trust me.

21

KIERNAN AND GABRIEL STUDIED THE ROADWAY and surrounding ground at the intersection north of Chipping Campden. Fletcher said Tony and Jeanette had been seen passing through the village on their way to Stratford-upon-Avon, but he could find no one who had seen them afterwards.

There were tracks of four or five vehicles on the main road. Only one coach, four horses with riders, and a curricle had traveled along the narrow crossroads. The ground had been damp enough earlier in the day to leave clear tracks—and footprints. Kiernan backtracked the footprints from the middle of the intersection to thirty feet down the road toward Chipping Campden.

Jordan, Thaddeus, and Mr. Norton stood some ten feet farther back. Behind them, forty men—the other house guests as well as workers and tenants from the Nortons' estate—waited for orders to begin the search. "Can you make any sense of it?" asked Norton.

Grimly, Kiernan nodded and motioned for the three men to join him. He pointed to one impression in the roadway. "These are the tracks of a two-wheeled vehicle, probably a curricle judging from the spacing. They were stopped here. The horses shuffled around quite a bit which likely means they were uneasy." He glanced at

Gabriel who moved slowly along the side of the roadway, carefully searching the grass.

"You mean someone forced them to stop?" asked Norton.

"Yes. Afterwards, the curricle turned to the right. There is only one additional set of carriage tracks on the other road, a four-wheeled coach that stopped in the middle of the crossroads. It was accompanied by four outriders." He pointed to the other hoof prints. "See how the riders came over here to the curricle?"

"Why, it looks like they surrounded it!" exclaimed Jordan. "Two in front of it and two at the back."

"Precisely," said Kiernan. "Two people, a man and a woman, got out of the curricle and walked to the coach. Some of the footprints have been destroyed by traffic, but you can see where they climbed down here and started toward the crossroads. There are matching prints by the coach tracks. Jeanette would never go off like that willingly. She wouldna lie or deliberately cause anyone worry. Someone else got into the curricle and drove it off in that direction."

"But how do we know it was Drake and Miss Macpherson?" asked Norton.

"I canna tell for certain looking at the tracks. But right now, it's the only thing that makes sense."

Gabe bent down in the grass a few feet from them. He straightened with a heartsick expression and looked at Kiernan. "It was Jeanie." He cleared his throat and held out his hand to Kiernan. "The lass had her wits about her." He glanced at the other men. "Kiernan gave her this for her birthday."

Kiernan took the silver perfume bottle, a cold knot of fear hardening in his stomach. *Oh, God, no! Dear God, dinna let them hurt her!* Pain and horror engulfed him, and he walked quickly away from the others to the hedgerow, keeping his back to them. *Why? How could you let someone take Jeanie? She's never harmed a soul in her life!*

271

Until they reached the crossroads and he read the tracks, Kiernan had barely considered the possibility of kidnapping. When he first heard they had not arrived at their destination, he had immediately dismissed the suggestion of elopement. Tony knew he approved of him. If Jeanie wanted to marry him, there would be no need to run away to Gretna Green. He had hoped they made a wrong turn, or that one of the horses had come up lame, or they had broken a wheel. His worst fear had been of a carriage wreck and serious injuries.

Not abduction! Dear, gentle, sweet lass. He ached to have Mariah with him to give him strength, to help him believe his sister would return safely.

He felt a hand on his shoulder and looked up to see Gabriel standing beside him. "When I think of what they might do to her—" Kiernan's chest tightened, and he could barely breathe. He clenched his fists and closed his eyes.

"We have to believe they willna hurt her. They want money."

"All they have to do is keep her alive until they have the money. What's to keep them from killing her and Tony then?" *Dear God, I wish you'd never let me inherit a farthing!*

"We have to trust God to keep them safe." Gabriel squeezed his shoulder. "Faith is all we have. Faith and a small army to search for them. We canna do anything standing here."

Taking a deep, ragged breath, Kiernan turned abruptly, striding swiftly back to Norton, Jordan, and Thaddeus. "They've gone to the northwest, but I want the whole area checked in case they doubled back somehow. Gabriel, Thaddeus, and I will follow the coach."

"Take as many of my men with you as you need," said Norton. "You don't know for certain how many you'll be up against."

Kiernan nodded. "Jordan, I'd appreciate it if you would stay with Mother and Mariah. Mother needs your faith and strength to see her through this. She's just now becoming herself again after my father's death. If something happens to Jeanie, I dinna know if she could bear it."

"Yes, my lord. I will do my best. I expect there will be some kind of message from the kidnappers. How shall I handle it?"

"Jeanette and Tony must be returned to us before I give them any money. I'll make the exchange at the same time if necessary, but they willna get anything unless I know Jeanie and Tony are safe."

"What if they want the money before you return?"

Kiernan considered the question. "They will know I dinna have a lot with me and will have to get it from the Bank of London."

"If there is a time problem, I will go ahead and pay the ransom," said Norton. "I have funds in a local bank."

"I will see to the exchange if we cannot locate you in time," said Jordan.

"I appreciate the offer, but that is a risk I canna let you take."

"We may not have any choice. God will go with me, sir. I will tell them I am your secretary." Jordan smiled slightly. "If they demand that you deliver it, I'll simply tell them you are unavailable. If they know anything about you, they will realize that you are looking for your sister, not sitting back and waiting for orders from them."

"Very well." Kiernan led them back to the other men, told them what they had concluded and gave instructions for the search. He asked for twelve men to ride with him, and because Lord Idington was an ex-military man, he put him in charge of dispersing the others. "Go by twos. Check every woods and thicket, every building—business, house, barn, corncrib—anywhere they might hide." He looked at Idington. "I would suggest that you run the search from Norton's estate. That will give them one central place to report what they find."

"Good idea. I'll keep a few men at the ready to send word to you.

You're going northwest, you say?"

"Yes. I'll send someone back to keep you informed of our general location." Kiernan slowly looked around the group of men, some wealthy, some not. When called upon to help, they came instantly and without question. "This may be dangerous. There is a chance you might be hurt or even killed. If you feel you canna take the risk, no matter what the reason, please return to the estate with my blessing. No one will question you or think ill of you. I thank you all and know my sister will, too, when we find her. Go with God."

They mounted the horses Norton had put at their disposal. When Norton's men joined them, Fletcher and Stanwell were with them. Kiernan and Delia's husband had become good friends so he was not surprised that he would ride along.

Fletcher's willingness to go did not surprise him, either. After the incident at the ball, Card would do anything to help Jeanie. Kiernan had become acquainted with the man over the past few weeks and thought highly of him. He might have made a fool of himself on the dance floor, but in every other situation, Fletcher had a level head and plenty of common sense.

"Goin' with you, milord," said Card.

Kiernan thanked him and the others as they started. They slowed at every adjoining lane to make certain the coach had not left the road. They soon realized the vehicle would be easy to follow as long as the ground had been wet enough to leave a clear impression. The coach's front right wheel wobbled slightly, making a distinctive track. Two riders had gone ahead of the carriage, and the one following it had preferred the middle of the road, leaving the markings left by the wheels completely untouched.

Picking up their pace, they rode for nearly an hour, stopping where the carriage had turned off the road. They followed the tracks down a bumpy lane into a small woods. Judging by the number of hoof prints stomped into the ground beneath the trees, the kidnappers had changed teams.

They returned to the road, easily picking up the trail again. They did not go far before Kiernan and Gabriel saw a new concern. Slowly but steadily, mile after mile, the wobbling grew worse.

Jeanette watched Gray as he stared out the window, his expression dark and brooding. He had not said a word and had barely looked at her the whole time they had been alone. He was unlike any man she had ever met, and he frightened her, but at least he had stayed on the other side of the coach. She worried about Tony riding on top with hardly anything to hold onto and wanted desperately to have him by her side.

Concluding that Gray did not intend to attack her, she relaxed enough to turn her attention to the passing scenery. They had gone through several villages and skirted around a larger town, but it was all new to her. The road was rougher, or maybe she was so exhausted it only seemed that way. Drawing her plaid tighter, she leaned her head against the padded side of the carriage and closed her eyes.

Sleep eluded her, but despite being jostled uncomfortably from side to side, Jeanie gained fragments of rest. She shivered as the late afternoon chill reached the inside of the coach.

Seconds later, warmth covered her, and she felt Gray's breath upon her cheek. Opening her eyes with a start, she met his gaze as he leaned over her, tucking his frock coat around her shoulders.

"You looked cold," he said, sitting back across from her.

"I am. Thank you."

"You're welcome." He watched her intently.

"Tony will be cold," she ventured. "He is only wearing a light jacket."

"It would be justice if the bloke froze." He scowled and looked out the window. Seconds later, his angry gaze was back on her. "He doesn't deserve you."

"Anthony Drake is a fine and decent man."

Gray snorted. "He's a part of this whole thing."

"Dinna be ridiculous." Jeanette glared at him.

He glared back. "Where was he last night? In Warwick on business for his father?"

"Yes, but you've obviously had someone spying on us. You had to so you'd know our plans."

"Meeting us was his business. His brother is deep in dun territory and made it worse by goin' to a moneylender. Now, he stands to lose everything he owns and all his father has, too. You weren't bein' swept off your feet fast enough so his father hired me and the lads to kidnap you. We had to meet with young Tony to work out the particulars. Why do you think he made sure you were the last to leave?"

"I dinna believe you." *I will do everything in my power to avoid hurting you.* Doubt gnawed at her as she remembered his odd expression before uttering those words and how relieved he was when she mentioned that she would have a generous dowry. *I truly care for you. I hope you know that.* Why had he insisted she go back for her parasol when she did not really need it? Was it just so they could be the last to leave? "Tony would no' hurt me; he wouldna put me through this. He cares for me."

"Aye, he does, and this hasn't been easy for him. But he cares for his family more."

An image of his miserable expression when he left for Warwick swam before her mind's eye. *He didna want to do this.* "He wouldna do this," she insisted in a broken voice. *He would do anything to protect his mother.*

"He was the one who ordered us to clean the privy, make sure there wasn't a spider or cobweb to be found. Said you hated spiders, was scared to death of 'em. He didn't want to frighten you," Gray said, wearing a bemused frown. "It almost seemed like he didn't think being kidnapped would scare you."

Tears welled up in her eyes. She shook her head in denial though he spoke the truth. Only Tony would have known of her fear. But how could he think abducting her wouldn't frighten her just as much?

Gray slammed the seat cushion with his hand and swore proficiently, but Jeanette was beyond being embarrassed by his words. Her pain was too great.

"How much do I have to hurt you to make you understand what he's doing?" asked Gray, shaking his head with a scowl.

I understand! She wanted to scream at him to stop but no words would come, nothing could get past the burning ache in her throat, the searing pain in her heart.

"He even told me to make advances toward you so he could look like a hero," said Gray quietly.

"Liar!" Sobbing, Jeanie went at him, fists swinging, but he anticipated the move and blocked her attack. Hauling her onto his lap, he circled her with his arms and held her still in spite of her struggling. "Did he tell you to kiss me?" she sobbed. "To hurt me?"

"No." He pressed her head against his shoulder. "I was only supposed to act like I was going to. I'm a blackguard; always have been. There's not much I wouldn't do for the right price. For all his fancy ways and noble play-actin', he's no better than me. Knowin' that you thought the bloke was grand because he got hurt supposedly trying to protect you irritated the spit out of me. When you risked your neck trying to help him, I lost my temper." He sighed wearily, smoothing his fingers lightly over her hair. "I'm sorry I hurt you."

277

The emotional explosion drained her. His revelations left her numb. She tried to sit up and was surprised when he let her, even more surprised when he lifted her across the carriage and set her down on the opposite seat.

He picked his coat up from the floor and handed it to her. "You're trembling. Put it on."

She looked down at her quaking body, hazily realizing she ached from the cold. Fumbling, she put on his coat. *He has to be lying. Tony wouldna do something so terrible.* But why would Gray say such mean things? She was so tired. All she wanted was to go to sleep and wake up in her bed in Scotland. Her eyes drifted closed. *Just a wee nap. Then I can think.*

She barely noticed when Gray leaned over and picked up the plaid, spreading it over her like a blanket. She felt him move across the coach and sit beside her, taking her hand between his, rubbing briskly.

"Sit up and talk to me before you faint," he ordered.

"Never faint," she mumbled, but she had the vague impression he might be right. She forced her eyes open and sat up, watching him rub her hand. "Why did you say those mean things about Tony?" she asked sadly.

He frowned and rubbed harder. "You still don't believe me?"

"I dinna want to believe you." But she did. Too many things confirmed what he said. "Why did you tell me?"

"Because you're probably goin' to marry him. Someday you'd find out what he did, and you'd be trapped." He shrugged. "Just didn't seem right."

"Then you're going to take me back?"

"Can't. There's too much money in it." He tucked her hand beneath the plaid and picked up the other one.

"You have a strange set of principles, Mr. Gray."

"Just Gray. No mister. The men expect to be paid very well for this job. If I tell them I've changed my mind and we're taking you back, they'd likely slit my throat and continue on as planned."

"My brother would pay you ten times as much."

"Your brother would see us hang from the nearest gallows."

"No' if you helped me."

"Maybe, maybe not. I can't take that chance."

She pulled her hand from his, slipping it under the plaid. Jeanie felt sick. She almost wished she could faint so her mind would not torment her. He had to be telling the truth. There was no reason for him to make it up.

A sudden jolt rocked the carriage, throwing Jeanie hard against Gray and slamming them both against the side of the coach. An eternity later, it came to a shuddering halt, leaning alarmingly to the side.

"Are you hurt?" asked Gray.

"No' much." She tried to move off him, but the tilt of the coach made it impossible. "Are you?"

"Not enough to worry about." He glanced out the window. "I'd say we broke a wheel."

The carriage tipped farther as the coachman and Tony climbed down. Gray grinned and put his arm around her. "No sense fightin' it. We're meant to be together."

"And the fairies dance in the moonlight," she muttered. Ignoring his soft laugh, she reached for the door handle, but he pulled her back.

"You'll fall on your nose."

Disgusted, she sat still, waiting for someone to help them out of the carriage.

The door flew open, and Tony glared at them, his face scarlet with rage. His furious gaze raked over her, from her disheveled hair to the coat she wore to Gray's arm curled around her. "Obviously, I've been worrying myself sick for naught. You seem to have made the best of the situation, my dear," he said sarcastically. "How irritating to discover I've trod so carefully all these weeks when I didn't have to."

Jeanette stared at him in disbelief.

He reached through the opening and hauled her out of the coach with a bruising grip on her upper arms. The instant her feet touched the ground, he released her. In one smooth movement, Tony spun back toward the doorway and punched Gray in the mouth. "You were only supposed to frighten her a little, not cozy up alone with her. She's mine! I want her untouched."

It's true! Like a fool, she had clung to a faint hope that Gray had been lying. A wave of dizziness and nausea swept over her. She took a deep breath and another. Anger came to her rescue, forcing despair momentarily aside. "I am no' yours, Tony Drake, and I never will be. No' after what you've done."

Startled, Tony looked at her. It was his turn to stare in disbelief.

"How much was the ransom, Tony? How much do you think I'm worth?"

The color drained from his face as he realized his error. He tried to dissemble. "I don't know what you mean."

"Do you take me for a complete addle-cove? It's obvious you're behind this whole mad scheme."

"That's ridiculous."

The driver wandered around the end of the coach in a daze, blood dripping from a deep cut on his hand. "What'll we do now, Mr. Tony? It'll be morning before we can get a new wheel."

Tony groaned and closed his eyes, shaking his head. "I told Father this wouldn't work."

Jeanette glared at him. "Give me your handkerchief before your coachman bleeds to death."

Tony pulled his handkerchief out of his pocket and handed it to her without a word.

She went to the coachman, noting a large, purple bump on his forehead. "Do you have a kerchief, sir?"

He nodded and winced. "In me coat pocket, miss."

She folded Tony's handkerchief into a thick pad and placed it over the wound, instructing the coachman to hold it there. Digging his kerchief out of his pocket, she tied it snugly over the pad and around his hand. "You had better sit down." She guided him over to a large rock beside the road. When he was seated, she went back to Tony. "That man needs a doctor. He has a lump the size of a goose egg on his head, and his hand needs stitching."

Tony waved away her concerns. "He's had worse and healed fine without a doctor."

"You must be well acquainted."

Tony sighed. "He is my father's coachman. Jeanette, I'm truly sorry for all this. I do care for you, but I had no choice." Behind him, Gray rolled his eyes and shook his head in disgust.

"There had to be a better choice than kidnapping me!"

"I favored a dash to Gretna Green myself," Tony said absently, pacing up and down beside the coach. He stopped and smiled. "That's what we shall do."

"You canna be serious. Tony, look at me." When he focused on her, she said very clearly, "I willna marry you. No' ever."

"Of course you will. If we elope, you'll have to. All that time on the road alone with me is enough to ruin you completely. The only way to save your reputation is to become my bride. Branderee will not want any more scandal, so he'll pay my brother's debts. It will all work out perfectly."

"You've gone daft."

Tony ignored her. "Gray, ride to Worcester and rent a good

coach." He pulled several bank notes from his pocket. "This should be more than enough to put us on the road. We can hire post horses for the rest of the trip."

Jeanette unbuttoned Gray's coat and removed it, handing it back to him. "Thank you, sir. I find I am no longer cold enough to need it."

Gray put on his coat. "I'll send Philips after the coach. I don't know how to drive one."

"Whatever. Just get it done quickly. We have no time to waste."

Gray nodded and walked over to one of the guards. After a brief discussion, the man mounted his horse and galloped off toward the last large town they had passed.

Jeanette leaned inside the coach and withdrew her reticule and plaid, wrapping it around her. Without a word, she turned and started walking down the road.

"Where do you think you're going?" shouted Tony.

"To Worcester."

"It's ten miles. Come back here." When she ignored his command, Tony ordered one of the guards to bring her back.

"I'll do it," said Gray, going after her. When he caught up with her, he fell in step beside her. "You'll never get there in those shoes. It will be dark in less than an hour and probably start raining in a few minutes. It's dangerous for a woman to be out on a road alone."

"I'm no' going to Scotland with him."

"It's a long way. There will be better opportunities to escape than this one."

A drop of rain hit her on the forehead. Then another. Within minutes, a light, steady rain was falling. With a resigned sigh, Jeanette turned back toward the coach. She took shelter alone on a stump beneath a tree. "Father, help me find a way out of this. I dinna know if Kiernan can track us past Worcester. There are too many roads there. Please send someone to help me. Someone I can trust."

Jeanette was not a person who could hold on to anger for very long, even when she wanted to. Misery soon overcame her. *How could he win my affection and then abuse it so? How can he still say he cares for me? Does he think this is some grand adventure I'll soon forget?* Tears filled her eyes, but she refused to give in to weeping, not yet. *I want to go home, Lord. Please send someone to take me home.*

The coachman sat huddled uncomfortably beneath another tree, while one guard stood beside him, watching the road and her. The other guard had taken up a position under a tree several hundred feet behind them. A few minutes earlier, Tony and Gray had decided to unhitch the team.

Though she was somewhat protected by the tree boughs, the rain soon soaked her skirt. The plaid had protected her head and upper body for a while, but in time it too grew wet. Cold and stiff from sitting, she decided to move around.

When she stood, the guard came toward her. "I'm going to move around a bit," she said. A shiver jarred her teeth. "I'm too cold sitting there. I'll walk a little way down the road and back around the coach." He nodded and resumed his place under the meager shelter of the tree.

Jeanie took a few steps and shook her legs in an attempt to speed up the circulation. She walked a little farther, rubbing her arms beneath the plaid, then turned back. Tony and Gray were talking as she approached the carriage. Moving quietly beside it, she stopped when she could understand them.

"She's exhausted and soaked," said Gray. "You're liable to have a sick bride on your hands if you make it all the way to Scotland. Don't see how you can anyway, with her brother hot on your heels."

"I am concerned about her health," said Tony. "Mine, too, with this nasty rain and cold. I've decided to spend the night in Worcester."

"Branderee may catch you there."

"I'm counting on it. We'll rent a couple of rooms, have a good meal, and see that she's nice and dry in a warm bed. When she's sound asleep, I'll quietly join her. Don't look at me like that. I don't intend to ravish her. All I need is for Branderee to find us together. He will have to agree to a quick wedding."

"And what if he doesn't find you?" snapped Gray.

"You will earn the rest of your money by letting it slip that we are together upstairs. There will probably be some members of the *ton* spending the night. Such an *on dit* will be impossible to pass up. You should even be able to persuade a gentleman or two to take a peek for themselves."

"And how am I supposed to do that?"

"With a wager. Jeanette has such a flawless reputation, they will instantly go against you if you're willing to put money on it."

"Gentlemen in a pig's eye. The whole lot of you are a disgusting bunch of rotters."

"Not all," said Tony dryly. "Why should you complain when you stand to make money off them?"

Jeanette did not wait around to hear the rest of the conversation. Head reeling, she walked back over to her spot beneath the tree. There she could quietly think out loud without anyone hearing. "I'll have to try and find a maid or someone to sleep in the room." She rubbed her reticule between her fingers, feeling the coins nestled in a small bag inside it. Kiernan insisted that she always carry money with her. A well of love filled her heart. "When I see you, big brother, I'm going to hug you so tight you squeak."

Her thoughts went back to Tony's plan. "Dear God, I'm trying so hard to trust you, but I'm scared. Surely, it isna your will for me to be forced into marriage with such a man. Show me the way out of this mess soon, Lord. Please, make it soon."

22

THE CURRICLE CAME DOWN THE ROAD at a fast clip. When Tony spotted it, he moved to stand beside Jeanette. "Be good, my dear. You don't want the gentleman hurt. I'm told Gray and his men can be quite ruthless."

"No more than you."

He shook his head. "Dear Jeanie, is that the way to talk to your intended? This all will pass. In time you'll understand why I had to take such drastic measures. You'll forgive me, and we shall make a go of it. I can make you happy, if you will but give me a chance."

She stared at him in amazement; he appeared to actually believe it. "The only way to make me happy is to take me home." She stood as the carriage approached, anxious to somehow relay her distress without being obvious.

Tony stepped closer and put his arm firmly around her waist. "Follow my lead, love, and play along."

"I'm no' your love, so dinna say it again." She watched the curricle slow and gasped when she saw who was driving. *Dominic!*

Tony laughed softly. "How sad to have your hopes dashed so soon. The notorious Thorne would never exert the energy to help a young innocent. Now, if you were a widow, I'd be worried. Still, we'll tell him a tale for his sake and to preserve the secrecy of our little endeavor."

Dominic drew the curricle to a halt in front of them. He tipped his hat to Jeanette, studying her intently. "Miss Macpherson."

"Mr. Thorne." She nodded but said nothing more as Tony's hand pressed harder against her side beneath the plaid.

With a mild frown, Dominic turned his gaze to Tony. "Drake, may I be of assistance?"

"Thank you, but no. I've sent a man into Worcester to secure another carriage. He should be back any minute. Thankfully, no one was seriously injured."

"Miss Macpherson, may I drive you into Worcester? I could take you to the Red Boar Inn. The innkeeper and his wife would be more than happy to see to your welfare and comfort."

Jeanie flinched as Tony's fingers dug deeper. "Thank you for your concern, Mr. Thorne, but as Tony said, his man should be back any minute now with another coach." She wiped a wet tendril off her forehead with a trembling hand and met his gaze. *Help me. I'm no' here willingly.*

Dominic's eyes narrowed minutely.

Help me. She tried to ease away from Tony, but he squeezed so hard she almost cried out.

Dominic glanced around. "What's this? No chaperon?" he asked with an unconcerned smile. "Don't tell me you managed to slip away from your brother and Mariah?"

"Wish us happy, Thorne. Jeanette has agreed to become my wife. We are on our way to spend the week with my parents who have not had the honor of meeting her. They are visiting some cousins in Stourbridge. We would have been there long ago if not for losing the wheel."

"How nice. I do indeed." He looked at Jeanette. "May your highest hopes quickly come true." He scanned the gray, rainy sky. "Such bothersome weather. Well, if you're certain I cannot be of assistance,

I'll be off. I'd hoped to make it home before nightfall, but it appears I'll be late."

As he drove away, Tony laughed and loosened his hold on Jeanette. "I wonder who he has waiting for him this time. I'd forgotten he has an estate around here somewhere. One of several, I believe."

Fighting tears, Jeanette sank despondently down on the stump, staring as Dominic disappeared around a bend in the road. *He drove away. How could he leave me here? Couldna he see something was wrong?* A savage chill shook her. *Lord, I'm so cold. So alone.* Her throat ached. Her whole body ached. *Where are you, God?*

I'm here, child. The words were a soothing balm to her heart. *I have not forsaken you.*

"Thank you, Father," she whispered. She leaned her throbbing head in her hand and closed her eyes.

"Yes, that's good. You rest a bit. I need to talk to Gray anyway."

Jeanette had no idea how long she sat on the stump with her eyes closed. A minute, a few minutes, maybe an hour. Her teeth chattered, and her feet and fingers were like ice. She remembered Kiernan being concerned because ladies' fashions were made of such lightweight material. He had insisted she have a heavy wool pelisse made up because the spring weather was so unpredictable. Unfortunately, that wonderful, warm coat was back at the Nortons' estate. "Mam must be sick with worry. Please comfort her, Lord."

Plunk. Jeanette opened her eyes, glancing at the ground. She couldn't see anything different. *Plunk.* There it was again, a quiet, out of the ordinary noise. *Thunk.* Startled, she sat up straight as something small bounced lightly off her back.

Smoothing back her sopping hair, she looked over at the men. Tony was talking to Gray, who appeared bored. The coachman snored beneath a tree. One guard stood across the road, staring in the direction of Worcester. The other sat on a log, half asleep.

She stood, stretching her back, and rotating her neck. Yawning, she turned around casually and searched the woods behind her. Dominic poked his head around a thick clump of trees.

Excitement and joy surged through her, and she barely held back a cry of relief. *Thank you, God!* Dominic ducked back behind the trees when she started walking slowly toward him.

"Jeanette, where are you going?" Tony asked sharply.

She turned around and glared at him. "To tend to private matters."

"Oh." He turned back to Gray, politely ignoring her.

She picked her way through the bushes until she reached Dominic. When she stepped behind the thick clump of trees, he gathered her in his arms.

"Do you need rescuing, my dear?" he asked in the kindest voice she had ever heard.

"Please." She clung to him and buried her face against his chest, remembering another time and place he had held her so gently. Her relief then had only been a fraction of what it was now.

His arms tightened. "Did they hurt you?" he whispered, wrath vibrating in every word.

She shook her head, not willing to put him in danger over a few minor physical hurts.

"Let us make haste before they come after you." He slowly released her.

"I'll see if they are looking." She stepped away from the tree. Tony still had his back to her, and Gray was gazing down the road, probably desperately wishing his man would hurry up. "It's clear."

Dominic stepped cautiously from behind the trees and took her hand. He pushed aside the long, straggly limbs of a bush, holding them clear until she moved past. Jeanie glanced back toward the road to find Gray looking straight at them. She stiffened, and Dominic halted, looking back, also.

A tiny smile touched the kidnapper's face as he gave them a faint nod. He shifted his position, turning his back to them.

They did not wait around for him to change his mind. When they reached Dominic's curricle, he quickly peeled off his greatcoat and helped her put it on. Lifting her into the curricle, he covered her legs with the coat before rushing around to the other side. He drove slowly down an old, grassy lane until they reached the main road some distance from Tony's coach.

"We must hurry in case he sends a rider after us. Can you hold on?"

"I'd hold on with my teeth if I had to."

He smiled and touched her cheek with his gloved hand. "I don't think that will be necessary. It is only about five miles to Thornridge. We will soon have you warm and dry."

A few minutes later as they sped down the road, she swayed toward him. He quickly put his arm around her. "Bear up a little longer, angel. I need my hands free to drive. Why don't you lean against me and hold onto my arm?"

When he moved his arm from around her, she did as he suggested. *Thank you for saving me, Lord. Thank you for this man and the goodness in him.* "I knew you'd come."

"Me?" Startled, he peered down at her.

"Well, no' you particularly, though I'm glad you're the one he chose."

He frowned. "He?"

"God. I asked him to send someone to help me. Someone I could trust."

He made an odd sound, but said nothing, merely flicked the reins to keep the horses moving. Several minutes passed. "You have been at the Norton house party, have you not?"

"Yes. Tony and I were going with the Templetons and Fletcher and Olivia to see Shakespeare's home today."

"Your brother and Mariah did not go?"

"No. The others were some distance ahead of us. Tony arranged for us to be the last to leave."

"To put his plan into action. Was he forcing you to elope?"

"No' at first. Tony's family is desperate for money, so he and those men kidnapped me. They were going to hold me for ransom. They made it look like he was being kidnapped, too. Later, I learned he was behind it." She briefly told most of what had happened. "When I found out about his part in the kidnapping, he decided to go to Gretna Green instead. I told him I wouldna marry him, but he was certain I would change my mind. I know Kiernan and others are out looking for us."

"I'm sure he is. He is not the type to sit and wait for you to turn up. I'll dispatch men to cover the roads coming into Worcester from the south. They should be able to intercept him and tell him you are safe."

By the time they halted in front of his large country manor, Jeanette had reached the limit of her endurance. A footman held the horses still while Dominic climbed over her legs and hopped to the ground. He lifted her from the curricle and carried her through the open door into the entryway. "Fetch Mrs. Hastings," he ordered a second footman.

Jeanie curled her arm around his neck and rested her head against his shoulder as he carried her up a long flight of stairs. Nudging open the door to a bedroom, he lowered her carefully into an armchair by a warm fire.

Wearily, Jeanie rested her head against the back of the chair, letting her gaze roam slowly around the room. It was a man's room, with heavy furniture and books by the score scattered about. She frowned, looking at him in confusion.

"Yes, this is my bedroom. It is the only one with a fire. I promise as soon as another room is warm enough, we'll move you." He slipped off her shoes and worked at the knot in one garter. "I don't think I can untie this. We'll have to cut it loose."

She was beyond caring. "Whatever," she mumbled.

He stood and walked over to his desk, rummaging around. In a moment he returned. Kneeling down in front of her, he slid the blade of a penknife between the woven garter and her skin. A slight pressure carried the knife through the cloth. He repeated the movement with the other leg and set the knife on a table by the chair.

As he rolled down her stocking, a middle-aged woman and a young maid rushed into the room. "Mrs. Hastings, this is Miss Macpherson. She is soaked through, chilled to the bone, and has been through a painful ordeal. Please get her into something dry and warm. Perhaps one of the maids wouldn't mind sharing a flannel nightgown." He slipped the stocking from her foot and started on the other one.

"Of course, Mr. Thorne. Penny, fetch a gown. And hurry."

Jeanette groggily watched the exchange. She thought the housekeeper seemed surprised at his request. *Probably thought he'd want something more seductive.*

"I'll have a fire laid in the green guest room. Put her in bed here. We'll move her when the other room is warm enough." He reached up and felt her face, moving his fingers in a light caress across her cheek. "As I feared, she's taken a fever. She had chills all the way here."

"Throat hurts," Jeanette said hoarsely.

"I'll send up some tea in a few minutes," said the housekeeper, unbuttoning Dominic's greatcoat. "It'll soothe your throat, and a bowl of broth will give you back a bit of strength. Lean up."

Jeanie obeyed, leaning forward and resting her head on Dominic's shoulder. He put his hands around her waist as the housekeeper pulled the coat down her back and tugged the sleeves from her arms. When she straightened, she looked into his anguished eyes. "Dinna worry so." Her hand shook as she smoothed his frown. "I'm strong. I will heal."

He caught her hand, holding it in his solid, reassuring grip. "And your heart?" he asked, his expression troubled.

Jeanie thought of Tony, her chest aching. The pain was great, but she had known greater hurt when her father died. "It will mend through God's grace," she whispered.

"Come, Mr. Thorne. Off with you so we can tend to business," said Mrs. Hastings. "You need to change out of your wet clothes, too."

He smiled and squeezed Jeanette's hand before lowering it to the arm of the chair. "I'll be back in a few minutes." He stood and turned to the housekeeper. "Make certain you or one of the maids stays with her."

"Yes, sir."

He grabbed some dry clothes and hurried out the door, closing the door behind him.

Mrs. Hastings turned to Jeanette with a kind smile. "Now, child, let's get you out of those wet things." She moved quickly and efficiently, peeling the layers of cloth away. She wrapped a towel around Jeanette's hair and briskly dried her with another.

Penny returned with the flannel nightgown and a nightcap. She hurried over to the fire, holding the gown up in front of it. "I saw Martha and Kent in the hall. She is heating some bricks and will bring them up. He's fetching some broth from Cook."

"Good work, gel. Hand me the gown and look over there in Mr.

Thorne's dresser and find those wool stockings I knitted."

Jeanie was shaking continuously by the time Mrs. Hastings pulled the nightgown over her head. Heated by the fire, the cloth surrounded her in blessed warmth. The housekeeper unwound the wet towel from her head, replacing it with a dry one. "We'll wait awhile for the nightcap." She guided her over to the bed. "Did you find the stockings, Penny?"

"Yes, mum. Here they are." The maid grinned as she held up the heavy red wool stockings. A row of knitted green holly trimmed the tops and toes. She knelt in front of Jeanette, pulling them on her feet.

"Does h-he w-wear them?" asked Jeanie through her chattering teeth.

Mrs. Hastings smiled. "At least once or twice during Christmas week for the past four years. He likes to wear them in the morning during breakfast and while he reads the paper."

Jeanette laid down on the bed, leaning back against three pillows, sighing when the housekeeper drew the heavy blanket over her. The maid quickly added two more. A minute later, another maid brought in warm bricks to go next to her feet. She was followed by a footman carrying a tray with a bowl of soup and two cups of hot tea.

Looking up, Jeanie saw Dominic in the doorway. He had changed into a dry shirt, trousers, and slippers. He stepped into the room, took a cup of tea from the tray, and walked over to stand by the fire. He said nothing until the maids and footman left the room. "I asked Cook to put honey and lemon in the tea and to cool it so it wouldn't scorch your mouth. I usually find that Mrs. Hastings' remedy eases a sore throat."

"Thank you." A chill shook her voice.

He frowned. "Are you warmer?"

She nodded. The housekeeper held the tea to her lips. Jeanie took a long drink and looked at him through drooping eyes. "It's good."

"Don't go to sleep yet, miss," said Mrs. Hastings. "You need some nourishment." She set the tea down and picked up the bowl. Dipping a spoon in the broth, she held it up to Jeanette's mouth. She kept spoon-feeding her until the bowl was almost empty. "There, doesn't that feel better?"

"Yes, ma'am." Jeanette did feel stronger, and the chills had stopped. She did not believe, however, that she had ever known such exhaustion. She yawned, meeting Dominic's gaze. "You have men watching for Kiernan?"

"Yes. I also sent men to try and apprehend Drake and his cohorts, though I doubt they will be easily found. I expect he fled when he discovered you had escaped."

"What will happen to him?"

"He will likely take the first boat out of England. Hopefully, the only one he will find is destined for India or darkest Africa. He will be an old man before he dares set foot on English shores."

"He canna come back?"

"Not without fear of being thrown in prison."

Poor Tony. His father forced him to do it. Sudden tears burned her eyes and spilled down her cheeks. *He deserves it. He kidnapped me and terrified me. He caused my family untold pain.* Her tears fell faster. *He'll never see his family again, and he loves them so.* She couldn't catch her breath. *He meant to...in Worcester....Oh, Tony, how could you?*

A deep sob broke free as her tenuous hold on her emotions gave way. The horror, pain, and sorrow burst forth in violent weeping.

"Oh, you poor child. What has happened to you?" cried Mrs. Hastings, putting her arm around her.

"She was kidnapped by the man she loved," said Dominic, his heart pounding in fear. *What did that devil do to her?* "Leave us, Sarah."

"Are you sure?"

"Leave us," he ordered harshly. He raked his hand through his hair as she jumped up from the bed and sent him a reproachful glance. "Stay close by and don't shut the door all the way. But by thunder, anyone who eavesdrops will be thrown off the property."

He sat down on the bed and pulled Jeanette into his arms. The towel tumbled from her hair onto the bed. He tossed it on the floor, cradling her head against his chest. "He can't hurt you anymore. You're safe. I have men posted all around the house. He couldn't get to you even if he were foolish enough to try." He ran his hand gently up and down her back. "Sweet Jeanette, don't cry so hard."

She clung to him, great sobs racking her body. He tightened his arms, whispering tender words against her hair. "Shhh, you're safe. Don't cry so hard, please."

"He w-won't ever see h-his family. He loves them so much...that's why he took me away. He did it for them."

"That doesn't make it right."

"I know." She looked up at him, tears streaming down her face, her body shuddering as she drew a convulsive breath. "My mother... I dinna know if she can bear this." Her expression filled with horror. "I have to get back to Mam."

He shook his head. "You are too exhausted and sick to travel. I've sent a carriage for her and Mariah and a letter telling them you are safe."

She buried her face against his chest, her tears and damp hair wetting his shirt. "They told me to stay away from you. They all said you were bad." She put her arms around him. "They were wrong. You're a good man, Dominic. So good to me. He is the bad one, no' you."

"What did he do to you, Jeanette?" he asked softly, dreading the answer, yet needing to know.

"Broke my heart."

"Did he hurt you any other way?"

She shook her head as a new round of weeping overcame her.

"What is it, dear one? What pains you so?" *Please, God, if you're up there, comfort her. Show me how to help her.*

"I heard him say we'd spend the night in Worcester." She took a deep, shuddering breath. "Rent two rooms. When I was asleep, he planned to come to my room. He wanted Kiernan to catch us together so I'd have to marry him. But if Kiernan didna find us, he told Gray to bring some gentlemen up to see me in bed with him." Her voice broke. "He was going to make sure everyone found out. How could he say he still cared for me and mean to shame me so terribly?"

Dominic shook his head, unable to give her an answer. He had never known such rage. He closed his eyes and clenched his teeth, fighting for control. *How could anyone hurt such a gentle soul? God, how could you let her know such fear, such pain?* "I swear to you, angel, I will track him down and put a bullet through his black heart."

"You willna have to," said Branderee, walking into the room, appearing weary and grim.

Dominic tensed, prepared to be upbraided for being alone with Jeanette, for holding her as if he had some right to do so. To his surprise, he felt no animosity from her brother as he approached the bed. Dominic expected her to pull away, but she held onto him tighter than before.

"Kier, you didna kill him?" she whispered, her face ashen.

"No, Posy, but someone else did."

"Oh, no! Please, God, no," she hid her face against Dominic's chest.

Branderee stood beside them, laying his hand gently on her shoulder. He looked sorrowfully at Dominic. "Your men found him beside the carriage. The old coachman said Drake had an argument with the man named Gray. Something about Gray letting you go?"

"He saw her leave with me but didn't give an alarm," said Dominic. "He just turned his back."

"The coachman said while they were arguing, Drake pulled a brace of pistols from a special compartment underneath the seat. He fired one at Gray but missed. Before he could get off the second round, Gray shot him. The coachman said it was clearly self-defense, which must have been hard for him to admit. The men said he was holding Tony in his arms when they found them."

Jeanette straightened, resting her hands on Dominic's chest. "Tony said the coachman had worked for his father for years. Poor man." She shook her head sadly. "Poor Tony. I think he was truly reluctant to be a part of this when they were planning it, but he wanted to help his brother and parents. Then he became caught up in the adventure." She looked up at Kiernan. "What happened to Gray?"

"He and his men had fled. We'll find them. They will pay with their lives."

Dominic saw an even greater need for vengeance than his own reflected in her brother's eyes. "I'll help you."

Branderee met his gaze, studying him intently. Finally, he nodded.

Dominic felt Jeanette pull away. He eased her back against the pillows, his heart plummeting at the desolation in her eyes. He closed his hand around hers. "We will see justice done, angel."

She looked at him, then at Kiernan and shook her head wearily. "Leave them be."

"No, Jeanie. I canna do that. They must pay for the crime."

298

"Kiernan, Gray helped me. He told me what was happening and proved to me that Tony and his family were behind the whole thing. He helped me get away by no' telling anyone else."

Dominic looked at Kiernan. "It must be the fever and exhaustion."

"It is no' the fever." She reached for her brother's hand. "Tony is dead. His family ruined. They have lost a son they loved. Let them go after Gray if they want to, though I canna see how they can have him arrested without exposing their part of this whole affair."

"I dinna know, Jeanie," said Branderee with a frown.

"Please. Gray is a scoundrel, but he showed me mercy. I can do no less for him."

When Kiernan's expression filled with resignation, Dominic shook his head. "No, it's not right."

"If you go after Gray and his companions, this will drag on and on. You may never find them. I just want to go home and try to put this all behind me. Let it end here and now, Dominic, I beg you." Moisture shimmered in her eyes. "Let me be free to go to Scotland. Let me heal."

Dominic sighed. "Very well. I do not want to see you hurt further." He did not want to see her go back to Scotland, either, even though he knew it was best. "I'll leave you two alone. I've sent my coach for your mother and Mariah, Branderee." He stood and stepped aside.

"Thank you," said Kiernan, his voice breaking. "Thank you for all you've done."

Dominic nodded.

Branderee sat down on the bed and embraced his sister, tears rolling down his cheeks. He leaned his dark head against her lighter one.

Dominic turned away and started to the door.

"Thank you, Heavenly Father, for answering our prayers, for bringing Jeanie back to us," Kiernan said quietly. "Thank you for watching over her and protecting her and for sending Thorne to her aid."

"Bless Dominic, Father," said Jeanette softly. "Thank you for his courage and kindness."

Dominic walked out into the hall where his housekeeper was wiping her eyes on her apron. "I told you not to eavesdrop," he said gruffly, knowing she probably heard every word that had been said.

She sniffed. "You also told me to stay close and not shut the door." They walked down the hall together, not as master and servant but as cousins and lifelong friends. "She's the one you were telling me about, isn't she? The one you caught at the ball?"

"Yes." *The one who captured my heart in an instant.*

"Now I understand."

"Understand what?" They started down the stairs.

"Why you roam the house in the middle of the night and stare out the window for hours on end during the day."

"Sarah, I'm not that bad."

"Almost. You haven't been yourself since you arrived a week and a half ago. You act like a man in love. Real love, Dominic, not a meaningless flirtation."

"I admit I'm fascinated by her and drawn to her, but nothing can come of it."

"Why not?"

"Because I'm nine-and-thirty. She's nineteen. She's pure and good. I'm wicked."

"Not completely." She smiled and straightened his lapel. "At the heart of the libertine lies a good and kind man. I've always known it. I believe she saw through your façade from the very beginning."

He shrugged. "I did feel as if she was searching my soul. Sadly, it's a dark, ugly place."

"Then let her fill it with light."

They were wrong. You're a good man, Dominic. So good to me. "She's young and naive."

"No, cousin. She is wise beyond her years." Sarah stopped at the drawing room door, meeting his gaze. "Don't let her slip away, Dominic. She is your redemption."

His harsh laugh held no humor. "I'm beyond redemption, Sarah. Past praying for."

"She doesn't think so."

Jeanette's sweet words echoed in his mind. *Bless Dominic, Father. Thank you for his courage and kindness.*

"I doubt God thinks so, either. You know how to make your peace with him," Sarah said softly as she turned toward the kitchen.

I knew you'd come...I'm glad you're the one he chose.

23

JEANETTE'S FEVER AND SORE THROAT lasted almost a week, but the doctor assured them her illness was not life threatening. They were all concerned, however, by her despair over Tony's death. Her grief seemed almost as great as when their father died, which deeply worried Kiernan.

A few days after Jeanie's fever broke, they met with the doctor in the drawing room. "I think we should return to Scotland as soon as she is strong enough," said Kiernan.

The doctor nodded. "I agree. She needs to be away from everything relating to this tragic event. Going back to London, even to collect her things, is out of the question. The strain would be too much for her."

"Miss Macpherson and her family are more than welcome to stay here as long as necessary," said Dominic.

"Good, though she should remain here only until she is strong enough to travel. Unfortunately, I expect even your home is a reminder of her troubles due to your connection to the incident, Mr. Thorne.

"But she is comforted by being here in the country, and by your kindness to her, sir. She was sitting by the window when I saw her just now, and she commented about how beautiful she found your gardens. It's a warm day. She would benefit from the sunshine and fresh air, although I don't want her walking down the stairs yet. You must guard her against tiring."

Dominic rose quickly. "With your permission, Branderee, I'll take her out to the garden."

"Go ahead. Jeanie loves flowers and the outdoors. We'll join you in a few minutes." Kiernan watched him hurry from the room. He suspected Thorne had slept even less than the rest of them during Jeanette's illness. She had been plagued with nightmares, especially during the fever. Every time she cried out, he had appeared, going to her if she was alone or hovering in the hall if someone else reached her first.

"Have the nightmares lessened?" asked the doctor, thoughtfully watching Dominic's departure.

"Only one last night," said Kiernan.

"Good. Perhaps soon there won't be any. It will help you all to have a few nights' uninterrupted sleep. Could she tell you what it was about?"

"Thorne reached her first. He said she was trying to stop Tony from being killed. The same thing as before. She's running toward them but can never quite reach them. Gray shoots Tony, and she wakes up screaming. She blames herself for his death; she's told me so. She thinks if she hadna escaped, it would no' have happened. We keep reassuring her that it wasna her fault; that even if she'd been there she probably could no' have stopped it."

"That's all you can do, I'm afraid." The doctor turned to Ailsa. "How are you holding up, madam? You have a bit more color this morning."

"I'm fine now that I know Jeanie is over the fever. I slept well last night until she had the nightmare, and it was close to morning anyway. It is hard to see her suffer such anguish over Tony's death, but I trust God to heal that, too."

"Your daughter is fortunate to have so loving a family, Mrs. Macpherson. I'm certain she will mend completely, though it may take time. Well, I must be off. Lord Branderee, would you mind seeing me out?"

"No' at all."

Walking to the door, they met Dominic carrying Jeanette down the stairs. "Such a lazybones," teased Kiernan.

Jeanie gave him a halfhearted smile. "I have to take advantage of the opportunity. It's no' every day I can have a handsome gentleman carry me around."

The doctor chuckled. "Enjoy it for the next three or four days. Don't take those stairs as long as you feel any weakness." He winked at Dominic. "See that she obeys my orders."

"I will," said Dominic without a smile. They went toward the gardens in back of the house as Kiernan and the doctor continued out the front door.

"I hope you will forgive me, my lord, if I speak out of turn. The people here hold great affection for Mr. Thorne. No other gentleman in this area takes better care of them, not only those on his estate but in the village, too. He is a fair landlord and a generous benefactor. He sees that no one goes hungry or without clothes, good shelter, or medical attention, not even the village drunkard.

"I am aware of his bad reputation with the ladies, but I daresay that should he ever take a wife, she would never find a husband more loyal." The doctor smiled. "Now that I'm done sticking my nose where I have no business, I shall be on my way. Force Thorne to rest, please. He pays well, but I'd rather see him over a game of cards at the inn than sick in bed."

"We'll do what we can." Kiernan returned to the house to find Mariah waiting for him in the hallway.

"Your mother and Gabriel have gone outside."

"Then we are alone." Kiernan smiled at her and caught her hand, leading her into Dominic's study and shutting the door.

"If you conveniently forget the horde of servants."

"They're off working. Willna even miss us." He leaned against the door and pulled her into his arms, resting his face against her hair. "I've needed to hold you all day."

She laughed and put her arms around him. "It's only two o'clock."

"Will you go with us to Scotland? I've been afraid to ask, but you know I want you to. I need you with me, Mariah, now more than ever. I need you to calm me when the anger takes over, when I want to go to Drake's father with vengeance burning in my heart. I need you to ease my fears when I worry about Jeanie. You would be good for her, too. She has few friends at Branderee, and I doubt anyone close enough to confide in. Will you come with me, my love?"

She met his gaze with profound tenderness. "I would not think of letting you go without me. If I can be of any help to you or Jeanie, I would not dream of staying in England. Besides, I want to see Moray Firth in the moonlight." She stood on tiptoe and kissed him lightly, pulling back when he would have deepened the kiss. "No, you don't. I refuse to go outside and have Gabriel give us that knowing grin."

Kiernan laughed, releasing her. "The one that says he knows what we've been up to?"

Mariah nodded. "Now, tell me what you plan to do about Dominic."

"I dinna know. I owe him too much to tell him to leave her alone." Kiernan sighed heavily. "I suppose I have to ask him what his intentions are. It isna hard to see how he feels about her. Even the doctor noticed and commented on it. He's worried about Thorne's health."

"He does look haggard. I've never known him to worry over anything, but I've come to realize I saw only one side of him, the side he shows to the *ton*. I think Jeanie knows him far better than I ever did."

"Was she seeing him when I didna know?" His temper began a slow simmer. Since Jeanie's abduction, anger came far more quickly than normal.

"No, I'm sure she did as we asked and stayed away from him. I'm certain there were no secret trysts. Did I ever tell you about our conversation the morning after the ball?"

"No." Kiernan calmed and listened as Mariah told him about Jeanie asking her to pray for Dominic and about his loneliness. "I should talk to her first before I speak to him. I would not want to give him any false encouragement. She may only feel the need to pray for him and nothing more."

They strolled out to the garden and joined the others. Dominic had set out chairs for all of them in the sunshine. He claimed one next to Jeanette while Ailsa occupied the other. Kiernan was pleased to see his sister smile even if her joy was fleeting. She occasionally participated in the conversation but mostly gazed at the brightly colored flowers, lost in thought.

After about an hour, Kiernan decided she looked tired. "Would you like to go back upstairs, lassie? You look a wee bit droopy."

"The sunshine is making me drowsy. I suppose I had better go up and rest before I fall asleep here and wake up with a face full of freckles."

"I'll carry you up," said Kiernan, mildly amused at the flash of irritation on Dominic's face. He scooped her up in his arms and headed toward the house before she or Thorne could protest.

"Are we runnin' a race?" she asked with a tiny smile, draping one arm around his neck and holding her hat on with the other.

"I just wanted some time alone with my little sister."

She frowned at him. "To give me a lecture?"

He laughed. "I dinna always have one in mind. What should I be talking to you about this time?"

"I thought maybe you dinna like Dominic carrying me outside."

"I have no objection as long as he does no' take you to some secret hideaway."

"I'd like to go to a hideaway," she said sadly, leaning her head against his shoulder. "Will we go home soon, Kier?"

"As soon as you're strong enough to make the trip. Gabe and I go to London tomorrow to take care of things there. I have a few business matters to attend to. Jordan should arrive there tomorrow or the next day with the things we left at the Nortons'. Then we will have everything packed and brought here. I expect within a few weeks you will be ready to travel."

"Will you ask Wilton to go with us?"

"I dinna know. I've been thinking about asking him to become my house steward. Since Fiske left, there is no one seeing after the place. It would give Wilton and Mother more time to become acquainted, though I suppose it could pose problems if their interest in each other waned.

"I'll ask Mother what she wants me to do. I know she's missed him. She wrote him after she got here, telling him what had happened. Dominic sent the letter by special messenger." He laughed. "I dinna believe she told him she was writing the butler, only a close friend. She received a letter from him this morning but she has no' shared what he had to say."

They reached her room. "The bed or the chair?" he asked, pausing in the middle of the room.

"The chair is fine for now."

Kiernan set her down in a comfortable chair and sprawled in one across from her.

She laughed. "I'm no' that heavy. All those parties have made you weak. Too much food and no exercise."

"Too many sweets," he agreed. "The only thing I'll miss about London is Gunter's ices and pastries. I'm thinkin' about hiring a pastry chef and taking him home with us."

"You do and we'll grow fat and lazy. Now, what did you want to talk about?"

"Dominic."

"He isna like everyone thinks he is."

"I know. Still, it is common knowledge no woman has ever kept his interest for more than a few months."

"I doubt those relationships were the kind to cultivate long-term devotion, nor do I think he wanted it."

"Do you know what he wants of you?"

A light blush colored her cheeks. "I would hope no' the type of liaison he is used to. He has never said or done anything improper. I suppose the high sticklers would say he should no' come to me when I have bad dreams, but I take great comfort in having him there."

"More than the rest of us? If so, I'll tell Mother and Mariah to stay in bed next time." Kiernan smiled, pleased to see a spark in his sister's eyes at his teasing. Even irritation was better than melancholy.

"You know I am thankful for all of you. I hate troubling you." She looked away quickly, but Kiernan saw tears glisten in her eyes.

"We would gladly stay awake all night long if we needed to."

"I know. For pity's sake, take shifts. There is no sense in everyone becoming ill because of me."

"We have been. All except Dominic. He comes running every time you cry out. I dinna know what to do about him, Jeanie. At the Altburys' ball, I ordered him to stay away from you."

"So that's why he barely spoke to me from then on."

"I dinna think he even heard me. He was oblivious to everyone but you." Kiernan hesitated, not wanting to push her toward Dominic. At the same time, he felt he should be honest with her. Honesty won out over caution. "He watched you walk away with Fletcher and quietly quoted a verse from Proverbs one-and-thirty."

"Proverbs?" Her eyes widened in surprise.

Kiernan smiled. "That was my reaction, too. It was the verse about the woman speaking with wisdom and kindness. Then he looked at me and said you were goodness itself, gentleness and honor."

"Oh, my."

"Indeed. A lot to grasp in a moment or two," he said with a wry grin. "But there was more. He said your price truly is far above rubies and told me to guard you well, to give you only to a man who would cherish you above all else."

She stared at him, dumbfounded. "He said that about me?"

"Yes. True and wise words, and from all appearances, heartfelt. Though I tried to heed them, I failed you on both counts, which I deeply regret."

"I dinna see how you could have known about Tony; no' about his financial problems nor that he might do something so cruel. I never would have guessed him capable of such a thing, and I dinna think anyone else did, either."

She sighed and gazed out the window. "I think his father must have held great sway over him. When Tony went to Warwick the day before the kidnapping, he was in a terrible state. He looked positively wretched when he left. He was torn between his loyalty to his family and his feelings for me. I know he held great affection for me, but as Gray said, he cared for his family more." She shook her head sadly. "He was convinced that I would readily forgive him for the whole miserable affair, and that we could be happy together in spite of it."

Kiernan frowned thoughtfully. "He almost sounds as if he was coming unhinged."

"I've had the same thought, even at the time. The whole scheme was strange, but some things..." Her voice trailed off as she stared out the window.

"What?" Kiernan anxiously leaned forward in the chair. "Jeanie, what did he do?"

"Had the necessary scrubbed." A tiny, sad smile touched her trembling lips.

"The necessary? Jeanie, what are ye talkin' about?"

She took a deep breath and looked at him. "We changed horses the last time at an old abandoned farm. They drove right into the barn. Gray told us to get out and walk around. He said one of his men had spied our picnic basket and put it in the boot. All part of the plan, I'm sure, though at the time, I didna know Tony was involved in it.

"We ate, then Gray took me out back and pointed to the privy. It was embarrassing to go out there with him watching, but I didna have much choice. He assured me they wouldna stop again. Every step, I dreaded opening that door, expecting it to be filthy."

"And full of spiders," said Kiernan quietly.

She nodded. "But it had been scrubbed clean, no dirt, spiders, or cobwebs. I was surprised but grateful, and it gave me hope that they wouldna greatly mistreat us the rest of the time. Gray told me later that Tony had ordered them to clean it because he knew I was afraid of spiders." Repeatedly smoothing her fingers across the velvet arm of the chair, she fell silent.

"Posy, what is it? What else happened?" he asked gently.

"Tony wanted to look like a hero. He told Gray to make advances to me so he could come to my assistance."

Kiernan felt sick as she grew even paler. *Oh, Father, no.*

"When I returned to the barn, Gray was waiting by the door. I thanked him for cleaning the necessary. He said something about me being easy to please, then put his arm around me."

Kiernan gripped the arms of the chair, squeezing so tightly he thought he might break them. He had tried to question her before, but she had refused to talk about what happened. *She said he helped her. Please, God, let that be the truth, the real reason she didna want us to go after him.*

He listened in trepidation as she told about Gray acting as if he were going to kiss her, Tony coming to her aid, and the kidnapper hitting him. He shook his head in disbelief when she said she had attacked Gray. When she told about Gray kissing her and forcing Tony to ride on top of the coach so he could be alone with her, Kiernan could barely contain his anguish.

"It terrified both of us. Tony wasna acting any longer. He truly feared for me. Once Gray and I were inside the coach, he treated me kindly. He gave me his coat when I got cold and told me about Tony's part in the kidnapping. He apologized for hurting me.

"I didna want to believe Tony was behind the whole thing, but so much of what Gray said made sense. I think I was about to faint. Gray thought so, too. He covered me with my plaid and moved over to my side of the coach. He was rubbing my hands when we lost the wheel. Then Tony opened the door and found us sitting side by side, and he accused me of making the most of the situation."

Kiernan jumped to his feet and walked to the window, putting his back to her so she would not see his rage. He regretted Tony's death less and less. He wanted to get his hands on Gray and wished he had not promised Jeanie he would not try to find him.

"I do think he had become unstable. Otherwise, I dinna believe he would have tried to shoot Gray. I wish it could have turned out differently. I was right to flee from him, though I will always wonder if I could have changed the outcome if I'd stayed."

Kiernan turned around to face her. "You might have been shot."

"I know." She wiped her cheek. "But he didna know the Lord, Kiernan. I'd talked to him about Jesus some, but I dinna think it was enough. I should have done more."

"We never know what seeds we have planted, Jeanie. All we can do is share about Jesus when the Lord leads. It is up to God and the Holy Spirit to finish the work. There is always the chance that in his last moments, he remembered what you said and gave his heart to the Savior."

"I hope so." She was quiet for several minutes. "I promised Dadie I would only marry a Christian. I wish he'd told me no' to let a man court me unless he knew the Lord. Something like this wouldna have happened then."

"Well, at least it's no' as likely. Will you tell Dominic his attentions are no' wanted?"

"I dinna know what to do. I have been drawn to him from the moment I met him. I knew God wanted me to pray for him, but I was attracted to him, too. I found myself thinking about him often. When we were at the same parties, I would feel him watching me. I would search the room until I found him, and sometimes it was almost more than I could manage no' to go to him. I stayed away because everyone said I should, but that didna keep me from wanting to be with him, to get to know him."

"Then you didna love Tony?"

"No. Everyone kept telling me how wonderful he was and what a good match we were. I admired and respected him and enjoyed being with him." She paused, blinking back tears. "Forgive me. I'm still much too weepy."

"Tears are a gift from God to wash away the pain, Posy. Dinna be ashamed of them."

She pulled a kerchief from her sleeve, wiping her eyes and blowing her nose. "I hadna thought of it that way. I still will be glad when they dinna come so easily."

She took a deep breath, exhaling slowly, regaining her composure. "I cared for Tony very much, but I didna love him. My continued interest in Dominic proved it. Tony destroyed my trust in him, and I lost a dear friend. That hurts. I grieve because he died and because he wasna the man I thought he was.

"It canna be wise to enter into another courtship so soon, but I feel God put Dominic in my life. I dinna know, maybe it was only because I needed him to rescue me. I asked the Lord to send someone to help me, someone I could trust. There are others I know far better who could have done the same thing."

"But would they have? He risked his life to save you. No' everyone would have. They might no' have even realized there was a problem since Tony said you were engaged."

"I'm confused about what to do about Dominic. There are many reasons no' to encourage him. He is much older, does no' know the Lord, and has lived a reprehensible life. Yet, I believe he is searching for God, and I know he will find him. He will be made new in the Lord and free from the sins of the past. I would make certain he understood about my promise to Father and to God from the beginning."

"And his age?"

"Right now, I find his maturity very appealing. But I'm no' sure of my judgment anymore. I was very mistaken about Tony."

"We all were. Go slow with Dominic. I dinna want to see you hurt again." He smiled and sat down, leaning his head back against the chair. "According to the doctor, most of the people around here think he is a fine man."

"I tend to agree with them."

"So do I. I also think you are more than a friend to him. I have been praying for him ever since I arrived and found you weeping in his arms."

"I will greatly miss him when we leave."

"Perhaps. You may discover when you get home that you dinna miss him as much as you thought you would. See how you feel shortly before we leave. If you are still interested in him, ask him to come visit us in a month, on one condition. Give yourself—and him—the freedom to change your minds. If, after you are home, you find that your feelings are no' strong enough to encourage his suit, then tell him so. Give him the same choice, with the promise of no ill feelings. Agree to be honest with each other from the start, and then follow through with it." He shook his head ruefully. "It is a lesson I learned the hard way."

That night before retiring, Mariah and Kiernan went for a walk in the garden. When they came inside, only Dominic was still downstairs. They found him at the back of the house in the small drawing room which he preferred to use with friends.

He looked up when they entered, nodded, and went back to staring at the fire. Sitting down on the sofa beside Kiernan, Mariah studied his forlorn expression and haunted eyes. "Jeanie was right," she said quietly.

Dominic glanced at her. "About what?"

"You."

He shook his head and turned back to the fire. "She's wrong. There is nothing good about me."

"You risked your life to help her.

He shrugged. "Anyone would have helped."

"I disagree." Kiernan started to say more, but stopped when she laid her hand on his arm.

314

"So do I, but that's not what I'm talking about," said Mariah. "The morning after you two met, I told her to stay away from you."

"Very wise." Dominic nodded cynically.

"You do have quite the reputation."

"Carefully cultivated over the years, I assure you," he said bitterly.

"She agreed to follow my advice, but she had a request of her own. She asked me to pray for you."

"What?" Frowning, Dominic tensed. "Why would she do that?"

"She said despair and loneliness are destroying you."

He shook his head, looking away in confusion. "How could she know?" he asked softly.

"God revealed it to her. You'll find he does that often. He did the same thing for you, showing you the kind of woman she is."

He frowned at them as if they had lost all reason. "And did you pray for me, Mariah?" he asked in a strained voice.

"Some, though I fear I'm not as diligent as she is. Jeanette has prayed for you every day since she met you."

He shook his head in denial. "Why would she care about me?"

"Because Jesus cares about you, and Jeanie loves Jesus with all her being. She has the kind of faith that can move mountains, Dominic, and a gentle spirit that heals broken hearts. She sees the hurts most of us miss."

He sprang out of the chair, pacing around the room. "What about her hurts? Her broken heart? If God is so loving, why was she kidnapped? Why did he let Drake treat her so cruelly?"

"I don't know. Being a child of God does not mean we will never have troubles or pain, but he gives us the strength to endure them and to overcome. He will heal her hurt and her heart, Dominic. God does all things according to his will. I can't begin to understand his purpose for letting her go through this terrible event, but I believe he is sovereign. He sees things on a far broader canvas than we do.

Perhaps someday we will understand why all this has happened. We may never know."

"We're just supposed to trust him with blind faith?"

"Sometimes faith and time are all we have," said Kiernan quietly.

Dominic turned around, his expression dejected. "And sometimes we have nothing." His eyes filled with sorrow. "Why did she have to fall in love with Drake when I would give everything I have to see her happy?"

"You do love her," Mariah said in amazement.

"Astounding, isn't it." He walked back to his chair and sank into it with a sigh. "I've always laughed at men who said they fell in love at first sight. I didn't believe in love. Lust, certainly, but not love."

He glanced at Kiernan. "That night at the Altbury ball, I had noticed her long before she landed in my arms. In fact, I found myself watching her much of the evening, but always with the reminder that she was too young and innocent for my tastes.

"Then, when I looked into her eyes, my only thought was how desperately I needed her gentleness and goodness, her acceptance. I felt as if she was the only person in the world who could save me from myself. I wanted to spirit her away from the ball and bring her here."

"Good thing you didna try," said Kiernan dryly.

"Sanity did prevail, though for a moment I wasn't sure it would. The thought of pistols at dawn shook me out of my fanciful notions. I haven't been able to get her out of my mind. Strange as it seems, I do love her."

Kiernan glanced at Mariah. "It's no' so strange. I'm learning that God and love dinna always act as we expect."

"I'm not worthy of her." He looked away.

Kiernan smiled at him. "I dinna think anyone is, but I'm her brother." He sobered. "Jeanie grieves for Tony, but she wasna in love with him."

Dominic's eyes grew wide. "No?"

"No."

Dominic shook his head. "I could never expect her to overlook my past."

"We all sin, and in God's eyes, no sin is greater than another. He can change you, wipe the slate clean through Jesus. All you have to do is believe in him and repent. I dinna think Jeanie is too concerned with your past. It is your future she cares about, both in this world and for eternity." Kiernan caught Mariah's hand and stood, pulling her up beside him. "Now that we've muddled his brain, I think it's time we left him to stew."

Dominic laughed, standing also. "I wish you weren't leaving for London tomorrow, Kiernan. I would like to get to know you better."

"Maybe we'll still have the chance."

Kiernan and Mariah bade him good night and walked upstairs together. They stopped in front of her door. "We'll probably leave before you're up in the morning," he said.

"I'll miss you." She slid her arms around his neck.

"I'll miss you, too." He kissed her tenderly. "But it's better if Gabe and I go to London alone. Is there anything else you want me to take care of or pick up?"

"Take the letter to Delia."

"I willna forget. And I'll pay a call on the Templetons and Nortons if they are in town. They will want to know the latest about Jeanie. I'm thinking about inviting all of them to come to Branderee later in the summer."

"That's a wonderful idea."

"It is if you'll be there to help organize everything. I dinna think Mother and Jeanie would want to try it on their own."

Mariah laughed. "I think I'm being bribed into an extended stay."

"We could have new visitors every month. We've met so many

people, it could last years."

"Sounds like too much work."

He pulled her a little closer. "But it would keep you there so long, you'd forget to leave."

"Right this minute, I'm not sure I will ever want to leave."

He leaned down, kissing her slowly and thoroughly. He brushed one last tiny kiss across her lips and searched her eyes. "I love you, Mariah."

"I love you, too," she whispered.

His heart soared to the heavens. He'd known it for weeks, even if she had been unsure. Her eyes shone with love when she looked at him, and he'd felt it time and time again in her touch. He had waited for the words, longed to hear her acknowledge what was in her heart. He crushed her to him. "Thank you."

"I wanted you to know before you left."

The thread of fear in her voice made him lean back and look at her. "Dinna worry about me, Mariah. It's only a trip to town."

"I'm nervous after what happened to Jeanie."

"I'm no' a young woman easily preyed upon—even if I do wear a skirt."

Her smile wobbled. "There are still highwaymen about."

"No' many. If they hold us up, I'll give them all my money without so much as token resistance. I willna let Gabriel argue with them, either. If he gets stubborn, I'll hit him over the head myself."

She laughed softly. "I know I'm being silly. The robbers would take one look at you two and run the other way."

He grinned. "If they dinna, I will play the pipes. That'll scare them away for sure." He kissed her on the forehead. "Now off to bed with you, lass." He released her and turned away. After a few steps, he went back, studying her thoughtfully. "Was that I love you and want to marry you? Or I love you, but I'm still no' quite sure about marriage?"

She made a little face, and he knew her answer. "I can't have any doubts, Kiernan. I have to be sure, not of you but of me."

"I'll wait." He tickled her chin with his knuckle. "But dinna take too long, love. The castle is cold in winter, and I canna think of a nicer way to keep warm than snuggling with you."

24

KIERNAN HAD ADVISED DOMINIC that his private secretary, Jordan Wylde, and possibly another gentleman, a friend of the family named Wilton, would return with them from London. Both men were with them when they arrived. Dominic quickly deduced that the expressive Mr. Wilton was a particular friend of Mrs. Macpherson's.

When Dominic and Jeanie drove out to see one of his tenants later in the afternoon, she confided that Wilton had been their butler in London. Such disregard for the strict social conventions ruling the upper class amazed and pleased Dominic. The longer he knew Kiernan Macpherson, the more he liked and respected him.

"Wilton was so kind to her and lifted her spirits when nothing we did seemed to help. She had been listless and depressed since Dadie left us. Wilton accompanied her to the park and often read to her." She smiled at him. "Which is as good as going to see a play, according to Mother."

"He was in the theatre?"

"When he was younger. He is from the gentry, a fourth son, so he had no expectations. He told Kiernan he had portrayed a butler in so many plays that fulfilling the role in life came easily."

Dominic chucked, delighting in the way her topaz eyes twinkled when she smiled. The past week had been both a joy and torture. Her strength had returned quickly. Within three days after Kiernan left for London, she was strolling up and down the stairs without difficulty.

Her emotions, however, were still rickety. She tried hard to be cheerful and lively, but sadness often lingered in her eyes. Depression occasionally defeated her efforts to keep up a good front, and she wandered off alone, either to her room or to walk across the grounds. On her return, her eyes were often red from crying.

He had driven her to every corner of Thornridge and introduced her to each tenant family. Not content to sit in the gig when the families came out to greet them, she would wander off with the tenant's wife, admiring the garden, the chickens, or the children.

Time after time, he watched in amazement as she knelt down to look the children in the eye when she spoke to them. Even the most bashful child took to her instantly. More than once she picked up a grubby little boy, much to his mother's worry over dirtying her dress.

Jeanette would laugh and tell the mother not to fret. "What's a wee bit of dirt compared to a child's hug?"

Without fail, she won the admiration and respect of every man, woman, and child on the estate.

"Wilton was certainly happy to see you up and about."

"He has been protective of me from the beginning of our stay in London. I'll never forget the scold he gave me when I ventured off to the park on my own."

"You went out alone?" Dominic frowned down at her.

She reached up, trying to spread the wrinkle between his eyebrows and end his frown. "You dinna need to reprimand me. Wilton did that sufficiently."

At her teasing smile and playful touch, he relented. He had to since he couldn't hold back his smile. "Baggage. Didn't you know better?"

"I had been advised no' to, but I didna see what harm it could do. At home and here on your estate, I go for walks by myself all the time."

"There is far less danger here."

"I know, but I'm afraid I can be stubborn sometimes. Kiernan was in the country—meeting Mariah," she said with a mischievous grin. "Gabe was sick with a terrible cold, and everyone else was busy. The park was only three blocks away, so it didna seem like too great a risk.

"The minute I saw Wilton marching toward me, I knew I was in trouble. No one else would have thought so, but his stern expression was quite daunting. He politely told me I was needed at home and escorted me back. Then he gave me the lecture, pointing out the dangers in a wee bit more detail than Kiernan had."

Sadness briefly touched her face. "He reminded me of my father. Dadie was always straightforward with me, sometimes to the point of being embarrassingly blunt. He said it was better to make my face red than let me be harmed because I didna know what to expect."

"Your father sounds like a wise man."

"He was. Unfortunately, I doubt he had ever met anyone like Tony," she added angrily.

"Family responsibility can force a man to do things he normally would not do, Jeanette. I have been fortunate not to face the same challenge as young Drake."

"Surely, you wouldna have resorted to kidnapping me."

Dominic enjoyed the flash in her eyes and her show of spirit. Fire and gentleness made an intriguing combination. "No, I wouldn't have. I would have pressed my suit with greater ardor," he said with a lazy smile.

"He did that, too."

Jealousy stabbed him. "Evidently, you did not succumb to his charms quite as quickly as he required." He glanced at her out of the corner of his eye, annoyed and worried when she blushed. "Or perhaps you did," he said softly.

"I did no more than kiss him," she said, looking away in irritation.

"That was not enough to engage your affections?"

"There are many kinds of affection." She took a slow, deep breath. "I told him from the beginning that I wasna looking for a husband. I promised myself before I left Scotland that I wouldna marry an Englishman."

Dominic's hope sank, but he carefully controlled his expression. "Only a Highlander will do, I suppose."

"It seems logical, but I have learned that one's heart does no' always heed one's mind."

He glanced at her, but she had looked away. He wanted to pursue the conversation, but they had arrived at the tenant's house.

The couple had a new baby boy, and Jeanette insisted on giving the babe a present. Dominic had taken her to Worcester the day before to shop. Remembering how she had searched for just the right gift brought a smile. He had teasingly grumbled after visiting each shop because she so sweetly entreated him to continue in their quest.

The young man came out to meet them. His wife followed, carrying the baby in her arms. "I didn't expect to see you again so soon, sir," said Mr. Smythe with a warm smile. He nodded to Jeanette. "Miss." Taking hold of the horse's halter, he steadied the animal while Dominic climbed out of the gig.

"Miss Macpherson wanted to see the baby one last time. Sadly, she is leaving us tomorrow." He walked around to Jeanette's side of the carriage and lifted her down, his gaze meeting hers. For a heart-beat, he did not hide his sorrow. Her eyes widened slightly, and her breath quickened.

"Are you going back to Scotland, miss?" asked the young mother.

Pressing her hand lightly against his shoulder, Jeanie turned away. "Yes. England is lovely, but we're all homesick." She walked over and peeped at the little boy. "Oh, he's awake! May I hold him?"

"Of course." Mrs. Smythe handed the baby to Jeanette, who took him with practiced care.

She smiled at the baby and made silly little noises, lightly touch-ing his cheek with one finger. "You're such a braw laddie. Aye, Georgie, you are." She smiled at Mrs. Smythe. "Such a sweet baby."

"Yes, he is," said his mother proudly.

Jeanette murmured several Gaelic phrases, and Mrs. Smythe sent Dominic a questioning glance.

"It's Gaelic, the language of the Scottish Highlands, but I have no idea what she said."

Jeanette looked up. "It's a prayer my grandmother used to say over me when I was small. I asked God to watch over the wee lad-die, to keep him safe and well, and to give him a heart that loves the Lord Jesus."

"'Tis a good prayer," said the baby's father.

"God has been faithful to honor it." Jeanette smiled down at Georgie and tickled his stomach. The baby cooed and grabbed her finger. "Oh, you're a stuffie lad," she said with a laugh. She looked at Dominic, her face glowing. "Come see how strong he is."

He would have preferred watching her hold the child, though it filled him with a strange longing. He'd never wanted a family—until now. Her children would know the touch of a loving mother. She would probably defy English tradition and fight to keep her sons from being sent to boarding school. Dominic thought that if they

324

turned out to be as fine as her brother, she would be right to keep them home.

"I haven't been around children much," he said quietly, stepping up beside her.

"Well, this wee laddie canna bite you yet," she said with a grin. She gently tugged her finger away from the baby. "Now, hold out your finger so he can reach it."

Dominic obeyed, and the baby grabbed onto his finger, curling his tiny hand around it. Dominic smiled, moved by the trusting touch of those small, perfect fingers. "He is a sturdy lad." The boy looked at him and gurgled with a quick smile. "He likes me."

"Dinna sound so amazed." Jeanette winked at the baby's mother. "He knows who to turn up sweet."

Dominic laughed, causing the baby to jump and release his finger. The little boy's face puckered up, but before he let loose with a wail, Jeanette raised him up, resting his cheek against her shoulder. Patting his back, she sang softly in Gaelic, and Georgie calmed quickly.

"You have a way with children, Miss Macpherson," said the tenant's wife.

"I do love them. I hope to have a houseful someday. But I'll be content with how many the Lord gives me." She kissed the baby on the forehead and handed him back to his mother. "We brought a present for Georgie." She hurried over to the gig and picked up the package.

Mrs. Smythe handed the baby to her husband and took the present with a shy smile. "You didn't need to go buying us anything."

"We wanted to."

"She dragged me all over Worcester looking for it." Dominic grinned at Mr. Smythe, who nodded in understanding.

Mrs. Smythe set the package down on a small worktable beside the door, eagerly untying the strings holding the wrapping paper closed. When she folded back the paper, she gasped in surprise and quick tears filled her eyes. "Oh, miss, it's beautiful." She reverently lifted the white silk christening robe from the wrapping. "Thomas, look what Mr. Thorne and Miss Macpherson brought for our Georgie. Did you ever see anything so fine? Just look at all the lace." A little cap, petticoat, and top were also included.

Mr. Smythe grinned. "Georgie will look grand enough to go to St. Paul's."

"But we'll settle for the village church. Thank you, Miss Macpherson, Mr. Thorne. It's the nicest gift you could have given us."

"And not the only one," said her husband, looking at Dominic. "The coins you slipped behind the water pail when you were here earlier were another nice surprise. Thank you, sir. We do appreciate it."

Dominic smiled, deriving as much happiness from Jeanette's pleased and approving smile as from his young tenant's gratitude. "I thought you could probably use a little extra. You are bound to have additional expenses." He offered Jeanette his arm. "We should be going, my dear. I don't want your brother to come looking for us."

"He wouldna, but you're right." Jeanette took one last peek at Georgie and slipped her hand around Dominic's arm. "Enjoy him."

"We will, miss. Thank you again for the gown. It's lovely. Me Mum will be so thrilled."

They drove back to the house, talking about the everyday workings of the estate, avoiding any mention of her leaving on the morrow. Dominic was tempted to stop the gig several times and tell her of his love, but his courage failed him. To think that such a young, wonderful woman might consider such a reprobate for a husband was ridiculous.

They spent the evening with the others, catching up on the news from London.

"The Templetons, Nortons, and Stanwells have all agreed to pay us a visit." Kiernan winked at Mariah.

"I'm glad." Mariah smiled at Wilton, who sat next to Ailsa on the sofa. "I'm also happy you will be there to help us oversee everything."

He bowed. "We shall do our best to make it memorable. Lord Branderee and I thought we might put them to work. The gentlemen could go out with the fishing fleet, and the ladies could work in the fields."

Mariah laughed. "I doubt they would be too enthused about such amusements." She turned to Kiernan. "Didn't you say there was a golf course not far away?"

"In Nairn. We would probably need to spend the night, but it would give them something different to try. Lord and Lady Templeton may be experts at the game since they spend so much time in Scotland."

"Olivia said they had only gone a few times. Did you invite Fletcher, too?" asked Jeanette.

"We did. He and Olivia are practically inseparable, so it seemed wise," said Gabriel. "Did Kiernan tell you about Clarissa St. John?"

"No. Has she made her catch?"

Gabriel nodded. "The marquis of Lenegall, a good solid Irishman."

Jeanette laughed. "Evidently she gave up on nabbing you or Kiernan. I dinna remember meeting him."

"From what I gather, he didna frequent too many parties until he was introduced to Clarissa at the theatre. Suffers from the gout."

Jeanette's smile faded. "Is he old?"

"Somewhere in his sixties, but rich as they come. He was more than happy to pay off her father's debts in exchange for her hand. Dinna look so sad, lass," said Gabriel. "They both know what they are getting."

"Did you see her? Does she seem happy?"

"Yes, to both questions. She told me she is quite fond of the old gent. They will be living in Ireland, which surprisingly pleases her. She confided that she would be happy to be such a distance from her mother." Gabriel's expression softened. "She asked me to tell you that she regrets being forced to end her association with you. She hopes your friendship can resume after she is married and under no obligation to do as her mother wishes."

"I hope so, too. She's flighty and can be obnoxious, but I do like her." Jeanie smiled at Mariah. "Most of the time."

"I cannot understand why her mother took such a dislike to me," said Mariah.

"Clarissa said her mother thought you would be ostracized on your return. By taking the lead in condemning you, she believed she would increase her status with Society's patronesses. Unfortunately for her, most people welcomed you, and she soon learned she didna wield the social power she thought she did."

"I suppose I should feel sorry for her," said Mariah. "But I don't."

"Maybe next time she willna be so quick to cast stones," said Ailsa. "Personally, I didna like the woman. I was happy when she quit coming to call, which by the way was before you came to London, Mariah."

Wilton laughed quietly. "After her second visit, I always told her you weren't at home." He shrugged when Ailsa looked up at him in surprise. "Her visits upset you, and I did not think you needed any added concerns. Since you didn't seem to mind Miss Clarissa, I was more lenient with her."

"How many others did you keep at bay?" asked Ailsa with a bemused smile.

"A dozen or so the first week, until it became clear to you and Lord Branderee that you were not up to much company. I did not

328

feel I could turn them all away without your consent, so I tried to weed out the more irritating ones. I was not always successful at reading their characters."

Ailsa laughed. "You did well enough."

Later in the evening, Jeanette stepped out onto the terrace, and Gabriel followed. Dominic was sitting by the door, and though he did not intentionally listen, he overheard their quiet conversation.

"Clarissa sent one more message, lass. She is thankful you are safe."

"So the word had gotten round already," Jeanette said with a heavy sigh.

"I'm afraid so. Most everyone we met expressed their horror at what happened and their hope that you are recovering. No one held you to blame, lass. They find it hard to believe Tony could do such a thing, but everything his coachman told the magistrate confirms what happened."

"Does anyone mourn him? Or has he become a complete villain?"

"He is mourned. Some remember his more redeeming qualities and wonder what happened. To others, he is a villain indeed."

"He did have some good qualities, you know," she said softly, her voice breaking.

Dominic ached to go to her but remained still as Gabriel put his arm around her.

"I know, lass. I liked him."

"What has happened to his family?"

Gabriel was silent for a minute. "They sold his brother's house and part of the estate to cover the debt."

"But I thought they stood to lose everything."

"Evidently, that is what his father and brother told Tony, but it wasna as bad as they portrayed. They wanted to keep the whole thing, so they lied to him."

"Their greed and lies cost him his life. How could they use him that way?" she cried angrily.

"I dinna know, Jeanie. Nor does his mother. She wrote a letter to Mrs. Norton giving her those details. She asked her to tell you that she tried to write you but could not."

"How she must hurt. Tony adored her."

"Which is the leverage his father used to persuade him to go through with the plan. Tony did it to protect her."

"How can she bear to be married to such a terrible man?"

"I dinna think she can. She has gone to live with her sister and vows never to return to him."

Jeanie was quiet for several minutes, resting her head on Gabriel's shoulder. Though Dominic wished he was the one to comfort her, he felt no jealousy or threat from Gabriel, who was like another brother to her.

"I'm going for a walk." Her voice was heavy with sadness.

"Do you want company?"

"No, thanks. I need to be alone. I'll just be in the garden. Tell Mam and Kiernan no' to worry about me. I'll go up to bed when I'm ready. The Lord and I have a lot to talk about."

Jeanie still had not come inside when Kiernan and the others retired. Dominic lingered downstairs, waiting for her.

Sarah came in and sat down next to him. "Did you talk to her?"

He shook his head morosely. "No. What can I say? There is nothing that will make her stay."

"I'm sure there isn't, but you should see how she would react if you decided to call on her."

Dominic smiled in spite of his gloom. "It's not like I can just drop by for an afternoon visit."

"No, a month would be more like it." Sarah stood, stifling a

330

yawn. "I hear Scotland is nice in the summer, and you've never been to the Highlands. I can't think of a better place to go on a trip. She's sitting next to the wall by the rose garden. I saw her there a few minutes ago when I went out for a breath of air. See you in the morning."

Dominic mulled over her suggestion for a while, finally deciding he might write Jeanette after she was home and inquire about a visit. He blew out the candles in the drawing room with a heavy heart, but did not leave the room. He had no intention of going upstairs until she was safely inside.

Untying his cravat, he unwound the long piece of linen from around his neck and tossed it onto a chair by the door. Unlike many fashionable gentlemen, he did not wear his coats tight enough to need his valet to help remove them, so his coat quickly followed the cravat.

Moonlight shone through three large windows, sending streams of gold amid the shadows. Unfastening the shirt button at his throat, he sat down on a settee in the edge of the light, hoping she would see him when she came inside. When she returned from the garden a few minutes later, he wasn't disappointed.

25

JEANIE STOPPED AT THE DOOR to the drawing room. Sometime during her walk she had removed the ribbon and pins from her hair. Instead of being caught up in curls at the back of her head, her hair lay across her shoulders, falling in loose waves. "I saw the lights go out and was afraid you had gone upstairs."

"I couldn't go up with you still out in the garden," said Dominic.

"How thoughtless of me. I beg your pardon for no' coming in sooner."

He stood and walked over to her. "That isn't what I meant. I could have gone to bed. My house steward always locks the doors, and he usually stays up late. I should have said I didn't want to go up until you came in. You are free to stay out in the garden as long as you wish."

"It's a beautiful night but growing cool. Would you mind if we sat down here and talked awhile? With the moonlight coming in the window, it's almost as nice as being outside, and it's warmer."

"I'd like nothing better." He followed her to a small settee, happy she chose that seat since it was made to hold only two.

"In a way, we both had the same thing in mind. I thought you might go out for a walk, so I waited for you," she said.

"For me?" He sat down with a smile. It might have been the

light, but her eyes seemed to glow with pleasure when she looked at him. "What did I do to deserve such an honor?"

"If I counted everything you've done, I'd run out of fingers and toes. You've been wonderful to me, Dominic. To all of us."

"I'm happy to help, believe me." He turned so he could look at her. "You greatly miss Scotland, don't you?"

She nodded. "Even more than I thought I would. I never believed I'd call Branderee home. Some people consider the northeast coast part of the Highlands, but I dinna think of it that way. We lived in the mountains before, and I still miss them. Since being in England, I've missed the coast and that big old castle as well. I can see why some Highland lords have purchased estates along the coast as a refuge from the mountain winters. Have you ever been to Scotland?"

"To the Borders and around Edinburgh, but not beyond St. Andrews. I tried my hand at golf but was not too successful."

"We've gone to the course in Nairn a few times and given it a try. Kiernan does well, though I beat him once." She smiled. "I still have no' decided if he let me win or no'. It's something he would do."

Dominic nodded. "Yes, I expect it is."

"He likes you. We all do."

"That's good to hear. I hate for my guests to dislike me. Makes for poor dinner conversation."

She laughed. "Better verbal daggers than real ones."

"Both can play havoc with the digestion. Thankfully, no one has drawn a knife on me yet. A few pistols and about a dozen flowerpots, but no knife."

"Flowerpots?"

He could have sworn her eyes twinkled, but he was afraid her smile would disappear in a second. "Yes, well, uh, years ago, I was under the impression that a new lady friend's husband was an understanding sort of fellow. Turned out he wasn't. He caught me nibbling on her neck in the garden, and the flowerpots were handy. He chased me, throwing every pot of primroses along the way as I fled down the path, coattails flying. I was younger and faster, so I easily outran him. A portly gent, he quickly became winded, but he had enough energy left to jump up and down a few times and shake his fist at me."

For a heartbeat, she attempted to look stern but failed completely. Soon a giggle escaped. In trying to stay quiet, she laughed all the harder. He sat still, enjoying simply watching her laugh. After several minutes, her giggles subsided and she sighed happily.

"Thank you. I needed to laugh. I hope you learned your lesson," she said with a small smile.

"Indeed, I did. From then on, I made certain the husbands were long dead."

She arched an eyebrow. "Well, I suppose that is something of an improvement. At least you willna be shot or have your head broken." Her smile held a trace of mischief. "I dinna know which is funnier, the image of you running for your life, dodging pots and flowers, or you nibbling on her neck as if she was a scone."

Dominic laughed out loud. "I assure you, my dear, it is nothing like eating a scone."

"No?" she asked innocently.

He narrowed his eyes. Was he imagining it, or was there a subtle invitation in her tone? "No crumbs, for one thing."

He was tempted to move closer and give her a demonstration. She was easy prey right now. In the past, he would not have thought twice about using that to his advantage. But he would never do that with her. *Not with Jeanette.*

He curved his hand around hers. "Someday, a man will show you what I'm talking about." In spite of his effort to make his comment light, his voice sounded low and husky.

"I dinna want someone else to show me," she whispered. "I want you to."

He fought to resist her, tightening his grip on her hand. "Angel, don't tempt me. Believe me, I would like very much to kiss you, and not just on the neck, but I'm not going to."

"Why?" She looked down, her hair veiling her face, her voice trembling with confusion and hurt.

"Because I'm trying very hard to be noble. You've suffered great anguish, and whether you realize it or not, you are quite tender right now. Your emotions are in a turmoil, and you're grateful because I helped you. All that makes you susceptible and reckless. You could easily be swayed to do something which at other times would be completely repulsive to you."

After a minute or two, she looked up at him, her eyes golden and trusting. "You're right. I should no' have asked."

They sat quietly for several minutes, holding hands, looking up at the moon as it seemed to rest on top of a lofty elm tree. He pictured her leaning back amid the heather on a lonely Scottish moor, captured in a moonbeam. "I'll miss you, angel."

"I'll miss you, too. I'll never forget how good you've been to me. Dominic, you canna know how I felt when I looked back and saw you behind those trees. Knowing you had come back for me..." Her voice caught, and she lifted his hand to her lips, kissing the back of it.

His heart skipped a beat. "I expect you were extremely relieved."

"To say the least. How did you know things were no' as Tony said? Why did you come back?"

"You begged me to. I saw it in your eyes, as well as fear, misery, and desperation."

"We do that with each other." She kissed his hand again, just a brief, light touch.

She has no idea what she is doing to me. "Jeanie..." She ignored his whispered warning and rubbed her cheek across his knuckles. He gripped the arm of the settee with his other hand to keep from hauling her into his arms. "Jeanette, stop," he ordered, sounding sharper than he intended.

She released his hand and crossed her arms. Her cheeks darkened in the pale light as she stared straight ahead. "I'm sorry. I dinna know what's come over me. It's just that I've thought about you so much and dreamed about you so many times the past month—"

"What?" His heart began to pound. He nudged her chin up with his fingers, gently lifting her face until she met his gaze. "What are you saying, angel?" he asked, lowering his hand to his thigh.

She sighed heavily. "My emotions may be at sixes and sevens, but I'm no' just grateful because you saved me. You've been on my mind far too much since I met you. Sometimes, even when I was with Tony, I compared him with you. Every time I saw you, I wanted to be with you—to talk to you, dance with you, hear your voice, feel your arms around me." She frowned. "Between my dreams and daydreams, I've probably kissed you a hundred times," she said irritably.

He grinned. He couldn't help it. He felt like shouting with joy but managed to contain himself. "And you wanted the real thing," he said softly.

"Yes." She glanced up, saw his grin, and her frown deepened. "I dinna think it's funny."

"I'm not laughing at you. Only pleased."

"You dinna think I'm foolish?"

"Not at all. I'm honored."

"I know I'm young and green, no' very experienced in the ways of the world."

"May it always be so. You are wise in the ways that count, Jeanie.

Far wiser than I." Reality intruded on his joy. "You're leaving tomorrow."

"Come with us to Scotland."

"I doubt your brother would be too keen on that idea."

"He told me to invite you so we could become better acquainted." Uncertainty clouded her expression. "But come with us only if you want to. Dinna think you have to. Drat! This is harder than I thought it would be. You must think I'm throwing myself at you."

"I'll catch you," he said softly, scooting closer. Easing his hand from hers, he put his arm around her.

She looked startled, then smiled shyly.

"I'd like to see your Scotland, and I'd like very much to further our acquaintance. No, that's not exactly correct. I'd like very much to court you, but I'm twice your age, Jeanie."

"And twice the man of anyone younger."

He smiled and took a deep breath. "You're going to make me puffed up with pride. I'm liable to split the seams in my coat."

She shrugged and smoothed an imaginary wrinkle on his shirt. "From what I've seen, you can buy another."

"Several." He grew serious. "I've done many things I'm ashamed of. I'm even more conscious of them since I met you. Jeanie, I have no idea how many lovers I've had. I never kept a count, though I think there is a list in the betting book at White's."

She winced slightly before breathing deeply. "Is there someone now?"

"No. I give you my word that there would never be anyone else as long as you and I were involved, whether it was courtship or marriage."

She smiled. "I give you the same promise."

He laughed softly. "As if you would do such a thing in the first place." He hesitated, then decided he might as well have everything out in the open. "I know your faith is very important to you."

"It's the most important thing. I promised my father and God that I wouldna marry a man who does no' believe in Jesus as his Savior."

"I've only gone to church for weddings and funerals."

"But you've been reading the Bible."

"Yes. Sarah suggested it a year or so ago. She thought I might find solace there."

"And did you?"

"Some, but I still have many questions and doubts."

"All of us do. Often the answers are there, though we may have to dig to find them." She paused. "Sometimes they come through living and seeing God work things out in our lives."

"Is that why Drake died, and you were kidnapped?" he asked angrily. "So God could work things out?"

"I dinna know why Tony died. I wish with all my heart that he hadna. All I can do is trust God that he had a purpose in allowing it to happen, and that he did it for a good reason."

Puzzled, he shook his head. "How? How do you so faithfully trust him?"

"I choose to. God has given us a will, Dominic. We have the freedom to make our own decisions, for better or for worse. He will lead and guide, but the choice is ultimately up to us."

"It is not always that simple."

"No, it isna. Our desires and emotions sometimes rule over our minds. I hate Tony's father. I hate him for what he did to me, to Tony, and Tony's mother. Scripture says we should hate the sin and no' the sinner, but right now, I canna do that. I wish he had been the one killed instead of Tony. I wish he'd kidnapped me or just sent Gray instead of involving Tony. He's a wicked, evil man."

She closed her eyes and leaned her head against his arm with a sigh. "I pray each day that God will take this hatred from me, that he will soften my heart toward this man and help me forgive him. I pray that he will help me understand why Tony died and help me to forgive."

"Forgive Tony?"

"No," she said faintly. "I've already done that. He was even more of a victim than I was. I need to forgive God. It's all very confusing." She shook her head. "I know Tony tried to kill Gray. His actions were what led to his death. I love God and trust him with my life, but in this I have a hard time accepting that he did the right thing. My mind knows God does no' make mistakes, but my heart canna understand why it had to happen."

"And your kidnapping? Have you come to any conclusions about that?"

"Yes, I have. I never believed God caused it; he does no' do things that way. But I think maybe he allowed it to happen because he knows how stubborn I can be and how much I dislike hurting anyone. I probably would have kept on seeing Tony because I enjoyed his company and didna want to hurt his feelings. I might even have married him, which would have been a grave mistake."

"Mariah said God reveals things to you, like my loneliness. Sarah says sometimes it's as if God whispers to her in her mind. Why didn't he just tell you to quit seeing Tony?"

"I think he probably did, but I had too many conflicting emotions to understand him. The only way left was for Tony to show me the other side of his character." She paused, her expression tentative. "There was another reason."

"What?"

She looked up at him, and he caught his breath. "You," she said softly. "God brought you to me that day, Dominic."

He dared not dream what he thought he saw in her beautiful

eyes. "You needed rescuing."

"He could have sent anyone, but he sent you. I'm no' certain of all the reasons, but he wanted us to be together, if only for a little while."

I want forever. He barely kept the words from tumbling out. "Mariah said you have been praying for me."

"Since the day we met."

"Why?"

"Because God told me to. He showed me your loneliness, your despair, that night. His love can take that away."

"It's your love I need." He could have bitten off his tongue. *Please, God, don't let her think I'm just trying to seduce her.*

"Maybe, but you need Jesus more. He can heal the wounds I canna touch." She turned toward him and laid her hand on his chest. "He can work miracles, Dominic. He can mend your heart, cleanse your soul. I canna do that.

"God also saw my loneliness. He reads our hearts and minds and knows our innermost thoughts, our secret longings. You won my deep admiration at the Altbury ball when you came out onto the dance floor and caught me before I could be hurt and terribly humiliated. You didna know me, yet you did me a great kindness. When you held me close, I didna ever want to leave the shelter of your arms. And no' just because everyone in the room was staring at me."

"I didn't want to let you go."

"I know." She turned her head, resting her forehead against his neck.

"I noticed you when you first arrived and had wanted to meet you all evening. You don't know how tempted I was to sweep you up in my arms and carry you out the door."

"That would have caused a bigger commotion. I admit it would have been thrilling, except for having Kiernan chase you, roaring in

Gaelic," she said with a laugh.

"The thought crossed my mind," he said, smiling.

"Will you come to Scotland?"

"Not tomorrow. I must take care of some estate business before I can be gone for such a length of time."

She looked up at him. "When?"

Her hopeful expression was almost enough to make him forget about the estate and order his valet to pack their bags. "I should be able to get away within a fortnight."

"A week."

He laughed softly. "Ten days at the most. Why the frown?"

"I just remembered Kiernan said we should wait a month after I got home. That way we would both know our feelings better. We'd have a chance to change our minds if we needed to, with the promise of no ill will between us."

"Your brother is a wise man." Dominic did not know how he could stay away from her that long. If she changed her mind, it would be the end of him.

"I think we should have the freedom to cry off if we dinna suit."

"I will agree to that." He didn't want to, but he knew it was best.

"I dinna want to wait so long to see you. Will you leave as soon as you can?"

"I'll tend to my business and be on the road as soon as possible. Do you think Kiernan would bar the door—or is it lift the draw-bridge—if I arrived too soon?"

She grinned. "No drawbridge. No' even a moat. He wouldna wait that long if he wanted to see Mariah."

"No, he wouldn't." Dominic brushed her cheek with his knuckles. "You need your rest."

"No' yet." She caressed his cheek, tears glistening in her eyes. "I'm going to miss you so."

"I'll join you soon." He caught a tear as it slid down her cheek and lifted his finger to his lips. "Don't cry, my angel." He kissed the tear away on her other cheek. "How can I not follow you, when you have my heart?"

He kissed her, not with the sensual expertise perfected with many others, but with the love he had never expected to feel, the love he had unknowingly saved all his life for her. Jeanie's gentle innocence surrounded him, filling his heart and soul with a sweetness almost too pure and beautiful to contain. He lifted his head and saw his wonder reflected in her face as she slowly opened her eyes and gazed up at him.

"I love you, Jeanette," he said quietly. "I've never said that to anyone else. I have cared for others but did not love them. No matter what happens between us—even if you decide you never want to see me again—I will always be here for you. If you ever need help, you can call on me."

"I dinna think I can leave you."

"I don't want you to go, but you should. You need to seek God's guidance without me hovering nearby. I want you for my wife, but I don't know if it is best for you."

"Then you believe he directs us to what is right?"

"I believe he can direct you. I'm not certain God wants anything to do with me."

"He loves you, Dominic. He loves all of us. Just reach out to him with a willing heart."

"I'll try, I promise. Now, upstairs with you, my angel. You'll be exhausted before you even start the trip." He stood and tugged on her hand, drawing her up beside him. With his arm firmly around her shoulders, they walked across the hall and started up the stairs, halting abruptly when they spotted Kiernan and Mariah sitting near the first landing.

"What are you doing up there?" Embarrassment flooded Jeanette's cheeks.

To his amazement, Dominic also felt his face grow warm.

"We're supposed to chaperon you, remember?" said Kiernan, his expression somber.

Dominic noted that Kiernan had his arm around Mariah. He grinned in spite of his embarrassment. "I think you need a little more training."

Mariah giggled and Kiernan smiled. "We made sure you didna get carried away." He met Dominic's gaze. "I assume you willna be taking my advice and waiting a month to come see us?"

"You assume correctly." Dominic and Jeanette continued up the stairs, stopping in front of them. "I should be able to leave in a week."

Jeanie shot him a glance and a quick smile.

He leaned close to her ear. "You are very persuasive," he whispered.

She giggled and turned her head toward him. He leaned down so she could whisper into his ear. "So are you," she said, kissing his cheek.

She stepped away, walking past Kiernan and Mariah. Stopping behind them, she winked at Dominic and reached down, ruffling her brother's hair. "You're doin' a fine job, laddie." With a laugh and a sparkling smile directed at Dominic, she raced up the stairs.

Kiernan grinned. "She's lucky I'm too tired to chase her."

"You could stay awhile longer," Dominic said hopefully.

"Thank you, but no." Kiernan smiled at Mariah as she told him good night and quietly rose, following Jeanie up the stairs. "I received a strange letter from a former employee yesterday." He stood and walked up the stairs with Dominic. "He was the house steward and acted as my secretary. He is a nervous little man, and we didna work well together. While I was in London, I decided to pension him off. He was more than happy with the decision and moved to Edinburgh immediately.

"His letters have never been wordy, but this one was only two sentences. He thanked me for his first annuity payment, then told me to go over the ledgers carefully, talk to the tenants about their rents, and keep a close watch on Macnair, my factor."

"Do you think Macnair is stealing from you?"

"Maybe. Unfortunately, I know little about running an estate or keeping accounts. I've tried to learn since I inherited the estate, and Macnair has been a willing teacher. Too willing. I've felt all along that something isna quite right. Gabe knows a bit more than me, but no' much. I'm hoping Jordan learned enough working with Sir Edgar to detect what is amiss."

Dominic did not like the thought of trouble waiting for them. He knew Kiernan would do everything he could to protect Jeanette, but he was not willing to leave her safety in his hands alone. "I inherited my first property when I was three-and-twenty and have been thoroughly involved in the business of my estates since that time. Things may work somewhat differently in Scotland, but I expect I could determine before long whether or not he is cheating you."

He mentally went over the list of things that should be done before he left and decided most could wait. If he lost that piece of land he had planned to buy, then so be it. Given some written authority, his estate manager could handle everything else. "If you will delay your departure by two hours, I can go with you."

Kiernan looked at him in surprise. "I thought you needed a week."

"My man can handle most of it. What he can't do will have to wait." They stopped at Kiernan's door. "Jeanie told me that your reception at Branderee has not exactly been warm."

"It has no'. I know it must be hard for the servants and tenants to accept a stranger when most of them have been there for years. My cousins and their families were well loved."

"Then you will need all the help you can find." The beginning of a plan quickly formed in his mind. "We can tell Macnair that I'm looking to buy a Scottish estate, which I am, if Jeanie decides to marry me. She'll want to live close to you and your mother. That way, I can make inquiries about how things are done there."

Kiernan studied him thoughtfully. "It would be that easy for you to move?"

"Thornridge is my only real tie here, and the estate manager is more than capable of running it on his own if the arrangements are made. I have other properties, but I only visit them once or twice a year. I rarely see my sister and her husband, and then only by chance at social events during the Season. She has never forgiven me for putting a frog in her bed when I was five. Everything I have done since has only strengthened her disapproval and dislike." He met Kiernan's gaze. "I meant it when I said I'd give everything I have to see Jeanie happy."

"I'd be grateful for your help and glad to have you come with us. I doubt it will hurt to wait one more day to leave. I could use the rest, and it would give you a little more time to make arrangements."

Dominic nodded and turned away. "I'll tell Jeanie I'm coming with you." When Kiernan's hand clamped down on his shoulder, he grinned. He looked back at him. "No?"

Amusement twinkled in the Scot's eyes. "I'll tell her. It's ill dune to teach the cat the way to the kern."

Dominic thought he had the gist of the proverb, something akin to not putting temptation in another's path, but he asked anyway. "Care to translate?"

SONG OF THE HIGHLANDS

"It's wrong to teach the cat the way to the churn."

Laughing, Dominic walked on past Jeanie's room. Though he had gone to her often when she had nightmares, the temptation to linger would now be much greater.

A verse from Shakespeare's poem "Venus and Adonis" came to mind:

Love comforteth like sunshine after rain,
But Lust's effect is tempest after sun;
Love's gentle spring doth always fresh remain,
Lust's winter comes ere summer half be done:
Love surfeits not, Lust like a glutton dies;
Love is all truth, Lust full of forged lies.

He had long agreed with the poet about lust, though it had not stopped him from partaking of its fleeting pleasures. There were enough happily married couples around to acknowledge the existence of love and the truth of Shakespeare's lines. Yet he had never considered applying them to himself—until an angel fell into his arms.

God, thank you for Jeanie and her family. Help me to be strong for her sake. Make me worthy.

Please let her love me.

Dominic made a list of things he needed to tend to before he left, and then blew out the candles. He walked over to the window, unbuttoning his shirt, and looked up at the heavens. "God, I guess I've believed in you for a long time. I thought you were up there somewhere, watching us mortals destroy ourselves and your creation, then handing down harsh judgments because of our idiocy.

"But I've seen the changes you've made in Sarah these past few years, the happiness you've given her. She says it's because Jesus loves her and she loves him. Jeanie loves and trusts you, even though she doesn't understand about Tony, even though she is angry with you. Seems as though lately several people have come into my life who love Jesus. Maybe you sent them?"

He rested his hands on the windowsill, his heart heavy. "They say all I have to do is repent of my sins, believe that Jesus is your Son, and believe that he died for me. I do believe he is your Son, God. I see that truth in the Bible and in those who love him. I know that truth in my heart.

"I don't want to continue living the way I did in the past. It holds only emptiness, loneliness, hurt, and regret. I want to marry Jeanie and be a good, faithful husband. But, God, even if I cannot marry her, I will not go back to having lovers and mistresses or spending my time gambling or drinking. So I guess that means I repent of my sins. Those are just the obvious ones. You'll have to show me what else I need to change."

He pressed his forehead against the cold windowpane. "The Bible says Jesus died for the sins of the world, that he became a sacrifice so we could stand before you blameless. It says he conquered death and rose from the grave so that we might have a way to heaven.

"God, I've lived a wicked life. My soul is black, and though Jeanie brings joy and sunshine to my heart, even she cannot completely dispel the darkness there. I feel lost, alone, and afraid. Afraid not just of going to hell, but of living another forty years—another day—with this wretched emptiness. Is it true, God? Do you love me? Did Jesus die for Jeanie and Kiernan and Sarah and just those who are good, or did he die for me, too?"

He sank to his knees, feeling as if the weight of his sins might suffocate him. "Can you make me a new person? Can you wash me clean and give me a new heart? A new life?"

I've already begun.

"Do you love me, Jesus?"

I always have.

"But how? How can you love someone like me?"

Because it is what I do, who I am. You were created for me to love.

With those gentle, inaudible words spoken to his heart and mind, Dominic chose to believe, and in the choosing came the knowledge, the certainty that it was right and good and true.

Love flooded his soul and overflowed, surrounding him, comforting him, washing the despair and loneliness from his heart and filling it with peace and joy. Tears poured down his face as he let go of the past—the mistakes, the hurts, the regrets—and accepted the promises of the future and a new life in Jesus.

The next morning, Jeanie received a note from Dominic asking her to meet him in his study. When she arrived, she found him, Kiernan, and Mariah looking at a map of Scotland.

"Good morning, angel." Dominic straightened and came around his desk to greet her with a kiss on the cheek. "How are you this beautiful day?"

Raising an eyebrow, Jeanette glanced out the window at the pouring rain and dark gray sky. "Fine, thank you. And you?"

He ran a finger lightly along her jaw, smiling mischievously. "Happy. Excited." His voice dropped to a whisper as he leaned closer. "In love." He grabbed her hand, leading her over to the desk. "Kiernan has been showing me the route to Branderee. I enjoy traveling, but I think this will be the best trip I've ever taken."

Kiernan laughed. "Because of the company, no doubt."

"Precisely." Dominic slid his arm around Jeanette, keeping her at his side when Kiernan and Mariah sat down. "We shall have hours and hours to all become better acquainted."

"More like days and days," said Jeanie with a smile, looking up at him. Her heart had been singing ever since Kiernan told her Dominic was accompanying them. She had barely slept for the excitement.

"Delightful." He met her gaze and held it for a moment.

Jeanie caught her breath at what she thought she saw.

He turned away, grinning at Kiernan. "I want to hear all about your estate, about the Highlands, and life with the Gordons." He looked down at Jeanie, his expression softening. "And what this lovely lady was like as a child. Did she get into mischief? Or was she busy doing kind things for others?"

"Some of both. She was also forever taggin' along after Gabe and me."

Jeanie studied Dominic's face, searching his beautiful emerald eyes, and looking into his heart. She caught her breath. Gone was the desolation of a lost and lonely soul—in its place, the radiance of pure joy and peace.

She touched his face, blinking back a tear. "You've met the Savior."

Moisture glistened in his eyes. "Last night. I was hoping you could see the difference." When she nodded, he smiled at Kiernan and Mariah. "That's why I asked you here, to tell you. I've believed in God for a long time, probably most of my life. These past several months as I've studied the Bible and talked with Sarah, I've accepted the truth that Jesus is God's son.

"What I had trouble believing was that he could love me at all, much less enough to die for me. But you gave me hope that perhaps he might cleanse even a soul as black as mine." He took a deep, ragged breath. "So last night I asked him if he loved me, if he could make me new. I don't know what I expected, perhaps a sense of acceptance or relief."

"But you experienced much more," said Kiernan with a smile.

Dominic nodded. "It was...is...incredible." He looked at Jeanie. "I have only to think of what has happened to you to know everything won't be perfect. There will still be trials and probably temptations, but I feel this overwhelming assurance that Jesus will be there with me. He told me he has always loved me, and when I asked him how he could, he said simply that it's what he does."

"Oh, Dominic." Jeanie put her arms around him and hugged him fiercely. "I'm so happy for you. I thank God for allowing us to be here with you now."

He wrapped his arms around her, sighing softly. "I thank him that he brought you into my life." A few minutes later, he pulled away and turned to Kiernan and Mariah. "All of you. Without your understanding and encouragement, I might never have come to believe."

"He would have used someone else," said Kiernan quietly as he stood. "But I'm glad he didna." He held out his hand to Dominic. "Welcome to the family of God."

Dominic shook his hand. "A mere thank you seems so insufficient to express my gratitude."

Kiernan grinned. "I'll think of something for you to do when we get to Branderee." He turned to Mariah. "Shall we go tell the others the good news?"

"If Dominic doesn't mind," she said as she stood and wiped a tear from the corner of her eye.

"I would like them to know, but I didn't feel comfortable sharing it with everyone all at once. Please feel free to tell them." He looked at Mariah, his expression sobering. "Years ago, who would have thought we would be standing here like this?"

"Only God." She walked over and hugged him. "I'm so glad you've found him."

"So am I."

When Kiernan and Mariah left the room, shutting the door behind them, Dominic gently drew Jeanie into his arms. "Thank you for praying for me, for giving me the courage to choose to believe."

Jeanie nodded, afraid to speak lest she betray the emotion welling up in her heart. Though it seemed suspiciously like love, she had to be certain. Staying there alone with him did not seem wise.

When she knew she would not give herself away, she eased from his embrace with a smile, edging backward toward the door. "We have so much for which to be thankful." She reached the door and turned the handle behind her. "Right now, I'm especially glad Fletcher Card was such a terrible dancer."

At his jubilant laugh, she winked and slipped through the doorway, thanking God from the depths of her soul for his love and grace.

26

WHEN KIERNAN'S TRAVEL COACH, followed by four others, drove up the lane of Branderee Castle, the footman opened the door, took one wide-eyed look, and instantly disappeared. A few minutes later, the housekeeper, Mrs. Laing, came hurrying out the door followed by a string of footmen and maids.

"Welcome home, Lord Branderee," she said, puffing as she dipped into a shallow curtsy. She glanced at the other carriages. "I see you brought company."

"Didna you get my letter? I wrote from London that we would be leaving in a few days and bringing guests."

Mrs. Laing shook her head. "No, but we'll manage well enough, unless someone needs to lie down right away. It'll take a bit to prepare the beds. Dinner might no' be as grand as it should be, but ye willna go away hungry."

"I doubt anyone will want to rest." He scanned the caravan, as Wilton had dubbed it, smiling at the excited chatter as everyone tumbled out of the carriages. "We stopped for luncheon no' too long ago and didna travel long today. I'm certain you'll handle it all with your usual efficiency, though I do regret that you were no' forewarned."

Mrs. Laing looked over the crowd and smiled, her eyes sparkling.

Kiernan didn't think he had ever seen her look so happy. "I take that smile to mean our unexpected arrival has no' distressed you."

"Oh, no, milord, it makes me proud to finally hear happy voices and see smilin' faces in Branderee again."

"Aye, Mrs. Laing, I feel the same. The time for grieving is past. God has brought healing and joy into all our lives on this trip."

His gaze fell on Jeanie as she talked with Dominic, pointing toward the back of the castle which faced Moray Firth, a wide sea inlet. She had not complained the whole way, but she looked pale and weary, her smile strained. Ailsa said Jeanie had dreamed of Tony the night before and had woken up sobbing.

He expected it was because they had reluctantly agreed over dinner to tell Mrs. Laing and Macnair they returned early because of what happened to her. Jeanie had suggested it to keep Macnair from becoming suspicious. Kiernan had objected strongly until Gabe had pointed out the news would spread even if they or the servants who came back with them never said a word. There were other members of the aristocracy living along the coast who were either still in London or knew someone who was.

"There has been sorrow and sickness, too," he said quietly. "I think my sister may need to rest after all."

Mrs. Laing followed his gaze, her brow wrinkling in concern. "Why, the poor lass looks exhausted. I'll have Mary Alice make your sister's bed right away, and your mother's, too. How is she?" She looked around until she spotted Ailsa standing with Wilton, comfortably holding his arm. He leaned down and said something which made her laugh. "Ah, now, isna that a wonder," the housekeeper said softly, reaching for the corner of her apron and dabbing her eyes.

"Yes, it is," said Kiernan, thinking how few times his mother had laughed at Branderee. He caught Mariah's hand as she walked past and drew her over to them. "We've all brought home someone special.

This is Lady Mariah Douglas, the love of my life. I have no' quite persuaded her to become my wife, but I'm working on it. Mariah, this is Mrs. Laing, our undauntable housekeeper."

Mrs. Laing dipped into another curtsy. "It's a pleasure to meet you, milady. To think the laird had to go all the way to London to find himself a pretty Scottish lass," she said with a wide smile.

Mariah laughed and linked her arm through Kiernan's. "I'm afraid he wouldn't have found me in Scotland even if he had been looking. I've lived in England since I was young. It's very nice to be back."

"We'll do our best to convince ye to stay. Now, if you'll excuse me, there is much to do. We'll have tea and a bite of something to eat for you soon, milord."

"Thank you." Kiernan nodded and watched the housekeeper take charge, sending servants scurrying in all directions.

"She seems like a nice, friendly woman," said Mariah, looking up at him. "What's wrong?"

"She's always been nice in a remote way, but never friendly. And she called me the laird."

"She didn't before?"

"No one has. They used my title and milord, but never the laird. They both mean the same thing, but somehow being called the laird seems more affectionate. It makes me feel closer to them, more like I belong here."

"I expect she has worked through her grief, too, and is ready to accept a new laird and family in Branderee Castle. It must have been hard for them to lose everyone at once."

"I know it was. None of them could speak about Malcom or his family without becoming choked up or shedding tears. Maybe now we can all make a new beginning." He surprised Mariah by leaning down and kissing her soundly. When he straightened, her face was scarlet, but she was smiling.

"Kiernan!" she scolded softly. "You shouldn't do that in front of everyone."

"Get used to it. I'm the laird, and I want everyone to know you're goin' to be my lady."

"There are more subtle ways of showing it. Besides, I haven't said yes."

"You will," he said with a confident grin.

"Oh? Why are you suddenly so sure?"

"Because you love me," he said tenderly. Putting his arm around her, he looked up at the rugged stone castle with its towers at each end and corbeled turrets at the corners. "And because you love this place. You have no' stopped smiling since you first saw it from the drive."

"I do love it. It's wonderful." She laughed when he assumed his best sad-eyed-puppy expression. "I love you, and I think you're wonderful, too."

"That's better. Come on, I'll show you the view of the firth. Everyone else is going around back anyway." They followed a wide walkway through trees, shrubs, and flower beds around a five-story tower and a lower wing that housed the kitchens, work rooms, and servants' quarters.

Moving past the building, they walked into an open grassy area bordered on three sides by a four-foot stone wall. A slightly shorter wing extended from the other end of the castle. "That's the chapel," said Kiernan. He smiled and made a sweeping motion with his hand. "And that's the view."

Beyond the wall, pale blue water extended to the horizon as the eastern portion of Moray Firth blended into the North Sea. Half a dozen seagulls glided by, dipping and swaying in the light breeze, calling for a handout. The water lapped gently on the shore below, making a soothing background for their cries.

As they walked toward the wall, the coastline to the west came into view. Inland, the ground was almost level and covered with long green grass which became shorter close to the shore. The ground sloped at a sharp angle down to the gravelly shore. From there a rough and barren stretch of rock spread out into the water. Gulls nested on the rocks, and their screeching calls drifted on the wind toward the castle.

They reached the wall, and Mariah peered down the cliff to the water nearly a hundred feet below. "Kiernan, I know you miss your mountains, but this is one of the most beautiful places I've ever seen." She took a deep breath of the fresh sea air. "It's so peaceful, so refreshing." Her contented expression said she could stay there forever.

"Peaceful now, but wait until a storm comes in. Sometimes I think the wind is going to take the castle right with it." He smiled and put his arm around her. "Mrs. Laing assures me that it's only the shutters rattling. True enough, the only damage done all winter was a shutter blown off one of the tower windows. These thick stone walls have withstood nature for centuries and probably will hold her at bay for several more. I do enjoy being out here, even at the beginning of a storm. 'Tis glorious to see the clouds churning and building over the sea."

"It must be." She gazed out at the water. "You said your cousin anchored his yacht here, but the coastline looks too rocky for a rowboat, much less a ship."

"It is, except right next to the castle."

She peered over the wall again.

Kiernan leaned forward, too, enjoying the feel of her body tucked comfortably next to his. "The water is deep all around the cliff. There are coves on either side of the castle, but you have to be next to the side wall to see them. Both are deep enough for a ship, though only one is wide enough. It is also the only one that can be reached from land."

He took her hand, leading her back to the west side of the yard so they could look over the top of the wall. "This is where Malcom moored his ship. There is a channel leading right to it, but I'm told it takes an experienced sailor to navigate it. It's an easy walk down the path to the dock. Malcom's cousin kept his yacht in a cove about a mile west of here. Most of the coastline in that direction is low-lying, with the land coming right down to the water. There are wee sandy coves and harbors all along it, nooks and crannies as the local people call them. Many of them can only be seen from the sea."

"Have you thought about buying a ship?"

"No' me. I have no interest in going on the sea. If I do any sailing, it will be in a small boat on Loch Laggan or another loch where I can see the shore."

They walked across the grass to the chapel side of the yard. The coastline to the east was not as rocky, but the land rose straight up from the water. The narrow cove next to the castle was bordered on two other sides by the cliff.

"There is no way to get down to it?" asked Mariah.

"No' that I can find. I thought there might be a way to reach it from inside the castle, but I have no' found a tunnel or anything that might lead to it. I've studied the castle from the other cliff and canna see any kind of entry, though the walls go down nearly to the water. I suppose with the good cove on the other side, they didna see any reason to use this one when they built the castle."

"I think I would have built a way out." She smiled impishly. "You never know when you might need another escape route."

"My thinking exactly. The dungeon is on this side, too."

"Beneath the chapel?"

"Under the tower section. The chapel was added later. They probably felt guilty about what went on in the dungeon. We'll have to explore it together. You might spot something I've missed." He leaned closer. "And it would give us a chance to be alone."

She looked up at the huge building. "I doubt we'll have trouble finding a hidden corner away from curious eyes. Maybe someplace nicer than the dungeon," she added with a grin.

"The sooner the better."

They strolled back to the middle of the wall, joining Jeanie, Dominic, Ailsa, and Wilton. Jordan was a short distance away, having a chat with a gull strutting along the top of the wall. Kiernan was pleased to see that Jeanie's cheeks had regained some color, and her eyes sparkled when she smiled. He tugged lightly on a curl that blew across her forehead. "I think you're glad to be here, Posy."

"I am. I've missed Branderee, especially the sea air and view of the firth. I began feeling better the minute we walked around the building."

Wilton struck a dramatic pose, one hand on his chest, the other flung upward toward the castle, proclaiming:

"This castle hath a pleasant seat; the air
Nimbly and sweetly recommends itself
Unto our gentle senses."

He bowed to Ailsa, then to the others.

"Well done, sir, and appropriate to use *Macbeth*," said Dominic.

"One of the more cheerful lines," said Jeanie with a laugh. She tugged on Dominic's arm. "Let's go see if Mrs. Laing has the tea ready. After we have a bite, we can take a tour of the castle."

"A wonderful idea." He looked at Kiernan and grinned. "If we're lucky, maybe we'll lose Kiernan and Mariah along the way."

"That might be arranged," said Kiernan as they all started toward the door.

"Just dinna be lost too long," said Ailsa with a small smile.

"Yes, ma'am," Dominic and Kiernan said in unison, making everyone laugh.

"I dinna know, maybe we should chaperon you two." Kiernan winked at his mother, grinning when she blushed.

"We're old and wise enough to take care of ourselves," said Ailsa.

When they stepped into the castle, walking directly into the great hall, Mariah gasped in delight. The room was sixty feet long and thirty wide, with an equally high arched ceiling. Heavy medieval tapestries hung over the stone walls, and each end of the room held a massive fireplace. Modest fires burned in both, displacing the coolness that lingered in the hall well into summer. "I feel as if I just stepped back four hundred years."

"Only two hundred. This section was built to look older so it would blend in with the towers. The first tower was built around 1360, and the second around 1570. There's no record why they didna just add a wing or build the second tower right next to the first one. Thirty years later, one of the earls added this to join the towers. He also built the wings which house the kitchen and chapel.

"The sword and targe in the center above the fireplace belonged to the first Lord Branderee. The ones flanking them belonged to each successive earl."

"There are only nine swords up there."

"I'll mount mine someday, but for now, I'm keeping it handy. I dinna have a targe, but neither did the last two earls."

Jordan was inspecting a polished suit of armor in one corner. He looked over at Kiernan and grinned. "I think it might fit."

"Try it if you want, but I'd hate for you to get stuck in it. You'd have to raise the visor every time you wanted to say something."

"Writing might be a chore, too. Not to mention walking." Jordan moved to a large glass case displaying numerous dirks, pistols, and muskets. "I'm glad the clans don't fight each other anymore."

"There are a few feuds still goin'," said Mrs. Laing, walking in ahead of four footmen carrying the tea service and several trays of food. "None locally. We're fairly civilized these days. Things are usually taken care of in the law courts, though now and again mischief has to be handled directly."

"England is much the same," said Jordan.

Dominic took Jeanie's hand. "Sometimes it cannot be called mischief."

"We have some of that, too. Thankfully no' as much as we used to. Now, here's some smoked salmon, bread and butter, a bit of fruit." She supervised the footmen as they placed the trays on a heavy, ornately carved Elizabethan table. Two mahogany couches upholstered in ivory silk sat near it. "Your room is ready if you are tired, Miss Jeanette, though you look a bit perkier than you did when you arrived."

"I'm feeling much better, thank you. But it's nice to know I can lie down if I feel like it."

After eating, they all toured the main floor together. A drawing room almost as large as the great hall ran beside it along the front of the castle. The plaster ceiling was flat and lower, with a beautiful coat of arms in the center. The blue velvet sofas and armchairs were complemented by gilt mirrors and tables made in the slender, graceful Regency style.

Mariah walked slowly around the room, admiring dozens of painted panels adorning the walls. Each depicted a different romantic Scottish landscape—ruined castles, the sea, mountains, lochs, and glens. "These are lovely, even prettier than the Scottish paintings my parents had. I like this one especially," she said, gazing at a loch framed by misty mountains.

Kiernan put his arm around her. "It's my favorite. It looks much like Loch Laggan." Glancing at the other scenes beside it, he smiled. "I enjoy them and often discover some small detail I've missed."

The music room was adjacent to the drawing room, with a billiard room beyond that. A short door at one end of the great hall led to a corridor and a two-person wide, spiraling staircase going up to the other floors. In the other direction, the corridor took them to the chapel. Kiernan's study and a huge library opened off the hallway between the stairs and the chapel.

At the other end of the main room were the dining room and a smaller breakfast room. Another staircase gave access to the upper floors, and a hallway led to the kitchen and various other work areas for the servants. Kiernan pointed to a heavy, arched door beside the staircase. "That leads down to the dungeon and wine cellar. We'll save it for later so you can see the other rooms before we lose the afternoon light."

Jordan stayed with Gabriel in the library while the others wandered through the rest of the castle. "I'll find my way around soon enough," he said, his eyes twinkling with good humor.

The three couples climbed the wide, elaborate mahogany stairway together, but when they reached the second floor, Ailsa and Wilton went one way while Dominic and Jeanie went the other. Kiernan grabbed Mariah's hand. "Come on, lass, I'll show you one of the towers that overlooks the firth."

She laughed as they walked up the next flight of stairs. "Kiernan, when I first met you, you said your castle was so big you couldn't find your way from one end to the other. This house plan is not very complicated. How can you get lost?"

"Well, I suppose I exaggerated a wee bit, though I do tend to be confused by some of the storage rooms. There's an arsenal on the second floor, guns for hunting and others for protection, even a small cannon. There are three rooms of clothes and furniture, and another room somewhere that is full of porcelain. Malcom's mother collected it, and his wife carried on the tradition."

"Is it simply sitting on shelves gathering dust or in display cases?"

"In cases. Seems like a waste to me, but I guess women like it. There is also a room for the silver on the third floor." He smiled as they continued up toward the top floor. "I know where that one is." He lowered his voice to a whisper. "And where the jewel vault is. Four centuries' worth. Bless Fiske, he might be a nervous old fellow, but he had a complete inventory of everything in the house, from the spoons to the diamonds."

Her eyes grew wide. "Diamonds?"

"And pearls, rubies, emeralds, sapphires, gold crosses. Probably every jewel known to man, some loose, some set in various trinkets. Fiske was the only one who knew where the safe was. If you're nice, I'll show it to you."

"I don't want to know. You can show me some of the jewels if you want, but do it in a different place than where they are hidden."

"Nae, lass. You're going to be my wife. Those jewels are security, as well as the coins and banknotes kept in another vault. I want you to know where they are in case there is ever an urgent need for funds, and I am no' here."

"You don't believe in banks?"

He grinned. "I have money there, too. Like the previous earls, I dinna believe in having it all in one place. I'll show you where everything is tomorrow."

"You trust me so much?"

"I trust you with everything I own, and everything I hold dear, including my heart and my life." He searched her face, wanting to ask how much she trusted him. With her heart? Her life? Remembering his promise to be patient, he kept silent.

The turret provided a round lookout room, though the view was not quite circular; a small part of it was blocked by being attached to the castle. Mariah went to the first window, which looked over much of the land east of the castle, as well as the shoreline and part of the firth. The grass-covered landscape sloped gradually upward away from the sea, giving rise to a small hill now and then. Black cattle grazed in the rock-fenced pastures. Half a mile away, a village nestled around a cozy harbor where several fishing boats were anchored.

"What is the name of the village?"

"Branderee," he said quietly. "Twelve fishing boats sail from there, and they keep us constantly supplied with fresh fish. Some of the villagers are involved in salting and drying huge quantities of cod, ling, skate, and haddock. We export much of it to Leith, Montrose, and Dundee."

"And the wonderful salmon we had with tea, do they catch it, too?"

"No, others own the fishing rights on the rivers. Sometimes we purchase it in Banff, but I prefer salmon from the Spey. It probably does no' taste any better, but we lived near the Spey in the Highlands so I think it does." Kiernan stood behind her and slid his arms around her, resting his jaw against the top of her head.

"Is the village on your land?" she asked quietly.

"Yes, it's at the edge of it. I'm thinking my cousin could have put more money into the estate. The houses for the villagers and the tenants are no' bad, but they could be much better. I've been considering building new ones."

"That should win them over."

"It might help. I want to plant trees, too. No' just some here around the house, but grow a real forest."

Mariah smiled. "Wouldn't it be simpler to buy yourself a house in the Highlands?"

"I'll probably do that, too. A wee one with ten or twelve rooms."

"That's not exactly small."

"A lot smaller than this, but big enough for family and friends to visit."

"This is certainly a nice place to come with a cup of tea first thing in the morning," she said with a contented sigh.

"The sunrises are beautiful, but it takes coffee to appreciate them."

She laughed and turned around to face him, looping her arms around his neck. "That early in the morning, it would indeed take coffee to keep my eyes open. I love your castle, Kiernan."

His gaze fell on her lips as he lowered his head. "I'm glad."

They had spent most of their waking hours together on the trip but had not been alone for two weeks. He drew her tightly against him, and she came willingly, longing for him as much as he longed for her. Kiernan stepped back, carrying her with him, until he was against the wall and well out of view of anyone below. He kissed her again and again, their passion increasing with each touch, each whispered word of love, until they both trembled with need.

Holding her close, he buried his face in her hair and fought for control. "Marry me," he whispered, his voice ragged. "I need you, Mariah. I want to see your face when I blow out the candles at night and again at morning's first light. I want to be able to hold you and kiss you anytime I feel like it. To fill Branderee with love and wee redheaded bairns."

"And black-haired ones, too," she said softly, kissing his throat. "You've won my trust, Kiernan, and made me believe that someone besides God can truly love me. Aye, my braw man, my love, my life. I'll marry you."

"Soon?" He looked into her eyes, his heart pounding wildly.

"Right this minute if you want. I'm sure we could find two people around here who would witness our pledge to each other."

Kiernan leaned his head against the wall and closed his eyes. There was nothing in the world he wanted more. By Scottish law, all they needed for a legal, irregular marriage were two witnesses to hear them accept each other as husband and wife. Afterward, he could carry her downstairs to his bed and love her in the way he desperately wanted.

Unfortunately, irregular marriages were more easily challenged than regular ones—those performed by a minister. The possibility of its being contested was heightened by the fact that he held a title. It probably would not happen in his lifetime, but after his death some distant relative might try to claim Branderee. As long as they lived openly as man and wife, Mariah and the children would likely win any lawsuit, but he was not willing to risk putting them through a legal hearing.

He looked down at her and caressed her shoulders. "Lass, if I were still a piper or even a forester like my father, I'd do it without a second thought. But my life is no longer simple. I have a title to pass on, and great wealth to be shared with you and our children. I must ensure that no one can question my son's right to become the next earl, or if we have no son, that the line can pass on through a daughter. I pray God will grant me a long life by your side, but I'll no' risk the slightest chance that you might be called into court to prove that ye were my true and honest bride."

"I suppose we can survive the few weeks it takes to post the banns." She smiled ruefully. "Though it will be difficult."

"Yes, it will." He pulled her close again, kissing her gently. "But God will give us the strength to use restraint."

"No more trips alone to the tower?"

He glanced around at the stone floor and the two chairs by the window. "I think we're safe here. When I make ye mine, it will be in comfort, no' on a cold, stone floor."

27

KIERNAN, JORDAN, GABRIEL, AND DOMINIC rose early the next morning, shutting themselves away in Kiernan's study to go over the ledgers. After inspecting the records for the last two years, both Dominic and Jordan agreed they could not find any obviously incorrect entries.

There were several expenses listed without supporting receipts, but Kiernan had caught those previously. "Macnair had an explanation for each one and showed me where he had made the improvements."

"We still need to check all the improvements he has listed and make certain they have been done," said Dominic. "His explanations are not as detailed as I would like."

"He could have listed purchasing material for two projects but only have done one," said Kiernan thoughtfully. He looked at the ledger again. "Each time there is a receipt missing, the same materials have been bought for a similar improvement."

"Like these two where he bought rocks to build fences," said Jordan. "Only he doesn't say where they were built."

"He showed me two sections of fence that had been replaced, but I have no idea whether or no' it took as much rock as he said it did."

"We should look into it. We should also check the price of materials. There is always the possibility that the supplier charged too much and split the excess with Macnair. I'll ride into Banff and see if I can find out anything," said Jordan.

"I'll talk to the fishermen and people in the village," said Gabriel. "Since he oversees the fish exporting, he might be altering receipts and pocketing some of the money."

"And I'll talk to the tenants," said Kiernan. "I want to hear directly from them how much they are paying in rent. I'll also ask him to show Dominic around the estate."

"I'll ask his advice on everything," said Dominic with a sly smile.

"Are you taking Jeanie with you?"

"No, I don't want to risk having her around in case I ask something that makes Macnair suspicious. Besides, she'd distract me too much, and I'd miss half what the man said. When we went driving around Thornridge, she visited with every tenant's wife and hugged every child. Needless to say, she won their hearts. I was deeply moved by her tenderness toward them."

"She's done the same here. Tenants that watch me with distrust break into smiles when they see her," said Kiernan. "I've asked Mariah to go with me. I want to show her Branderee, and it should keep Macnair from noticing that I'm visiting everyone." He glanced at the clock. "Time to put away the records and look like fools. Macnair should be here any time."

When someone knocked on the door a few minutes later, Gabriel opened it. "Come in, Mrs. Laing, Mr. Macnair." He looked back at Kiernan. "Jordan and I will be on our way." Turning to Mrs. Laing, he asked, "Do you need anything from the village, ma'am?"

"No, thank you, Mr. Macpherson. I'll go to the market in Banff on Friday." Entering the room, she smiled affectionately at Gabriel, who had charmed her months before. "Which lass are you goin' to sweet-talk today?"

"All of them," he said with a roguish smile.

"I'm going into Banff to find my way around," said Jordan. "Is there anything that cannot wait until Friday?"

"I dinna believe so, but I thank you for asking."

Kiernan introduced Jordan to Macnair before he left.

"He's such a nice man," said Mrs. Laing as Jordan shut the door behind him.

"Yes, he is. Until he became my secretary, he was the vicar in Lady Mariah's local parish. He is a kind and knowledgeable man, but hated giving sermons. I consider myself fortunate to have him. Please sit down. Mr. Macnair, may I introduce my friend, Dominic Thorne."

Dominic and Macnair exchanged polite greetings. Kiernan thought the factor seemed uneasy.

"Mr. Thorne is courting my sister and hopes to have a good reason to buy an estate near here soon." Kiernan winked at Dominic. "Judging from the way Jeanette looks at him, I'd say the odds are likely that he will. Since you are our local expert, Mr. Macnair, I was hoping you might take him around Branderee this afternoon and answer some of his questions about how things are done here." He shrugged and sat down. "I fear there are many things I canna tell him."

Macnair sat up a little straighter. "I'd be happy to, milord. I ken you've got the right of it. Nothing goes on around here that I dinna know about."

"Splendid," said Dominic. "I do so want to provide a good home for Jeanette. Don't want to make a muddle of things right off, you know."

"How are things, Macnair? Are there any problems I should know about?" asked Kiernan.

"No, sir. Everything is runnin' smooth. We had twenty new calves when I counted yesterday and should have several more within the week. The fishing has been good. Sent another shipload of dried fish to Montrose on Monday last."

"Excellent. I'm happy to hear you've had no problems. And the tenants, are they all well?"

"Mrs. Storrie had twin boys this morn. They are all fine."

"I'll have to pay them a call and congratulate them," said Kiernan, glancing at Dominic who was shaking his head with a smile.

"Two more for Jeanie to cuddle," said Dominic.

"She'll be a good mother, that one," said Mrs. Laing. "Such a sweet, gentle lady she is. She brings out the good in people."

Kiernan tapped his fingers on the desk. He did not want to talk about what happened to Jeanie, but he had decided Gabriel was right. It would be better for the servants and others to hear the accurate version, even if condensed. He sighed heavily. Thinking about what she had been through still hurt.

"Unfortunately, not in everyone, Mrs. Laing. We have decided it would be best to tell you both the reason for our early return so you can correct any erroneous gossip should you hear it. From the start of the London Season, Jeanie had numerous men vying for her attention. She favored one young man, Tony Drake, in particular. We all liked him. He was friendly, well-mannered, highly respected, and came from a good family.

"Jeanie told him from the beginning that she wasna looking for a husband, but Tony was intent on changing her mind. Unknown to us, his family was in financial difficulties, and his father counted on Jeanie's dowry to bail them out. When Tony wasna able to convince my sister to marry him right away, his father arranged for Tony and some hooligans to kidnap her."

Mrs. Laing gasped and covered her mouth. Tears sprang to her eyes.

Macnair scowled and shook his head. "To think anyone would hurt that sweet lass."

"Thanks be to God, she wasna harmed physically, but emotionally it has been a very difficult experience. At first, they made it appear Tony was being kidnapped, too. Things didna go as they had planned, and she found out he was a part of it. Because she considered him a dear friend, it was very hard on her."

"Did you catch up with them, Lord Branderee?" asked Mrs. Laing, wiping her eyes.

Kiernan shook his head. "We were trailing them, but they were several hours ahead of us. God intervened in the form of a broken wheel." He looked at Dominic. "And by sending someone else to rescue her. Dominic had met Jeanette several weeks earlier. He has an estate near where their coach had broken down. When he came along, he sensed all was not right despite Tony's assurance that they needed no help.

"Being outnumbered four to one, he drove on, but came back by way of another road behind them. He attracted Jeanie's attention, and she managed to slip away from the others. Dominic hustled her into his curricle and took her to his estate. He then dispatched men to apprehend Tony and the others and to intercept us so that we would know Jeanie was safe.

"In the meantime, Tony and one of the other kidnappers had an argument. Tony was killed, and the others fled, all except for the family's old coachman. He stayed with Tony's body and told Dominic's men what happened."

"Did you capture the others?"

"No. They have vanished, probably hiding in London's underworld."

"What about the young man's father? Did you file charges against him?" asked Mrs. Laing.

"Jeanie asked me no' to, and I didna want to see her suffer any more. She only wanted to come home, to put it all behind her. It probably would have done us no good anyway. I expect Tony's father would have blamed it all on him, saying it was his son's misguided way of trying to help them."

"But wouldna the coachman tell what happened?"

"He might, but Tony's father is a viscount. He would be tried by his peers, not in a regular court but in the House of Lords. Who do you think the lords would choose to believe? The magistrate is looking for the men who did the actual kidnapping and killed Tony, but he says it isna likely they will ever be found."

"After Tony's coach broke down, they waited in the rain for one of the men to bring another one," said Dominic. "Jeanie was soaked when I found her. She took a fever and was sick for several days."

"Which is why I was so concerned about her when we arrived yesterday," said Kiernan. "She occasionally has nightmares and falls into the dismals. She is doing better every day, but I wanted you to know the situation."

"Thank you for telling us, sir. We'll set any gossips straight if we hear anything," said Macnair. "May I wish you happy, Lord Branderee? Mrs. Laing tells me you are engaged."

"I am. Thank you for the good wishes. I'm no' sure Lady Mariah is up yet. If she isna, we'll probably see you this afternoon. I'm taking her for a drive around the estate and introducing her to the tenants."

"I look forward to meeting her. If that will be all, sir, I should be off to work."

"I believe that is everything. Thank you for coming by."

Macnair nodded and looked at Dominic. "Shall I come back around one o'clock, sir?"

"That would be fine, Mr. Macnair. Thank you."

Both employees stood, but Kiernan asked Mrs. Laing to stay for a minute. After Macnair left the room, Dominic closed the door.

"Is there a problem, Lord Branderee?" she asked.

"That is what I'm hoping you can tell me, Mrs. Laing. I received a letter from Fiske before we left England. He told me to keep a close eye on Macnair. Have you noticed anything unusual or heard anything strange from the tenants?"

"Well, they didna take too kindly to you raising the rent right off, I can tell you that."

Kiernan glanced at Dominic. "Understandable. Anything else? Has Macnair done anything that strikes you as odd?"

"He came in last week and did some bookkeeping, then he went upstairs. He was gone for a long time. When he came down, I asked him what he was doin' up there. He said he'd been up in the tower enjoyin' the scenery. It struck me as a wee bit odd, but since I've done the same thing, I didna question him anymore.

"That night, one of the maids said she had seen him coming out of the room where all the weapons are kept. I didna see him carrying any guns, but he might have had them hidden beneath his coat. Now that I think of it, while you were gone, he's come by two or three times to borrow a musket for hunting. I canna remember him bringing them back. I should have said something to you, my lord, but in all the excitement of you comin' home, I forgot about it."

"Dinna worry about it, Mrs. Laing. I appreciate you telling me now. I trust you'll keep our conversation just between us?"

"Of course, sir."

"Is there anything else?"

"No' that I can think of."

"Let me know if anything comes to mind." Kiernan stood and escorted the housekeeper to the door. "Thank you."

After she left, Dominic met Kiernan's gaze. "I didn't notice that you raised the rent."

"I didna."

Dominic frowned thoughtfully. "My estate manager has keys to almost everything. Does Macnair?"

Kiernan nodded grimly. "Including the castle."

After sharing a second breakfast with Mariah, Kiernan took her upstairs to the third floor. "The silver is in here," he said, unlocking the door.

Mariah entered a tiny room, expecting to see a display cabinet. She held up the lamp they had brought with them. The room was empty. "Kiernan, there is nothing here."

"This is the antechamber. I'll have to unlock the other door." He turned sideways and scooted by her, stopping long enough to give her a kiss. "Sweet," he said softly, feathering another kiss at the corner of her lips. "The perfect breakfast dessert."

She patted his hard stomach as he straightened. "Better for you than apricot tarts."

He nodded and sorted through the keys on a large ring.

"Kiernan, you're supposed to say it tastes better, too."

"I am?" He would have looked as innocent as a small boy except for the impish twinkle in his eyes. When she nodded, he grinned. "But I greatly like apricot tarts."

"Ohhh." Narrowing her eyes and fighting back a smile, she tried to tickle the one place on his ribs she had discovered made him squirm.

He dodged her fingers and caught her hand, holding her at bay. "However," he said, emphasizing the word, "no' as much as I like you. I could live without apricot tarts but no' without you."

"Much better." She smiled as he released her hand and unlocked the door. The doorway was arched and low, a defense tactic built into many medieval castles. Attackers had to bend or crouch down to enter a room, which gave those inside the advantage of striking the first blow before their adversaries could straighten.

Mariah ducked through the door. When she stood up, she stared at the room with her mouth hanging open. Perhaps a dozen display cabinets lined the walls and formed two back-to-back rows down the center of the room, each filled with silver of every kind. There were tea, coffee, and chocolate sets, candlesticks, salt cellars, compotes, and serving platters. There were also dinner plates and goblets by the score, as well as numerous bowls and half a dozen silver baskets. One cabinet was completely filled with chests of flatware.

"Someone certainly liked silver," she said, mildly dazed.

Kiernan laughed. "Mainly the fifth through eighth earls, according to Fiske. We could have a hundred to dinner and eat off silver plates."

"The dining table would hold that many."

"And has. Mrs. Laing said Malcom and his wife entertained the local aristocracy and gentry regularly, even if they didna like to go to London."

"How does she keep it all polished?" She peered closely at an intricately engraved compote. "There isn't a speck of tarnish on any of it."

"The maids work up here several days a month."

Mariah looked over the display, going slowly from one case to another. There were some curious empty spaces and arrangements on the shelves. "Mrs. Laing must keep some of it downstairs."

Kiernan frowned. "I dinna think so. Mother prefers the china tea service. Why do you think so?"

"Look at these two cabinets. See how everything is neatly arranged? Even artistically?"

"Mrs. Laing is very particular about how things are put away. She does have an eye for makin' things look pretty."

"Now, look at this one. It looks out of balance, like things have been moved around to make it look fuller than it is."

"They have." Kiernan studied the heavy silver in the cabinet. "I remember these because they are the oldest pieces. Most belonged to the fifth earl, but many were old when he bought them. There were two pairs of candlesticks and two goblets adorned with a ring of rubies. The earl and his wife each had a set of the candlesticks in their bedchambers. According to family legend, if he was home, they drank a toast to each other every night before retiring, using the goblets."

"Do you think Macnair took them when he was up here last week?"

"He might have. They would be heavy, but he wears a large coat much of the time. We'll check the arsenal when we go back downstairs." They left the room, locking the doors behind them. He pointed to a room across the hall. "That's either where the porcelain is or some of the clothes. I have no' been in there since Fiske showed them to me."

They walked on, and he stopped at another room midway down the hall. When he unlocked the door and opened it, Mariah glanced around. It was full of wardrobes and trunks. "Clothes?"

"From the fifteenth and sixteenth centuries. You know how frugal Scots are; we never throw anything away."

She laughed, watching with interest as he walked directly toward two ornately carved wardrobes sitting side by side. A row of rosebuds and Scottish thistles, intertwined with ivy, had been carved across the top and bottom of the front. Matching carvings framed each side of the wardrobe, and three horizontal rows of the flowers divided the side into panels. "Those are beautiful."

He stood in front of them, tipping his head to one side. "They are. Fiske said he believed they were made for the third earl, but he wasna quite sure." He turned to her and held out his hand. "Please come here, lass."

She did as he asked, taking his hand. He drew her up beside him. "Now, love, count down five thistles from the top on the right side and press on it."

Mariah stepped around to the side of the wardrobe and counted the thistles, pressing it. It moved slightly beneath her fingers, but she couldn't see anything else happening.

"Now, go to the back row of carving on the right side and count down fifteen rosebuds."

She followed his instructions. When her fingers hovered over the fifteenth rosebud, she looked at him. "Press it?"

He nodded. "Now come around to the front and on the left side, count up ten leaves from the bottom and nudge it upward. When you do that, look carefully between the wardrobes toward the back and see what happens."

Mariah complied, noting that there was just enough space between the wardrobes for a man's fingers. She nudged up the leaf and focused on the space between the wardrobes. A block of wood some two inches square moved slowly out of the wardrobe on the right and pressed up against the other piece of furniture. She heard a faint click, and the block of wood moved back to its original place.

"Come around here," said Kiernan, clasping her hand. The lower panel on the outer side of the left wardrobe had swung open, revealing a hidden compartment. He kneeled down, lifting out a heavy, locked wooden coffer and set it on top of a trunk.

"Jewels?" she whispered.

"Jewels." He took a small key from his sporran. "I keep the key behind one of the stones in the fireplace in my bedchamber. I'll show you where in a minute." He unlocked the chest and lifted the lid. "If you see anything you particularly like, help yourself."

Mariah couldn't seem to catch her breath. She had never seen so many sparkling gems in her life, not even on all the ladies gathered at one of London's most elaborate balls. The strand of pearls and single emerald pendant and earrings she had inherited from her mother seemed paltry indeed compared to such splendor.

"Much of it is old and gaudy by today's fashions. Fiske's list noted the things Malcom had bought his wife, and what she had brought into the marriage. I gave them back to her family. But there are a few baubles I thought you might enjoy." He peeked at her face. "Dinna you see anything you like?"

Speechless, she nodded.

He chuckled and picked up a strand of creamy pearls. "These would look nice with that peachcolored dinner dress." He fastened them around her neck and picked up a small gold cross on a gold chain. "This would look nice with your brown frock, or any of your other day dresses." He dug around in the pile and took out a heavy emerald necklace. "How about this one?"

"Too heavy," she croaked, then cleared her throat. "Is there one with smaller stones?"

"I think so. Look and see. This tray comes out. There are more beneath."

Mariah carefully lifted the top section out of the chest, setting it on the trunk. The second tray was neater than the first, and she quickly found a lovely emerald pendant attached to a gold chain adorned with smaller emeralds. "This one is beautiful. It doesn't look outdated at all."

"I think there are matching earrings."

She dug around some more until she found the earrings, setting them aside with the necklace. "The set is lovely." There was also a pretty ruby set, with necklace, earrings, and bracelet. The stones were a little larger, so it was heavier, but she liked it. She set those aside, too.

"What else is there?"

She caught a distinct note of eagerness in his tone and glanced up at him.

He grinned. "Having fun?"

"I've felt like Cinderella ever since you swept into my life," she said with a smile. Standing on tiptoe, she kissed him lightly. "Now, even more so."

"That makes me a prince." He laughed. "I dinna think ol' King George would like that." He turned her back around toward the coffer. "I think I saw some sapphires in there once."

"I don't see any." She carefully shifted the heavy necklaces and bracelets. "I like this gold bracelet, though." She slipped the engraved band on her arm.

"Maybe they're in the next section. I'll move this one out of your way."

The only things on the next layer were a sapphire necklace with matching drop earrings and a bracelet.

"Kiernan, they're breathtaking." She picked up the necklace, each oval stone the same size and color, and held it up to the light. "These are not old."

"I went to the jewelers the day after you wore that pretty cream-colored dinner dress. They are made just for you. I wanted to give them to you then, but I knew you wouldna take them."

Tears burned her eyes. "You loved me even then?"

"Lass, I told you I started falling in love from the very beginning."

"And the emeralds?"

"I bought them a week later."

"After I wore the pale green dress."

Blinking back tears of happiness, she picked up a tray and set it back in the chest.

"What are you doing?" he asked, grabbing her hand gently when she reached for another.

"I've seen enough for today. I can't stand anymore."

"No' even diamonds?" he asked, dropping a light kiss on the nape of her neck.

Pausing, she took the tray back out. "I suppose I could stand seeing the diamonds."

He laughed and took out the next section, revealing three small cloth bags. "These are the loose stones." He pointed to the bags in turn. "Emeralds, rubies, and a mixture. No diamonds." He lifted out the tray. "Those are here."

She peered into the chest. A flat walnut box sat on top of several layers of gaudy diamond jewelry with huge stones. "Those would be too heavy to wear," she said, picking up the box with trembling fingers and handing it to him. "Please open it for me."

"This willna be too heavy." He opened the box, revealing a short necklace made of half-carat diamonds. Strands of varying lengths, mounted with smaller diamonds, hung from it like a delicate waterfall. Earrings of the same shape rested on the black velvet above the necklace.

She buried her face against his chest as tears began to fall.

He set the box down and put his arms around her. "You dinna like it?"

She nodded and put her arms around him.

"You do like it?"

She nodded again and took a shaky breath. "I've never seen anything so beautiful. Is that the necklace you mentioned? The one you teased me about?"

"It is. I kept thinking about it so I went back and bought it."

"Were you so sure I'd agree to marry you?"

"No, but I didna want someone else to buy it. It would have made me angry to see it around some other woman's neck. As far as I was concerned, it was made for you." He held her close. "And I wanted to replace the jewels Shelton took from you."

"My dear, wonderful man, I only had two necklaces: a string of pearls, and a small emerald pendant with matching earrings. One of these old baubles would more than make up for those. But I do thank you, love. For all of them, but especially for the ones you bought for me."

"I have one condition in giving them to you."

"Yes?"

"Every time you wear them, let them be a reminder of how much I love you."

"I will. I also ask something of you. Whenever I wear them, please know how much I appreciate them and how much I love you for giving them to me. But also know that the only thing I truly need is you. If you lost all your wealth and the title, I would still be happy with Kiernan Macpherson, piper, forester, or shepherd."

He wrinkled his face. "No' shepherd. I'd take care of cattle but no' sheep. Right now, we need to put your trinkets away and get on to other things." He took a smaller chest from the hiding place. "I thought you'd want to keep the things you like separate from the rest so they are easier to find."

"That will hold a great deal more than what you've given me and what I picked out."

He shrugged, opening the second chest. "You might find other things you like in there when you have more time. And I intend to buy you more baubles over the next fifty years."

"I won't need new baubles when I'm nearly eighty."

"We'll see," he said with a tender smile.

They put everything away and closed the secret door. When shut, it was indistinguishable from the other panels on the cabinet.

Stopping by the arsenal, Kiernan discovered several muskets and pistols missing, as well as powder cartridges and shot. "He must have taken two or three pistols when he came by for a musket, as well as when he was here last week. He's up to no good."

Kiernan took her to his bedroom and showed her where he kept the chest of banknotes and coins. Opening this safe was simpler. He pushed one stone on the side of the fireplace and a small section of the wall slid to the side, revealing the money coffer. He also showed her where he hid the key to the jewel chest.

"There is another money box in my study," he said a few minutes later, leaning against the doorjamb to her bedroom while she picked up her bonnet. "Enough for small household expenses. We have accounts with the shops in Branderee and most in Banff. Those are settled monthly, as is most of what we buy for the estate." When she walked toward him, tying the bonnet ribbons beneath her chin, he smiled. "That's the hat you wore to the village when you lived at Stillwater."

"Is it good enough to wear out with you?"

"It is. It is also my favorite of all the ones you have. Reminds me of the day I saw you walking along the road and how pretty you were." He moved into the hall and offered her his arm. "Ready to play Bow Street Runner?"

"Ready."

On the way out, they met Ailsa and Wilton leaving for a walk to the village.

"Where is Jeanie?" asked Kiernan.

Though his sister was doing much better, Mariah knew he did not like to leave her alone.

"She drove over to see Mrs. Storrie and her new bairns. Took

381

them a pot of stew and some baby blankets and wee gowns from the stack she bought in Edinburgh." Ailsa smiled as she absently adjusted Wilton's cravat. "She has enough to gift every tenant's next three or four babies."

"Perhaps she was thinking more about having some of her own," said Wilton. "I hear wedding bells every time she looks at Mr. Thorne."

"Maybe so. What do you think of him, laddie?"

"I'd be pleased to have him for my guid-brither. Despite his past, I dinna think anyone could love her more. Now that he is a believer, I see no reason for them no' to marry."

"If he asks her and if Jeanie wants to," said his mother.

Kiernan grinned and opened the front door. "No' if. When."

28

BY THE TIME KIERNAN AND MARIAH returned from seeing all the tenants, he was threatening to throw Macnair in the castle dungeon for a year or two before turning him over to the authorities. "No wonder the tenants disliked me so much." He pounded on the desk in his study. "I ought to put him on the rack. With a bit of grease, it would work fine."

"Now, laddie, torture isna a Christian's way," said Ailsa calmly. "Let the authorities handle it."

"Maybe they'll transport him to some rat hole," said Dominic, entering the study with a scowl. "Not only has he been cheating you left and right, he thinks I'm a complete idiot."

"Then you must be a great actor, for no one in their right mind would take you for an idiot," said Jeanette, going to greet him with a hug.

Surprise flashed across his face at her action, but a smile instantly replaced it as he returned her embrace. "Thank you, angel, for restoring my self-esteem so quickly." He kissed her on the forehead. "And for putting me in a better humor."

"You're welcome." She turned and slipped her hand around his as they sat down. "Now, tell us what he has done."

"We guessed correctly about those entries without receipts. The work had been done on those, but not on some of the others. That braggart drove me around in all directions and showed me the same section of repaired fence three times, calling the pasture a different name each time. I also counted thirty new calves instead of the twenty he told you about, and I assure you, ten of them were not born this morning. What did you find out?"

"He raised their rents by 20 percent before we even arrived here and blamed it on me."

Dominic whistled softly. "From what I saw, some of your people cannot afford that kind of increase."

"No, they canna. As soon as he is in custody, I'll make it right. He was also supposed to have made some repairs to the houses while we were gone. They hadna been done but were noted as expenses in the ledger. He must think I'm an idiot, too."

Gabriel and Jordan arrived at the same time. "You can rest easy about the fish exports," said Gabe. "I talked with the men who took the fish to Leith and Montrose. Since Macnair didna go with them, they keep their own records to protect themselves. Their records for amounts sold and moneys received match yours."

Jordan said, "I checked with the two merchants in Banff who supply stone and lumber, asking about the cost for similar repairs. They both quoted basically the same as what he shows, although one was slightly higher. I did not tell them I was representing you. I merely said I wanted some estimates. From your unhappy faces, however, I gather there are some problems."

Kiernan told them what he had learned about the rents and the missing repairs, as well as what Dominic had discovered. "There are also two sets of old, valuable silver candlesticks and two silver and ruby goblets missing." He sat down on the corner of his desk. "What troubles me even more is that four muskets, eight pistols, and ammunition are missing from the gun room. Mrs. Laing said one of the maids saw him coming out of there last week."

"He had borrowed a musket on two or three occasions to go hunting, but she could not remember him returning them," said Dominic. "I'm worried about what he may be planning."

"If we're going to confront him, it should be soon. We asked more than enough questions today to arouse suspicion," said Gabriel, taking the cup of tea Mariah handed him. "He must have at least one friend who would warn him."

"We need to go well armed," said Jordan quietly.

Mariah had been listening to the discussion with growing apprehension. It was especially disconcerting to hear Jordan talk about taking weapons. She expected Kiernan and Gabriel, even Dominic, to think along those lines, but for her gentle friend to consider arming himself brought home the danger of the situation.

She knew they needed to act promptly but did not want them to take the risk. Standing, she walked over to the window, crossing her arms protectively over her chest as she stared unseeingly at the countryside. When Kiernan moved to stand beside her, she looked up at him. "Can't you let the constable handle this? I don't want to be a widow before I have a chance to be a wife."

"I dinna intend for you to be, lass, but we canna wait for the constable." He put his arm around her shoulders. "We'll be careful." He leaned close and whispered in her ear. "I'll have Jordan stay here."

"Thank you. But I'm just as worried about you. Macnair didn't take all those weapons to use by himself."

"I've thought of that. Dinna worry, love. I'm no' about to get shot." He hugged her shoulders. "I'm good at duckin' bullets, remember?"

"You'd better be."

Kiernan released her and turned to the others. "Jordan, Wilton,

I'd like for you to stay here and protect the ladies. Macnair's a bold one; he might come here if he suspects we are going after him. I'll arm the footmen and station guards outside, too. I think I can trust them, but I *know* I can trust you." He looked at the two men. "Can you shoot?"

"It's been a few years, but I was once a crack shot," said Wilton. "I believe I can still load and fire in the general direction of a villain."

"I can shoot," said Jordan somberly. "I've never pointed a gun at a man before, but I could do it if necessary."

"I'm counting on you and Wilton to keep the other men alert. Come upstairs with me for your weapons."

"I want a pistol, too," Mariah said quietly.

Kiernan looked at her in surprise.

"I didn't live alone all those years without a way of protecting myself. Thaddeus taught me how to shoot."

Kiernan held out his hand to her. "I'll keep that in mind next time I stir up your temper."

Jordan smiled as he stood. "You should. She put as many rabbits and pheasants on the table as Thaddeus or I did."

Mariah took Kiernan's hand. "I can fish, too, but I doubt Macnair would be too concerned if I waved a rod and hook at him."

"You could always pelt him with worms," said Kiernan with a grin.

Mariah shook her head and looked at Ailsa. "I think he is enjoying this."

"He does have a fondness for adventure. Always has had. He's no' likely to change."

"I guess I'd better get used to it."

Kiernan and his men approached Macnair's house openly but with caution, pistols drawn. Catching him unaware was impossible, since he owned a small mutt that always barked furiously whenever anyone rode into the yard.

They were met with eerie silence, though a thin trail of smoke rose from the chimney. The front door stood ajar, and the wind flapped a curtain against an open window. Kiernan looked around slowly, noting every detail outside the house and around the grounds. Macnair's curricle sat beside the house, but the farm wagon was gone. So were all four horses.

Gabriel eased his mount up beside him. "He's gone."

"Probably." Kiernan signaled for the men to circle the house. When they had it surrounded, he shifted in the saddle, drawing the reins a little tighter. "Macnair!" he yelled. "Come out!"

No sound. No movement.

"Macnair, give it up."

Silence.

Kiernan and Gabriel dismounted, watching the house closely. Dominic raised his pistol, ready to fire. The other men followed his lead, some watching the house, some scanning the grounds.

Running to the front of the house, Gabriel took cover to one side of the front door, Kiernan to the other. Gabe nodded when he met his gaze. Kiernan stepped in front of the door, kicked it in, and rushed into the room. Gabe was right behind him.

Quickly scouting the four rooms, they confirmed that Macnair had fled. A glass of milk sat on the table beside an empty plate. A flat pan still hung over the dying coals in the fireplace where he had cooked oatcake bannocks. One of the round, flat cakes remained in the large semicircular toaster rack curving around the front of the coals. It was hard and toasted black on one side.

Gabriel went to the front door, telling the men Macnair was gone. Dominic came inside, peeking in the bedroom as Kiernan searched the room. "Looks like he left in a hurry."

"And I dinna think he plans to come back." Kiernan flipped the toe of a stocking hanging over the edge of an empty drawer. "Even if he did miss a few things." He moved back into the kitchen and put his hand around the glass of milk. "It has no' been too long. The milk is still a wee bit cool."

Kiernan shut the window and closed the door behind him. He instructed most of the men to scour the estate and surrounding countryside in case Macnair decided to hide and wait until dark to escape. A few accompanied him to the castle. Everything there was as they had left it, with no sign of the factor.

The others returned from their search shortly before dark, saying Macnair had been sighted earlier rushing past the village, using all four horses to pull the wagon. They found a few people in Banff who had seen him drive into town, but he seemed to have disappeared after that.

Kiernan stationed guards, working in two-hour shifts, around the sides and front of the castle as well as at the doorways in back of the building.

"Do you think he has left the district, Son?" asked Ailsa at dinner.

"Maybe, but several things worry me. Why would he use the wagon when it is faster to travel in the curricle? It didna look as if he had taken anything but his clothes and the dog. I dinna think he stole the guns to sell them, though that's possible." He glanced around the table. "He has keys to the house, and the locksmith is out of town for a couple of days."

"Do you expect him to try to rob us?" asked Jeanette.

"He must believe you have a trunk full of money, if he thinks he needs the wagon to carry it," said Gabriel.

"Maybe he wants more guns or silver," said Jordan.

"Or something else," said Kiernan thoughtfully. "Something hidden here in the castle that no one else knows about."

"But where?" asked Mariah.

"That, lass, is the problem. Whoever knows about a hiding place is no' telling." He looked at Jordan. "How would you like to be the new factor?"

Jordan paused with his fork halfway to his mouth. He looked at Dominic, then Mariah, who smiled encouragingly. Setting the fork down carefully on his plate, he met Kiernan's gaze. "I'm not sure..." He stopped and cleared his throat. "Do you think I can do it?"

"Yes. If you make any mistakes, they will be honest ones. We can seek advice from some of the other gentlemen around." He glanced at Dominic. "What Dominic does no' know, we'll ask the earl of Findlater or the earl of Fife. They're both noted for the improvements they've made to their estates, and they are reasonably close."

"They have no' exactly been friendly, Kier," said Jeanie quietly.

"They were friends of Malcom's, and I'm a stranger. But it's time they accepted me as the new earl and their neighbor. We didna hide from Society in London. It's time to quit hiding here."

"One of the best ways to win a man's friendship and respect is to ask his advice," said Jordan. He took a deep breath, releasing it slowly. "I'd be honored to be your factor, Lord Branderee. If after a trial period you feel I am not up to handling the position, I trust you will tell me so and find another to replace me."

"If it does no' work out, you can resume your duties as secretary."

"I would hope, sir, that I am allowed enough time in the new position to warrant you hiring another secretary."

Kiernan smiled. "I intend to give you plenty of time. Mariah has agreed to help me for a while. She has neater handwriting than I do." He winked at her. "People will actually be able to read our letters. We are both going to oversee the household accounts. It should no' be hard to follow Fiske's record-keeping method. He was very exact.

"I want to work closely with you, both in planning and in record-keeping, so I will have a clear understanding of how everything is run. Then, when you are away on business, I canna make a muddle of things."

"I doubt you would have any problem, my lord, but it seems a wise way of doing things."

Kiernan waited until the footman had removed his dishes and left the room. "One more thing, Jordan."

"Yes, sir?"

"You've been Mariah's friend a long time. Now, you are mine. My friends call me Kiernan. No' milord, sir, or Lord Branderee."

"I'll remember that at the appropriate times." Jordan smiled benignly. "You may not particularly like your title, but sometimes it is a necessity."

Kiernan laughed, nodding in a slight bow. "Well said."

They all moved to the great hall, sitting comfortably around the fireplace, discussing various ideas for improving Branderee and becoming better acquainted with their tenants and neighbors.

When it was time to retire, Kiernan stood and stretched his arms above his head. He and Dominic would be up another two hours, until they finished their turn at guard duty. "Ladies, did you ask your maids to sleep in your bedrooms tonight?" Mariah and Jeanette both nodded. Ailsa, however, merely took Wilton's hand and started for the stairs. "Mother?"

They stopped, and she looked back at him, her expression calm. "Yes, dear?"

"Did you ask Sukey to stay with you?"

"No, laddie, I didna. James will be there to protect me."

"Wilton?" Kiernan frowned, glaring at the older gentleman.

Wilton looked down at Ailsa, his eyes twinkling merrily. "We forgot something, my dear."

"He's such a stickler for propriety." She glanced quickly at Kiernan, then looked expectantly at Wilton.

Wilton smiled down at her, his eyes glowing with love as he took both her hands in his. "Ailsa Mary Elizabeth Macpherson, I take you to be my lawful wedded wife. I promise to love you always, forsaking all others, and to keep to you as long as we both shall live."

"James Elliot Wilton, I take you to be my lawful wedded husband. I love you and promise to forsake all others and keep only to you as long as we both shall live."

Wilton leaned down and kissed her gently. Ailsa smiled at him, then turned to look at Kiernan. "That should do it. We have more than enough witnesses. Next time the four of us go into Banff, we can fill out the certificate."

Kiernan stared at them in disbelief. He had expected them to marry—eventually—but he thought his mother, of all people, would want a regular marriage officiated by a minister.

"Son, dinna you wish us happy?"

His mother's joyful radiance snapped him out of his shock. "Of course I do, Mam." He walked over to Ailsa and kissed her cheek. "I just hadna expected you to be married so suddenly."

"I'm learning that it does no' hurt to be impulsive every once in a while."

Kiernan shook hands with Wilton. "Welcome to the family, James."

"Thank you." Wilton laughed as Jeanie wiggled in between them and gave him an exuberant hug.

Kiernan stepped back as the others gathered around his mother and her new husband. *Thank you, God, for sending Wilton to love her. I dinna think Dadie would mind.* His gaze settled on Mariah, and he envied his mother her freedom to be impulsive.

"So that's how it is done," said Dominic thoughtfully. "I had wondered."

"It's one way," said Kiernan. There was another—if a woman allowed a man to make love to her because he promised to wed her, they were married in the eyes of the law—but Kiernan didn't think he would mention it.

Dominic watched Jeanie as she laughed with her mother. He met Kiernan's gaze with a wry smile. "Well, it does make one think of the possibilities."

"Just dinna forget the witnesses."

"Don't worry. If Jeanie agrees to marry me—when I get up the courage to ask—we'll post the banns and be married by the minister. With my past, I want everyone to be very clear about my intentions."

29

JEANETTE PUT HER EAR AGAINST MARIAH'S BEDROOM DOOR, listening intently. When she heard someone moving around, she called softly, "Mariah, are you still awake?"

The door opened quickly. "I won't be able to sleep until I hear Kiernan come upstairs."

"I'm having the same trouble. He and Dominic should have been up thirty minutes ago. I didna hear any kind of commotion. What could be keeping them?"

"They are probably downstairs talking, without a thought that we might be up here worrying ourselves silly." Mariah glanced at Jeanie's heavy robe, similar to the one she was wearing. "Let's go see about them."

Jeanie nodded, waiting as she went back to the bedside table and picked up the small candle and holder.

Elise roused on her cot along the wall, raising up on one elbow. "Is something amiss, milady?" she asked with a yawn.

"I doubt it, but Jeanie and I can't sleep until we know our men are safe and sound. We are going down to give them a scold for keeping us awake. Go back to sleep."

"G'night, milady. Call if you need me." Elise was asleep before Mariah reached the door.

Jeanie shook her head and grinned. "Sometimes it pays no' to love someone."

"Yes, it does." Mariah closed the door quietly behind her. "So you've decided you love him?" she whispered as they tiptoed down the hall.

"Yes, more and more every day. I canna wait to wake up in the morning to see him, and if we are apart during the day, I count the minutes until we are together again. When I pray about marrying him, I feel a deep peace. Even though I was very fond of Tony, I always had doubts about sharing my life with him and felt confused when I prayed about it. There is no doubt or confusion with Dominic."

"I think he has always been a good man at heart, but for some reason he hid it from most people. Something must have happened when he was young to cause him to live the kind of life he has. God has changed him. So have you. I never thought I'd see the day when Dominic Thorne truly loved someone, but even a stranger could see how he feels about you."

They moved quietly and cautiously down the stairs until they were next to the great hall. Listening at the closed door, they could hear men talking. It only took a minute to determine Kiernan was speaking. Hearing quiet laughter, Mariah opened the door.

Kiernan and Dominic jumped to their feet when they saw them and hurried across the room. Jordan and Gabriel stood also, looking alarmed.

"Is something wrong, lass?" asked Kiernan.

"Only that we're upstairs listening for you to come down the hall, praying our brains numb, and you're down here telling war stories."

"Sweetheart, I'm sorry. We didna think about you waiting up for us." He glanced sheepishly at Dominic. "I guess we have some things to learn."

"Forgive me, love," murmured Dominic, lifting Jeanette's hand to his lips. "I thought you would be sound asleep long ago."

"I would have been if you two hadna been outside guarding against who knows what." She frowned at him. "Knowing you're down here talking is one thing; worrying about you gettin' shot is another."

Dominic put his arms around her and held her close. "Angel, no one has ever worried about whether or not I might be shot," he said quietly, his voice thick with emotion.

Jeanie hugged him, then leaned back and looked up with a knowing smile. "No' even the women whose husbands caught you?"

Dominic choked and turned red.

The others grinned.

"There was only one," sputtered Dominic. "And he didn't have a gun."

"Oh?"

"Only flowerpots," he mumbled.

Mariah giggled as Kiernan and Jordan laughed. Gabriel collapsed on the sofa, laughing so hard tears ran down his cheeks.

Jeanette peeked around Dominic at Gabriel. "You'd better point him toward bed, Jordan. He's so tired, he has the sillies. He can go on like that for a half hour. Just when you think he's stopped, he'll start whooping again." She grasped Dominic's hand and started for the door leading to the stairs.

Kiernan's laughter abruptly changed to a frown. "Jeanie, where are you taking him?"

"To the top of the tower. If he's nice, I might no' lock him in." She winked at her brother. "In case you have no' noticed, the moonlight is shining across the firth. And it's too late to go to the dunes."

Kiernan grinned. "Chilly, too. Which tower?"

"We're goin' to the east one." She smiled sweetly up at Dominic.

"You can go wherever you want."

Dominic picked up a candle and held it in front of them as they climbed the stairs. When they reached the turret, he set the candle on a small table in the hallway and followed Jeanie inside, shutting the door.

She stopped in front of the window facing directly toward the firth, and Dominic stepped up behind her. The moonlight shimmered across the water, frosting the waves with silver.

"It's beautiful," said Dominic softly, putting his arms around her and leaning down so the side of his face touched hers. "Well worth the climb."

"Before we went to London, I used to come up here often at night to look at the stars and the water and dream."

"About what?"

"Oh, the usual things one thinks about in castles this old—fearless Highland warriors fighting to save their ladies and their homes. Sometimes I'd imagine how it must have been when the Vikings stormed the coast, plundering and pillaging."

"And stealing the women?"

She laughed. "Well, I thought about it once or twice. Of course, the Viking who stole me was fairly polite. He didna drag me away by my hair."

"Just threw you over his shoulder?"

She nodded, her cheek rubbing against his. "Bouncing around like that is hard on the stomach."

He laughed, giving her a light squeeze. "I don't suppose you ever dreamed of an Englishman capturing you?"

"I'm afraid no'. Would an Englishman throw me over his shoulder like a Viking, or pull me up in front of him on his horse like a Highlander?"

"I thought the Highlanders always charged into battle on foot."

"No' always. Even if they did, they still had horses to ride back home, at least the chiefs and their captains did."

"I see. Well, an Englishman would be more gentle."

"Ha! I've heard how gentle the English were with our fair lassies."

"I'm talking about a modern Englishman. We're much more refined these days." He lifted her hair with his hand, laying it over one shoulder.

The night air cooled her neck; his breath warmed it.

"We've learned that the art of persuasion is much better than brute force." He trailed one knuckle down the side of her neck.

Jeanie's heart did a somersault. She instinctively leaned her head slightly to the side and forward. When he brushed his fingertips across the nape of her neck, her legs turned to jelly. Warmth rushed through her, yet she shivered. *No wonder he thought it unwise to nibble on my neck that night in his drawing room.* Thinking she might die if he didn't kiss her, she breathed his name, and he understood.

He turned her toward him, kissing her urgently, kindling her passion as never before. Whispering words of love against her lips, he kissed her again and again. Yet she sensed his restraint, and she loved him all the more.

When he slowly raised his head, Jeanie stared up at him in dazed wonder. "I love you, Dominic."

"Are you sure, angel?" He searched her face, his eyes turbulent with longing and uncertainty. "Is this passion speaking or your heart?"

"Both. I want to be with you every minute. I go to sleep thinking about you and wake up early in the morning anxious to see you. Which must mean I love you because I've never liked to get up early."

He smiled, but uncertainty still clouded his eyes.

"What is it, love?" she asked gently. "What troubles you?"

"People will tell you things about me, about my past. Some may even have good intentions and want to warn you about what to expect. Others are only malicious."

"What will they tell me, Dominic? About your women?"

"Yes, probably who they were, where I took them, and what they imagine we did."

"And about your gambling?"

He nodded. "Though they wouldn't have much to complain about since I usually win."

"Because you dinna drink when you play cards."

He blinked. "How do you know that?"

"Mariah told me. I'm no' sure how she found out." She rested her hands on his chest. "Have you ever killed a man in a duel?"

"No, I've never fought one."

"Will they tell me that you are a thief and a liar? That you seduce your maids and whip your footmen?"

"No," he said emphatically.

"They might say you are a notorious flirt, but I didna see you being outrageous."

"It's hard to flirt with someone else when I only have eyes for you."

"So your only sin is being England's greatest lover."

He chuckled and shook his head. "I wouldn't go that far. And it's certainly not my only sin, but it is the most obvious one."

"If anyone begins a litany of your past transgressions, I will calmly—or maybe no' so calmly—point out those things are indeed in the past. You are a new person. Because Jesus is a part of your life now, you are a new creature. If God can forgive you and wipe the slate clean, so can I. So should they.

"I will tell them you are a brave and noble man. That you are loving, kind, and generous. Women will probably still throw themselves at you because you are such a braw man. I may dump pudding over their heads, but I willna be worried because I know you love me. You honor God and you will honor our marriage. And if the gossips are still persistent, I'll confide that I never worry about you sharing someone else's bed because you sleep in mine every night."

He grinned. "Every night? You mean we are going to be unfashionable and share a bedroom?"

"We are. I've often thought there wouldna be so many unhappy marriages among the wealthy if the houses were no' so big. Love and understanding canna grow if a husband and wife are seldom in the same room."

"How true. We probably should have separate dressing rooms. I'd be embarrassed to have Molly there while I was dressing."

"I doubt you've ever been embarrassed by a gawking woman. It would be a wee bit awkward, though, having your valet shave you while I'm running around the room in my shift."

Dominic laughed and hugged her close. "You would distract him so much he'd probably cut off my ear."

"I like your ears, so we will definitely have separate dressing rooms." She kissed his jaw, his chin, his mouth. "Now, hurry up and propose."

He laughed softly and slid his fingers into her hair, framing her face with his palms. "Will you be my wife, Jeanette?"

"Yes."

He kissed her tenderly, and when they drew apart, their eyes were misty. "God is good," he whispered, holding her comfortably close.

"Yes, he is." She settled her face against his chest, wishing she could stay there all night. Suddenly, a movement below caught her attention. "Dominic, what is that in the water? Down in the little cove?"

Dominic released her and peered out the window. "I can't tell. Blast! When did that cloud cover up the moon?"

Jeanie glanced at the sky. "Patience, love. It's almost past." A few seconds later, the moonlight began drifting across the water. "Oh, my stars! It's a boat!"

"A rowboat heading out to the firth. What in blazes?"

Jeanie squinted in the darkness, blinking in surprise when a moonbeam fell across the cove like light from a lantern. "It's Macnair. There, see his long nose and pointed chin when he turns to the side? Another man is with him, but I canna tell who it is."

"They have crates in the boat. Kiernan is right. There must be an opening into the castle, and Macnair is hiding something in there." Dominic grabbed her hand as the boat silently slipped out of the cove and disappeared around the cliff. "Come on, we need to talk to your brother."

They picked up the candle and hurried down the stairs to the third floor, racing along the hallway as fast as they could without the candle going out. When they reached the other tower they rushed up the stairs.

"Kier, we need to talk to you," called Jeanie as she rounded the last section of the stairway.

"Yes, you have my blessing. Now go away."

"We just saw Macnair and another man in a rowboat leaving the small cove."

The door opened instantly. "Was there anything in the boat?" asked Kiernan.

"Crates."

"I knew it." Lost in thought, Kiernan absently rubbed the side of his face. A lock of hair on the back of his head stuck straight up.

Holding back a grin, Jeanie glanced at Dominic's beautiful golden hair. One of the silver wings drooped over his ear, but the rest was still neatly combed.

Mariah calmly moved beside Kiernan and reached up, smoothing down the wayward curl. "It's too late to search for hidden rooms and passages tonight. I suggest we start in the morning when we are more alert."

"I agree." Kiernan draped his arm across Mariah's shoulders. "Right now, I'd miss the passage even if it had a big sign on it. It will be light before too long. I doubt he will come back tonight." He looked thoughtfully at Jeanie and Dominic. "Is there something you'd like to tell me, Posy?"

Jeanette put her arm around Dominic's waist, smiling with joy. "We are going to be married."

Kiernan beamed and hugged her. "About time you got him to come up to scratch." He held out his hand to Dominic, and when he took it, Kiernan pulled him into a bear hug. When Dominic stepped back with a grin, Kiernan asked, "Do you know what brother-in-law is in Scots?"

"No."

"Guid-brither." Kiernan smiled. "I know you will be just that, a good brother."

"I'll do my best," said Dominic, his grin fading. "I used to wonder how it would be to have a family that cared for me." He clasped Jeanie's hand. "Now I know."

"We've been blessed, haven't we?" said Mariah quietly, meeting Dominic's gaze.

"Yes, we have."

As they walked downstairs, Jeanie talked silently to her heavenly Father. *Thank you, God, for bringing these two wonderful people into our lives and for the happiness you've given us all.*

Later that morning, Kiernan stood in the middle of the dungeon, hands on hips, studying the stone wall. Gabriel, Dominic, Jordan, and Wilton were with him.

The women had stayed upstairs, meeting with the servants so Mariah could discuss ideas for the house party they planned for later in the summer. Since they suspected Macnair might have an accomplice working in the house, the main purpose of the gathering was to keep the servants occupied in the hope they would not notice where the men were.

"This canna be the outside wall," said Kiernan. "There has to be another room on the other side of it."

"Do you have any idea how to find the entry?" asked Jordan, grimacing as he looked up at a man-sized cage hanging from the ceiling.

"With everything else I've found that's hidden, you have to push on something. Start at the door and push on the stones from as high as you can reach to the floor. Pull on the chains or anything else you come across. Gabe, you try some of the equipment."

Gabe raised an eyebrow. "Kiernan, no' even for you will I stretch myself on the rack."

Kiernan looked at him, mildly amused. "I didna say try it out."

"Good. If I manage to fasten myself to something, promise no' to leave me here."

"Dinna tempt me."

"Everyone stand still, please," said Wilton, holding his lantern high and studying the floor. "We could simply follow the footprints."

Kiernan turned toward his new stepfather, waiting to move farther until Wilton beckoned him.

"If you look closely, you will see footprints in the dust."

Kiernan looked at the floor and shook his head. "I think you were a butler too long. I dinna see any footprints."

"It does take a keen eye and one used to perfection," said Wilton. "Or perhaps a different angle. Come stand here, and I think you will see what I mean."

Kiernan changed places with him and stared at the floor, nodding. "Footprints."

The trail went from the stairway over to a wheel on the wall which aided in raising and lowering the cage. A heavy chain ran from the iron cage in the center of the room to the wall, then down to the wheel and wrapped around it. A long crank attached to the wheel enabled someone to turn it and tighten or loosen the chain. "It canna be as simple as lowering the cage because I've done it," said Kiernan.

"Perhaps the trail leads somewhere else." Wilton walked over to the wheel, careful to avoid disturbing the faint prints. He lowered the lantern toward the floor. "Someone took four steps in that direction, then came back."

Gabriel joined them, also avoiding the impressions on the floor. He followed the second set of footprints. "He didna turn around here." He squatted down and ran his finger along the stone. "No' enough dust to leave a sign. I think he went farther in this direction. But why?"

Kiernan borrowed Wilton's lamp and followed Gabe. Lifting the light, he scanned the area, looking over the junk piled in the corner. "The jailer was no' very tidy, was he?"

"What do you do with worn-out manacles?" asked Gabe, picking up a length of chain with a thick metal band attached to one end. "The clasp is broken. Maybe someone escaped." He rummaged around some more. "Here's a spare thumb screw. Know anybody with three thumbs?"

"We could use it to hold your mouth shut," murmured Kiernan.

Gabe grinned and kept digging through the odds and ends.

"This may be what we're looking for." Kiernan picked up an iron rod about four feet long and an inch in diameter. "Gabe, come take my lantern." When Gabriel complied, he picked up a second rod, identical to the first and carried them to the middle of the room. "We'll lower the cage and see if these fit where I think they will."

He unfastened the lock holding the wheel and slowly turned the crank, lowering the cage to the floor. "If I remember correctly, there are some holes in the bars that these rods may fit through."

When the cage touched the floor, Gabe picked up one rod. "You're right." He slid the end into a hole in one of the bars and through the cage. Jordan reached his fingers through the space between the bars and guided the end through another hole. The rod fit perfectly, sticking out about six inches on each side. They did the same thing with the second rod, putting it through holes slightly lower than the first ones.

"Everybody move to the stairway. There is no tellin' what this may do, if anything." When the others were safely hiding in the stairway, Kiernan turned the crank, raising the cage. When it was almost to the ceiling, he heard a click. He stopped and looked around the shadowy room but could not see or hear anything else.

He turned the wheel another rotation and heard a second click, then a creak as a four-foot-wide section at the top of the opposite wall began to slide slowly downward. The muffled rattle of chains accompanied its descent. He threw the locking brake on the wheel, securing it, and prepared to dive into the stairwell if necessary.

Suddenly, he saw another part of the wall move, only this one was near the floor and going up, making a wide, tall opening. The other men hurried from the stairway for a better view. When the first section of wall touched the floor, the second one stopped.

Kiernan double-checked the brake on the wheel before carrying the lantern over to the entry, illuminating the immediate area on the other side of the wall. "The floor looks like solid stone."

Dominic held his lantern up to the top of the opening, inspecting the hidden door. "Well, this isn't. It is wood with a stone veneer on this side to make it look like the wall."

Kiernan took a deep breath. "Let's see what Macnair has stashed away." He held the light through the doorway, making certain of his footing before he actually stepped through. "The floor feels safe."

The others followed him, each carrying lanterns and flooding the area with light. They beheld a large room filled with stacked crates of varying sizes and over twenty wine casks.

"My stars," breathed Dominic. "It's a smuggler's den, a veritable warehouse. No wonder Macnair would risk sneaking in last night, even with the castle guarded. This is worth a fortune."

"Paid for with six pieces of silver, I'd wager," said Kiernan. "Candlesticks and goblets." He shook his head sadly, losing the slim hope he had held for possibly retrieving the heirlooms.

Another wheel and crank were mounted on the warehouse side of the dungeon wall, along with a second set of chains running to the counterweight and door, so it could be opened or closed from inside the room. On the interior side of the castle's outer wall was a similar arrangement to gain entry there.

Gabriel walked around the wooden boxes. "It looks like this has been a steady business. All of this couldna have come from one ship."

Kiernan nodded. He knew that, due to import taxes on all kinds of goods, smugglers, or free traders as the Scots called them, had long enjoyed a thriving business in both England and Scotland. During the seventeen years Great Britain had been at war with France, taxes had increased. Many commodities had been in short supply, particularly after Napoleon declared a blockade against the country. What was available often cost dearly. Even the wealthy sometimes resorted to purchasing smuggled items to avoid the taxes or to buy what they could not obtain otherwise.

"We have soap from Ireland, lace from Belgium, and silk from China," said Gabriel.

"Tea, coffee, sugar, salt, even a crate of raisins." Dominic moved to the casks. "Mostly Madeira and port, though here is one of sherry."

Kiernan examined the goods with growing discomfort. In his storage room beyond the dungeon were identical cases of sugar, salt, and tea, as well as an extensively stocked wine cellar.

"Kiernan, what's wrong?" asked Dominic, laying a hand on his shoulder. "Similar supplies in your own storeroom, perhaps?"

"Aye. Especially the wine cellar. There is a door on the other side of the dungeon that opens directly into the castle's main storage area. I think I know how my ancestors made some of their money. This room had to have been included when the first part of the castle was built."

"If the earls were notorious smugglers, wouldn't it be well known in the area?" asked Jordan.

"Maybe. But if they moved everything in and out at night using the firth, they might have been able to keep it from the authorities. It is impossible to see the entryway from the outside of the castle. I have no' climbed into a boat and rowed around to it, but I have examined it from the cliff with a spyglass. I canna see how anyone could detect it."

"This may have been built originally more for safety than for smuggling," said Wilton. "It would be a perfect place for the women and children to take refuge if the castle was under attack."

"Which it sometimes was in the early years." The thought consoled Kiernan. "If the castle was about to be taken, the earl and his people could have hidden down here and escaped during the night. There is plenty of space to store small boats."

"And the outside entry is big enough for them to fit through," said Jordan.

"I think I'll favor that story over a history of smugglers." Kiernan frowned thoughtfully. "Though there is a wide passageway leading from the dungeon into the main storeroom. I suppose it could have been added at any time."

"Or used to transport prisoners to and from the dungeon without taking them through the house." Gabriel smiled mischievously. "I doubt the countesses would have tolerated bodies, dead or otherwise, being dragged through the great hall."

"I think we had better take Gabriel back upstairs," said Jordan, his eyes twinkling. "The dungeon brings out a strange side of him."

"Strange is his normal side," said Kiernan with a teasing smile.

"What do you plan to do next?" asked Dominic.

"Notify the magistrate and the excise men that we're going to set a trap." He did not expect Macnair and his cohorts to give up easily. Looking at the stacks of smuggled goods, Kiernan knew he would have to tell the authorities about the suspicious items in his own supplies. "And pray we dinna get caught in it."

30

TELLING THE SERVANTS THAT HE HAD DECIDED Macnair was not stupid enough to try to break in, Kiernan did not post guards around the castle that evening. Jordan had discussed the situation with the authorities earlier in the day, so when Kiernan went for a walk around eleven, he met the constable and excise men in the woods near the house.

"We have three ships anchored along the coast and out in the firth," said Bell, the government agent in charge of the small group. "I doubt if he is moving the goods to another ship, but we are prepared just in case. We also have men stationed on land along the coast in both directions to nab his cohorts."

"I have several men in the castle to help us. We should outnumber him and his men," said Kiernan. "This trail will take us down to the main cove and dock where there is an entry into the castle. You can wait in the storeroom until I come downstairs in a few minutes."

"Wylde said you thought there is someone in the castle helping him," said Bell.

"I think there has to be. I dinna know how he could get in without someone opening the entry from the inside. We're going to pretend to retire for the night, then go to the dungeon by another set of stairs. Hopefully, we will be ahead of Macnair's partner. Macnair left the castle after two last night, so I dinna expect him to arrive before midnight."

Kiernan led the five men along the trail through the woods and down the slope to the cove, keeping low and hidden in the shadows. Though the moon was almost full, clouds blocked the light most of the time, aiding in their stealthy run across the dock and up the stairs to the storeroom entry. Jordan opened the door at Kiernan's light tap.

When the men were inside and the door closed, Jordan turned up the wick on a lamp he had hidden away from the door. "Good evening, gentlemen. Have a seat," he said with a half smile, waving his hand toward several crates. Gabriel, Dominic, and Wilton waited with him.

Bell studied a crate containing raisins for a minute before sitting down on it. "This is the first time I've actually sat on the goods to catch the smuggler."

Kiernan winced. "I was afraid you would say that."

"Do you have receipts for these items?" asked Bell.

"No' for the raisins, a crate of sugar, one of salt, and five casks of Madeira."

"Lord Branderee—the previous earl—was quite fond of Madeira," said the constable sadly. "Sorrowful thing to discover he was part of the operation."

"I'm no' sure he was," said Kiernan. "I talked to the housekeeper this afternoon. She said Macnair brought these things after we went to London. Said I had ordered them from Edinburgh, but I hadna. He may have wanted to implicate me or perhaps bribe me if I found out he was smuggling."

"Which is why Fiske was only too happy to be pensioned off," said Jordan. He met Bell's questioning gaze. "Fiske was the former house steward who advised Lord Branderee to look carefully at his accounts and to watch Macnair."

"Fiske did his job thoroughly, so I'm sure he knew Macnair was lying," said Kiernan. "Macnair probably threatened him to keep him quiet. Fiske was a nervous man and always seemed under great stress when Macnair was around. I think he suspected or knew what Macnair was up to even before we left. Now, I'd best be on my way. Macnair's partner might become suspicious if I'm gone too long."

Kiernan slipped out the door and pulled it closed. He left it unlocked but pretended to lock it in case someone was watching. He walked casually down to the dock and stood there for a few minutes, watching the clouds float across the sky. Strolling up the path at a comfortable pace, he walked around to the front door and entered the castle.

"Did you have a nice walk?" asked Mariah as he stepped into the great hall.

"I did. It's a pleasant night. I thought we might be in for a storm but now it does no' look like it. I checked all the doors to be on the safe side. Everything is locked up nice and tight." He wondered if anyone was eavesdropping and yawned for their benefit as he stopped in front of her. "I think I'll go upstairs." He smiled at her. "Someone kept me up too late last night."

"It's your own fault," she said, stifling a yawn. "Why is it yawns are contagious? I think we all were up too late last night for country hours. Everyone else has already retired."

"But you stayed up?"

"I was waiting for you. I thought you could walk me to my door."

"I'll be glad when I'm walking you to *our* door." He took her hand when she held it out to him and tugged her to her feet.

"I will, too." She leaned over and blew out the lamp on the table beside the sofa.

Kiernan walked across the room and snuffed several candles on the mantel. "Ready?"

She nodded, picking up the lone candle still burning. They left the darkened room and walked up the stairs arm in arm.

When they reached her bedroom, he stepped inside and closed the door behind them. He leaned down and kissed her gently. "I love you."

"I love you, too." She caressed his cheek. "Please be careful," she whispered.

"I will. You have your pistol loaded? I pray there is no reason to need it, but I want you prepared."

"It's ready. Jeanie, your mother, and our maids are in the storage room. I'll go up in a few minutes."

They had decided it would be safer if the women did not stay in their own rooms. Thaddeus, the coachmen, and the valets—men Kiernan could trust—were by now guarding the entries to the castle. Still, he did not want the women easily found. "If Macnair or one of his men comes after you, dinna be afraid to shoot."

"I won't be."

"I'd feel better if one of the men was with you."

"You need everyone down there. Sukey has a pistol, too. She says she knows how to use it. We'll be fine."

Though he did not like leaving them alone, he had no real choice. His uncertainty of whom to trust had limited the number involved in his plan. He barely had enough men to cover the outside doors, the dungeon, and the smuggler's den. He rubbed her cheek gently with his knuckles. "Be very careful."

"You, too." She stood on tiptoe and kissed him quickly. "God be with you."

Kiernan went to his room for his weapons. He slid a dirk into his stocking and buckled on his sword. Though they had taken twenty

411

loaded pistols down to the storeroom earlier in the day, he tucked two more under his belt. Blowing out the lamp, he paused for his eyes to adjust to the darkness before going down the hall to the stairway that led to the dungeon.

Holding his sword against his side, he moved quietly down the stairs, pausing on the ground level to listen before cracking open the door leading to the dungeon. No light glowed in the darkness below, so he stepped into the passageway and closed the door behind him. Feeling his way along the cold stone wall, he moved carefully down the steps. Moisture dampened his fingers as he reached the dungeon. The doorway to the storeroom was on his right, all the way across the room.

He moved cautiously, keeping one hand slightly in front of him on the wall. It was a straight, unobstructed path, but since the room was pitch black, he did not hurry. He stopped when he thought he was close. Gabe was supposed to wait in the passageway with the door opened a crack so he could watch for the accomplice. "Gabe?"

"I'm here. Careful, I'm opening the door. I'll fetch a light."

Kiernan heard his soft footsteps move away on the stone floor. The door at the other end of the corridor opened, sending a shaft of light though the darkness. A minute later, Gabe stepped into the dungeon, carrying the lantern. "About time you joined the party."

"I was hopin' you wouldna start without me." Kiernan nodded to Bell and the others as they followed Gabriel into the room. Gabriel went after the two iron rods while Kiernan lowered the cage. They inserted the rods into the cage and raised it.

When the door to the outer room opened, Bell whistled softly. "Ingenious."

Kiernan nodded. "We think it might have been originally built as a safe hiding place and a means of escape if the castle was overrun."

"Wouldn't someone have to be on this side to close it?"

"No, it can also be opened and closed from the inside."

"A smuggler's paradise."

Kiernan, Dominic, Gabriel, and the four excise men went into the smuggler's storeroom. Scattering around the room, they took cover behind the crates and casks and placed their weapons close at hand. Jordan, Wilton, and the constable remained in the dungeon, so they could return the cage and rods to their normal positions. They would then hide in the passageway, planning to move into the dungeon at the appropriate time to block the way into the regular storeroom and upstairs.

Kiernan watched Jordan lower the cage. Wilton removed the rods and put them back in the corner. When Jordan raised the cage again, the door to the outer room slid closed, leaving them in total darkness.

Stretching out his legs, Kiernan tried to relax. His mind raced through a dozen ways the confrontation might unfold—if one happened at all. He prayed for God's protection on his household and those involved in apprehending Macnair and his men.

Perhaps ten minutes later, Kiernan tensed as the door began to open. He shifted position, kneeling on one knee, and picked up a pistol. A man carrying a lamp stepped into the smuggler's den. Kiernan recognized him as one of the under footmen, a lad named Reed. *Young enough to be easily swayed by exciting tales of a free trader,* he thought sadly.

The footman hurried to the outer wall of the castle. Standing beside the wheel that opened the outer door, Reed listened intently, his ear practically touching the wall.

Kiernan saw the shadowy silhouettes of Jordan, Wilton, and the constable steal out of the passageway and creep across the dungeon. Wilton went to a small alcove beside the stairway. Jordan took shelter behind the rack, and the constable ran across to the wall between the dungeon and the outer room.

Three distinct taps sounded on the outside wall. Reed released the lock on the wheel and turned the crank, raising the door. When it was secured, he went out to the flat rock beside the castle wall. He appeared again, holding one end of a rope, which he tied to a hook next to the door. He went out a second time, returning with another rope and tied it in the same way.

Two boats, mused Kiernan. He expected they planned to move as much as possible on this trip and leave the rest. Reed stood by nervously as four men entered. Kiernan waited with a frown, but no one else came inside.

Macnair was not with them.

The men immediately set to work. They were scraggly-looking, the kind to be found in the worst inns along any major waterfront.

Kiernan took a deep breath. When most or all of the men were occupied carrying goods, he and the others would make their move. The first two men rolled a cask of wine toward the door. The other two picked up a heavy crate, swearing at the weight. One snarled an order at Reed, and he jumped to carry a box of tea.

The instant he picked it up, Kiernan and everyone helping him stood, staying behind the crates for protection.

"Halt in the name of the King!" cried Bell.

Reed dropped the box of tea and fell to the floor, covering his head with his hands.

The men with the cask released it, pulling their pistols from their belts and diving for cover. Gabriel fired, and one of them slumped to the floor, the round hitting him in the chest. The second man rolled behind the row of wine casks. When he raised up to shoot, Bell fired, but the man ducked. The smuggler scrambled toward the cove door, waving a second pistol in the air and firing wildly, barely missing Gabriel.

Kiernan took careful aim at the smuggler as he lunged for the opening. He didn't miss.

The other men dropped the crate, immobilizing one of them when it landed on his foot. As he fumbled for his pistol, Dominic pressed his gun against the smuggler's side. "Hands up!"

The man obeyed instantly.

Bell and his men surrounded the other smuggler as he raised his gun. He let it drop from his fingers and put his hands in the air.

Kiernan looked around for Reed. He was crawling toward the dungeon. "It will do you no good, lad. The constable and two others are waiting for you."

Reed looked up toward the door. When he saw the constable standing there, blocking the way, he dropped his head to the floor with a groan.

Kiernan walked over and jerked Reed to his feet. He grabbed the man's shirt, pulling his collar tight around his throat. "Where is Macnair?"

"Silver," he wheezed. "Your lady. Hostage."

Kiernan's blood froze. He shoved Reed aside and ran for the stairway, almost knocking the constable over. "Where are Jordan and Wilton?"

"Went upstairs when the shooting stopped."

Kiernan raced up the stairs. The door to the hall was open, and he bolted through.

"Kiernan, stop!" ordered Wilton in a loud whisper. When Kiernan skidded to a halt, the older man put his hand on his shoulder. "Stealth would be more appropriate than thundering up the stairs."

"He's after Mariah." Kiernan tried to jerk away, but Wilton's grip was surprisingly strong.

"All the more reason to move with caution. Your head must rule now, not your heart."

Jordan came hurrying down the hall. *Silently,* Kiernan noted with chagrin. "Did you see him?" he asked Jordan in a whisper.

"No, but I heard him. He's on the second floor, going from room to room, and he's not quiet. Can't be with all that silver crammed in his pockets."

"Where is he?" asked Dominic as he and Gabriel joined them.

"Second floor." Kiernan nodded to Dominic, Jordan, and Wilton. "You three go up these stairs to the second floor. Gabriel, come with me. We'll take the other stairs."

"What if he gets to the third floor before we catch up to him?" asked Dominic.

"I'll go up after him," said Kiernan.

"I'm going, too." Dominic's tone and expression were implacable.

Kiernan nodded, understanding his need, trusting his ability. "If we see no sign of him on the second floor, Dominic and I will go on up. The rest of you guard the stairs at the second floor in case he gets by us or is hiding there."

They split up, moving as quickly as possible without making any noise. Reaching the second floor, they stopped. Kiernan listened for movement—and heard the creak of a board in the hallway above him. He looked at Gabe and whispered, "Pray." Gabe nodded.

Kiernan moved to the next flight of stairs. *Protect them, Lord. Please, keep them safe.* He repeated the prayer over and over as he crept up to the third floor.

Though several of the rooms were used for storage and were locked, Macnair had keys. Locked doors would not stop him, but if he started at the right end of the hallway, they would slow down his search. The women were in a room midway down the hall, containing furniture, trunks, and boxes of odds and ends. With care, they should be able to hide from him even if he went into the room.

Kiernan carefully peeked around the corner and down the hall.

Macnair stood in front of a door, unlocking it. From where he stood, Kiernan could not tell exactly which room it was. He raised his pistol and took aim, knowing he could not miss. In his fear and haste, he had only brought one loaded pistol. He had one shot. He prayed Dominic had more.

Macnair disappeared into the room before he could fire. Grimacing, Kiernan tucked the pistol back in his belt and slowly unsheathed his sword. *Please, Lord, I want a long life with her.* Tiptoeing down the hall, he quickly realized Macnair was in the same room as Mariah and the other women.

He stopped beside the open door and listened. Judging from the silence, Macnair had not spotted anyone inside the room. Moonlight shined through the doorway. *Mariah, why didna you close the drapes?* he thought desperately.

Dominic moved silently toward him, pistol drawn, and stopped on the other side of the doorway.

Macnair's shadow moved across the light. "Where are you, milady?" he asked softly, the silver jingling with each step. "Come out, pretty lass. I willna harm you. I just want your company for a wee while. Safe passage, y'are." The floor squeaked as he took another step. "I know you're in here," he said irritably. "I checked all the other rooms."

Kiernan waited, his sword poised to strike, praying that Macnair would give up and move back into the hall. Cursing softly, Macnair kicked over a chair and shoved a box. His shadow stopped in the moonlight. He turned his head as if listening.

Kiernan held his breath.

A delicate, muffled sneeze came from inside the room.

"So you're over there," said Macnair, turning toward the left side of the room. "What's wrong, milady? No' used to the dust?"

"Leave her be, Macnair," said Mariah quietly.

As Kiernan stepped into the doorway, Macnair turned back toward the window. Kiernan's heart lodged in his throat as Mariah moved into the light, holding her pistol leveled at Macnair.

"Put the gun down, Lady Mariah. You willna shoot me."

"I will if I must." Her voice shook mildly, but her hands were steady.

Kiernan took a careful step forward, angling the sword upward above his right shoulder.

Macnair pulled his pistol out of his belt but did not cock it. "I can shoot you and take Branderee's sister. I hear she knows all about bein' kidnapped. I expect she'd be real cooperative."

"Then you expect wrong," said Jeanie from the darkness.

A small click from the opposite corner filled the silence. Macnair looked quickly from one side of the shadowy room to the other.

"I'm not the only one with a gun," said Mariah.

Kiernan took advantage of Macnair's confusion, moving forward rapidly, laying the blade against the other man's throat. "But I'm the only one with a sword. Drop the gun, Macnair." When the man hesitated, Kiernan pressed the blade a fraction harder. "It's over. Your men are in custody. Drop the gun and put your hands up where I can see them. Now."

"You wouldna slit my throat."

"I'm a Highlander," Kiernan said softly. "I honor the old ways."

Macnair swallowed hard, almost cutting his throat himself. Holding the pistol downward, he let it drop to the floor and put his hands in the air.

"We're going to back out of the room slowly." They moved backward, one careful step at a time, with Kiernan's sword still touching Macnair's throat.

When Macnair reached the hallway, Dominic, Gabriel, and Bell were waiting for them. Dominic and Gabe held their guns on

Macnair as Kiernan moved the sword away from the man's throat and stepped out of the way.

"Hands behind your back. Nice and slow," ordered Bell, clamping handcuffs around Macnair's wrists when he obeyed. "We have him," called Bell.

Jordan and Wilton came running from one direction, an excise man from the other. Wilton rushed past them into the room, gathering Ailsa into his arms. Dominic followed him into the room.

"Good work, Lord Branderee," said Bell. "We'll meet you downstairs."

Kiernan nodded and slid his sword into the sheath. As he stepped into the storage room, he noted someone had opened the drapes on the other window, filling the room with moonlight. Wilton cradled Ailsa gently against his chest, and from the way Dominic held Jeanie, he doubted he would ever let her go. His mother's maid, Sukey, comforted Jeanie's young maid, Molly.

As he walked by, Molly looked up at him, tears pouring down her cheeks. "I-I'm sorry I sneezed, my lord."

He patted her on the shoulder. "Dinna worry about it, lass. He likely would have found one of you anyway," he said, glancing at the open drapery behind Mariah.

"The cord was tangled," said Sukey. "We couldna close it."

Mariah sat on a trunk in front of the window, her head bowed. Elise stood by her side, her arm around her mistress's shoulders. He stopped in front of them. "Thank you, Elise."

She nodded and walked unsteadily toward the door. Kiernan heard Gabriel speak to her and knew he would take care of her. Out of the corner of his eye, he saw Jordan put his arms around Sukey and Molly and escort them from the room. He sensed the others quietly leave the room; he could not hear them over the pounding of his heart.

Kiernan knelt in front of Mariah, and with trembling hands, gently lifted her face so he could look into her eyes. "Brave lass. It's over."

"I would have killed him, Kiernan," she whispered, her face filled with anguish. "If you had not been there and he had tried to take one of us, I would have pulled the trigger."

"Defending yourself or others isna wrong, Mariah. If you had been forced to kill him, you might have saved other lives." Uncertain of who trembled more, he put his arms around her, holding her close. She clung to him, her tears wetting the side of his neck. "I was afraid I would lose you," he whispered.

"When I saw you behind him, I knew you would stop him. I knew I wouldn't have to kill him."

"I didna know if I could be quick enough."

"I heard the gunfire and was so afraid you'd been shot."

"It will take more than a smuggler's lousy aim to keep me from you." He eased his hold minutely. She looked up at him, and he touched her lips with his, pouring all his love and turbulent emotions into the kiss. When he finally drew away, he gazed down at her tenderly. "You'll make a fine countess."

"It won't be hard. I'll be the wife of a fine earl. You may not have been born to this position, Kiernan Macpherson, but no one deserves the title more. As your people come to know you, without Macnair causing problems, they will honor the tenth earl of Branderee."

"I dinna want their honor, only their respect and affection." He looked out the window at the dark line of the distant hills. Beyond them, to the southwest, lay his beloved Highlands. He missed them and supposed he always would, but for the first time, he felt as if he truly belonged at Branderee.

31

ON THE FOLLOWING SUNDAY MORNING, the minister in the parish church proclaimed to the congregation the intent of the earl of Branderee and Lady Mariah Douglas to marry. It was also proclaimed that the earl's sister, Miss Jeanette Macpherson, and Mr. Dominic Thorne intended to become husband and wife. The minister advised the congregation that if anyone knew a valid reason why either of these couples could not be married, that person should speak to him privately.

Normally, the banns had to be proclaimed on two separate Sundays in the presence of the congregation before the marriage could take place. A Scottish minister, however, had the right to waive the second reading of the banns if he was satisfied there was no impediment to the marriage.

Kiernan and Dominic pled their cause with the minister, and after talking to Ailsa, whom he trusted implicitly, he agreed one Sunday would suffice. They still had to wait forty-eight hours for the certificate. There were no objections to either marriage, and the certificates were granted Tuesday, a few minutes after noon.

Unlike English weddings, which had to be performed in the morning and in the parish church, there were no such restrictions in Scotland. The marriages took place in the chapel of Branderee at three o'clock Tuesday afternoon in the presence of the servants, tenants, and villagers of Branderee.

Since no specific wording was required, they chose a simple ceremony, each speaking from the heart. Kiernan and Mariah stood on one side of the minister. Kiernan wore a white shirt and silk cravat, black velvet evening jacket, and his best kilt of finely woven wool. In the pocket of his jacket was a simple gold band he had found at a shop in Banff. Mariah wore a creamy silk evening gown trimmed with lace and the sapphire necklace, bracelet, and earrings Kiernan had given her.

Dominic and Jeanette stood on the other side of the minister. Dominic wore his finest dark green evening jacket and buff pants with an emerald waistcoat that matched his eyes. Jeanie wore a white satin gown with a lace overskirt and a simple gold cross her father had given her on her seventeenth birthday.

The minister looked at the two couples and smiled. "Let us say a prayer to begin. Father God, we ask you to bless this ceremony. Let our hearts and minds dwell not only on these two couples but also on your boundless grace and love. In Jesus' name, amen." He turned his attention to Kiernan and Mariah.

Kiernan took Mariah's hand in a firm grip, gazing at her tenderly. Her eyes glowed with such love, he felt like shouting praise to the Father.

"Lord Branderee, do you take Lady Mariah to be your lawful wedded wife?"

"I do, joyfully. I shall love you and be faithful to you all my days, in good times and bad, sharing all that I have. I will never leave you, forsake you, nor send you away. These things I promise in the name of the Father, Son, and Holy Ghost."

"Lady Mariah, do you take Lord Branderee to be your lawful wedded husband?"

"I do, with gratitude and joy. I shall love you and be faithful to you all my days, in good times and bad, sharing all that I have." Tears of joy pooled in her eyes, but her voice was strong. "I accept your promise never to leave me, forsake me, or send me away, and I vow to you the same, in the name of the Father, the Son, and the Holy Ghost."

Kiernan withdrew the gold band from his pocket and slipped it on her finger. "With this ring, I thee wed, giving you my love and my life."

The minister placed his hand over their joined ones. "By the laws of Scotland and before God and these witnesses, I declare you to be husband and wife in the name of the Father, Son, and Holy Ghost. And may it always be so." He smiled happily. "You may kiss your bride."

Kiernan put his arms around her, kissing her gently but thoroughly. They looked at each for a moment, silently proclaiming their love, then turned to watch Dominic and Jeanie become man and wife.

A lump formed in Kiernan's throat as he thought of how God had brought these two together. *Thank you, God, for this man, for his salvation, and his love for my sister.* If anyone had ever questioned the sincerity of Dominic's love, those doubts were banished by the joy and tenderness on his countenance as he looked at her. Her love was just as obvious as she gazed up at him in adoration.

"Do you, Mr. Thorne, take Miss Macpherson to be your lawful wedded wife?"

Dominic held both of Jeanie's hands, looking into her eyes. "I do, with great joy and humility. God saw my pain and sent me an angel. He saw my sins, great as they were, and forgave me. The love of Jesus made me clean and whole, that I might be worthy of you." Dominic brushed away a lone tear that trickled down her cheek. "In the name of God, Jesus Christ my Savior, and the Holy Ghost, I make you this promise. I will love you forever. I will be faithful to you in every way and will forsake all others both in thought and deed for as long as I live. All that I have is yours, and I will cherish you above all else."

The minister cleared his throat, and Kiernan saw that his eyes, too, were moist. "Miss Macpherson, do you take Mr. Thorne to be your lawful wedded husband?"

"I do, with happiness and thanks to God for sending you to me. You have my trust, my heart, and my love forever. I shall be faithful to you in every way, forsaking all others for as long as I live. I will cherish you above all else and be honored to be your wife. I pledge these things in the name of the Father, the Son, and the Holy Ghost."

Dominic fumbled a little as he withdrew the ring from his pocket, but he smiled as he slipped it on her finger. "With this ring, I thee wed."

The minister placed his hand over theirs. "By the laws of Scotland and before God and these witnesses, I declare you to be husband and wife in the name of the Father, Son, and Holy Ghost. May God bless you." He smiled kindly at Dominic. "You may kiss your bride."

Dominic cradled Jeanie's face in his hand and kissed her tenderly. When he ended the kiss, he leaned toward her ear and whispered something that brought a blush to her cheeks and a sparkle to her eyes.

Mariah laughed softly. "Scores of women will go into mourning when they hear he has married," she whispered to Kiernan, making him laugh, too.

When they turned toward the others in the chapel, Kiernan slowly looked around the room at the smiling, happy faces. "Thank you all for sharing in this most joyful day." He had already returned the excess rents Macnair had taken, but he and Mariah had a few surprises for the people of Branderee.

"As you know, I never expected to inherit Branderee. It has been a big change for all of us, and it has no' been easy. I still have much to learn about running an estate and being an earl. I'll make mistakes, but hopefully, no' as many as I have this last year. Now I have trustworthy friends to guide me.

"To celebrate our marriage and that of my sister and guid-brither, my lady and I have some gifts for you. For the tenants and villagers, repairs and improvements to your homes will be made immediately." He grinned as the audience cheered and held up his hand for silence. "Mr. Wylde will be visiting each tenant in the next few weeks to go over the terms of your leases. Some of them are fine, but others are no'. We want to set up something fair to all. In addition, no rent or fishing income will be charged for the remainder of the year."

His declaration was met with stunned silence, then hushed whispers. Finally, a lad of thirteen stood up. Kiernan recognized him as a boy who had become a man overnight when his father had deserted the family six months earlier. "None, sir?" he asked cautiously.

"None."

The lad sat down and glanced at his mother's worn dress, grinning broadly.

Kiernan felt Mariah's hand tighten on his, confirming that they were doing what was right. He looked at Mrs. Laing and the other employees. "My long-suffering staff will receive a bonus and a raise. We will also see if any improvements need to be made to your quarters." He glanced at Mariah. "Did I forget anything?"

"The party."

"Ah, yes, the party. We hope all of you can stay. Mrs. Laing and the staff have been working for days, preparing wonderful things for us to eat. I know many of you brought food to contribute, too, for which I thank you. We'll have an afternoon of music, dancing, and celebration."

With a happy smile, and Dominic and Jeanie beside them, he escorted Mariah from the chapel as the people of Branderee stood and cheered.

During the course of the afternoon, they laughed, ate, sang, and danced as one of the fishermen played the fiddle. Far more at ease than he had been in London, Kiernan danced several Scottish reels with his bride. It seemed everyone sought them out, wishing them well and thanking them for their generosity.

The only sadness for Kiernan came after he had played several tunes on the bagpipe. The songs tugged at his heart as always, and when he glanced at Gabriel and saw the faraway look in his eyes, he knew his friend would be leaving soon. He found him a short time later up in the tower gazing toward the distant mountains, his expression lonely and troubled.

"When are you going?" Kiernan braced his hands on the windowsill and looked out across his lands.

"In a few days. You have a new best friend now."

"Gabe, no one will ever take your place, no' even Mariah. You and I have been together our whole lives."

"I know, but you need time alone with her. I'm happy for you, I truly am. She's a wonderful woman. I pray I find someone like her." Gabe glanced at him. "I was all too happy to come here with you when you inherited Branderee, partly because I felt adrift at home. I was in the regiment too many years, gone too long. Now I need to find my place."

As a second son, Gabriel would inherit no lands from his father. He had inherited a generous fortune, however, from his grandmother

426

and stood one day to inherit more from an uncle.

"You could buy something around here," said Kiernan, knowing the suggestion was useless but wishing it were not so.

"Nae, my friend. The Highlands bid me come home. I've felt the call since we left London, and it grows stronger day by day. I think God wants me there, though I'm no' sure why." Gabe turned to him with a smile. "It's no' all that far. We can see each other often."

"We're planning to buy a house there. Maybe I'll wait until you settle in somewhere and find something close by."

"I'd like that."

As Kiernan looked at him, his mind traveled back through the years. He saw them racing across the heather, climbing mountains and hills, swimming in the cold loch. Together they had studied, laughed, prayed, and found the Savior. Together they learned about life, both good and bad. They had made mistakes, but God in his grace had always brought them back to what was right. They had fought side by side and looked into the face of death many times, but God had seen them through. *So we might serve him.*

"I'll pray that you can clearly see what God has for you," said Kiernan. When Gabe nodded, he gave him a big hug. "I'll miss you."

Gabe hugged him and patted him roughly on the back. "I'll miss you, too." He pulled away, his eyes misty. "But right now, I expect your wife is wondering where you are. Go on, enjoy your party. I'll be down in a minute."

"You'll always be welcome here, or wherever we may be."

"I know. Pray that God will send me the right woman soon. With all my friends walking around in a love-struck daze, I'm starting to think seriously about finding a wife."

Kiernan slapped him on the back and shoved him toward the door. "We'll look, too. Right now, I canna think of any lass with the patience of Job."

∽◦∾

Later in the evening, Kiernan and Mariah slipped away from the festivities, walking arm in arm upstairs. Dominic and Jeanie had disappeared a short time earlier. "It's been a wonderful day." Mariah leaned her head against his shoulder. "I don't think I've ever seen so many joyful people."

"It's time they had something to be happy about. Time we all did." He kissed her forehead. "I love you, Lady Branderee."

"And I love you, Lord Branderee." Mariah's heart swelled with love and thanksgiving as she looked up at him. "I never expected God to give me a man like you."

His smile held a hint of self-satisfaction. "I'm glad you like his choice. I always knew he'd give me the bonniest, most wonderful lass in all of Scotland."

"I wasn't in Scotland."

"A minor detail. You're a Scot, and that's what counts."

"What if I'd been English?" she asked as they stopped at the master bedchamber door.

"I would have given the matter some thought." His eyes twinkled as he opened the door. "For maybe a minute, then I would have graciously bowed to his wisdom."

He swept her up in his arms and carried her into the room, kicking the door closed behind them. Mariah's laughter rang out as he tossed her on the bed. As he stretched out beside her, resting his head on his elbow, a gentle breeze blew through the castle like a contented sigh.

"I think even the castle is happy."

"It should be." He gazed down at her, his smile bright with love, his eyes dark with passion. "It is no longer an empty shell, but a home filled with love and laughter. 'Tis a place where God dwells."

Dear Reader,

Several years ago, my husband took a business trip to England. We were remodeling our kitchen at the time, but given the opportunity of meeting him in England, it was easy to wait for new appliances and other things.

We couldn't afford to stay very long, so we crammed one of the most memorable times of our lives into eight glorious days. England's beautiful countryside, quaint villages, towering cathedrals and castles were a delight. The age and history of so many buildings are awe inspiring. In several cathedrals, the stone stairs have been worn down by the steps of worshippers over the centuries. It served as a joyous reminder that the love we hold for our Lord has been shared by so many.

Then we took the train to Scotland—and felt as if we were home. Not surprising since we both always get misty-eyed when we hear bagpipes. Except for spending the night in Borthwick Castle seven miles from Edinburgh, we spent most of our time in the city. But Scotland and its wonderful, hospitable people captured our hearts—like the lady who helped us with a bus schedule, then after she paid her fare, turned around with her open hand full of change in case didn't have the right amount. Practically everyone on the bus became involved in helping us find the correct stop, then waved when we got off and told us not to spend all our money in one place.

Writing *Song of the Highlands* has been like renewing old friendships and visiting England and Scotland all over again.

A high point of this past year and a half has been all your wonderful mail. My thanks to everyone who has written to say how much you enjoyed *Love Song* and *Antiques*. I never expected to hear from so many of you! Unfortunately, pressing writing commitments and a lengthy family illness earlier this year have kept me from answering many of them, for which I sincerely apologize. I'm not sure I'll ever get caught up. If I don't, I hope you will consider this a personal message—I am greatly blessed to know the books have touched you and thank God for allowing me the privilege of writing for him and for you. I thank each of you for taking the time to write and for your encouragement.

God bless you,

Sharon Gillenwater

PALISADES...PURE ROMANCE

Promise Me the Dawn, Amanda MacLean (Premier)
Kingdom Come, Amanda MacLean (March, 1997)
Betrayed, Lorena McCourtney
Escape, Lorena McCourtney
Voyage, Elaine Schulte

A Christmas Joy, Darty, Gillenwater, MacLean
Mistletoe, Ball, Hicks, McCourtney
A Mother's Love, Bergren, Colson, MacLean (March, 1997)